The
Summerhouse

Books by Jude Deveraux

Published by POCKET BOOKS

Jude Deveraux

The Summerhouse

BOOKSPAN LARGE PRINT EDITION

POCKET BOOKS
New York   London   Toronto   Sydney   Singapore

This Large Print Edition, prepared especially for Bookspan, contains the complete, unabridged text of the original Publisher's Edition.

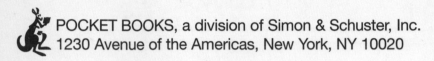 POCKET BOOKS, a division of Simon & Schuster, Inc. 1230 Avenue of the Americas, New York, NY 10020

ISBN: 0-7394-1827-0

POCKET and colophon are registered trademarks of Simon & Schuster, Inc.

Printed in the U.S.A.

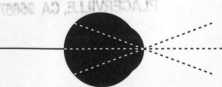

This Large Print Book carries the Seal of Approval of N.A.V.H.

*I'd like to thank Dr. Donna Twist for her expert help with writing about the treatment of an injury like Roger's. We walked and talked and had many laughs together.
Thank you.*

Part One

One

Leslie Headrick looked out her kitchen window at the old summerhouse in the back. Now, in early fall, the vines and twisted stems of the old roses nearly covered the building, but in the winter you could see the glassed-in porch well. You could see the peeling paint and the cracked glass in the little round window above the front door. One of the side doors was hanging on one hinge, and Alan said it was a danger to anyone who walked past the place. In fact, Alan said that the whole structure was a danger and should be torn down.

At that thought, Leslie turned away from the window and looked back at her beautiful, perfect kitchen. Just last year Alan had gutted her old kitchen and put in this one. "It's the best that money can buy," he'd said about the maple cabinets and the solid-surface countertops. And Leslie was sure that it was the best, but she missed her ratty old Welsh dresser and the little breakfast nook in the corner. "That table and those chairs look like something kids made in a shop class," Alan had said, and Leslie had agreed—but their perspective of what was beautiful differed.

As always, Leslie had given in to her husband and let him put in this showplace of a kitchen, and now she felt that she was ruining a piece of art when she baked cookies and messed up the perfect surfaces that scratched so easily.

She poured herself another cup of tea from the pot, strong, black English tea, loose tea, no wimpy tea bags for her, then turned back to again look out at the summerhouse. This was a day for reflecting because in three more days she was going to be forty years old—and she was going to celebrate her birthday with two women she hadn't seen or heard from in nineteen years.

Behind her, in the hallway, her two suitcases were packed and waiting. She was taking a lot of clothing because she didn't know what the other two women were going to be wearing, and Ellie's letter had been vague. "For a famous writer, she doesn't say much," Alan had said in an unpleasant tone of voice. He had been quite annoyed to find out that his wife was friends with a best-selling author.

"But I didn't know that Ellie was Alexandria Farrell," Leslie had said, looking at the letter in wonder. "The last time I saw Ellie she wanted to be an artist. She was—"

But Alan wasn't listening. "You could have asked her to speak at the Masons," he was saying. "Just last year, one of my clients said that his wife was a devotee of Jordan Neale." Everyone in America knew that Jordan Neale was the lead character that Ellie, under the pen name of Alexandria Farrell, had created. Jordan Neale was someone women wanted to imitate and men wanted to . . . Well, the series of romantic mysteries had done very well. Leslie had read all of them, having no idea that the writer was the cute young woman she'd met so long ago.

So now, in the quiet of the early morning, before Alan and the kids came downstairs, Leslie was thinking about what had happened to her in the last nineteen years. Not much, she thought. She'd married the boy next door, literally, and they'd had two children, Joe and Rebecca, now fourteen and fifteen years old. They weren't babies any longer, she thought, sipping her tea and still staring out the window at the summerhouse.

Maybe it was the letter and the invitation from Ellie, a woman she hadn't seen in so very many years, that was making Leslie think about the past so hard. But, as Ellie had written, their one and only meeting had had an impact on Ellie's life and she wanted to see both Leslie and Madison again.

Yes, Leslie thought, that meeting had had an impact on her life too. Since that afternoon nineteen years ago, she'd often thought of Ellie and Madison. And now she was going to fly all the way from Columbus, Ohio, to a tiny town in Maine to spend a long weekend with the other two women.

But what was it about the summerhouse that was holding her attention this morning? She'd been so restless that she hadn't been able to sleep much last night, so, at four A.M., she'd got out of bed, dressed, then tiptoed downstairs to put together the ingredients for apple pancakes. Not that anyone would eat any of them, she thought with a sigh. Rebecca would be horrified at the calories, Joe would come down with only seconds to spare before he made the school bus, and Alan would only want cereal, something high-fiber, low-calorie, low-cholesterol, low . . . Well, low-flavor, Leslie thought. Attempts at gourmet cooking were wasted on her family.

With another sigh, Leslie picked up a warm pancake, folded it, and ate it with pleasure. Last week when she'd received Ellie's letter, she wished she'd received it six months earlier so she would have had time to get rid of the extra fifteen pounds she was carrying. Everyone at the Garden Club said they envied Leslie her figure and how she'd been able to keep it all these years, but Leslie knew better. Nineteen years ago she'd been a dancer and she'd had a body that was supple, muscular, and hard. Now, she thought, she was soft, not fat really, but her muscles were soft. She hadn't thrown her leg up on a ballet bar in years.

Overhead she could hear Rebecca's quick step. She'd be the first one down, the first one to ask why her mother had made something that was guaranteed to clog all their arteries with one bite. Leslie sighed. Rebecca was so very much like her father.

Joe was more like his mother, and if Leslie could get him away from his friends long enough, they could sit and talk and "smell the roses," as she used to tell him. "Like your wallpaper," he'd said when he was just nine years old. It had taken Leslie a moment to figure out what he was talking about, then she'd smiled warmly. In the summerhouse. She'd put up wallpaper with roses on it in the summerhouse.

Now she remembered looking at her son on that long ago day and seeing his freckled face as they sat across from each other in the old inglenook at one side of the sunny kitchen. Joe had been such an easygoing child, sleeping through the night when he was just weeks old, so unlike Rebecca, who seemed to cause chaos and confusion wherever she was. Leslie wasn't sure if Rebecca had yet slept through a night of her life. Even now, when she was fifteen, she thought nothing of barging into her parents' bedroom at three A.M. to announce that she'd heard a "funny noise" on the roof. Leslie would tell her to go back to bed and get some sleep, but Alan took "funny noises" seriously. The neighbors were used to seeing Alan and his daughter outside with flashlights.

Leslie looked back at the summerhouse. She could still see some of the pink paint on it. Fifteen years later and remnants of the paint were still there.

Smiling, she remembered Alan's expression when she'd bought the paint. "I can understand if you want to paint the place pink, but, sweetheart, you've bought five different shades of pink. Didn't those men at the store help you?"

Alan was a great believer in men taking care of women, whether it was at home or in a paint store.

At that time Leslie had been five months pregnant with Rebecca and she was already showing. She didn't know it then, but Rebecca was going to be early in everything, from letting her mother know she was there to . . . well, letting the world know she was there.

Laughing, Leslie had told Alan that she planned to paint the summerhouse using all five shades of pink. Now, fifteen and a half years later, she could still remember the look on his face. Leslie's mother had said that Alan didn't have a creative bone in his body, and, over the years, Leslie had found out that that was true. But, back then, when they were both so young and so happy to be on their own, the colors she wanted to paint the falling down old summerhouse had been cause for laughter.

It had been Leslie who'd persuaded Alan to buy the big Victorian house that was in an old, unfashionable neighborhood. Alan had wanted something new, something that was white on the outside and white on the inside. But Leslie couldn't stand any of the houses that Alan had liked: perfectly square boxes set inside a bigger perfectly square box. "But that's what I like about them," Alan had said, not understanding her complaint.

It was Leslie's mother who had given her the strength to stand up to her new husband. "The house belongs to the woman," her mother had said. "It's where you spend most of your time and it's where you raise your children. It's worth a fight." In her family, her mother had been the fighter. Leslie was like her father and liked to let things find their own solutions.

Later Leslie said that it was having

Rebecca's fierce spirit inside her that had given her the courage. She played her trump card: "Alan, dear, we are buying the house with money my father left to *me*." Alan didn't say anything, but the look on his face made her never, ever again say anything like that.

But then she'd never before or since wanted anything as much as she'd wanted that big, rambling old house that needed so very much work. Since her father had been a building contractor, she knew what needed to be done and how to go about getting it done.

"That has to go," Alan had said when he'd seen the old summerhouse, hidden under fifty-year-old trees, nearly obscured by wisteria vines.

"But that's the most beautiful part of the house," Leslie had said.

Alan had opened his mouth to say something, but Rebecca had chosen that moment to give her first kick, and the argument about the fate of the summerhouse was never completed. Later, whenever Alan had said anything about the house, Leslie had said, "Trust me," so he'd left it to her. After all, Alan had just started selling insurance and he was ambitious, very, very ambitious. He worked from early to late. He joined clubs and attended meetings. He was quite happy when he found out that the most fashionable church in town was within walking distance of the horrible old house that Leslie had persuaded him to purchase.

And it was at church that he found out that people were pleased with him for having the foresight to buy "the old Belville place" and restore it. "Sound invest, that," some old man said as he clapped Alan on the shoulder. "It's unusual that a man as young as you would have that much wisdom." Later the man bought a big policy from Alan. After that, Alan took as much interest in the house as Leslie did. And when Leslie had her hands full with two babies under the age of three, Alan took over supervising the restoration of the house.

At first there had been fights. "It isn't a museum!" Leslie had said in exasperation. "It's a home and it should look like one. Joe's going to ruin that expensive table with his trucks. And Rebecca will draw on that silk wallpaper."

"Then you'll just have to keep them under control," Alan had snapped.

And Leslie had backed down, as she always did at a confrontation. Like her father, she'd rather retreat than fight. Which is why her mother had ruled her childhood home and Alan ruled their home. So Alan had filled the wonderful old house with too many antiques that no one could sit on or even touch. There were three rooms in the house that were kept tightly closed all year, only being opened for cleaning and for Alan's huge Christmas party for all his clients.

The kitchen had been the final holdout, but last year Alan had had his way on that room too.

Leslie finished her tea, rinsed out her cup, then looked back at the summerhouse. That was to have been hers. It was to have been her retreat from the world, a place where she could keep up with her dancing, or curl up and read on rainy afternoons.

Now, looking at the building, she smiled. Before she had children, a woman thought of what she wanted to do on rainy afternoons, but afterward, her hours filled with "must" instead of "want." She *must* do the laundry, *must* get the groceries, *must* pull Rebecca back from the heater.

Somehow, Leslie had lost the summerhouse. Somehow, it had gone from being hers to being "theirs." She knew exactly when it had started. She had been eight months pregnant and so big she'd had to walk with her hand under her belly to support Rebecca's constant kicks and punches.

They'd just torn out the living room in the house and there was a leak in the roof. Alan had invited his brother and three college friends over for beer and football but it was raining that day, so there was nowhere for them to sit and watch the game on TV. When Alan had suggested that he set the TV up in the summerhouse for "this one afternoon," she'd been too grateful for the peace and quiet to protest. She'd been dreading a house full of men and smoke and the smell of beer, so she was glad when he said he'd take the men elsewhere.

On the next weekend, Alan had taken two clients into the summerhouse to discuss new life policies. It made sense, as the living room was still torn up. "We need a place to sit and talk," he'd said, looking at Leslie as though it were her fault that the roofing materials still hadn't arrived.

Two weeks after that, Rebecca was born,

and for the next year, Leslie hadn't been able to take a breath. Rebecca was insatiable in her demands for attention from her tired mother. It was three months before Leslie could get herself together enough to get her squalling baby out of her pajamas. By the time Rebecca started walking at ten months, Leslie was pregnant again.

When she was three months pregnant with Joe, Leslie made the trek out to the summerhouse. In the months since Alan had first set up a TV in the place, Leslie had almost forgotten that her retreat still existed. But from the first day, Joe was an easier pregnancy than Rebecca, and Leslie's mother had started taking her granddaughter on short jaunts about town. "There's nothing more uninteresting than a nursing baby," her mother had said in her usual forthright style. "When she starts walking and looking at something besides her mother's bosom, then I'll take an interest in her."

So, on her first afternoon of freedom, for that's the way it felt, Leslie had made her way out to the summerhouse. Maybe this time, she'd be able to stretch out on the wicker chaise lounge she'd found in an antique shop and read a book.

But when Leslie pushed open the door, her breath stopped. Vaguely, she'd wondered why Alan had used the summerhouse only a few times, then never said anything about it again.

Someone had left the doors open and it had rained in on her furniture. Before she was first pregnant, she'd made the slipcovers for the little couch and the two chairs. She'd made the matching curtains and hung them herself. But now mice were nesting in the stuffing of the couch, and it looked as if a neighboring cat had clawed the arms of the chairs.

Turning away, she felt tears come to her eyes. She didn't even bother to close the door as she ran back to the house.

Later, she'd tried to have a confrontation with Alan, but he'd expressed such concern that her anger was going to harm the baby, that Leslie had calmed down. "We'll fix it up after you've had the baby," he said. "I promise. Scout's honor." He'd kissed her then and helped her with Rebecca and later, he'd made sweet love to her. But he didn't fix the summerhouse.

After that, Leslie had been so busy with children and helping Alan establish himself within the community that she wouldn't have had time to get away even if she'd had a place to go. And as the years followed each other, the summerhouse became a storage shed.

"So how's my old girl this morning?" Alan asked from behind her. He was two months younger than Leslie and he'd always found jokes about their age difference to be amusing. Needless to say, Leslie didn't see the humor.

"I made pancakes," she said, keeping her face turned away to hide her frown. She hadn't yet come to terms with the idea of turning forty. Hadn't it been only last week when she'd boarded a bus and headed to big, bad New York City, where she was going to turn the town on its ear with her dancing?

"*Mmm*," Alan said. "Wish I had time, but I have a full schedule today."

When she turned around, he was looking down at the newspaper, absorbed with the financial section. In the seventeen years that they'd been married, Alan hadn't changed much. Not physically anyway. His hair was now gray, but on him it looked good. He said that an insurance agent was considered more trustworthy if he looked older. And he kept in shape by going to the gym regularly.

What had changed about him was that he no longer seemed to actually *see* any of them, not his wife, not his two children. Oh, Rebecca could throw one of her look-at-me fits and she could get his attention, but Joe and Leslie, with their easygoing ways, were mostly ignored by him.

"You ought to leave him," Leslie's mother said, even more outspoken now than she had been when her husband was alive. Widowhood agreed with her. "If you left him, he'd find out how much he needs you. You need to shake up his perfect little world. Show him what matters."

But Leslie had seen what happened to women her age who left their handsome, successful husbands, and Leslie had no desire to live in some dreary little apartment and work at the local discount store. "Mother," Leslie often said in exasperation, "I have no skills to make my own way in the world. What would I do? Go back to dancing?" That she had failed at her one and only attempt at success in the world still haunted her.

"Where did I go wrong with you?" her mother would moan. "If you left him, he'd fall apart. You're the man's entire life. You do everything for him. If you left, he'd—"

"Run off with Bambi," Leslie said quickly.

"You were a fool to let him hire that little tart," her mother had snapped.

Leslie looked away. She didn't want her mother to know how she'd fought her husband's hiring the beautiful, young girl. "You hired a girl named Bambi?" Leslie had said, laughing in disbelief, at the dinner table the first night he'd told her. "Is she over twelve?"

To Leslie, it had been a joke, but when she looked at Alan's face, she could see that he didn't think his new secretary was a joke. "She is very competent at her job," he'd snapped, his eyes drilling into his wife's.

As always, Joe had been sensitive to any disagreement and he'd pushed his plate away. "I got some homework to do," he'd mumbled, then left the table.

Rebecca never seemed to see anything outside her own realm. "Did I tell you what that dreadful Margaret said to me today? We were in chemistry class, and—"

Leslie had at last looked away from her husband's eyes, and she'd never again made a snide remark about Bambi. But Leslie had been curious, so she'd called a woman she'd gone to high school with who worked in Alan's office and invited her to lunch. After lunch, Leslie had gone home and made herself a strong gin and tonic and taken it to the bathtub with her. She'd been told that Alan had hired Bambi six months earlier and that she was more than just his secretary, she was his "personal assistant." Paula, who'd been on the cheerleading squad with Leslie in high school, warmed to her story and seemed to enjoy "warning" Leslie. "If he were my husband, I'd put an end to it, I can tell you that," Paula had said with emphasis. "That girl goes everywhere with Alan. All I can say is that it's a good thing we don't have one of those unisex bathrooms or she'd—"

"Would you like to have some dessert?" Leslie had said rather loudly.

Now Bambi had worked for, with, "under," if the gossip were to be believed, Alan for over a year. And, quite frankly,

Leslie didn't know what to do about it. Every friend she had had an opinion and freely gave it to Leslie.

One day Rebecca had overheard some women giving Leslie advice about this young woman who worked so closely with Alan, and later, Rebecca had said, "Mother, you ought to tell them to go to hell."

"Rebecca!" Leslie had said sternly, "I don't like that kind of language."

"It's possible that your husband is having an affair with his over endowed secretary and you're worried about bad language?"

Leslie could only stand there and blink at her daughter. Who was the adult? How did her daughter know—?

"It's all over the church and at the club," Rebecca said, sounding as though she were thirty-five instead of just fifteen. "Look, Mom, men stray. They get itchy pants. It's normal. What you ought to do is tie a knot in his—"

Leslie gasped.

"All right, go ahead and live in the nine-teenth century. But that Bambi is a bitch and she's after Dad and I think you should *fight!*"

At that Rebecca had left the room, and all

Leslie could do was stare after her. Leslie hadn't the least idea of how to deal with a child who had just said what her daughter had, so Leslie pretended that it hadn't been said.

In fact, that's what Leslie seemed to be doing a lot of lately: pretending that nothing was wrong, that nothing bad had happened. She couldn't go so far as to, say, call Alan's office and tell his assistant to remind him of so and so party. No, instead, Leslie just worked around the whole idea of Bambi by pretending that the young woman didn't exist. And when the women at church or the club tried to warn her, Leslie perfected a little smile that let them know that she was above such low suspicions.

But now, looking at Alan as he bent over the newspaper, she wondered if he wasn't eating her pancakes for fear that he'd put on weight and Bambi wouldn't like that.

"So, Mom!" Rebecca said as she came into the room, "what are you old ladies going to get up to this weekend? Think you'll have an orgy with lots of bronzed young men?"

Part of Leslie wanted to reprimand her smart-mouthed daughter, but another part, the woman part that was separate from being someone's mother, wanted to joke with her daughter. "Ellie is bringing Mel Gibson and Harrison Ford," Leslie said as she glanced at her husband.

But Alan didn't seem to hear. Instead, he looked at his watch. Even though it was only seven A.M., he said, "Gotta go."

"Are you sure you wouldn't like a pancake or two?" Leslie asked, knowing that she sounded whiny. What she wanted to say was, "You can damned well spend an hour with your family before rushing off to your bimbo."

But Leslie didn't say that. Instead, she tried to smile invitingly.

"Sounds good, but I'm meeting some clients this afternoon and we have lots of paperwork to go over before the big meeting."

Even though the name was hardly ever said, all of them knew that "we" was Alan and Bambi.

Alan walked over to Leslie and gave her a kiss on the cheek. "I hope you have a good time," he said. "And, about your birthday . . ." He gave her a little-boy look that years ago she'd found irresistible.

"I know," she said with a forced smile. "You'll get me something later. It's all right. My birthday isn't for three days anyway."

"Thanks, hon," he said, kissing her cheek again. "You're a brick." Grabbing his jacket off the back of a chair, he left the house.

" 'You're a brick,' " Rebecca mimicked as she ate a spoonful of some cereal that looked like extruded sawdust. "You're a chump."

"I won't have you talk about your father like that," Leslie said, glaring down at her daughter. "Or me."

"Nice!" Rebecca said, coming out of her chair. She was as tall as her mother, so they were eye to eye across the breakfast table. "All you care about is *nice*! Nice words, nice manners, nice thoughts. But the world isn't *nice,* and what Dad is doing with that leech isn't *nice.*"

Suddenly, there were tears in Rebecca's eyes. "Don't you know what's going to happen? That woman is going to break us up. She wants what we have, not the family, but the money. She wants the silver tea set and the . . . and the fifty-thousand-dollar kitchen that you hate but were too cowardly to tell Dad that you didn't want. We're going to lose everything because you're so damned *nice.*" With that, Rebecca ran out of the kitchen and up the stairs.

And in the next moment, a car horn blew outside and Leslie knew that the shuttle bus that would take her to the airport was there. For a moment, she hesitated. She should go to her daughter. Her daughter was upset and needed her, and a mother always gave, didn't she? A good mother was always there for her children, wasn't she? A good mother—And a good wife, Leslie thought. That's what she was: a mother and a wife.

Suddenly, Leslie didn't want to be anyone's wife or anyone's mother. She wanted to get on a plane and go see two women she hadn't seen since she was very young, since before she was anyone's wife or mother.

Leslie practically ran out of the kitchen, grabbed her handbag off the hall table and her two suitcases from the floor, then opened the front door. She yelled, "Goodbye. See you on Tuesday," up the stairs to her two children, but she didn't wait for an answer. A minute later and she was in the van, the driver was pulling away, and it was then that Leslie realized that she hadn't brushed her teeth. She doubted if she'd missed an after-meal brushing of her teeth since she was three years old, and she almost told the driver to stop and go back.

But then Leslie leaned back against the seat and smiled. Not brushing her teeth seemed to be a sign that she was about to start on an adventure. In front of her were three whole days that were hers and no one else's. Freedom. She hadn't been on a trip by herself since she'd gone to New York nineteen years ago. What was it going to be like to not have people asking, "Where's my tie?" "Where's my other shoe?" "Hon, could you call down and order me something to eat?" "Mom! What do you mean that you didn't bring my red shorts? How can I have any fun without *those* shorts."

For a moment Leslie closed her eyes and thought of three days of freedom; then a laugh escaped her. Startled, she opened her eyes to see the driver looking at her in the mirror, and he was smiling.

"Glad to get away?" he asked. They were the only people in the van.

"You can't imagine," Leslie said with feeling.

"Whoever takes care of you better not

leave you alone too long," the man said, still looking at her, his eyes flirting.

Leslie knew that she should give him her best "Mrs. Church-Lady look," as Rebecca called it, after the comedian on TV. But right now Leslie didn't feel like giving that look. The driver was a good-looking young man and he'd just paid her a compliment. She smiled at him, then leaned her head back against the seat and closed her eyes, feeling the best she'd felt in a long, long time.

Two

Ellie Abbott leaned back against the seat of the airplane, closed her eyes, and thought, What the hell have I done?

Leaning forward again, she picked up the plastic cup of club soda from the fold-down tray, but when she tried to bring it to her lips, she saw that her hand was shaking. Putting the cup down, she tried to calm her nerves by looking out the window.

She was on a propeller plane flying into Bangor, and she was glad that the plane wasn't divided into classes because no longer did she travel in first class. In Ellie's mind she didn't deserve such perks as first class because she was no longer Alexandria Farrell, the writer who had caused such a storm when her books first came out, five of them, one after another. Boom. Boom. Boom.

No, it had been three years now since Ellie had written a word. It had been three years since the stories inside her head had stopped. Three years since her divorce and what had been done to her by the courts, by the American "justice" system.

Again Ellie tried to drink from her cup, but her hand was trembling too much to keep from spilling the drink. Nervously, she glanced at the man sitting across the aisle from her, but he hadn't seemed to notice anything. And, thankfully, he hadn't given any sign that he knew "who" she was.

Or used to be, Ellie thought. Like those old movie stars who were stopped on the street and asked, "Didn't you used to be so and so?"

Well, Ellie was still Ellie, Abbott again, back to her maiden name, no longer using her married name, but she didn't feel that she was still Alexandria Farrell the writer.

"You can't go through this birthday alone," her therapist had said. Jeanne was now the only person Ellie saw on a regular basis. For three years now Ellie had re-treated from the world, telling people that she needed time to "recover." But about eight months ago, after her second attempt at obtaining justice had failed, Ellie had sought professional help.

"I don't want to see anyone," Ellie had said. "Everyone knows me as I once was."

Jeanne had sighed. No matter what she said to Ellie, nothing seemed to penetrate the wall she'd put around herself. "You still are who you always were. It's time you got over this and went forward with your life."

"But who would even recognize me as I am now?" Ellie said heavily.

Jeanne narrowed her eyes at Ellie. "You can lose the weight. You need to go to a gym. Who knows, you might meet someone there and—"

"Not again!" Ellie had exploded. "I'll never, never go through that again. And who would want *me*? I'm fat and I'm *rich*!"

Jeanne had blinked at Ellie a couple of times, then they both laughed at the absurdity of what Ellie had just said. Not many people looked on having money as something bad.

"You know what I mean," Ellie said. "After what was done to me I'm afraid that people only want me for what they can get from me."

"Yes, I know," Jeanne said, surreptitiously glancing at the clock behind Ellie's head. In these months they had made little progress in getting Ellie past what had happened to her, and the trauma was making Ellie stand still in life, unable to move forward. Three years ago, Ellie had been on top of the world with her great success as a writer, but now she rarely left her apartment. And to make matters worse, she'd given up nearly all forms of physical activity, so she'd put on forty pounds, and forty pounds on someone just five foot one was a lot of weight.

But, try as she might, Jeanne couldn't get Ellie to *move,* to go anywhere, to try to get out of what was turning into a serious depression.

"All right, there must be someone you could spend your fortieth birthday with. If you don't want to be with your publishing friends, how about someone from your hometown?"

"Richmond? You mean I should call up an old high school buddy and ask her to share a pink birthday cake with me? Think I can get someone who'll wear her old cheer-leading skirt?"

Jeanne knew too well the trap of Ellie's sarcasm. "There must be *someone*," she said forcibly. "Someone *somewhere*!"

"Actually . . ." Ellie had said, looking down at her nails, which were no longer professionally manicured.

"Yes," Jeanne said encouragingly.

"On my twenty-first birthday I met two other women at the DMV here in New York. It was their twenty-first birthday also, and we . . ."

"Yes?" When Ellie didn't say anything more, Jeanne pushed. It was the first time Ellie had mentioned these women, and if there was any possibility that Ellie would spend time with them and get out of her apartment, then Jeanne just might write the invitations herself. "Who are these women?" Jeanne asked. "How can you get in touch with them? Can you three spend your birthday together?"

"I really don't know where they are now. We met that one day and spent a few hours together. It was, you know, just one of those things that happens to people. We were at the DMV for hours because—" Ellie broke off and gave a bit of a smile at the memory, and it was that smile that made Jeanne pounce.

"Call them. Find them. You know their names and their birth dates. Get on the Internet and find them. No, better yet, give me their names and *I* will find them. You can have a party together, the three of you. Talk about old times."

Ellie gave her therapist a look of disgust. "One was a dancer with the most incredible body you've ever seen, and the other was a model." What Ellie didn't say was that she couldn't possibly see them looking as she did now.

Jeanne gave Ellie a hard look, then pulled a photo album off a shelf behind her and opened it. She passed the album to Ellie.

Ellie looked at the picture but didn't understand. It was a photo of a ballet dancer, tall, thin, graceful. Beautiful. It took Ellie minutes before she understood. She looked up at the therapist. "You?"

"Me," Jeanne said.

Ellie gave her a weak smile. Jeanne was now in her sixties and had a body the shape of a potato.

"A person is more than her body," Jeanne

said. "If they liked you then, they'll like you now. And, besides, it's been nineteen years. Have you seen either of these women's faces or names plastered on billboards?"

"No . . ." Ellie said softly.

"Then obviously they didn't make careers out of dancing and modeling. So who's to say what they look like now? Maybe they've put on a hundred pounds and—"

"And married the town drunk," Ellie said, visibly cheering up.

"Yes," Jeanne said, smiling. "Think on the bright side. Maybe worse things have happened to them than have happened to you."

Ellie thought about that for a moment. "Maybe . . ." she said.

Jeanne sat there looking at Ellie for a moment; then she pushed the button on her telephone. "Sarah, cancel my luncheon date." She then turned to her laptop on her desk and opened it. "Ellie, my dear, you and I are going to get on the Net and see what we can find out about these women; then you're going to invite them to spend your birthday with you."

"Is a therapist supposed to be this controlling?"

"She is when she cares about her clients

as much as I care about you. And, besides, I want to read more about Jordan Neale. Hey! I tell you what, you can have my house in Maine for that weekend. There are only two bedrooms, but there's a sofa bed in the living room, so one of you can use that. Now, what were their names?"

And that was how Ellie came to be sitting on a plane that was flying toward Bangor, Maine, and why two women she hadn't seen in nineteen years were going to meet her and the three of them were going to spend their collective birthday together.

But now that she was actually on the plane and was, eventually, going to land— but, given her luck of the last three years, maybe they wouldn't land. No! Jeanne had made Ellie take an oath that for one whole weekend she was going to do her best not to be negative.

Anyway, now that she was actually flying toward the meeting, she couldn't believe she'd allowed Jeanne to bully her into it. Ellie was sure that the other women were both divinely happy and that she was the only one with a sob story for her life.

I must stop. I must stop, Ellie chanted to herself. I must force myself to look at the positive and not the negative. If nothing else, doing that will make people stop telling me that idiot story about the half-full and half-empty glass of water, she thought, then told herself to cut out the sarcasm.

Think of something good, she thought. Think happy thoughts. Think . . .

Leaning back against the seat, she closed her eyes. Legs and Face, she thought, then smiled in remembrance. "And I was . . ." she whispered aloud, smiling broadly.

The plane engine seemed to make a cocoon of sound, so that Ellie could hear nothing else but the roar. In the background she could hear a man with a monotone voice droning on and on and on. Glad I'm not married to him! Ellie thought as she began to visualize the first time she'd met the two women.

It had all started with that nerdy little man at the New York Department of Motor Vehicles, Ellie thought with a smile. And she'd never forget his name: Ira Girvin. His name was on a little badge on his chest and it was right at Ellie's eye level, and considering how short Ellie was, that meant he couldn't have been more than about five feet four.

"Sit over there and wait," the little man said to Ellie, and she could see that he loved having the power to make people wait.

With a fake smile, she took the forms from under the cage and turned around. There were some people standing between her and the bench along the wall, but when they moved, Ellie saw them. Sitting at opposite ends of a short green bench, looking in opposite directions from each other, were two of the most extraordinary women Ellie had ever seen.

The one on the left had on a black leotard with a long dark green silk skirt clinging to her legs. With her dark auburn hair pulled tightly back in a knot, she looked as if she was probably a dancer, just off the exercise floor, and she had a body that any sensible woman on earth would kill to have. She was like an illustration of what the human body *can* look like.

She had a pretty face, and her long neck curved gracefully down to wide, strong shoulders, then small breasts atop a stomach that looked as though it could flip coins over. Slim, strong hips topped legs that had to be seen to be believed: long, muscular, graceful. Even the way the woman was sitting was as though it had been choreographed, with elegant feet pointed, her hands in liquid repose.

Astonishing woman! Ellie thought; then she dragged her eyes away to look at the other woman. While the one in the leotard was graceful, this one was beautiful, so beautiful, in fact, that Ellie had to blink a couple of times to be sure she was seeing correctly. The woman was at least six feet tall and she was quite thin, but thin in a way that made you want to look like her. And she was beautiful. No, there had to be a term that didn't sound so run-of-the-mill. There were lots of women who were beautiful, but this one was . . . was . . . Well, she was perfection.

She was wearing a simple little summer dress, something with ruffles down the front of it, something that had probably been bought in some tiny Midwestern town and would usually have looked out of place in sophisticated New York. But this woman made the dress look like couture. There was something about her that made that plain, ordinary dress look as though it were grateful to be worn by this divine creature.

The woman had long, dark blonde hair that fell silkily down her back in big waves. Her face . . . Her face was that of a goddess, Ellie thought as she gaped at the woman. She had high cheekbones, a perfect nose, full lips. Her eyes were almond shaped, with thick black lashes set under brows that were perfect arches. Flawless skin, perfect hands and nails, and encased in little sandals were feet that looked like something off a marble statue.

For a moment Ellie just stood there looking from one woman to the other. Then, slowly, she turned back to Mr. Nerd, Ira, her eyebrows raised in question, as though to say, Are they for real?

Ira gave her a little shrug and a smile, then nodded his head toward them as though to tell Ellie she was to take her place between those two.

Slowly, Ellie walked toward the bench. The two young women had their backs to her and paid no attention when she sat down between them. Ellie tried to place the form on her knee without touching either of the two gorgeous creatures, but it wasn't easy. She twisted and turned but couldn't seem to find a way to sit and write at the same time. When she did manage to squeeze herself in tightly and raise her knee to use as a desk, the cheap pen she had wouldn't write.

For a moment Ellie raised her eyes skyward. Why, oh why, hadn't she renewed her driver's license before she'd left home? But today was her twenty-first birthday and if she didn't renew her license today, it would expire. It wasn't as though she were going to need a driver's license in New York, but if she should ever make it as the world's greatest painter, she might need to be able to drive, and who wanted to have to take that test over again?

She looked up at the counter where Ira was marking other people's applications. If she went to him, she was sure he'd tell her that the New York DMV was not a free-pen-lending institution.

"Excuse me," Ellie said weakly to the two backs on either side of her, "but do either of you have a pen I could borrow?"

There was no reply from either of the backs. "Great," she said under her breath.

"What did I expect, brains behind the beauty?"

She hadn't expected anyone to hear her. She'd grown up in a small house with four older brothers, all of whom seemed to be in a permanent contest to see who could make the most noise. Ellie's only defense against them had been to make snide remarks under her breath. It had always been an exciting game because if any of her brothers happened to hear one of Ellie's biting little remarks, she'd get an Indian head rub, a twisted-skin-arm, anything her jock brothers could come up with.

But the women beside her did hear, and it took Ellie a few seconds to realize that they were laughing. She could see ripples in the muscles of the dancer's back, and the ruffles around the neck of the other one seemed to move in a nonexistent breeze.

With her head down, Ellie smiled. "Can either of you read?" she said in a tiny voice. Slowly, Ellie felt the dancer turn and when Ellie looked up, the dancer was smiling mischievously.

"I can read a bit," she said, smiling, her eyes laughing.

Ellie smiled back. It was on the tip of her

tongue to blurt out, Where did you get that body of yours and can I buy one too? but she restrained herself. Before she'd left for New York, her mother had had one of her little talks with her daughter about keeping her mouth shut and thinking before she spoke.

But before Ellie could say a word, she felt The Gorgeous One on the other side of her turning. The dancer's head lifted as she looked over Ellie to the blonde creature beside her. When Ellie turned, her breath stopped.

Was it possible that the woman could be more beautiful up close than from across the room? She didn't wear any makeup, yet her skin was what makeup was all about. People paid millions to try to get that perfect, creamy texture to their skin, that delicate blush, that—

Suddenly, the girl smiled, a huge, radiant smile—and Ellie's eyes opened wide in shock. One of her front teeth was missing! There was a great black hole where her front tooth should have been. That this perfect woman should have such a flaw was . . .

"Cain't read. Cain't write," the beauty

said in a hillbilly accent, then grinned broadly.

While Ellie was still in shock, she heard the laughter of the dancer seated behind her.

"Madison Appleby," said the beautiful thing; then she stretched her hand around Ellie to shake the dancer's hand.

Ellie knew that something was going on that she wasn't in on, but she hadn't yet caught on.

The beauty looked down at Ellie, then extended her hand. "Madison Appleby," she said, but Ellie didn't move.

Then, bending, the beauty took something out of her mouth, and smiled at Ellie.

It was then that Ellie realized that the tall woman had stuck what looked like a black eraser cap over her front tooth to make it look as though one tooth was missing. And, Ellie, ever gullible, hadn't caught on as fast as the dancer. But when Ellie did understand, she smiled—and she liked the woman instantly. That someone as beautiful as this woman was could make fun of her own pulchritude made her Ellie's kind of person.

She shook the woman's hand. "Too bad

about the tooth," Ellie said, smiling. "But I think everyone should have a flaw."

"Brainlessness isn't a flaw?" Madison asked, eyes laughing.

"I thought we were just penless," the dancer said from behind Ellie.

"Penless and Brainless," Madison said. "Maybe we should go on the road."

Between them, Ellie sat blinking. Usually she was the one making the jokes, but they were beating her. "How about Legs and Face?" Ellie said.

"And what would *you* be?" Madison shot back, looking down her perfect nose at Ellie.

"Talent," Ellie answered instantly; then the three of them laughed together.

And that's how we felt about ourselves, Ellie thought as she snuggled deeper into the airplane seat. She'd pulled the shade down and had propped a pillow against the window so she could close her eyes and give herself over to the memory of that day when she'd first met Madison and Leslie.

After the dancer had lent her a pen, Ellie had filled out her form and taken it to Ira. "So what brings you two to New York?" Ellie asked when she'd returned to the bench. "Street cleaning?"

Leslie smiled. "Broadway lights," she said dreamily. "I left the boy back home at the altar." After she said the last, her eyes opened wide in shock. "I don't mean I really left him at the altar, but . . . but it was close enough that I know that it was a dreadful thing for me to do." She sounded as though she were saying a memorized speech.

"And you look sorry that you did it," Madison said solemnly, then the three of them laughed again. "Small town?"

"Suburb just outside Columbus, Ohio," Leslie said. "And you?"

"Erskine, Montana. Ever hear of it?"

Ellie and Leslie shook their heads no.

Ellie looked up at Madison. "Should I assume that we'll be seeing your face on the cover of magazines?"

"I just got here yesterday, so I haven't had time to do much of anything. I'm to go today and present my photos and—"

"Do you have them with you? Could we see them?" Ellie asked eagerly.

"I guess," Madison said without much enthusiasm, then she bent down and picked up a large, flat, black plastic zip-around notebook and handed it to Ellie.

Eagerly, Ellie unzipped the portfolio and opened it, Leslie peering over her shoulder. There were about a dozen photos of Madison, tastefully made up, her hair neat and tidy. There were head shots and a couple of full-length pictures, all of them perfectly composed and perfectly lit. On the side of each photo was the name of a photographer in Erskine, Montana.

"You're prettier than this," Ellie said, frowning as she closed the portfolio. She wasn't going to say so, but they were a spectacularly boring set of photos.

Madison just shrugged and looked ahead to where Ira was still stamping people's papers.

While they sat there, Ellie became aware of people looking at them. They would come in the entrance door, do a double take, look away, then look back again. Or they'd just plain stop and stare until someone jostled them and made them come out of their stupor and move.

"I'm beginning to feel like I should charge people for looking at you two."

" 'Two?' " Leslie asked, looking at Ellie in astonishment. "I think you mean three."

"Right," Ellie said sarcastically. "I must look like a gnome between you two." Now that Ellie was growing just a tiny bit used to the beauty of Madison, she realized that there was a calmness about the young woman that made her feel good.

"Don't you realize what that little man has done?" Madison asked.

"Who?" Leslie asked.

"You mean Ira?" Ellie asked.

"Yes, him." Ira glanced up just as Madison looked at him, and for a moment he paused, his hand raised mid-stamp. "He put us here so he could look at us."

Ellie gave a little laugh. "You two for sure, but not me." She expected the two of them to agree, but they didn't.

Madison looked down at Ellie in that cool way that Ellie was already becoming used to. "But you're lovely. Sort of like Goldie Hawn, that kind of soft, adorable loveliness."

Ellie blinked for a moment. Having grown up with four older brothers, she hadn't received many compliments in her life. Mostly her brothers had told her she was a pest and to go away or they'd make her sorry. "Me?" she finally said. Madison just looked at her, so Ellie turned to Leslie.

"I believe the saying is, Cute as a speckled puppy," Leslie said, smiling.

"*Hmmm*," Ellie said, thinking about this. "But cute doesn't last. Can you imagine what Goldie Hawn will look like when she's fifty?"

Madison was looking at Ira again. "My guess is that he's going to keep us here awhile. And I'll bet that he stations women here every day."

Ellie started to say something, but at that moment Ira motioned for her to come forward. He was holding up three driver's licenses. In a way, Ellie was glad that Madison was wrong, but she felt some regret that she couldn't spend more time with these women. She knew no one in New York, and she was beginning to feel a kinship with these women, as all of them were starting a new life.

And, besides, she would really like to hear Leslie's story about leaving a man at the altar. If she loved anything in the world, it was a good story. Ellie felt that Madison's story was written on her face, but obviously,

Leslie had worked long and hard to get that body of hers.

Ellie was the first to get up. "I'll get them," she said, then went to the cage, took all three licenses from Ira, then turned back to the bench. Leslie had a sweater over her arm and a huge black cloth bag, in preparation for leaving with her new license. But Madison hadn't moved an inch, just sat there looking at Ellie.

"Here we go," Ellie said as she looked down at the licenses. The one on top was Madison's. Even her driver's license photo was gorgeous.

But as she handed it to her, Madison said, "Check it."

"What?"

"Check the license. Make sure it says what it should."

"Okay," Ellie said slowly, looking at Madison as though she were a bit off her rocker. "Madison Aimes, born October the ninth, 1960. We have the same birthday."

"I have the same birthday too, but not the same last name," Leslie said. "*Aimes* is my name."

At that Ellie looked down at the licenses and saw that the three names were mixed up. Hers said, "Ellie Appleby," and Leslie's read, "Leslie Abbott."

Ellie looked at Madison with wide eyes. "How did you know?"

Madison shrugged. "Happens to me all the time. Any delay, any excuse to keep you there," she said, then looked away.

Ellie gave a glance to Leslie, then took the licenses back to Ira. At least he didn't pretend to be sorry for the mistake he'd made. "I guess you three will just have to wait a little bit longer, won't you?" he said with a smile. "Right there on that bench. And you better not leave the building in case I need to ask any of you any questions."

Ellie opened her mouth to tell him what she thought of him, maybe even to demand to see his supervisor, but then her vanity got the best of her. To be singled out to sit with two women like Leslie and Madison, to be a sort of living photograph, well . . . It didn't exactly make her feel bad. In fact, when she walked back to the bench, she was walking a little straighter than before.

She took her place between the two women. "So," she said, then turned to Leslie, "tell us all about the boy you jilted."

Leslie laughed. "Are all New Yorkers as blunt as you are?"

"I have no idea. I'm from Richmond, Virginia."

"Then we're all newcomers," Leslie said. "And are we all here to try to make our fortune?"

"Not try," Ellie said. "We're going to *do* it, right?"

"Yes!" Leslie said firmly, but Madison didn't say anything.

Ellie turned to Madison. "What about you? How many devastated young men did *you* leave behind?"

"None. Actually, I was dumped by my boyfriend."

Madison didn't say anything else, so Ellie stared at her in silence. She was too shocked to speak. After a moment she looked at Leslie and saw that she, too, was shocked. "No offense, Leslie," Ellie said, "but I need to hear this story *first*."

For a moment Madison was silent; then she said, "Oh, what the heck? Everyone in Erskine knows what happened, so it isn't exactly a secret."

Ellie bit her tongue to keep from remarking that everyone in Erskine could probably be told the secret of life, but it would still remain a mystery to the world.

"It was a case of high school love," Madison said. "Roger went to a high school about fifty miles from mine, but I was a cheerleader and—"

"Me too!" Leslie said; then they both looked down at Ellie in question.

"Not quite," Ellie said. "Debating team. Latin club."

"*Mmmm,*" Madison said. "So anyway, Roger and I met and were a couple all through high school. I never dated anybody but Roger. Our plan was that after we graduated, we would go to college together, then get married and live happily ever after. We even had the names of our kids picked out."

For a moment, Madison looked away, and when she turned back, her face was as composed as before, but there was pain in her eyes. She's used to hiding her emotions, Ellie thought, and for a moment she could see past Madison's beautiful face to see the real person inside.

"I should have known that there would be problems. You see, Roger's family is rich and my mom and I weren't."

"What about your father?" Ellie asked, heedless of manners and her mother's constant admonitions to not snoop into people's private affairs.

Madison shrugged one shoulder in a beautiful way. She should be on the movie screen, Ellie thought.

"Married man," Madison said. "He walked away—well, ran actually—the moment my mother told him she was pregnant. All I know about him is that his last name is Madison. My first name is my mother's revenge. She couldn't have his name, so she gave it to me. She said he couldn't deny her that small part of him."

For a moment the air was heavy with the anger that was in Madison's voice.

"Beats 'Ellie,' " Ellie said cheerfully. "My mother said she was sick of big, husky boys and she wanted a little girl, so she gave me a girly little name."

"Your real name isn't Eleanor?" Leslie asked.

"Nope. Plain ol' Ellie. I think I'll change it to Anastasia. So what happened to Roger?" Ellie asked Madison.

Madison let out the breath she'd been holding. Ellie's light remarks had broken the tension. "Two weeks before my high school graduation my mother was diagnosed with breast cancer."

"*Yeow!*" Ellie said.

Leslie put her arm across the back of the bench and gave Madison's arm a squeeze.

"Along with Roger, my mother was my life," Madison said. "She and I were a team. She'd raised me herself, working two jobs to make ends meet. At night she worked as a checker in a grocery and since she couldn't afford an evening baby-sitter, I used to go with her and hide in the back storage room. I can tell you lots about how a grocery is run." She had meant this as a joke, but neither Ellie nor Leslie was smiling.

"Anyway," Madison continued, "after Mother became ill, college had to be postponed." Again, Madison looked away for a moment. "To make a long story short, my mother died, but it took her four years to do it. By that time my college money had been spent on doctors and hospitals."

There was nothing Ellie could say, and judging from Leslie's silence, she felt the same way. "And Roger?" Ellie asked softly.

"Good ol' Roger, the love of my life, returned from college—where he'd gone on a full football scholarship, I might add. His parents are rich, but they have to be the cheapest people on the planet—and he had a fiancée on his arm."

"A what!?" Ellie said. "Why would any man marry someone other than *you*?" She didn't realize that she'd said this quite loudly until an entire line of people turned to look at them in interest.

"Beauty isn't everything," Madison said with a little smile.

"I'm not talking about beauty. You gave up your education to stay home and nurse your mother. That's beauty on the inside!"

Madison looked at Ellie in surprise; then she smiled until her whole face lit up. "I think I like you," she said, and Ellie smiled back.

"Go on," Leslie urged. "What did you do? And I agree with Ellie; why would he want someone else?"

Madison took a deep breath. "He said that since he'd graduated from college, he needed someone he could *talk* to. Someone educated."

At that, Ellie turned to look at Leslie, then back at Madison. "Castration would have been too good for him," she said softly.

Madison made a little face of agreement. "I thought so too at the time. Especially considering that all through high school I did most of his homework for him. He used to drive to my house three times a week and he'd always have a box full of schoolwork I was to 'help' him with. The truth was that he'd watch football on TV while I worked. Our dates often consisted of my doing his homework while Roger tossed a ball with somebody. And in college if he had a paper to write, he usually sent me the assignment and I wrote it."

"Could he get away with that?" Leslie asked. "Surely he would have been caught when he took his exams. You couldn't very well do those for him."

"No?" Madison asked, an eyebrow arched. "Roger was the best football player his high school had ever seen. He pretty much single-handedly won each and every game. The principal told the teachers that if Roger didn't get grades good enough to get him into college, then that teacher would stand a chance of losing his or her job, with or without tenure. I wasn't there, but I think the attitude at college wasn't much different."

"Well, that's fair," Ellie said, turning to Leslie. "Don't you agree?"

Leslie laughed. "So you got him into college, then helped him stay there, and all the while you were a saint."

At that Madison laughed. "A saint for nursing my mother? You know something, I enjoyed it." When the other two started to speak, Madison put up her hand. "No, no, I didn't enjoy my mother's suffering. But I was interested in the medical side of her illness. I even took a part-time job at the hospital. I had to drive seventy-five miles to get there, but—"

"Every day?" Ellie asked.

"Only three days a week. But Montana isn't like Virginia," Madison said, smiling. "You can put your foot on the gas pedal and go to sleep. More or less, anyway. During those four years Roger was away, I learned a lot. In fact, one of the doctors suggested that I go into nursing as a career, but later he . . ."

"Let me guess," Ellie said with a grimace. "He chased you around the desk."

Madison looked down at her hands. "Around the bed of a patient in a coma. But he really should have noticed that I had a full bedpan in my hands. I 'accidentally' spilled the contents all over the front of him."

At that Ellie exploded with laughter, causing the people to again turn and look at them. Leslie put her hand over her mouth as she laughed too.

"So if you liked nursing, why didn't you pursue it?" Leslie asked.

"Because . . ." Madison trailed off. How could she tell them what her life had been like? Maybe it was vain of her to think that she was beautiful, but all her life people had loved to *look* at her. Her mother said that even as a newborn she'd been extraordinary and people had noticed her. In school Madison had always been chosen to be the princess in the play. In the fifth grade she had begged to be allowed to be the witch, and she was thrilled when her teacher said yes, she could be the witch and wear the pointed hat and cackle. Madison had always loved to cackle. But then her teacher had gone home and rewritten the play so that at the end the witch turned out to be a beautiful princess in disguise. When Madison had protested, she was told that her face would sell tickets, so she had to stop complaining.

As Madison grew older, her beauty stayed with her and she grew to her present five feet eleven and a half inches tall. "I am *not* six feet tall!" she often said. Her mother had said that half of Madison's attraction to Roger was that he was taller than she was.

How could Madison tell these two women what it was like being a tourist attraction in her small town? Because during her teen years, that's what she had been— or at least that's what the girls who had graduated with her from high school had called her. There wasn't much going on in Erskine, just a few stores lining the main street. But Erskine's main street also happened to be part of the route to a major tourist area: winter skiing and summer outdoor sports. About six of the town's businesses had formed a council to try and come up with a way to get those cars that sped through their town to stop and buy. The council came up with several ideas of how to achieve this. One was to build a big jail and give lots of speeding tickets. They could put the driver in the jail, then, while his family waited for his release, they could shop in Erskine. That idea was discarded because it would probably make the tourists too angry to shop. "Not to mention that it's probably illegal," one of the council members had added.

There were more ideas tossed about, such as a couple of carnivals, and a film festival. "Spielberg doesn't show up just because you invite him," someone said. "Who wants to come to Erskine?" "We don't want them to come; we just need them to *stop*." At that someone had mumbled, "Too bad we can't get Madison to stand in the middle of the street. *That* would stop them."

From there the idea had taken hold, and the next thing Madison knew, she was being offered the job of handing out advertising brochures to passing motorists. "All I have to do is pass out brochures?" she'd asked. "That's it," had been the reply.

So the local businessmen had put up a red light smack in the middle of Erskine's one major street, and next to it they had erected a little shelter, rather like an old-fashioned bus stop, and when the cars stopped at the red light, Madison was to hand them the brochures.

It had all seemed simple enough and the

work was only on weekends, when the traf-
fic was heaviest, so she'd taken the job. But
it had all nearly backfired when so many
cars stopped in Erskine and so many men,
on their way to a weekend of merrymaking,
had hit on Madison that the local sheriff had
had to assign two deputies to sit near her. In
the end, Erskine decided that it was safer to
put up a billboard with a picture of Madison
on it. She was wearing cutoff denims, a red
shirt tied around her waist, and she was
inviting people to stop in Erskine and look
around.

To Madison, the whole thing had been a
great embarrassment, but she needed the
money for her mother's medical bills and
what with Roger in college, she was lonely,
and it had been nice to talk to the people
who were driving through on their way to
somewhere else.

"So what happened?" Ellie urged. "What
made you come here to New York?"

"The town council thought that they
owed me for something." Madison waved
her hand when Ellie started to speak. "It
doesn't matter now for what, but after
Roger dumped me, they decided to send

me here to New York so I could become a model."

Madison didn't tell them what her pastor's daughter had spat at her in an angry fit one day. The girl had always been jealous of Madison, because not only was Madison beautiful, but she was smart, and when people could get past her beauty, they liked Madison a lot. It was too much for the spiteful girl to stand, so she told Madison a secret she wasn't supposed to know. It was true that the town council had put up the money to send Madison to New York. "If she becomes famous, it will put us on the map," they'd reasoned. But the girl's father, the pastor of the church that Madison and her mother had always attended, said that the money they had gathered wasn't enough. The girl just "happened" to have picked up the telephone one day when her father was dialing and she'd heard a child's voice say, "Madison residence." Her father the pastor had said, "I'd like to speak to your father, please." A moment later a man came on the line. "Yes?" he said. "Your daughter needs ten thousand dollars. Now. Send it to me here at the church. You remember my name and address?" There had been a pause on the line, then, "Yes, I re-member." After that there was a click and the phone went dead.

But Madison didn't tell this part of the story about her father sending money. That was private and not to be told. Instead, she summed up by saying that the town council had sent her to New York to become a model, and left it at that.

Ellie sensed that Madison was leaving out some information, so she'd fired off lots of questions. But Madison had smiled in a Mona Lisa way and not answered them.

"What about you, Leslie?" Madison had asked in a way that made Ellie know that no amount of coaxing was going to get her to reveal more. "What about the man you left behind?"

"Alan," Leslie said, and tried to look sad, but there was such a gleam of happiness and anticipation in her eyes that Ellie didn't think anything could make her sad. "We were going to get married, but I chickened out. I know I'm already twenty-one and quite old enough to settle down and start producing babies but . . ."

"You want to see *life*," Ellie said enthusi-astically.

"Oh, yes!"

"So you ditched the boy and came to New York," Ellie said, smiling.

"More or less. Although, Alan was pretty angry about it. He said he could have done some things in college if he'd had any idea that I was going to turn out to be a—" Leslie looked down at her hands. "It wasn't a pretty scene."

For a moment the three of them were silent; then Madison said, "You have his address? Maybe Alan and I could get together."

It was what was needed to lighten their mood, and the three of them laughed hard. "What about you?" Leslie asked, looking at Ellie. "So far we have one jilter and one jiltee. What are you?"

"Nothing," she said, then quickly added, "I mean, nothing one would associate with romance, that is. I've wanted to be an artist since I was a child. All I ever wanted for any Christmas or birthday was paints and crayons and colored pencils, anything that I could draw with. In high school I think I went on three dates. I had four big brothers, all of whom have rocks for brains, I mean, I love them and all and they're good guys, but—"

"Stupid," Madison said.

"Yes," Ellie said with a sigh. "Big, good-looking, great at all sports, but my mother had to use a whip over them to get them to open a book. Like your Roger, they—"

"Please," Madison said, "not *my* Roger."

"Right. Sorry. Anyway, like you, their girl friends did their homework for them. And I mean that as two words: 'girl' and 'friend.' They had girlfriends to date, pretty girls who could fill out a strapless dress, but they also had some mousy little thing to do their work for them. That's why when I first saw you, I . . ." Ellie trailed off and looked away from Madison.

"Why you assumed that I was as dumb as the girls your brothers dated. Don't worry about it; it happens all the time."

"But you didn't have a boyfriend?" Leslie asked Ellie. "But you're—"

"I know, so cute," Ellie said with a sigh. "I guess I had more testosterone than I could handle in my house, so I didn't want any more. I just wanted to draw, so that's what I did in college. I graduated with a degree in fine arts in May, and this summer I lived at home and worked in an art gallery in Richmond. There was an old shed in back of our house that my mother used to call her 'summerhouse' because she planned to nag my father enough to get him to add some doors and windows and make it a place where she could sit and read. But, so far, she's been nagging for nearly thirty years and hasn't made any headway." Ellie said this with a smile, as it was a great family joke. At least it was a joke to everyone in her family except her mother.

"She should remodel it herself," Leslie said firmly. "My father is a building contractor and sometimes he would take me to work with him. I can use a hammer and a screwdriver as well as any man."

Both Ellie and Madison smiled at Leslie, because the way she said this was so very defiant.

"I am *woooooomman,* hear me roar," Ellie sang under her breath, and the three of them laughed.

"Anyway," Ellie said, "I used the old shed as a studio this summer and worked every minute that I wasn't at the gallery. And in the end . . ." She trailed off and looked down at her hands.

"Someone here in New York saw your work," Madison said softly.

"Yes!" Ellie said, and her eyes were sparkling as she looked up at Madison. "Yes, yes, and double yes! Miranda, who owned the gallery, sent photos of my work to a friend of hers here, and, well, one thing led to another and I was offered a studio loft apartment in the Village to sublet for one year. It's ugly and damp and has an elevator that looks like something out of a horror movie, but it has good light and lots of space, and—"

Ellie broke off so she could take a breath. "It's a chance," she said after she got her composure back. "My parents are forking out all the money. Only one of my brothers went to college, so my parents said I could have the college money of the other three, but I think that . . ." Again she broke off and looked down at her hands.

"They're helping you because they love you," Leslie said softly, then squeezed Ellie's shoulder.

Smiling, Ellie looked at Leslie and thought, She's a romantic. All the way through, she's a romantic.

"More or less," Ellie said, smiling. "My mom and I say we have to stick together against the boys."

Madison was looking at Ellie intently. "There wasn't one boy you were interested in? All the way through high school and college?"

"I'm not a, you-know-what, if that's what you mean," Ellie said. "I've been out on dates, but the men I liked physically couldn't tell a Renoir from a Van Gogh. They thought Rubens played for the Dallas Cowboys. And the guys in the art department . . ." She raised her hands, palm up, and grimaced. "Half of them liked each other, and the other half looked like they'd never had a bath."

Madison leaned back against the bench. "I can't imagine not being with a man," she said softly. "Maybe it was seeing how hard life was on my mother, but I grabbed on to Roger and never let go. Even when he broke up with me, I—" She broke off, then looked at the other two. "I asked him not to," Madison said with a little smile, and again Ellie saw that pain in her eyes.

Ellie wanted to get Madison's mind away from her past. "But now we're here and all that's behind us." She turned from Leslie to Madison. "You got away from Alan, and you got away from Roger. And good riddance to both of them."

"She's going to be the first of us to fall for some man and leave her art behind," Madison said solemnly. "Three years from now she'll be living in a tiny house somewhere and have half a dozen kids."

"If not more," Leslie said.

"Ha!" Ellie said. "The only man who could win me is one who had a thousand times more talent than I do. So . . . Unless I meet the reincarnation of Michelangelo, I'm safe."

"Wasn't Michelangelo gay?" Madison said to Leslie.

"Or was he the crazy one who cut off his ear?" Leslie replied.

"Okay, okay, you two. You can give me all the grief you want, but now we're on equal terms."

"Wait a minute!" Leslie said. "Speaking of equal, isn't today our birthday? I know it's mine, and isn't it—"

"Mine too," Ellie said, and Madison echoed her.

"We have to have a cake," Leslie said firmly.

"She's going to make a great mother," Ellie said to Madison, deadpan.

Leslie ignored them. "I'm going to ask lit-tle rat-fink Ira where the nearest bakery is, and I'm going to buy us a birthday cake."

At that she got up, and the words that Ellie and Madison were about to say stopped on their lips, for to watch Leslie walk was to watch beauty in motion. She moved as though she were floating, the sheer skirt clinging to her long, shapely legs.

"Wow," Ellie said under her breath when Leslie reached Ira's window. "Wow."

"Exactly," Madison said, her eyes wide.

Leslie waved as she walked out the door; then Ellie and Madison were left alone. And when they were, they found that they hadn't much to say to each other. For all that Leslie was the quietest of the three, there was something about her that enabled the three of them to talk. There was something warm, some easiness within Leslie that created an atmosphere that made it okay to reveal se-crets.

The silence made Ellie nervous, but Madison just leaned back against the bench and closed her eyes. Ellie was all kinetic en-ergy, while Madison seemed to have the pa-tience of the ages.

When Ellie looked up a few minutes later and saw Leslie coming toward them with a white box, she was surprised. It certainly hadn't taken her long.

"You'll never believe this," Leslie said as she sat down beside Ellie and opened the box. Inside was a small cake with fluffy white frosting; their names were written on the top in pink icing.

"That was fast," Ellie said, looking up.

Leslie's eyes were laughing. "There's a bakery next door, and every day they make a cake for 'Ira's Girls.'"

Ellie blinked at her. "You mean us? We are now called 'Ira's Girls'?"

Leslie was laughing. "You were right, Madison; the little twerp chooses two to three young women every day and makes them sit here on this bench while he makes a thousand mistakes on their licenses so they have to wait. Since so many people go to the DMV on their birthdays, it seems that a lot of them come up with the idea of sharing a cake."

"Does he get a kickback from the bakery?" Ellie asked. "And why does the City of New York let him get away with it?"

Leslie leaned forward and lowered her

voice. "That's what I asked them. Not about the kickback, but why he's allowed to do it. See that little window up there?" she said, turning her head and looking up at the wall behind Ira.

Above their heads, directly above Ira's caged window, was a small window, so dirty that it was a wonder anyone could see out of it.

"Ira's boss works up there," Leslie said. "From what the women in the bakery said, nothing has ever been said one way or another, but Ira's allowed to get away with this because his boss likes the view as much as Ira does."

"I'm sure I should be furious about this," Ellie said, "but then, today I've met you two, and . . ." She shrugged. "So what kind of cake is it?"

"Coconut. The woman at the bakery said that chocolate was too messy. And look, she gave me plates, napkins, and forks. So, Ira's Girls, let's dig in."

And dig in they did.

Three

"Please fasten your seat belts to prepare for landing," came the voice over the speaker, and Ellie came back to the present.

What had happened to that beautiful, beautiful girl? Ellie wondered. In the intervening nineteen years Ellie doubted if she'd ever looked at a fashion magazine without thinking of Madison. "She isn't as pretty as Madison," Ellie had said so many times that her ex-husband had said, "Let me guess: Whoever or whatever it, she, or he is, isn't as pretty as Madison." After that remark, Ellie had never again mentioned her aloud, but that didn't stop Ellie from thinking of Madison. Had Madison returned to her little hometown in Montana and gone to nursing school? Maybe she'd married a doctor and had half a dozen kids.

At the thought of children, Ellie pushed up the shade and looked out the window. Children was a place she'd better not go. In fact, children had been what had ended her marriage. The day after Christmas, the day after her ex had thrown yet another of his all-day tantrums about how Ellie never "gave" him enough, "did" enough for him, Ellie had looked at her husband and thought, I gave up children for this selfish man. She didn't know it then, but that was the moment when she left him. Left him in her mind, that is. The physical leaving and the courts would take nearly a year of her life, but her mind left him in that one instant.

As the plane touched down, Ellie's nervousness returned. It really was a foolish thing to make a date to see women you hadn't seen in so many years. It was like those horrible high school reunions. You return with pictures in your mind of how people were, so the lines on their faces and the rolls on their bodies were shocking. Then you go to the rest room and see yourself in a mirror and you realize that you have the same lines and the same rolls.

When the plane had stopped, she picked up her tote bag and stood up. As she waited to exit, her mind went back to the day at the DMV. Madison had been hiding something that day, she thought. Back then, Ellie had been so full of herself, so sure that she was going to set the world on fire with her art, and she'd been so positive that both Leslie and Madison were going to do the same thing. Looking at Madison, you thought you knew all about her. She would have been the prom queen and the most popular girl in school. Of course she would marry the captain of the football team.

Madison had fulfilled part of this scenario, but things had changed for her. Why hadn't she made it in the modeling world? Ellie wondered. Why hadn't Ellie been seeing pictures of Madison for the last nineteen years? It seemed to Ellie that all Madison would have to do is walk on the streets of New York and some photographer would beg her to model for him. Didn't that kind of thing happen all the time? Weren't models still discovered sitting in restaurants and in drugstores or wherever?

The people across from Ellie moved into the line in the aisle, and Ellie stepped behind them. As she waited for the line to continue moving, she thought about Leslie. A dancer was more difficult to keep track of, especially since Ellie didn't get to see too many Broadway shows. Had Leslie danced on Broadway, then met some fabulously wealthy man and married him? Or had Ellie been watching too many old black-and-white movies?

As the line began to move, Ellie took a deep breath. This was it, she thought. When she'd invited the other two women, she'd asked that if they said yes, to please send her their plane information. This had been Jeanne's idea. Using the flight information, Ellie had arranged for cars to meet the women at the airport and take them to Jeanne's house on the coast, northeast of Bangor.

Maybe it had been cowardly of her, but Ellie had arranged a flight that made her the last one to arrive. It would probably mean that she got the sofa bed instead of a bedroom, but she was willing to pay that price. When she got to Jeanne's house, Leslie and Madison should already be there.

As Ellie walked into the airport, a man in a black uniform was standing there with "Abbott" written on a piece of cardboard. She handed him her tote bag and her luggage claim tags, then followed him to the baggage carousel.

When they were finally in the car and he'd pulled away from the airport, Ellie wanted to tell him to turn around and go back. How could she tell them about her life? She had been a success, but now all that was gone. She had let a man beat her, let a court system beat her. All Ellie's life people had said that she was a little bulldog, that she never let go, that when she wanted something, she went after it. "And heaven help anyone who gets in her way," her mother used to say. But Ellie had given up. Ellie hadn't held on and, in the end, Ellie had failed.

But now, Ellie didn't tell the driver to turn back. In the last three years she had lived with constant, never-ending fear, and now was the time to start fighting back.

Some fight, she thought as she turned to look out the window at gorgeous Maine. The tree leaves were aflame with red and gold. Was it the same with everyone that their birth month was their favorite? October was certainly Ellie's favorite month, when the air was cool and the leaves turned brilliant shades of color. After the lethargy of

the summer, autumn seemed to wake people up.

It will be all right, she told herself. I am
nineteen years older and so are they. Even
Madison must have aged. Maybe if I don't
tell them what was done to me, they won't
feel sorry for me. Maybe if . . .

"Ever been to Maine before?" the driver
asked, snapping Ellie out of her thoughts.

"No. Do you live here?"

"All my life."

"So tell me everything," she said, wanting
something to take her mind off the coming
meeting, and a chatty driver would work as
well as anything else.

Ellie saw them before they saw her. And
when she saw them, it was as though a
thousand pounds of worry was taken off her
chest. She gave a great sigh of relief and
took a step forward, but then she halted,
wanting to give herself time to look and to
think.

The driver had taken her to the address
she'd given him, then took her bags out of
the trunk while Ellie had a look at the house.
Jeanne had said that the house was fairly

old, built by a ship's carpenter in the 1800s, but she hadn't told Ellie that it was so charming. It was small, two-story, with a deep porch in the front. What made the house stand out was the beautiful gingerbread trim around the exterior. It looked like something that a guidebook would caption, "Most Photographed House in Maine." Just looking at the house made Ellie smile. Jeanne had said that the caretaker would leave the house unlocked so all three of them could arrive when they wanted and not have to worry about being locked out. That the house could be left unlocked said everything about the little coastal town.

Once Ellie had tipped the driver, she picked up her case and quietly opened the front door. There were three unpacked suitcases on the floor in the little living room, so no one had yet chosen a bedroom.

The living room was charming, a few Colonial antiques, interspersed with lots of local crafts and a couple of pieces of real art. There was a big model ship above the entrance doorway, and one wall of the room was taken up by an enormous stone fireplace. The rest of the furniture looked vaguely Colonial, but, more important, it looked very comfortable. The colors of dark green and rust, with touches of yellow here and there, matched the exterior autumn splendor perfectly.

"No wonder you lent this," Ellie whispered aloud, thinking that her therapist wanted to show off the place.

Straight ahead was a wide doorway, where Ellie could see the kitchen with its cheerful yellow cabinets, and through there she could see into the back garden. And that's where two women were sitting under a tree that was covered in magnificent dark red leaves. The women were facing the house, with what looked like a pitcher of lemonade between them on a small wooden table, and they were quietly talking.

Ellie stepped through the living room, into the kitchen, and paused at the sink to look out the window. She expected the women to see her instantly, but because the sun was behind them and reflecting on the glass, they didn't. When she realized that she could see and not be seen, Ellie couldn't resist the temptation to stand and look.

Leslie was no longer extraordinary. She looked like a middle-aged, middle-class housewife. She was still slim, but she had lost all definition to what had once been a body-to-die-for. Her hair seemed to have lost its auburn glow and was now just a sort of brown, and judging by the many gray strands running through it, she didn't color it. Her skin was good, but it showed the lines about her eyes, and there were deep channels running from her nose down to her mouth.

She's very unhappy about something, Ellie thought.

Ellie kept looking at Leslie and remembering the girl she had once been. Now, the only thing that remained of the Leslie she'd met so long ago was her posture. Leslie still sat upright, her back as straight as a yardstick.

I wouldn't have known her, Ellie thought, frowning.

She knew that, sooner or later, she was going to have to turn her head and look at Madison. But Ellie didn't want to. She'd seen more than she wanted to when she'd first glanced at that once-beautiful woman.

For a moment, Ellie closed her eyes and gave a little prayer that asked for strength;

then she opened her eyes and turned to look at Madison.

Seeing Madison now was like being handed a Monet that someone had left in the rain and snow for nineteen years. She was something unbelievably beautiful that had been destroyed by neglect and time.

Madison was still tall, but her spine was slightly curved now, as though she spent a lot of time hunched over a desk. And she was smoking. In the few minutes that Ellie had been standing there, Madison had finished one cigarette and started another. In front of her was a big glass ashtray that was full of filter stubs, and there was a pack of cigarettes and a throwaway lighter beside it.

If Ellie looked hard, she could see the beauty that Madison had once been. But now there were dark circles under her eyes. Her skin, which had once glowed with health, was now almost gray. Her hair was still long, and even though it was pulled severely back off her face, Ellie could see that there was no luster to her hair.

Whereas once Madison had been slender, she was now gaunt. She wore a thin, long-sleeve knit shirt that clung to arms that were too thin, too lacking of muscle. Her legs didn't fill out trousers that were stovepipe style.

To Ellie's eyes, Leslie looked unhappy, but Madison looked as though life were a Mack truck and it had run over her.

Jeanne's words that maybe the other two women had had a harder time than Ellie'd had, came to her mind. And with this thought, came relief to Ellie. She wasn't going to be judged by these women. She wasn't going to be condemned because she'd gained a whopping forty pounds. And she wasn't going to be ridiculed because she'd lost her success, and lost her direction in life.

Nor did she think she was going to receive pity—and that was an enormous relief.

For a moment Ellie looked away from the two women sitting under the tree and waiting for her. How did she play this? Did she put on her happy face and say that they hadn't changed a bit? Did she lie and say that she was well and happy and working on a new book that was, like the others, sure to be a best-seller?

For a moment Ellie thought back to the day in the DMV. That day she'd been sarcastic and arrogant. Oh, yes, the arrogance of believing in herself, knowing that she was going to conquer the world. In other words, she'd been herself. And they had liked her then. So now she was going to be herself again.

After taking a deep breath, she put her hand on the knob of the back door and opened it.

When she walked outside, the other two stopped talking and looked up at Ellie. She could see the shock on their faces at the size of her. She was a great deal heavier than she'd been when they last saw her.

Leslie was trying hard to collect herself so she could speak, but Ellie beat her to it. "Too bad we didn't offer a prize for which of us looks the worst," Ellie said with great cheerfulness.

"I'd win," Madison said. She was sitting on a chair, the cigarette between her fingers, her long legs extended before her, and she smiled at Ellie. And when she did, Ellie could see part of the original Madison, the one who could outshine the sun with her smile.

"I don't know about that," Ellie said as she sat on the chair next to Leslie. There was a third glass on the table and she filled it with lemonade. "I think fat is pretty shocking. It shows a lack of discipline."

"At least you've made a success of your *life*," Madison said. "You're a big-deal writer. The whole world buys your books, but I work in a vet's office. If a dog is sick, I'm the one who cleans it up. No husband, no kids. Zip."

Her words were dreadful, but they were said with such cheerfulness that they made Ellie smile. It was good to hear that someone else had problems. In the last years it seemed that everyone she met had a wonderful life with no problems at all. They were all probably lying, but even that thought hadn't penetrated Ellie's misery.

But now she could smile about it. "You think that's bad? I'm a has-been. Dried up. Haven't written a word in three years. I had nearly everything I'd earned in ten years of writing taken away from me in a divorce court, all of it given to an ex-husband who did nothing all day."

"At least you had something to take away," Madison said happily. "I never did anything to earn a lot of money. I never had anything that anyone could take away."

"But isn't that better?" Ellie asked. "You don't have a world asking about what you used to be."

"Oh, no," Madison said seriously. "It's better to have been than never to have been at all. I think Nietzsche said that."

"Plato," Ellie said firmly. "It was Plato who said that, but I agree with Socrates. He said that—"

While Ellie was making up something, she thought, I love this. I love this back-and-forth, teasing dialogue. And I have missed it. And it was so, so, oh, so very, very good not to see pity in someone's eyes. There was nothing in Madison's eyes that said she felt sorry for the Ellie she used to know, the slim one, the one who didn't have eyes full of pain. In fact, seeing herself reflected in Madison's eyes, Ellie could almost believe that she was still that girl who had her life before her.

"Excuse me," Leslie said.

Ellie and Madison stopped their dialogue about whose life was in worse shape to turn and look at Leslie.

Leslie gave the two of them a very sweet smile. "I married the boy next door and had two kids. Now most of the town is telling me that he's having an affair with his new assistant whose name is Bambi. I live in a huge Victorian house that my husband fills with untouchable antiques. Last year he tore out my kitchen and made it into a work of art. My mother wants me to divorce him. My daughter wants me to 'fight back,' whatever that means. And my son runs away and hides at the mere hint of conflict—which means that I rarely see him. And as for what I do now, I dedicate my life to the three of them, and if I left, I wouldn't have the slightest idea how to get a job, much less keep one. And . . ." She paused, as though waiting for a drum roll. "I am on *three* fund-raising committees."

For a moment Madison and Ellie sat there and blinked at Leslie. Then Ellie turned to Madison, then back to Leslie.

"You win," Madison said.

"Or lose. Depends on how you look at it," Ellie said.

"So how about dinner?" Madison said. "I'm starved."

Ellie narrowed her eyes at her. "If you tell me you're one of those women who eats everything and never gains weight, I will kill you."

"Get out your gun, sweetie," Madison said with a big smile.

Before another word could be said, Leslie stood up. "Come on, you two, and stop trying to outdo each other. My country club is giving a charity dance next month and I need a theme for it. You two can help me come up with some ideas."

As Ellie stood up, she again looked at Madison. "Definitely the worst," Ellie said.

"Yes, definitely." Madison looked at Leslie. "A country club? Please tell me that you at least give dancing lessons to children. Something!"

Leslie smiled. "My big Victorian house came with a beautiful, romantic summerhouse. It was falling apart, but years ago I fixed it up. While I was pregnant. But my husband moved a TV in there. Then he—"

"Stop! Stop!" Ellie said, putting her hands over her face as though to shield herself from arrows. "I can't stand any more. What do you say to our going out and getting drunk? Unless one of you has become an alcoholic, that is."

Madison held up her cigarette. "These are my only vice."

Ellie put her hand on her hip. "Chocolate."

The two of them turned to Leslie. "No vices at all. None," she said, smiling.

Both Madison and Ellie groaned. "She always has to win, doesn't she?" Ellie said.

Leslie stuck both her arms out, elbows bent. "Shall we go find someplace to paint the town red?"

Ellie and Madison linked their arms with Leslie's; then the three of them headed toward the little gate by the side of the house to make their way to the street.

Four

They'd had dinner, lobster of course, at a restaurant with the word "main" in the name. And after dinner they had walked about the tiny town and looked at the wharf, at the boats in the harbor, and read the signs on the buildings that proclaimed they had been owned by so-and-so sea captain.

"Were they all named Josiah?" Ellie asked.

After having made such intimate contact before dinner, once they were in the company of others, they'd seemed to lose that feeling of knowing each other well. It had started when they'd entered the restaurant and some woman had squinted at Ellie and said, "Aren't you—?"

Ellie had cut her off sharply. "No," she'd said firmly, then walked ahead of Leslie and

Madison to follow the hostess to a table. But the woman had been seated near them and she'd kept staring so hard at her that Ellie'd not been able to enjoy her meal or the company of the others.

And the presence of the people in the restaurant and the woman's staring seemed to take away the feeling that they were just old friends. The truth was that one of them was a celebrity.

"So tell us about your children," Madison said to Leslie in a formal voice.

The easy camaraderie was gone. They were strangers to each other now, each woman with a very different life from that of the others. Leslie, with her life of church and schools and committee meetings, was very different from Madison, with her life of dating and looking for Mr. Right. And Ellie's life was the most removed from either of theirs. Neither of them had ever been asked for her autograph.

"Shall we get out of here?" Ellie asked after a short time.

Since neither of the other women wanted to be reminded of Ellie's mega-success, they agreed readily. How could you relax with a woman who the First Lady had said was her favorite author?

Once they were outside, the tension didn't relax, and as they wandered around, looking in the store windows, both Ellie and Madison grew silent.

It was Leslie who was the peacemaker, the one who smoothed over the situation. "I thought we were going to get drunk," Leslie said.

Neither Madison nor Ellie answered her, but just gave little smiles, then turned back to the windows. They both seemed to be fascinated with a shop that carried wooden birds.

"Ellie, you're the celebrity, so *you* pay for the booze," Leslie said, and that made Ellie smile.

"Maybe she could pay for it with an autograph," Madison said, and there was a hint of something not very nice under her voice.

"Only if it's on a credit card slip," Ellie shot back, then looked at Madison with some defiance.

"If you two get into a cat fight, who do you think I should bet on?" Leslie asked, and that relieved the tension in the air.

"I'm hungry," Ellie said. "That woman made me so nervous I couldn't eat."

Smiling, Leslie pointed to a little grocery store that was still open and a liquor store across the street. Thirty minutes later, the three women, their arms laden with food and a bag of bottles, were laughing as they made their way back to the little gingerbread house.

Once inside the house, their good mood returned. Outside the house, they were aware that they didn't know each other, that they'd led very different lives that had ended up in different ways. But inside the house they were once again those three girls—Ira's Girls, they'd reminded themselves—and they were equal. Their futures had yet to be made.

Ellie unpacked a couple of plastic containers of dip and three bags of chips while Leslie rummaged in the kitchen for a corkscrew. Madison threw pillows on the floor in front of the couch, pulled out a couple of packs of cigarettes, then plopped down on the pillows.

Ellie took one look at the cigarettes and opened a window near Madison. Leslie returned from the kitchen with glasses and an opened bottle of white wine.

"Okay, who's first?" Leslie asked as she, too, tossed pillows on the floor then sat on them. Ellie stretched out on the couch behind Madison.

"Who's first with what?" Ellie asked.

Leslie's eyes twinkled. "As though you aren't dying to hear all about everything."

Ellie smiled and scooped up a big glob of a cheesy dip. "What happened to your dancing?"

Before Leslie could reply, Madison looked through a cloud of smoke and said, "Why don't we get down to it and talk about men?"

"Nothing to tell on my part," Ellie said as she ate more dip.

"Me neither," Leslie said. "I married Alan and that's it. I've been absolutely faithful to him all these years."

That announcement seemed to bring the conversation to a halt.

Ellie turned onto her back and looked up at the ceiling. "Did you ever think about the one who got away? About the man you *could* have hooked up with and didn't?"

When neither woman spoke, Ellie turned

onto her side and looked at them. Both Leslie and Madison were studiously looking at their hands and not meeting each other's eyes.

"Am I good or what?" Ellie said, smiling as she picked up her glass. "I've already found a story and I've only been here a matter of hours. So who's first?"

"How about *you* going first?" Madison said, narrowing her eyes at Ellie.

Ellie opened her mouth to speak, then seemed to think better of it, so she turned to Leslie. "What about you? Do you have lots of regrets?"

Leslie smiled complacently. "Not really. I'm happy with my life. Sure, my husband and kids pay no attention to me and I sometimes wonder if they'd step over my body if I fell dead in the kitchen, but—" She stopped to laugh at the looks of horror the other two were giving her. "Okay, so I'm a doormat. I admit it, but I really do *love* them."

"There isn't anything you'd like to change?" Ellie asked, obviously not believing her.

"No, not change . . ." Leslie said.

"But what?"

"Alan is the only man I've ever been to bed with."

"I won't even comment on that," Madison said as she stubbed out her cigarette.

"There was a boy in college who was interested in me, but . . . Well, he was rich."

"Is there a downside to this?" Madison asked.

"Not rich like a computer nerd but old-money rich," Leslie said. "Kennedy rich. Truthfully, his family frightened me so much that I turned down his invitation to spend spring break at his family home."

"What happened to him?"

"He's a senator now. Some say he's a president in the making."

"My goodness. Well, Mrs. President . . ." Madison said, lighting another cigarette.

Ellie was looking at Leslie intently. "What else?" she asked.

Leslie took a long drink of her wine. "That's it. Nothing happened. After I turned down his invitation, he lost interest in me and I never thought about it again. Except . . . In the last year, every time Alan mentions Bambi, I wonder what would have happened if I'd taken that young man up on his invitation. If nothing else, I think it would have been good for Alan to have had some competition."

"He didn't? Not ever?" Madison asked.

"None," Leslie said; then her eyes lost that faraway look and she smiled again. "So how many men have you two had?"

"Thousands," Ellie answered instantly. "Oh, yes. Thousands at least. Celebrities have access, you know."

Laughing, Leslie turned to Madison. "And you?"

"Same with me. Thousands."

"I see. You know, you two aren't very good liars."

Both Ellie and Madison laughed.

"Okay, so maybe it's really two," Ellie said. "My ex-husband and a guy in high school."

"Three," Madison said. "I was married for a few years and there were a couple of others."

"We aren't exactly advertisements for the sexual revolution, are we?" Leslie said.

"What about you?" Madison asked Ellie. "What about the man who got away in your life?"

"There wasn't one."

Both women scoffed at this. "Sure, sure. You're just not telling," Madison said.

"No, really, I'm still waiting for my Jessie," Ellie said.

"And who was he?"

"No one yet. In the movie *Romancing the Stone*, the Kathleen Turner character writes romances and the hero of all of them is named Jessie. She says that she's waiting for him to appear. And so am I."

"There wasn't one man in your past, other than the man you married, who . . . ?" Madison wiggled her eyebrows at Ellie.

"Nope," Ellie answered, and they could hear the sincerity in her voice. "All the men in my life are in my head. And I write them down and sell them. I share all my fantasies with the entire U.S. With the world if I'm lucky."

"So why do I feel that you're hiding something?" Leslie said, staring at Ellie in the same way that she had been stared at.

Ellie picked up her wineglass, and when she spoke, her mouth was a hard line. "Actually, there was a man once who inter-ested me. I liked him a lot, admired him a great deal. He was married with two small daughters and when he asked his wife for a divorce, everyone vilified him. They couldn't believe he'd do such a rotten thing to his darling wife. But I defended him. I told him that I understood. And I defended him to people who cut him down. I think I had fantasies about his telling me what a great person I was, then he'd whisk me away from my unhappy marriage and . . ."

Ellie put the glass down and shrugged. "Didn't happen. He married someone else and moved to another state."

Leslie looked at Madison. "*You* must have turned down a million men."

"I wish," Madison said, as though what they were saying was a joke.

But Ellie and Leslie didn't laugh. Instead, they stared at her.

"Okay, so I've had a lot of offers, mostly indecent ones, but there weren't any that appealed to me." Madison looked down at her cigarette, then back up at the women. They were looking at her without a shred of belief on their faces.

"All right, there was one man," Madison said as she lit another cigarette, "but it was a long, long time ago, and I think it was the circumstances more than the actual events. I don't think he would have paid any attention to someone like me if we hadn't been thrown together that summer."

Ellie jumped on that statement. "What does that mean? 'Someone like me'? Do you mean, someone beautiful enough to make the stars jealous?"

Madison laughed. "I can see how you make your living. No, I don't mean that. I mean, someone uneducated. He had just finished his third year of medical school, and I was . . . Oh, well, it's a boring story."

"Doesn't sound boring to me," Ellie said as she picked up a handful of corn chips. "Sound boring to you, Leslie?"

"Not in the least. In fact, compared to the alternatives, an empty bed or the TV, I think this story sounds downright fascinating."

Again Madison laughed. "You two are good for my ego. All right, it was right after I miscarried and—"

"What?!" both women yelped together.

Madison took a long, deep drag off her cigarette. Both women noticed that there was a bit of a tremor to her hand as she lifted the cigarette to her lips, but neither said anything. Madison drew in the smoke, then leaned back her head and exhaled slowly. "I've never been to therapy—not that I didn't need it, mind you, I just couldn't afford it—but I think maybe being with you two is like a group therapy session."

"So tell us everything," Ellie said eagerly.

"All right," Madison said as she pointed her cigarette at Ellie, "but if I read one word of this in one of your books, I'm suing you."

Ellie looked away for a moment, as if she had to think about that, and when she looked back, both Leslie and Madison were holding in their laughter. "Okay, I agree," Ellie said, pretending reluctance, but she loved to hear a story as much as she loved to tell one.

"The miscarriage really has nothing to do with the story, but—" Madison put up her hand when both Leslie and Ellie opened their mouths to protest.

Madison took a deep breath, then an even deeper drag on her cigarette. "It was an accident, just one of those things that happens. Roger was still in a wheelchair, and—"

"Wait a minute!" Ellie said. "Wheelchair? Roger? Is this Roger the same guy who you did all his homework for and who dumped you for a college girl?"

Madison smiled into the smoke. "You

make me forget an entire nineteen years. I might as well be sitting on that bench back at the DMV. Yes, this is the same man. Not long after I got to New York, Roger was in an accident. He was riding a bicycle and was hit by a car. It ran over his pelvis and crushed all the bones."

"*Yeow!*" Ellie said.

"And you left New York and modeling to go back to him?" Leslie asked softly.

Madison stubbed out her cigarette. "Yes. But before you two start thinking of what I gave up, I want to remind you that modeling wasn't my idea. It was the town's idea."

"You wanted to be a nurse," Leslie said.

"Yes." Madison smiled at them. It was nice to be remembered so well. "Roger called me from the hospital and said that he'd been told that he'd never walk again. Then he told me that he still loved me, that he'd sent his fiancée packing, so I went running home. It wasn't any great sacrifice for me to give up the idea of modeling. I hated . . ." Pausing, she lit another cigarette.

"I didn't like modeling," she said after a moment, "so I was glad of any excuse that allowed me to return home. And Roger said all the right things. He blamed his dumping me on his father, saying that his father had threatened that if he married an uneducated girl like me, he'd be disinherited."

"No wonder you have a chip on your shoulder about not having gone to college," Ellie said under her breath.

Madison pretended she hadn't heard Ellie. "So I went home and I married a man who was in a hospital bed in a body cast. Then, let's see . . . How should I put this? Then I entered hell. Yes, I think that's about right."

Madison looked at Ellie and Leslie to laugh, but they didn't.

"Roger was a horrible patient. He'd always been very physically active, so he didn't take well to being confined to a bed. And his parents—" Madison stopped for a moment to take a deep drink of her wine; then she looked up at the other women. "Roger's parents were very rich, but they were also extremely cheap. They wouldn't shell out any money for Roger's rehabilitation. I'll never know for sure, but I think my ex-father-in-law got Roger to marry me so I'd be a free nurse. After all, I'd had years of experience with my mother. I'd even worked in a hospital."

Ellie and Leslie could see that Madison was trying to make light of what had obviously been a horrible situation, but the women didn't smile; they couldn't. It wasn't fair that Madison had had to give up college to nurse her mother, then she'd given up a chance at modeling to nurse a husband.

"What about the 'one who got away'?" Leslie asked as she refilled Madison's glass.

"Oh, yes," Madison said, and there was a genuine smile on her face. "Thomas."

As she picked up her glass, Leslie looked at Ellie and raised an eyebrow. There was something about the way that Madison said the name . . . Thomas.

"Roger was injured, but he could still, you know," Madison said as she set down her glass, "so I was six months pregnant and Roger's parents were away that weekend, so—"

"You were living with your in-laws?" Ellie asked in horror.

"Oh, yes. Roger didn't have any money and I didn't either. I mean, I had the money the town had given me for modeling, but that was soon gone."

Ellie opened her mouth to explode at that, but Leslie put her hand on her arm and stopped her. Madison had given her college money to her mother's illness; then it seemed that she'd given her modeling money to a rich, whining, ungrateful—

"That weekend Roger's parents were away, so we were alone, and, as I said, I was six months pregnant. What happened was very simple really. I was rolling Roger to the bathroom when one of the wheels of the chair caught on one of those expensive rugs his parents had everywhere. I was afraid that the rug was going to move and topple one of their vases." Madison's still-beautiful mouth hardened into a line. "His parents would make me beg them for money for rails in the bathroom, but they'd go to New York and pay ten thousand dollars for some old Chinese vase."

She had to light another cigarette before she could speak again, and the other two women watched in silence. Already, the air was full of Madison's pain, and no matter how much she tried to pretend that she wasn't still angry, she obviously was.

"Roger's legs were healing and they had spasms where they'd kick out of their own accord. I had several bruises on my ribs from being in the line of them during a spasm. To this day I don't know why I didn't think of those legs as I bent down and pulled the rug out from under the wheel."

She looked up at the other two women. "You see, I had paused at the head of the stairs, and when Roger's leg kicked out, it knocked me off balance and I went headlong down the stairs."

At that she stopped for a moment and concentrated on her cigarette. The other women just watched her. There was nothing they could say, as "I'm sorry" was wholly inadequate.

"I was unconscious, so Roger had to get to the only phone on the second floor, in his parents' bedroom. He couldn't get the chair through the doorway, so he had to drag himself across the room. His upper body was strong, but, still, it took him a while. And I . . . was bleeding." Madison took another deep drag, then slowly let out the smoke. "The nearest hospital was—and is—over fifty miles away. And it was winter in Montana. Roger managed to get hold of some neighbors and they came, but there was nothing they could do. Except soak up the blood, that is."

Madison looked down at her full ashtray.

"By the time the ambulance got there, I was in labor. He didn't live very long. He was so tiny."

Madison turned to look out the window for a moment. "When I did get to the hospital, the only way the doctors could get the bleeding to stop was to remove my uterus."

At that Ellie reached out to take Leslie's wrist. She didn't dare touch Madison, as she guessed that this proud woman wouldn't want to think someone was feeling sorry for her.

After a long moment, Madison looked back at the two of them and gave them a strained smile. "So now you know why I never had kids. But weren't we talking about something else?"

"The summer you met a man," Leslie said softly as Ellie withdrew her hand.

"Ah, yes. It was the summer after the miscarriage and I was still pretty low. I'd lost a lot of weight and I admit that I was looking pretty bad. And I'd been having more fights than usual with Roger's parents. They were embarrassed by their son's injuries. He no longer fit in with their idea of the perfect son, so they kept him, and me with him, locked away on the second floor. There was no wheelchair ramp built—not that I hadn't tried to get one, but they said it would destroy the 'lines of the house.'"

"So you and Roger were kept prisoners," Leslie said.

"More or less. And I can tell you that we were sick of each other's company. But, to be fair, I think it was more my fault than his. I was pretty, well, I guess . . . sad about the baby."

"Suicidally depressed?" Ellie asked.

"Exactly!" Madison answered, and gave a bit of a real smile. "Truthfully, I was going crazy with grief and loneliness. And I was so tired that my hair was beginning to fall out."

"Now *that's* tired," Ellie said, and was glad to see that Madison smiled wider at her joke.

"Yes," Madison said, and her voice was lighter. "Anyway, when some college friend of Roger's called and asked us to fly to Upstate New York to spend two weeks with him and his family at their summerhouse, both Roger and I were ecstatic. The man had been Roger's college roommate and he'd recently fallen over a washtub while playing touch football and broken his leg. He was in a cast, and by that time Roger was using two canes, so the two of them planned to commiserate together."

"With you waiting on both of them," Leslie said in a voice that said she knew all about waiting on people.

"Actually, that's just what I thought would happen. In fact, I was so sure that that's what the trip was going to be that I begged Roger to go without me."

"You mean you were asking him to feed himself, clothe himself, get himself on and off a toilet, all by his widdle self?" Ellie asked in sarcasm.

Madison laughed. "You're reading my mind. I was so depressed and so tired that all I could think of was sleep. I told Roger that I'd throw the biggest fit the earth had ever seen in order to get his parents to hire a nurse to go with him, but to please let me stay there and rest." Madison stubbed out her cigarette, then drew up her knees and clasped them to her chest.

"But Roger could be persuasive when he wanted to be. He said he couldn't go without me, that I was his whole life, and that he wasn't sure if he wanted to live if I didn't go with him."

"Been there, done that," Ellie said bitterly. "So you went with him."

"Yes," Madison said softly. "I went, and it wasn't anything like what I thought it was going to be. You see, the truth is that I was afraid of going. This boy was from Roger's college and his parents both had degrees and there was an older brother in medical school. When I heard the credentials of these people, I wanted to turn tail and run."

She smiled as she stared at the floor. The bad memory of the miscarriage was fading and in its place was the wonderful memory of that time at Scotty's parents' summerhouse. And Thomas. The beautiful memory of Thomas.

Looking up again, Madison continued. "By the time the plane landed in Upstate New York, I was a nervous wreck. I was sure these people were going to take one look at me and know that I had no education and therefore think that I was worth nothing." For a moment, she closed her eyes in memory. "But they weren't like that, not at all. Scotty's mother was what my mother had always wanted to be, except that my mother had no husband and a daughter to support. Mrs. Randall loved to feed people, loved to take care of everyone. I had nothing at all to do."

"Except wait on Roger hand and foot."

"Oh, no," Madison said, grinning at the women. "Roger couldn't stand me. Once we got there, he wanted nothing to do with me. He said I reminded him of the months when 'someone,' meaning me, had to change his diapers."

"Why, that ungrateful—" Ellie began, but Madison interrupted her.

"No, no, by that time it was a relief. I never had the courage to be absolutely honest, but I was truly sick of Roger, tired of looking at him day after day, month after month, with no company but him. He was worse than taking care of triplets, what with his complaining and his—" Madison laughed. "Oh, well, that's over with now."

When she didn't say anything else, the women stared at her.

"So?" Ellie said. "What happened?"

Madison smiled. "I spent most of the time I was there with Thomas, Scotty's older brother."

Ellie was about to say something, but Leslie put her hand on her arm. "What did you do?" Leslie asked softly.

"We went white-water rafting, hiking, spent the night together in a tent."

Smiling, Ellie said, "I want to hear every single word. In chronological order."

Madison hugged her legs tighter to her chest. "Okay," she said slowly, then closed her eyes for a moment. "They were rich and their summerhouse was huge, built in the 1840s and added onto by generations of Scotty's family until the thing had about eight bedrooms. Only two baths, mind you, and that sometimes caused problems, like the time Mr. Randall . . . No, you said, chronological order, didn't you? Okay, let's see. Where do I begin? Scotty's father met us at the airport in a pickup truck, a horrible old thing that was nearly rusted through. I thought he was the gardener, but Roger gouged me in the ribs and told me the man was a professor of medieval history at Yale. Head of the department, even. But Mr. Randall didn't seem like what I thought a professor would be, and we hit it off right away. In fact, he put Roger in the back of the truck, while Mr. Randall and I sat in the front. I can tell you that Roger didn't like that one little bit. No, he didn't like that at all."

Five

"Look, the man is a full professor," Roger said as though Madison were too stupid to understand the full importance of this fact. "At Yale. Do you understand what that means, Maddy?"

"I can't very well forget, can I?" Madison snapped. "You keep reminding me every ten minutes."

"I knew it was a mistake to bring you," Roger muttered under his breath.

Madison opened her mouth to reply, but then Frank Randall got out of the truck and approached them. He didn't look as though he were a college professor, Madison thought, certainly not one who had a half-mile-long list of abbreviations after his name, as this man did. Instead, he looked like someone's father in his old plaid flannel shirt and his worn-out denims. There were lines at his eyes that Madison was sure he'd acquired from smiling so much.

Madison liked him right away, and her smile told him so. "Hello," she said warmly. "Did you have a long drive to get here? We could have rented a car and—"

"Wouldn't hear of it," Frank said, but he was looking from Roger, on his canes, then to Madison as though something were wrong. He knew Roger from other summer visits with his son Scott, but he'd never met Madison.

Again, Frank smiled, then stretched out his hand in welcome. "I didn't know Roger was bringing his girlfriend."

After a startled moment in which she realized that Roger had not told their hosts that she was coming, Madison said tersely, "Wife"; then she took Frank's hand. She didn't dare look at her husband or she would have killed him.

"Congratulations," Frank said, as he turned to smile at Roger. "You should have told us. Newlyweds are always welcome."

"We've been married over two years," Madison said, still not looking at her husband.

"I see," Frank said good-naturedly, then turned away to hide his laugh, for he could see that Madison was furious and that Roger was going to catch it. "I'll just put your luggage in the back of the pickup."

As the older man carried two suitcases to the truck, Madison turned to her husband. "You didn't tell them I was coming?" she hissed.

"Could we talk about this later?" Roger said, motioning his head toward Frank's back.

Madison wasn't about to stop. "You didn't even tell them that you're married." Madison had to calm herself or she thought she might explode in anger. "If you didn't want to admit to having a wife, then why did you put on such a show to get me to come with you? I wanted to stay in Montana."

"Look, it's complicated, so I'll explain later."

"You're damned right you will," Madison said as Frank turned back toward them.

"Sorry about the mix-up," Roger said to Frank, "but I couldn't very well leave the ol' ball and chain at home, now could I?"

His attempt at humor fell flat with

Madison. When she glared at her husband, all the anger she felt showed in her eyes.

As Frank picked up another suitcase, he slowly looked Madison up and down. "Roger, you must be getting old if you can forget to mention something like this extraordinarily beautiful woman."

At that, Madison smiled at Frank in gratitude. It had been a long time since anyone had called her "beautiful." And she wasn't sure anyone had ever added "extraordinarily" onto the word. And considering that, to her eyes, she was too thin, her hair was scraggly, and her sadness showed on her face, she was especially pleased by the compliment.

"Madison, my dear," Frank said, "why don't you sit up front with me? Roger can get in the back with the luggage."

"I'd love to," Madison said happily.

But Roger moved forward on his canes and placed himself between Madison and Frank. "I think that, under other circumstances, that would be a great idea, but . . ." He gave a sigh and his face was full of sadness. "But I think that after what has happened to me, I would be much more comfortable sitting inside the truck rather than on the hard metal truck bed. And the luggage being loose like that might further injure me."

Madison, who was more than used to this, just gave a quick look skyward, then put her hand on the back of the truck, ready to vault over the gate and place herself next to the luggage.

But Frank's laugh halted her. "Boy, you have one enormous case of self-pity, don't you? Well, we don't allow pity, self or other-wise, up here. You can get in the back of the truck, and this gorgeous young lady can sit up front with me."

For a moment, all Madison could do was blink at him. Since her marriage, just after Roger's injury, she'd been isolated in Roger's parents' house, with just Roger and his parents for company. An oxymoron if she ever heard one, she'd often thought. His parents were all concern for Roger and none for her. If Roger kept her awake all night, they cared only for his pain, not that she'd had to run up and down stairs for eight hours. After the miscarriage, they'd said, "Well, maybe it was for the best." She'd nearly lost it then. "Best?" she'd shouted. "Best for whom? For you? If I had a child to care for, maybe you'd have to shell out the money for a nurse for your son. If I had a child, it might cost you as much as you pay for one of your vases, wouldn't it?" At that his parents had left the room and Roger had put himself in the doorway so she couldn't follow them. Madison had locked herself away for two whole hours and cried.

But now here was a man she'd never met before *not* giving pity to Roger. What was more, he hooked his arm around Madison's, led her to the passenger side of the truck, opened the door for her, and helped her climb up to the seat. He left Roger alone to get into the back of the truck all by himself.

Once Frank was behind the wheel and had started the engine, Madison began to apologize. "I'm sorry about the mix-up," she said. "I didn't know that I wasn't expected, and I know that an additional guest will be a burden on your hospitality, so—"

Frank heard her words, but he was listening harder to her tone, and he cut her off before she could finish her apology—before she could offer to leave. "Our family has known Roger for years, so I know he and my younger son are a great deal alike. They want to be thought of as men of the world, so they don't want anyone to think that they got 'caught' by a woman. Mark it down to immaturity."

Madison turned away, quick tears coming to her eyes. He is a very kind man, she thought, and he was making something awkward and embarrassing into nothing. And he was taking her side over Roger's!

"My eldest son, Thomas, is studying medicine, and he explained to us about Roger's accident and what kind of rehabilitation it's taken. I'm sure that you've been a great help to him." When Frank said this, he glanced at Madison to see her expression.

But she looked away for a moment so he couldn't see her face. No doubt this sweet man believed that Roger had round-the-clock nurses and a wife who played tennis at the country club, only returning occasionally to check on the progress of her injured husband. It was something that Madison had encountered all her life: people assumed that beauty gave you an easy life.

"So, Madison, how tough are you?" Frank asked as they pulled onto the highway and headed north.

"Tough?" she asked, puzzled. "You mean, can I play touch football with the guys? That sort of tough?"

Frank laughed. "Not at all. I think that if you played football with the guys, there'd be one big, collective tackle and that would end the game."

"You're wonderful for my ego. Want to have an affair?"

At that Frank let out a shout of laughter that made Roger, who was sulking in the back and holding suitcases away from his legs with his canes, turn and glare at them through the back window.

"I would love to," Frank said, "but I don't think my heart could take it."

"Or your wife," she said, smiling and loving the teasing. It had been so long since she'd talked of anything except Roger's physical problems.

"She'd probably be glad to get rid of me for the day, or the week, however long I lasted."

"Now, why do I doubt that?" Madison said, leaning back and looking him up and down.

Frank was looking out the windshield of the truck, but he was smiling and his face was warm from the pleasure of flirting with a pretty girl. "No, I mean 'tough' as in what you can take in the way of jealousy."

"Jealousy?"

"I think I better prepare you. In college my son and Roger had quite a few girlfriends." He gave her a glance out of the corner of his eye to see how she would take this.

"I've known Roger for years. You're not going to tell me anything about him that I don't know. *I* used to be the one who did his homework for him."

"I have a daughter a year younger than Roger and Scotty, and she brought a distant cousin and a girlfriend with her. The three of them will be staying at the cabin with us."

Madison waited for him to go on but he didn't, so she looked out the window and thought about what he'd told her. After a while, she smiled, then turned to him. "I see. They don't know that Roger has a girlfriend much less a wife, and they certainly didn't know that she was arriving with him, so there might be a little . . . What should we say? Cat hair flying?"

Turning, Frank grinned at her. "You're smart, aren't you?"

"I thought you were a college professor.

Don't you know that it's a law of physics that a beautiful woman *can't* be smart?"

"You'll do all right," he said, looking out the window again, his hands on the steering wheel.

"How much time before we get there?" Madison asked.

"About fifteen minutes," he answered.

"Could you make it twenty?" she asked as she picked up her tote bag from the floor and began to rummage in it.

When she withdrew a tube of lipstick, Frank said, "There's a diner on the way. How'd you like a rest stop?"

"Thank you," she said, and five minutes later, Frank pulled off the highway into the gravel parking lot of an old-fashioned diner. He waited outside, standing beside Roger and vaguely listening to his complaints, while Madison went inside.

Inside the diner, Madison asked where the rest room was. The woman behind the counter frowned. She didn't like tourists to stop and use her rest room without ordering anything. Grudgingly, she nodded her head toward a small door to the left.

Once inside the tiny rest room, Madison put her tote bag on the toilet seat and unzipped it. Maybe it was Frank's flirting, maybe it was the idea of facing three young women who had the hots for her husband, but Madison wanted to do what she could to look her best when she walked into that assembly.

As she looked into the tiny mirror with the single bulb over it, Madison wasn't sure she remembered how to apply makeup. For years now her only concern had been Roger and his recovery; she hadn't had time to think about making herself look like a woman.

But when she touched an eye pencil to her lid, her memory returned. Not too much, she thought, just enough to emphasize and enhance. Quickly, she applied pencil, mascara, a bit of base, lined her lips, then filled in the color. She bent over, which, for someone who was almost six feet tall, was nearly impossible in the tiny room, but Madison managed to hang her head down enough that her hair, unleashed from the elastic band, nearly touched the floor. She sprayed her roots, then swung her hair to dry it, then flipped her head back and voilà!—lion's mane.

She unbuttoned her blouse enough that

the tiny bow on her bra was exposed, then lifted the back of her collar. She let her denim jacket fall back on her shoulders just a bit, then straightened her shoulders, stiffened her spine, and left the rest room. As she walked through the diner, she kept her eyes straight ahead, but she knew that she had the attention of every person in the small restaurant.

When she opened the door to the outside, both Frank and Roger looked up. Frank's mouth dropped open and Roger frowned. As though Roger weren't there, Madison walked toward Frank.

"Am I ready to meet them?" she asked softly.

For a moment all Frank could do was stare at her; then he threw back his head and laughed. "My wife is going to enjoy this *immensely.* And to think, just last week she suggested that we go to Paris this summer instead of to the cabin. She said the cabin was too much of the same thing, year in, year out."

In answer, Madison just smiled at him, then started to open the door to the passenger side of the truck, but Frank beat her to it. When he had closed her door, he walked around the front of the truck.

Roger, who was still in the back of the truck, as it was too much trouble to get in and out, leaned over the side toward Madison's open window. "What do you think you're doing? You're not going to some sleazy bar, you know. These people are—"

Smiling, she looked at her husband. "You know something, Roger? Educated men like pretty girls too." With that she rolled up the window, then turned and smiled at Frank as he got into the truck and shut the door.

Six

The "cabin" was just as Madison had imagined it would be. It looked like something the Roosevelt clan had owned. It was one story, made out of logs that had aged a deep brown. On the front was a porch that had to be twenty feet deep and at least sixty feet long. Lots of old log chairs and benches were scattered about, each one covered with fat chintz-covered cushions that were fashionably weathered.

"Not even their upholstery looks new," Madison said under her breath; then Roger glared at her as though to remind her not to betray her origins. For a moment, Madison halted and she thought about asking Frank to take her back to the airport so she could go home. But then she thought, Where is home? With her mother gone her only home was with Roger.

Frank's arm under her elbow made her come back to the present.

"Nice place," she said with a weak smile at him as she followed Roger up the stairs. She'd started to help her husband, but he'd jerked away from her, so she walked beside Frank.

As Madison stood on the porch, she looked at the lake that ran behind the house, crystal blue water as far as she could see. Great trees and boulders dotted the shoreline. There were no other people or cabins in sight. Nor were there boats on the water, and Madison was sure that Frank's family owned everything within their vision.

"It'll do," Frank said with a little snort. "It's from my wife's family, not mine," he said under his breath. "My dad was a plumber."

It was as though he were reading her mind, and in thanks, Madison turned a dazzling smile on him.

For a moment Frank blinked at her. "And my mother took in washing," he said, making Madison laugh. She knew the last statement was a lie and that he was saying it just to get her to smile again.

"And I have an uncle who's a taxi driver."

Madison was still laughing when she got to the door and she was glad because she needed to laugh. Running out of the house, their attention a hundred percent on Roger, were two pretty girls—and the very look of them cried out, "Money!" They had on those colorless clothes that looked the same in the store as they did after ten years of wearing. But Madison knew that they were clothes that cost what her mother had earned each year at three jobs.

The girls were pretty but not in an obvious way. If they wore any makeup, it was so light that it was impossible to detect. They were girls who lived by rules such as, Get dressed, then remove one piece of jewelry. Of course the jewelry they owned was real and it had been given to them by their grandparents.

Standing back and looking at them, Madison suddenly felt too tall, too made-up, too flashy. Once again, she wanted to run away from this place. She didn't belong here.

Then, from out of the cabin came another girl, this one small and trim, with short, dark hair, big brown eyes, and as she stepped forward, the other two moved out of her way.

"Roger, darling," she said quietly; then with what was certainly a practiced gesture, she stood on tiptoe, hooked one arm around Roger's neck, drew his head down, and kissed him on the lips.

Beside her, Madison could feel Frank stiffen, but the odd thing was that Madison felt nothing. There was part of her that was standing to one side observing this action and remarking on it. "There's a woman kissing my husband. I should be wildly jealous. I should be pushing her away." But instead, Madison just stood there watching. When Roger had returned from college with a fiancée on his arm, Madison had been nearly insane with jealousy. Just to see the woman standing near the man Madison was so madly in love with had nearly pushed Madison over the edge.

But now all Madison thought was, Maybe someone else will look after him and I can have some peace and quiet.

It was Frank who broke them up. "Terri!" he said loudly, "I think there is someone here you should meet. This is Roger's *wife*."

At that all three of the young women

turned to look at Madison. Terri still had her hand on Roger's shoulder, and she didn't look as though she meant to remove it.

"Wife?" one of the girls whispered, looking at Roger.

All Roger did was shrug, as though a wife were something that had happened to him and it wasn't his concern.

As smoothly as he could, Frank introduced the three young women. There was his daughter, Nina, her cousin Terri, and Nina's friend, Robbie.

When the three girls looked up at Madison—she was, after all, several inches taller than they were—she sighed, for there was hostility in their eyes. All Madison thought was, Too bad, for she would have liked to have made friends with them.

I don't want this, Madison thought. It's been too long a day for a cat fight. Turning, she smiled at Frank. "I think that flight has tired me out. Maybe you could show me . . . *our* room?" Her ego couldn't resist that one little emphasis.

"Certainly," Frank said, then made his way through the girls, Madison close behind him.

The inside of the "cabin" matched the exterior, with big, comfortable couches and chairs, Native American rugs that were probably now worth the earth scattered across the pine floors. They walked past a living room the size of a bus station. At one end was a fireplace made of rocks that had to have been set in place with a crane.

Down a hall, Frank opened a door and motioned her inside. There was one bed, one small clothes cupboard, a couple of little tables, and a chair. "We'll have to switch rooms for you, since we didn't know . . ."

"It's fine," she said, letting him off the hook.

"Don't let them bother you. They've known Roger a long time, and he's . . . well . . ."

"He's a catch," Madison said, smiling at Frank. "I know. He's rich and he's good-looking. What else could they want?"

A frown crossed Frank's face for a moment; then he gave her a small smile. "If you need anything, let us know," he said as he put her suitcase on the floor, then left the room, closing the door behind him.

Within moments, Roger entered the room. Madison glanced up from her unpacking and saw that he was ready to start a fight.

"I don't see why you couldn't have been polite. These people are used to courtesy. Maybe you don't know about manners like theirs, but—"

She wasn't going to take his bait. Long ago she'd learned that when Roger knew he was in the wrong, he compensated by attacking. When she spoke, it was with a quiet, calm voice. "What I don't understand is why you didn't tell them that you were married and that you were bringing your wife."

She'd heard Roger coming down the hall and he had been swift and sure on his canes, but now that they were alone in the room, he was limping. As though in great agony, he lowered himself onto the side of the bed. "I'd appreciate it if you didn't start one of your fights."

She had to swallow a couple of times before she could reply to that. But again, she was not going to be bullied by him. Roger wasn't an impulsive person; everything he did was for a reason. "I just want to know why, that's all. I came here thinking that I was an invited guest, but I get here and find that they know nothing about me."

"All right, calm down," Roger said, as though Madison were on the verge of hysterics. "I never told Scotty or his family about you because, well, it's just a guy thing. We—"

"Being unmarried made you more macho?" she asked softly. Oddly enough, she wasn't angry at him. In fact all she was feeling was curiosity.

"Yeah!" Roger said. "So what's the harm in that? I haven't felt very male in the last years, so what if I let my best friend think that I was still a free man?"

"Free man?" she said under her breath, and it went through her mind all that she'd given up for him. "If you want your freedom, just let me know."

"Maddy, honey, you know that I didn't mean to hurt you." He reached out for her, but she stepped away.

"No, Roger, I don't know that you didn't mean to hurt me. In fact, lately I've thought that most of the pain you inflict on me is intentional.

Roger ran his hand over his face as though in extreme exasperation. "Couldn't

we have just a few days without your nagging? Is it possible for you to enjoy yourself? Look, I know you're upset about the
baby, but—"

"Not just one baby, Roger, all babies.
Forever."

"Is that my fault? Is that what you're saying? I did the best I could to get to a telephone. I—"

Madison turned away as tears came to
her eyes. Would she ever get over this feeling that her life was over? She was missing
a uterus, true, but she had other things.
People didn't have to have children to have
a full life.

She turned back to face Roger. "All
right," she said. She couldn't bring herself
to apologize, but maybe she could soothe
the situation. Anyway, she was too tired to
fight. "Okay, we'll call a truce. No fights for
as long as we're here. How does that
sound?" Roger looked relieved.

Suddenly, Madison couldn't bear to be in
the same room with him. If she stayed near
him much longer, she'd start screaming. But
she paused, her hand on the door latch.
There was something she *needed* to know.
"If you knew you'd not told them you were

married, why did you insist that I come here with you? I wanted to remain in Montana." For a moment Roger just sat there on the edge of the bed and didn't say anything.

She knew him so well. "Out with it," she said.

"Mom and Dad said they needed a break."

"I see," Madison said, then turned away. She wasn't going to allow herself to dwell on the injustice of that statement. She had left New York to return to Montana to nurse *their* injured son. She'd spent her days and nights waiting on him. The only "time off" Madison took was to read textbooks lent to her by her friend Dr. Dorothy Oliver, in an attempt to learn how to better rehabilitate *their* son. But yet his parents had declared that they "needed a break" from Madison.

"Maddy?" Roger said, and she turned back to look at him, but he didn't say anything else.

"What else?" she said, because she knew that he had something big he wanted from her.

"Let me have a good time," he said softly. "Just for the time we're here."

It took her a moment to understand what

he meant. A "good time" to Roger meant drinking and laughing and being the high school football hero again. And that meant girls, lots of them, all looking up at him adoringly. All of them imagining what a great lover he was. But Madison knew that most of Roger was show. He liked sex now and then, but he liked it short and over with quickly. What he liked best was the adoration—something that Madison no longer gave him.

"Sure," she said. "Have a good time. I'll—" She didn't know what she was going to do with herself, but if she could sit down on a rock and look at the water for one uninterrupted hour, that would be more than enough for her. "I'll leave you alone," she said after a moment. "Anything else?"

"No," he said, then smiled at her in a way that he hadn't done in years. For a moment she was the head cheerleader and he was the captain of the football team and everything was perfect. Madison smiled back at him. "Thanks," he said.

"You're welcome," she answered and meant it; then she opened the door and left the room.

Maybe it was cowardly of her and it was

certainly being a bad guest, but Madison found a side door and slipped outside without searching out her hostess to say thank you. Outside was what looked like a deer trail between the trees, and Madison took it. This had been one of her problems in New York City: she was a country girl and she wasn't used to a place that had no wilderness. She liked to walk for hours alone in a forest, drifting about, looking at the trees and the tracks left by the animals.

She walked for about an hour, then decided that she'd better get back to the cabin. No doubt they had dinner at a certain hour, and no doubt she was being discussed now as being a bad guest for not helping, et cetera, but her walk had done her good. It had been a shock to arrive at a place, uninvited, unwanted. And Roger's reasons for begging her to go with him had been a shock, but now, as she stood under a tree that had to be a couple of hundred years old and looked down at the sparkling water, she thought, What the hell? She hadn't wanted to go with Roger because she hadn't wanted to nurse him. She'd wanted a break from twenty-four-hour-a-day nursing and now she was going to get it.

When she got back to the cabin, she was feeling much, much better.

"You must be Madison," said a woman who greeted Madison the moment she stepped inside the door, and instantly, Madison knew that she was Mrs. Randall, Frank's wife, the woman with the old, old money. She was small, and beautifully preserved. No surgeon's knife had ever touched her face, but her skin was an example of what happened after a lifetime of care. What lines she had were confined to about her eyes, and her skin was soft and flawless. She wore lightweight wool trousers that had to be ten years old but Madison knew they must have cost a thousand dollars when new. And they had probably been made just for this woman. A pale pink cashmere twinset topped the trousers.

Later Madison couldn't believe she'd said what she did, but maybe it was the fresh air on top of Roger's taunts that she not embarrass him, but before she could stop herself, Madison said, "What, no pearls?"

The moment she said it, Madison put her

hand over her mouth in horror, but Mrs. Randall laughed, then companionably clasped Madison's arm to hers. "Frank said you were a delight, and now I see why. Oh, do come inside and liven up this place. All the girls are after your husband."

"Whatever for?"

At that Mrs. Randall stopped and looked up at Madison, her face serious for a moment. "Oh, my goodness. Well, *hmmm*," she said thoughtfully.

"I didn't mean—" Madison began. "I mean—"

"No need for apologies, dear," Mrs. Randall said, again starting to walk. "Are you hungry? Please tell me that you aren't dieting to keep your slim figure."

"No," Madison said, smiling. "I work off any food I have time to eat by lifting Roger in and out of the bed."

"I see," Mrs. Randall said seriously. "I had no idea, but then I know Roger's parents somewhat. Not socially, of course, but I have met them. And one hears things. I believe they like to spend their money where it can be seen."

"Yes," Madison said, and that's all she

could say. It was either that one word or she'd start talking and never stop.

"Well, dear, you stay with us and have a nice long rest. The girls will take Roger off your hands."

"That would be kind of them," Madison said, feeling better by the moment. This woman, who reeked good manners and old money, was making her feel better than she had in a long while.

Again, Mrs. Randall gave Madison a sharp, quick look. "Come in to dinner. And prepare to defend yourself."

"I'll do my best," Madison answered as they entered the dining room.

Everyone was about to take a seat, but when they looked up and saw Madison, it was as though the proverbial wet blanket had been tossed over the room. The three young women, who were clustered around Roger and a blond man who was on crutches, broke apart, guilty looks on their faces.

Madison wanted to say, "Don't stop on my account," but she didn't. Instead, she took the seat that Mrs. Randall pointed to and sat down. When everyone was seated, Mr. and Mrs. Randall at each end, Madison found she was next to Mrs. Randall, across from Terri, the young woman who had so lustily kissed her husband. The blond man, who introduced himself as Scotty, was next to Terri, and Roger was at the end next to Frank.

The huge pine table was loaded with great bowls of steaming hot food, all in plain blue-and-white china that looked as though it could have been purchased at Sears. But at the top of each plate was a *W,* which, without being told, Madison guessed was the initial of Mrs. Randall's maiden name.

After everyone had helped themselves from the bowls of food, Mrs. Randall said brightly, "Thomas arrives tomorrow."

When that announcement seemed to shock the whole group into stillness, Madison looked up from her plate. A feeling of gloom seemed to have descended on them.

"And who is Thomas?" Madison asked.

"My elder son," Mrs. Randall answered, and there was laughter in her voice.

Curiously, Madison looked at the others at the table. Mr. Randall's eyes were dancing in amusement, but Roger, Scotty, and the three young women had their noses almost to their plates.

This sight cheered Madison up considerably. "Tell me all about him," she said happily, smiling at Mrs. Randall.

"How should I characterize my eldest son?" Mrs. Randall said, holding her fork aloft.

"He's a throwback to an earlier generation of my wife's family," Frank said.

"Yes," Mrs. Randall said. "The Wentworths seem to be divided into two groups, those who earn money and those who spend it."

"I thought money was not to be spoken of at the table," said Nina, who Madison had learned was the Randalls' third and youngest child. Uncharitably, Madison thought that it was a good thing that she had money because upon closer view, the girl was not attractive. She gave the illusion of being pretty, the illusion that time and money gave a person, but . . . well, Madison thought, ten years from now she was going to look much more like her father than her mother.

"That's in public, dear," Mrs. Randall said. "In private we may speak of what we want." She turned back to Madison. "What my husband is saying is that my eldest son is one of the earners. Thomas has his nose to more serious matters than the rest of us have. My son has finished his third year of medical school. He's going into rehabilitation medicine."

"And will probably do something great and noble," Scotty said under his breath; then the others, including Roger, snickered.

That Roger was close enough to the family that he knew their private jokes made Madison angry. In the last two years she'd tried to get him to talk to her about something other than what was hurting him and how miserable he was. Why couldn't he have told her about the Randalls?

"He sounds like a nice man," Madison said, looking at Mrs. Randall.

"I think so, but then I'm prejudiced. Nice or not, Thomas is certainly unique. You know how mothers say, 'Johnny didn't smile until he was four and a half months old. I was ready to give up'? I'm still waiting for my elder son's first smile."

At that everyone at the table laughed politely and Madison knew that it was an oft-repeated story, but she was still intrigued by this other brother. Maybe right now she was feeling an affinity with him.

"Thomas will *hate* you."

Turning to the speaker, Madison said, "I beg your pardon?"

Everyone was looking at Robbie, aghast at her rudeness. "I meant nothing personal. It's just that Thomas isn't interested in pretty girls."

"Speaking from experience?" Scotty asked, then, like a junior high kid, looked at Roger to share the joke.

"Why would I be interested in Thomas?" Robbie snapped at him. "I'm not a masochist."

Scotty looked at Madison. "What Robbie is in a snit about is that she made a pass at my big brother last year, but he turned her down. Not enough brains for his taste."

"I'll have you know that—" Robbie began, but Scotty cut her off.

"My brother got the brains, but I got the looks," he said, then nudged Roger in the ribs. "But looks like ol' Roge and I have gets us through, doesn't it? The two of us barely made it through college. If it hadn't been for the girl Roger was—" At that Scotty broke off at a look from his mother. "Anyway,"

Scotty said, "she did all our homework for us."

Turning to Scotty, Madison smiled at him with such warmth that she could almost see him melt. It had been years since she'd been looked at as Frank and his son were looking at her now.

"Tell me everything about the two of you in college," Madison said in a deeper-than-usual voice, then lowered her eyes seductively. When she looked back up, Scotty was staring at her with his mouth hanging open, Roger was grinding his teeth in anger, all three of the girls looked as though they could happily have scratched her eyes out, Mr. Randall was looking at her adoringly— and Mrs. Randall looked as though she were about to burst into laughter.

As for Madison, she felt beautiful and she hadn't felt beautiful since . . . Well, actually since that day over two years ago when she'd sat on a bench at the DMV in New York City beside two other young women.

For the rest of the meal, Madison listened to the others talking, but she was in her own world. It was finally beginning to sink in that she really was in this gorgeous place and she would *not* have to take care of Roger. It was obvious that the Randall summerhouse came equipped with servants, so Madison wouldn't be required to help peel potatoes as she often did at Roger's house. But then, sitting in the kitchen chatting with the cook was a relief from the sickroom.

Vaguely, she heard more talk of this oldest brother, Thomas. It seemed that he was good at anything he tried.

"Of course Thomas wouldn't attempt anything he wasn't going to be the best at," his sister, Nina, said with contempt in her voice, making Madison look up at her.

"Better than changing majors every semester," Scotty shot back.

"Why do we have to talk about Thomas?" Robbie said in a little-girl whine. "So he was the captain of the Yale soccer team. So he's top of his class in everything he does. Does that mean he's lovable?" At that she looked at Mrs. Randall in horror at what she'd said. "I mean . . ." Her face turned red.

Scotty looked at Madison. "You've seen that my sister's friend does little else except put her foot in her mouth. Last summer she made a fool of herself over my older brother, but Thomas didn't so much as look at her."

"I did not!" Robbie said, tears in her voice. "I thought he looked lonely, so I talked to him, that's all."

"Yeah. Sure," Scotty said. "And that's why you bought four of those . . . What do you call them?"

"I believe they're called string bikinis," Mrs. Randall said, smiling.

"I'm not going to listen to any more of this!" Robbie said as she shoved her chair back and ran from the table.

Picking up the bread basket, Mrs. Randall offered it to Madison. "Now, dear, you see why I don't wear pearls. If I did, I might be tempted to strangle someone with them."

At that Madison laughed hard at the joke that only she and Mrs. Randall understood.

I like these people and I like this place, Madison thought. Not the girls, but the parents, anyway. As she looked about the room at the old hunting prints on one wall and the blue-and-white checked curtains over the big window, she thought, Yes, indeed, I like this place.

And it was at that moment that she vowed that she was going to have a good time. She was going to ignore whatever

Roger did and she was going to enjoy her-self. Now, as she glanced down the table at him, she could see that he was flirting with Nina. Since Terri was at the other end of the table, now it was Nina.

What kind of wife can sit and watch her husband flirt with another woman and feel nothing? Madison thought to herself. And instantly, she knew the answer: A wife who wants out, she thought.

With that thought came a great feeling of relief to Madison. She had made a mistake in returning to Roger. She'd left what could have been a lucrative career in modeling to return to a man who said he loved her, but it had been a mistake.

And she'd paid the price for that mistake. She had given up everything she had for Roger over these years. She had even lost her ability to have children, she thought, but she couldn't dwell on that. That hurt was too deep.

But now, as she watched her husband flirting, she felt a wonderful lightness. She was still young and she was still pretty, not as pretty as she had been before she'd given years of her life to nursing a sick mother, then a crippled husband, but she was all right. She still had hope, anyway.

"Madison, dear," Mrs. Randall said as she put her slim hand on Madison's wrist, "are you all right?"

"Actually, I am *very* all right. Would you mind if I went fishing tomorrow?"

"Fishing?" Mrs. Randall asked in surprise. "I would never have guessed that you . . ."

"Liked to do anything except slather beauty products on my skin?" Madison asked, amused.

Mrs. Randall's eyes sparkled. "We have a lot to learn about each other, don't we?" she said softly so the others wouldn't hear. "But, yes, of course, do whatever you like. Would you like someone to go with you?"

"No. Just by myself. If that's all right."

Mrs. Randall knew what Madison was asking. Did she have to be part of group social activities? Did they all get together and decide that two would do this, four that, et cetera?

"It's quite all right," Mrs. Randall said. "And tomorrow I want you to meet my son Thomas. He also likes to fish."

Madison gave a glance down the table at

Roger. He now had both Nina and Terri leaning across the table toward him as he told some story. Probably about some mad escapade that he'd had in high school, Madison thought. She turned back to Mrs. Randall. "Thank you, but I think I'd like to have a holiday from men."

"I understand completely," Mrs. Randall said with a smile. "My home is yours. On one condition, that is."

"Which is?" Madison asked cautiously.

"That you call me Brooke. All my friends do."

For a moment Madison blinked at the woman. She'd felt a bond with both her and her husband, but she hadn't realized that the feeling was mutual. Also, Madison knew that Robbie, who was about the same age as Madison and who had visited the Randalls many times before, was still calling this woman Mrs. Randall. But she was asking Madison to call her Brooke, and she was saying that Madison was her "friend."

"I would be honored," Madison said softly, then exchanged a smile with the woman.

"How about tea on the porch? You go get a heavy sweater while I get the brandy."

"Perfect!" Madison said as the two women got up, leaving the three men and two women sitting at the table. And as Madison went back to her room, she thought, Why couldn't my in-laws be like these people?

Seven

Madison saw Thomas before he saw her. And right away, she knew that she'd never been as attracted to anyone in her life as she was to him. Her mother had always disliked Roger. Her mother had said that Madison stayed with Roger because he didn't demand too much from her. "He isn't a challenge to you in any way. And he makes you fit in," she'd said to her daughter. Her mother said because Madison had spent most of her life either alone or in a succession of day-care centers, Madison wanted to belong to someone somewhere. So Roger was safe. Being with him had guaranteed that Madison was included in all the "right" parties in high school. And Madison had had the insight to know that if she hadn't had Roger, her height and her

looks would have made her ostracized by
the girls and a target of lecherous little
games by the boys. Yes, Roger had been
safe.

But if she were truthful with herself,
Roger had never made her heart jump into
her throat as it did when she saw Thomas
Randall.

And it was odd that she was attracted to
him because Thomas didn't have the appearance of a man who would inspire passion in a woman. He wasn't like the hero in
a romantic novel. For one thing, he had
what had to be a permanent scowl on his
face. Maybe his eyes were round and the
color of sapphires, but no one could tell because Thomas's forehead was drawn down
into a frown that made two deep creases
between his eyes and drew his eyes into
mere slits.

However, his eyes were topped by lashes
so thick they looked like the false ones
glued onto the eyes of dolls. He had a short
nose, then what may have been soft full lips,
but like his eyes, Thomas kept his lips
pulled into a tight line.

As for his body, Thomas was tall, about
six feet, and well proportioned and muscu-

lar, and from behind, he was delicious. He had broad shoulders, a muscular back, a slim waist, and legs made heavy from years of playing soccer. And, from what Madison had heard, his body had enticed many women to approach him. But so far, not one of them had been able to stand up against what they saw when Thomas turned around. His deep, permanent scowl frightened people away.

But it wasn't the scowl that sent Madison scurrying into hiding. No, it was the way she felt drawn to him. She had been about to step into the kitchen, which at five A.M. was already bustling with activity. After all, it took time to cover the sideboard with eggs prepared three ways, pancakes, waffles, two kinds of potatoes, fish caught that morning, and four kinds of bread.

"Master Thomas," said the huge woman who was the Randalls' cook and whom Madison had seen only briefly the day before. When Madison had asked Roger about her, she'd been told that the woman had worked for Scotty's mother's family "forever."

"Adelia," Thomas said, frowning at the woman. "Anything to eat?"

At that Madison wanted to weep in frustration. She'd wanted to leave the house without anyone seeing her. Roger was still asleep, since he'd sat up with Scotty and "the girls" until three A.M., drinking beer and reminiscing about people Madison had never met. She'd had no inclination to spend the evening with them, so she'd excused herself and gone to bed. This morning, she'd hoped to sneak out of the house before anyone was awake, so she'd tiptoed about, picked out some fishing gear from where Brooke had shown her it was stored, and set out.

Unfortunately, she'd decided to go through the kitchen, having no idea that it would have anyone in it that early in the morning. And Madison was sure that Adelia was one of those women who'd faint at the thought of someone stepping outside without a full belly, so, to keep from being seen and losing time, Madison had slipped into a space between the refrigerator and a pantry. She was willing to bet that the kitchen hadn't been renovated since about 1910, and from the roar of the motor of the refrigerator, Madison was sure that that machine was from that era too.

Madison had peeked from behind the refrigerator to see when she could safely escape to the outdoors when the door opened and in walked the man who was undoubtedly Thomas Randall, the elder son. And after seeing him, Madison hadn't moved a muscle.

"Why sure, honey, I always got lots to eat," Adelia said, and her tone was that of a woman talking to an adult whom she'd known since babyhood. "You sit here and I'll fill you a plate."

"No bacon," Thomas said.

"Do you think I don't remember that?" Adelia said, sounding hurt. "And where's my kiss?"

When she said that, Madison saw Thomas's face soften. And it was then that she saw the man he could be. Or was, she thought. He was another man under that scowl, and the sight of that man almost made Madison's knees give way. His eyes were indeed round, and his mouth was as soft as a baby's.

"Good to see you," Thomas said, then he hugged Adelia as though he meant it and he planted a hearty kiss on her cheek. "Are you well?"

Adelia pushed him away. "You are not gonna practice your medicine on me. Now, sit down and eat and I'll tell you everything about everybody."

To Madison's horror, Thomas sat down at a beat-up old pine table directly in front of her. Now what was she to do? Step out and say, "Excuse me, I was just hiding because I didn't . . ." Didn't what? Want to eat? Right now the plate of food that Adelia set before Thomas looked and smelled awfully good. But Madison was trapped. If she stepped out now and they saw that she'd been hiding like some six-year-old, she'd never recover from her embarrassment.

And, besides, the truth was, she didn't really want to leave. She wanted to see and hear more of this man who was doing funny little things to her stomach.

"So who's here?" Thomas asked as he picked up a fork and scooped up buttery scrambled eggs.

Madison watched those eggs all the way to his mouth. He had his scowl back on, so his mouth was back to being a tight line.

"Your mom and dad, Scotty and Nina, of course, your cousin Terri and also Robbie." At that name Adelia paused and smiled at

Thomas. She was standing on the other side of the table, across from him, smiling down at the top of his head fondly.

"*Hmph*!" Thomas said, not bothering to look up. "She bring any clothes with her this time?"

Adelia laughed. "I hope so. With you around she'll freeze to death. I don't know what you don't like about her. It's time you settled down."

"Robbie is a spiteful little brat with too much money and time on her hands. How's Mom?"

"Your momma is good. She looks real good. She likes the tall girl a lot."

At that Madison sucked in her breath and held it. If she was going to make an honorable escape, now was the time to do it. But she knew that if a rattlesnake had bitten her big toe, she still wouldn't have been able to move.

"Tall girl?"

"You know that boy Roger, the one that was here a few years ago?"

"Scotty's clone?" Thomas asked derisively. "The football hero?"

"That's the one. He's usin' a couple of canes now. Your momma said he was hurt real bad, but he's better now, so what with Scotty and his broken leg—"

"The two of them can feel sorry for themselves together," Thomas said, and Madison had to bite her tongue to keep from laughing out loud.

"So Roger is here?" Thomas asked.

"Him and his wife," Adelia said with aplomb, glad to deliver this juicy bit of gossip.

"What kind of nincompoop would marry Roger?"

This time Madison had to stick both sides of her tongue between her back teeth and clamp down. Now I understand, she thought. How many other women had felt attracted to him, then been speared by his cynicism? It was one thing for Madison to feel she'd had enough of Roger, but what right did this man have to judge him—or her, for that matter?

"She's a looker, I can tell you that," Adelia said. "Beautiful doesn't begin to describe her. I wonder what they feed them out there where that boy lives, because she's at least three inches over six feet."

Thomas gave a snort of laughter as he

picked up a piece of pancake and ate it. "Roger isn't that tall, is he?"

Taller than you, you little toad, Madison wanted to say to him. Six feet three indeed! She was half an inch short of six feet.

"So Roger married some tall Montana cowgirl and now he's here sucking up to my little brother. What's he want?"

Adelia seemed to consider that for a moment. "Not his tall wife, that's for sure. Hardly looks at her. My guess is that he wants either your sister or Terri. You know Roger. He spent a whole summer chasing after Lucy, but she wouldn't have him."

"No. He's too stupid for Lucy. But Terri might take him. She'd like a man who ignored her. So if he wants to dump his cowgirl, why'd he bring her with him? Why not leave her home with his mom and dad? He still lives with his parents, doesn't he? I can't imagine that Roger would ever leave them and their money. Roger never struck me as the type to go out and get a job."

"As far as I know, he's still livin' with his folks, and he's been hurt too bad to have a job. But I can't say why he brought his big, gorgeous wife with him. There's no love lost between 'em. She looks down her nose at Roger like this."

To Madison's disbelief, Adelia tipped her head back and looked down her nose at Thomas. There was a lot said in that gesture, and when Madison saw it, all the blood seemed to drain from her head. No wonder Roger was angry with her if she was looking at him like that!

"And how does Roger look at his wife?" Thomas asked.

"Like she's ain't even there," Adelia said. "If it was me and a man looked at me the way Roger looks at that beautiful creature, I'd throw him in a vat of boiling oil. Or maybe I'd take his canes away and hit him with 'em. Or maybe—"

"So how's Dad?" Thomas asked.

"Enjoyin' it all. I think he's half in love with that tall girl. He said that your mom didn't want to spend another summer here, but now they're glad they came. Last night that girl Robbie threw a fit and ran out of the dinin' room. And later after the tall girl went to bed, Terri was all over Roger. And I can tell you that he wasn't pushin' her away."

"And who was the tall girl with?"

At that Madison almost stepped from behind the pantry and told him what she thought of him.

"Nobody. She went to bed."

"By herself?"

"All by her lonesome," Adelia said. "You interested in takin' her husband's place? She looks hungry to me."

"You think the world is hungry," Thomas said, pushing away his empty plate.

"They are. Hungry for food of one kind or another. So how long you plannin' on stayin' here this time?"

"Not long. I have exams to study for."

"A genius like you?"

"Unlike my brother, I don't pay someone else to take my exams for me. I'm going to bed now. I was up most of the night studying, then I drove here. Tell Mom and Dad I'm here, but don't let anyone wake me."

"That include Miss Robbie?"

"Most especially that little tart." Standing, he stretched, then asked Adelia if she'd ask Charlie to get his suitcase out of the car.

"He's still asleep now, but he'll get it when he gets up." With that she turned and left the kitchen.

Madison, still wedged into the small space, was aware that she was now in the kitchen alone with Thomas. Of course he didn't know she was there, but she did. She held her breath for fear that he'd hear her, and she didn't move so much as an eyelash.

After a moment of standing by the table, his back to her, he walked to the door, and Madison almost let out her pent-up breath. But he stopped in the doorway, his back still to her. "Next time you want to snoop, you should hide where your shadow doesn't hit the floor," he said; then he left the room.

For a moment, Madison stood paralyzed. Then, slowly, she turned her head and looked at the kitchen floor. High above her head was a little window, and with the angle of the early morning sun, it had caught the back of her head and made a round shape on the floor. To someone unfamiliar with the kitchen, the shape on the floor wouldn't have been noticeable, but Thomas Randall had spent a lot of his life in that kitchen and he knew every shadow.

Feeling very foolish and wishing she could die from embarrassment, Madison moved out from between the pantry and the refrigerator, then stepped into the kitchen. For a moment she didn't know what to do.

Should she find the man and apologize? Explain to him that she hadn't really been snooping? Or should she just go to Frank and tell him that she absolutely positively *had* to return to Montana *now*.

Madison looked down at the fishing pole still clutched in her hand. On the other hand, she could just get out of the house and spend a day by herself near a stream somewhere and not think about Thomas Randall or her husband or any other man in the entire world.

In the end, fishing won out. She grabbed half a dozen biscuits from the sheet that had just been taken from the oven, and with a defiant little smile, she also took six slices of bacon, a couple of napkins, and left the kitchen. On the way out, she saw Adelia and the skinny little woman she'd seen with her yesterday, the one who seemed to be named Pretty, and Madison waved to them as she headed in the direction that Brooke had pointed out to her last night.

Thomas stepped through the trees and stopped dead in his tracks. Ahead of him, standing in his favorite fishing spot, the spot that had been his since he was six years old, was . . . was . . . Botticelli's Venus was the first thing that came to his mind.

Standing with her back to him, she looked like something from a fishing magazine that would be titled "Lust Fantasies Issue." She was tall, slim, curvy. She had on snug, worn jeans and green thigh-high waders. Above the boots was a round, firm rear end that curved up into a tiny waist that was encircled with a wide leather belt. She had on a denim shirt and a vest that must have been his brother's years ago, as it was too small for her. It reached only halfway down her back.

She had yards of honey blonde hair that hung down her back in huge waves, and when she swirled the pole around, her hair floated about her like some erotic cloud.

All Thomas could do was stare at her. He couldn't seem to move forward or backward—and what was worse, he couldn't seem to think. Instead of thoughts, his head was filled with visions. There was the vision of him walking toward her, taking her in his arms, undressing her, then making love to her on the rocky stream bank. Another vision showed them making love in the grassy meadow that was about half a mile from the cabin. Then there was horseback. And there was that big pine table in the cabin. And there was—

He put his hand over his eyes to hide the view of her.

"Control, man," he said to himself. His whole life had been about control and he couldn't lose it now. He wasn't going to become like his brother and sister, or like his grandfather who had nearly bankrupted the family with his self-indulgences.

Thomas took a couple of deep breaths, then looked back at her. She was so involved in casting her line that she was unaware that anyone was near her. What kind of woman liked *fishing*? he thought angrily. When Thomas had been younger, he'd had several girls tell him that they loved fishing, but he'd soon found out that what they loved was an invitation to the summer home of the Wentworths. Had this woman heard about Thomas's love of fishing, then wheedled his mother into revealing the site of Thomas's favorite spot?

As he watched her, trying to keep his eyes off her body, he saw that she knew what she was doing with the rod. Of course the rod she had was old and she'd never catch anything with it, but she looked as though she'd cast a line a few times.

Turning away, he took a couple of steps back down the path. He wasn't in a good mood. He'd been up all night and he'd wanted to sleep, but Adelia's words about the goings-on at the house had disturbed him too much to sleep. He didn't like Roger because Roger encouraged Scotty to be all the things that Thomas hated: vain, lazy, self-absorbed.

So now Roger was back, and this time he had a new bond with Scotty, with their both having trouble walking. So what was Roger after this time? Last time it had been Cousin Lucy, who had laughed at the brainless jock and sent him away. But Terri was another matter. Last year she'd been jilted by some big, good-looking guy who was up for the Olympics, and now Terri seemed determined to get a man somewhere somehow. But Roger was married. Was Thomas the only one who thought that it was odd that this man would bring his wife with him when he went courting other women? Turning back, Thomas looked at the tall woman standing ankle deep in the stream. She was moving out deeper now and casting her line further out. All his life he'd been told that he was too suspicious, but Thomas had found that no matter how suspicious he was, it was never enough. He had seen this woman's shadow on the floor in the kitchen and known she was hiding and listening. Why had she been spying? Were she and Roger working together? Maybe he was going after Terri, a Wentworth cousin, or Nina, Thomas's sister. So who was this woman after? Scotty?

Or me, Thomas thought; then a slow smile spread over his face. But it wasn't a smile that extended to his eyes.

"If she thinks she's going to get me, she's in for a surprise," Thomas said aloud; then he removed the smile from his face and walked toward her.

"Catch anything?" said a voice behind Madison, making her jump.

"You scared me!" she said as she turned and saw the man. Madison wasn't usually attracted to men. Usually, she spent her time trying to hide from them, but, just like this morning, when she looked at Thomas, she felt that little fluttery thing in the region of her heart. To cover herself, she looked down at her fishing pole. "A few," she said. "What about you?"

"You're in my spot," Thomas said.

"Oh. Sorry. I didn't see any signs," Madison said, realizing that it was a stupid thing to say. He was looking at her so hard that he was beginning to make her nervous.

Taking a deep breath, she looked at him. There was about twenty feet separating them, and the sound of the stream and the birds was loud. "Look, I'm sorry about this morning. I wasn't meaning to spy. I just wanted to sneak out of the house without being seen, so when I saw the cook come in, I slipped into—"

"Adelia. Her name is Adelia."

"Oh. Sorry. When Adelia came in, I hid. Then you came in and—"

"You stayed to hear what you could."

She blinked at him a few times. He was making it sound as though she had pur-posefully hidden herself so she could eavesdrop. "I didn't really mean to hear any-thing," she said. "It just happened. One cir-cumstance led to another." He was glaring at her, the lines between his eyes deep.

Madison wanted to lighten the air. "Anyway, all I heard was that everyone thinks I'm six feet four, so I learned my lesson." She said this with a smile.

But Thomas didn't return her smile. "Three. Six feet three. And you also heard that your husband is enamored with my cousin Terri."

For a moment Madison stood there with her mouth opening and closing like the fish she was catching. "I see," she said at last. "And what do you think I'm going to *do* with this information?"

"Name her in a divorce case. Or perhaps suggest that she give you a gift in order to keep her name out of the papers."

It took Madison a full minute to comprehend what he was saying. "Blackmail?"

"If that's what you want to call it."

The whole idea was so far from anything that had ever crossed Madison's mind that she laughed. She just stood there and laughed at him; then she turned and began to reel in her line. "You know, I used to feel sorry for myself because my mother and I weren't rich. I used to hunger after the pretty clothes that the other girls had and I drooled over Roger's rich house. But then I grew up and I've now lived in Roger's rich house. It has lots of expensive decorations in it, but it has no *love* in it. Not one bit."

She put her rod in one hand, then reached down into the water and lifted a string of fat fish. It was more than Thomas had ever caught in three days, but she had caught them all in just a couple of hours.

"So now here I get a vacation with a bunch of rich people and what am I accused of? Blackmail, that's what." She looked down at the fish, then back at him. "You know something, Mr. Randall? You can keep your money and you can keep your fishing hole." With that she threw the whole mess of fish smack in his face, then turned and walked back the way she'd come.

"Thomas," his mother said softly, but there was steel in her voice. "This time you've gone too far. Whatever you said to her has made Madison ask that your father drive her to the airport so she can return to Montana. Immediately."

"Perhaps," Thomas said calmly, "but I could have been right in what I assumed."

Mr. Randall was standing to one side of

the two of them, the three of them alone in the small sitting room. "Assume: makes an *ass* of *u* and *me*," Frank said under his breath.

Brooke Wentworth Randall calmed herself. She was the only person on earth who could get to Thomas. He was so stubborn. "Do you know who called me last night?"

Thomas gave her a look that said he wasn't going to play guessing games. "My sister called to ask how I was getting on with her dear friend Madison."

At that Thomas's eyes widened in surprise.

"Yes, my sister," Brooke continued. "Dr. Dorothy Oliver. You do remember her, don't you?"

Thomas stood still, ignoring his mother's sarcasm.

Frank stepped forward and put himself between his son and wife. He was the peacemaker in the family. "To us, this visit was just a normal thing of Scotty's asking his old college friend to visit, but it seems that there was a lot that we didn't know. Over two years ago when Roger was first injured, it seems that he called Scotty, as Scotty had mentioned that he had an aunt who worked with physical therapy. Roger told Scotty that he needed 'the best.'"

"Which you know that my sister is," Brooke said in pride.

"Yes, but . . ." Frank hesitated and looked at his wife. "Roger's parents are . . ."

"Skinflints," Brooke said. "I'm sorry to say it, but they are. What they did is . . . Well, it's abominable. You tell it, Frank, or I'll get too angry."

"It seems that Roger's parents consulted with your aunt Dot about their son's massive injuries. They even flew Dot out to Montana, but after she told them what was needed to rehabilitate their son, and even then he might never walk again, and—"

"And how much it was going to cost," Brooke added. "They told my sister, 'Thank you, but no thanks.' Dot said that it was six months before they paid her consultation fee."

Thomas knew that his parents were going somewhere with this story, but he couldn't guess where.

At times like this, when Brooke was so angry, it could be seen where her son got his scowl. "Dot thinks that Roger's parents encouraged their son to call his old girlfriend, Madison—a girl he had crassly jilted, by the way—and beg her to return to Montana, just so she could be his free nurse. She'd had previous nursing experience, so they knew she could do the job."

For a moment his parents were silent, and Thomas knew that he was to see something that he wasn't seeing. "So?" he said.

"So she did it," Brooke said. "That poor girl went back to Roger, married him, and has spent that last couple of years doing nothing but rehabilitating him."

Thomas hadn't graduated from medical school yet, but he had been interested in the extent of his brother's friend's injuries at the time, and he'd found out about them. Thomas knew the monumental amount of labor that must have been done to get Roger up on canes in a mere two and a half years.

Thomas gave a low whistle under his breath. He was impressed.

"Right," Frank said. "And during the rehabilitation, it seems that young Madison and your aunt became friends. Three times Dot and her family flew out to Montana on vacation, and she always spent as much time as possible with Madison."

"Smart," Thomas said. "That way she could deduct most of the trip."

Frank narrowed his eyes at his son in warning; then he continued. "Your aunt thought it was unethical to tell us about her clients, so we never knew any of this. However, Dot saw that her friend needed—and deserved—a holiday, so she planted the idea in Scotty's head to invite his old friend Roger here to the cabin. Of course your aunt never dreamed that Roger wouldn't have told Scotty about his marriage. The idea was to give Madison some time off—a rest."

"I see," Thomas said softly. "But now *I* have changed the situation."

"So what do you propose can be done to change it back?" Brooke asked her son, her eyes narrowing into slits that resembled his.

"I will apologize to her, of course," Thomas said. "It was really just a misunderstanding anyway. She was . . ." Now that he thought about it, her explanation that she had slipped behind a cupboard to escape being seen so she could go fishing early made sense. The truth was, Thomas had often climbed out his bedroom window in order to evade all the people his parents invariably had at the cabin, just so he could get to his favorite fishing hole early. "It will be a heartfelt apology."

"And then what do you think she will do?" Brooke asked.

Thomas looked surprised. "I have no idea. I don't know the woman. I assume she'll unpack and . . . and do whatever it is that women like to do."

Brooke shook her head at her son. How could he have lived this long and know so little about women? "Let's see. She came here thinking she was an invited guest. But she found out that her husband hadn't told anyone that she was coming. Actually, he hadn't even told anyone he was *married.* Your sister, your cousin, and their little friend Robbie have done nothing but look down their noses at her since she arrived because, as even you have probably noticed, Madison is beautiful enough to make a goddess jealous. Then she—"

"Venus." When his mother squinted her eyes at him in disapproval for his having interrupted, he said, "Botticelli's Venus."

"Well, I am glad you noticed," Brooke said sarcastically. "In addition to the abominable way my other guests have treated her—as well as that philandering husband of hers—I find that my eldest son has done something so intolerable that she is now asking to leave. If it wouldn't be too much to ask, could you please tell me what you said to her?"

Thomas looked down at the floor. His shoes needed to be polished. He looked back at his mother. When he was a child, she was the only person on earth who had ever been able to frighten him. And right now he felt about four years old and that he'd just done something he shouldn't have. "Blackmail," he said softly.

"I beg your pardon," Brooke said, her voice full of disbelief.

I should have studied law, Thomas thought. Maybe if he had, he'd be able to think of a clever defense of himself, but medicine didn't prepare one for defenses. He put his shoulders back. "It was a natural mistake to make," he said. "I thought that she was probably—"

Brooke put up her hand to cut him off. "I can't bear to hear this. That lovely girl, and you . . . you . . ." Stepping backward, she sat down on a heavily padded club chair, and when she looked up at her son, she looked as though she might cry. "Twenty-four hours ago I would have sworn that if I had taught my children nothing else, it was good manners. I know that you children grew up in a different age than I did, but we had—"

"Flagpole sitting and swing dancing," Frank said loudly, looking at his wife. "I think we should cut out the melodrama," he said, then turned to his son. "Look, the situation is that you've once again put your foot in it and now that beautiful girl is leaving. If she does, for one thing, it will make it very boring around here, but the major problem is that your mother is going to be in hot water with her sister. Thomas, you're young and you don't yet fully understand what you have to do in this world to keep peace in a family. If that girl storms out of here and your aunt Dot finds out about it, then one of those annoying family feuds is going to start, and those things can take years to die down. Every Thanksgiving and Christmas for years to come is going to be filled with 'what-you-did.' And I can tell you from experience that it makes for extremely unpleasant get-togethers."

Thomas's frown deepened. "I told you

that I'd apologize to her. I don't know what else I can do. If I apologize and she still decides to leave, that isn't my fault, is it?"

Brooke, still seated, opened her mouth to speak, but her husband beat her to it. "Son, there's logic and there's women. They don't have anything to do with each other."

"Really, Frank!" Brooke said. "What a dreadful thing to teach your son."

"Someone should teach him something!" Frank snapped back. "Come on, Thomas, you're smart; what can you do to make her *want* to stay?"

For a moment Thomas looked blank. His mother thought that it was nice to see him without his perpetual frown, but she did wish he hadn't been so very *stupid*. Unfortunately, Frank was right and her younger sister was going to be livid when she heard that her protégée had walked out after spending less than a day with them.

"Buy her a new fishing pole?" Thomas said.

For a moment neither Brooke nor her husband spoke; then they looked at each other and started laughing.

It was Brooke who recovered first as her husband turned and looked out a window.

He was shaking his head in disbelief and exasperation.

"Thomas, darling," Brooke said, and all her earlier annoyance was gone. "How shall I put this? You made the mess, so now you have to clean it up. When Madison does leave here, I want her to tell my sister that she had a wonderful time. Actually, I want her to say that she had the best time of her life."

Thomas did not like being laughed at. He wasn't about to explain that he'd seen Madison fishing and that she would probably really like a full set of fishing gear. Instead, he thrust his hands into his pockets and the crease between his eyes deepened. "I see. You would like me to leave."

Frank turned back to face them. "Just the opposite. After what we saw yesterday, I'm sure that Madison was going to want to leave within a day or two anyway, even if you hadn't shown up and insulted her. Her husband seems determined to ignore his beautiful wife, and you know your brother; he'll want to stay up every night partying. If Madison goes out with them . . ." He looked at his wife.

"I see," Thomas said. "You want her to

have a good time, but you don't want her going out with that wild crowd my brother hangs around with when he's up here. You don't want someone as dishy as this Madison exposed to limitless alcohol and—" He gave his mother a hard look. "And whatever else that Scotty and his crowd do. I don't know much about her, but I doubt if a girl raised in the backwoods of Montana is prepared for the crowd my little brother runs with."

Neither Frank nor his wife liked to admit out loud the truth about their younger son, but they couldn't deny it. "Exactly," Frank said at last.

"So," Thomas said stiffly, as he was still smarting over their laughter, "you want *me* to show her a good time and to keep her away from Scotty's crowd. And, while I'm at it, I'm to keep her away from jealous little twits who will make her visit hell with their backbiting and snide remarks. And what else? Since she and her husband seem to despise each other, I assume I'm to keep her away from him too. Is that about it?"

Brooke gave her son a weak smile. "I think you have it perfectly."

"What I wonder," Thomas said, "is what

the two of you would have done if I *hadn't* insulted her?"

"Begged," Frank said cheerfully. "Thomas, you're the only one who can do this. She's young. She won't want to spend time with us old folks. And Scotty's friends will eat her alive. We were going to talk to you about this morning, but then you—"

"Got to her first." Thomas turned away from them both. He loved his aunt Dot. She was the one who'd encouraged him to go to medical school. His father said that Thomas's brains came directly through his mother's family. Brooke's younger sister, Dot, had a medical degree and two PhDs. She was a dynamo in the world of physical therapy, having written the textbook that was used in medical schools all over the country.

So what would Thomas say to this aunt who had done so much for him when Dot heard that this girl she'd taken under her wing had left after just a few hours as their guest? *"I thought she was maybe working with that husband of hers in a blackmailing scheme, and I told her so two minutes after*

I met her." No, he didn't think that would get him off the hook.

He turned back to his parents. "All right. I'll fix it. Leave it to me," he said, then he left the room. He'd had enough of feeling four years old.

Eight

✿

"You've been what?" Madison said, staring at Thomas Randall. He had knocked on the bedroom door, and she'd said, "Come in," expecting Frank to be there to help her with her suitcase. Instead, a solemn, scowling Thomas had opened the door, stepped inside the room, then closed the door behind him. Madison had walked around him and opened the door.

Now, her hand still on the knob, she glared at him. "You've been what?" she said again, this time in a lower voice.

"Ordered to be your slave for as long as you're here," he said without the slightest bit of humor in his voice.

She didn't know him, but there was something about the way his eyes darted off to one side that was suspicious. "So why don't I believe you?" she asked.

At that Thomas let out a sigh and walked further into the room. "Look, if I promise not to molest you, could we close the door? This could become embarrassing."

"For you or for me?"

"Me," he said.

"Good," she answered, then closed the door, but she didn't move away from it. "Tell me what you have to say quickly. Your father is waiting for me."

"He is and he isn't," Thomas said.

She had a feeling that this man she was seeing now wasn't a man that many people saw. She had an idea that the real Thomas was sure of himself most, if not all, of the time, but now he was acting as though he'd rather face a firing squad than be here in this room alone with her. Just what my ego needed, she thought.

"First of all, I owe you an apology," he said. When she didn't answer, but just stood there with her arms folded across her chest, he threw up his hands and sat down on the chair by the window. "Okay, so how'd you like the truth?"

"It would make for a change around here."

At that Thomas gave the tiniest bit of a smile. "Do you know Dr. Dorothy Oliver?"

"Yes," Madison said tentatively. "But what does she have to do with my blackmailing your cousin in a divorce settlement?"

"*Mmph!*" Thomas said as though she'd hit him. "She's my aunt, my mother's sister, and it seems that you and your husband were invited here so *you* could have a good time."

At that astonishing statement, the hostility left Madison, and she sat down on the corner of the bed. "Me?" Her mind was whirling. Since she'd arrived, she'd felt as though she were an intruder here, as though she didn't belong, but all along, it had been her and not Roger who had actually been the guest.

"Why don't you start at the beginning?" Madison said, then watched him as he explained. When he'd finished, she said, "So you're going to be in serious trouble if I leave?"

"Well, it's not as though the IRS is going

to audit me or that I'm failing my courses or that—"

"When will you see your aunt next?" Madison asked, smiling.

Thomas grimaced. "Probably Thanksgiving." He looked at her. "And if you leave now, *I* will be the turkey that's served for dinner."

Madison laughed. "I see. So what has your family told you to do?"

"When you *do* leave here, they want you to honestly be able to tell my aunt that you had the best time of your life."

For a moment Madison just stared at him, blinking; then she stood and paced back and forth a few times, thinking about this. Halting, she looked at him. "So exactly what does this mean?"

"My mother wasn't specific, but I think it means that I'm to give you anything you want."

"Carte blanche at Bergdorf's?"

"If that's what you want," he said stiffly.

"Or does it mean that you are to 'show me a good time'? Wine and dine me, that sort of thing?"

"Whatever you want. We can fly into New York and go shopping. We could go out to some clubs there; then we could return here and I could take you out to some places where you could wear whatever you've bought in the city."

Turning away, she pretended to be considering what he'd just offered. She could tell that that's exactly what he expected of her, or, rather, what he would expect of "someone like her," as he'd probably put it. "All right," she said as she turned back to him. "I'll tell you what I want."

He lifted one eyebrow. "And what is that?"

"Nothing," she said. "I don't want anything. I just want some time off from responsibility. I want to lie about in a hammock all day long. I want to read trashy novels. I want to work jigsaw puzzles. I want to eat too much, then do nothing but lie around in the sun. The most strenuous thing I want to do is lift a glass of lemonade."

From the look on his face she knew that she'd startled him. Obviously, it wasn't what he'd expected her to say. In a way, it was rather like having a genie offer you three wishes, then turning them down.

"Are you sure?" he asked softly. "My brother will be going to parties and I'm sure that Roger will go with him. You'll need something to wear, so I can—"

"No, I won't need anything to wear to parties because I won't be attending any parties. Look, I know that everyone in this house sees that there isn't much left between Roger and me. I don't think anyone can go through what we have and still be 'in love,' so you might as well know that Roger and I have agreed to take a vacation from each other. He may go to all the parties he wants, but I was never one for large gatherings and I have no interest in them."

She could tell that he wasn't believing her. In exasperation she said, "From the moment you saw me, you've thought nothing but bad about me. What in the world could I have done to give you such an opinion of me?"

His voice was very quiet when he spoke. "Usually girls who look like you think only of diamonds and places to wear them."

That made Madison laugh. "Maybe that's true in the world you live in, but not in my world. Believe it or not, Mr. Randall, there's a person inside here."

He was staring at her in a way that made

Madison think that she'd forgotten to put on her clothes.

"You know, I think maybe there is," he said, then, slowly, he stood up and walked to the door. "I will see that you have everything you want," he said, then left the room.

After he left, Madison seemed to deflate. There was something about him that, when she was near him, made her feel charged with electricity. If she got angry, she seemed to get *extremely* angry. And if he made her laugh, she seemed to laugh all the way to her toes. And when he gave her a compliment, Madison was sure that it was the best compliment that she'd ever had in her life.

Roger's boots were sticking out from under the bed and Madison kicked them. "Down, girl!" she told herself. "You're married and . . . and . . ." She couldn't think of anything else, except that a man like Thomas Randall, from a family like his, wasn't for her.

Madison lasted a whole twenty-four hours before she was bored out of her mind. For the last two years, she'd read nothing but medical textbooks and she'd desperately wanted to read something light and happy, something that didn't go into detail about what awful things could happen to the human body. But as soon as she picked up what was best described as a "beach book," she was bored. How could she believe in romance? How could she believe that an ending could be "happily ever after"? After marriage was nothing but work. After marriage, people didn't even *talk* to each other anymore.

She'd promised to give Roger his freedom and not interfere in his life while they were on this trip and, at the time, it had seemed like a wonderful idea, but as she lay in the hammock that was several feet away from the big heated swimming pool, she almost wished she could join the others who were noisily laughing and splashing. In the water, Roger was no longer handicapped by his canes, so he leaped and played like a kid. All done with "the girls" of course.

Late yesterday, Madison had tried to join them. She'd been alone in their bedroom, trying to read her romantic novel, but she could hear the squeals of laughter from outside. So she'd put on her white swimsuit, a plain, one-piece thing, put on one of

Roger's shirts over it, and walked out to the pool. But her appearance had stopped all the laughter. Madison in jeans was a sight to behold, but Madison in a white swimsuit, the legs cut up to the waist, was a show-stopper.

Ten minutes after she arrived, Roger was pulling himself out of the pool. "Why did you have to ruin it?" he said, so Madison had turned away and gone back to their room. She hadn't seen Thomas sitting on the out-skirts of the group, a textbook open in front of him.

Early the next morning, Madison edged out of bed, not that she was fearful of waking Roger, as he was snoring loudly, after all— once again, he'd been out all night—but she just wanted to slip out of the house unno-ticed. She pulled on jeans, a T-shirt, an old corduroy shirt, then laced on her nearly worn-out hiking boots. But all her tiptoeing was almost for nothing when she opened the door and was nearly hit on the head by a long green canvas bag that some idiot had propped against the door.

But Madison caught it before it fell and

woke the household. And the minute she touched it, she knew that it was a new fishing rod. Even through the canvas she could feel that it was one of those divinely lightweight things that could pull in a marlin without snapping. It was the kind of rod she'd drooled over in sporting goods stores.

And she knew exactly who had put it there.

Tied to the handle with pink ribbon was a little envelope. She opened it. *"This is an apology gift. Please accept it. Meet me at the hole. I have a proposition for you."*

There was no signature, but there didn't need to be one. In an instant Madison went from dreading a day of nothing to do to having excitement running through her veins. She practically ran through the house to get to the storage closet where Brooke kept the other gear she'd need. And when Madison opened the closet door, she gasped. Inside were new waders, and she knew without checking that they were her shoe size. The pair she'd used before had been so big she'd had trouble walking in them. Also, there was a new vest, the kind that had lots of little pockets to store lures and hooks.

And on the floor was one of those old-fashioned basket creels, the kind that look so
good but cost twenty times as much as a
plastic bucket. Like the pole case, it had a
pink bow tied around the strap.

"I shouldn't do this," she whispered even
as she tried on the vest and picked up the
creel. "I shouldn't accept gifts from
strangers. I shouldn't—Oh, the hell with it,"
she said, then grabbed the tall boots and
went out the side door, avoiding the kitchen,
where she knew that people would be
bustling.

Within minutes she was near "the hole,"
as Thomas called it, and as she neared it,
she hesitated. What had he meant by
"proposition"?

As she stepped through the shrubs, she
saw that he wasn't there and immediately,
her heart sank to her knees.

"Good morning," he said from behind
her, making her jump.

"Do you always have to do that?" she
snapped, annoyed with herself that she was
so happy that he really was there.

"I like to keep the upper hand. You want
something to eat? Or did you sneak around
the kitchen before you came?"

"Very funny." As he walked off, she followed him, her hands full of his gifts. When he stopped at the stream edge and picked up his own pole, she said, "Look, about these things. I couldn't possibly keep them. How about if I just use them while I'm here?"

He didn't look up from the tiny artificial fly he was attaching to the end of his line. "Whatever you want," he said. "Food's over there. I brought hot chocolate, so I hope you aren't dieting."

"Never," Madison said honestly, then put down the boots and pole and went to the cooler; a big thermos leaned up against it. She poured herself some of the steaming hot chocolate, then took a brioche from the cooler and a couple of strawberries. Thomas hadn't moved from the stream edge, and now he had his back to her and was starting his first cast into the water.

With her food in her hand, Madison sat down on a boulder near him. "So what's this proposition?" She tried to sound light-hearted, but she could hear the edge to her voice.

"It's not what you think," he said, concentrating on his fishing and not looking at her. "But then, I guess you get hit on a lot."

"Yes," Madison said simply.

His line became entangled in something, and it took him a few minutes to free it; then he put down his pole and walked to the cooler just behind her. After handing her another roll and taking one for himself, he sat down on the rocky shore. "I think that you and I are a couple of misfits."

Madison started to protest that, but she couldn't, so she didn't say anything.

"At least here we are. This place is ruled by my little sister and brother and their friends. It wasn't always that way, mind you. When I was a kid, I loved spending my summers up here. I've hiked every inch of this place in a twenty-five mile radius. And fished most of the streams. But as my siblings grew up . . ."

Shrugging, he leaned back on his arms, and Madison looked at him. He had a beat-up old canvas hat on and it shaded his eyes, but she could swear that as he looked at the water, the frown lines between his eyes were less deep.

"Anyway, they prefer parties to the great

outdoors. In fact, there's a party planned for tonight."

At that Madison sighed. To her parties meant drunken men trying to put their hands on her body parts.

"Yeah, me too," Thomas said. "I can't stand parties. Look, I was wondering if maybe . . . I mean, I know that you said that all you want to do is lie around the house and read, but I thought maybe you'd like to go hiking with me."

Part of Madison wanted to yell, "Yes!" but there was another part that kept her silent. How many times had tourists passing through Montana asked her to go "hiking" with them?

"On one condition," Thomas said. "Nothing romantic."

"I beg your pardon?" Madison said, coming out of her reverie about her hometown.

Turning his head, he looked up at her. "Women keep wanting to marry me."

"Really?" Madison said. "How awful that must be for you."

With a grimace, he looked back at the water. "I thought maybe you'd understand. What is it that Jane Austin said, 'that a man with a fortune must need a wife'?

Something like that. Well, I'm rich and the minute women find that out, they start planning the wedding. And from what I've seen about you, whenever a man sees you, he starts planning—"

"The honeymoon?" Madison said.

"Exactly."

She, too, looked at the water. "I hadn't thought of it that way, but I guess you're right, we are misfits. So what do you propose? Or is that a bad choice of words?"

"Freedom for both of us. In my entire life I've never had what I'd call a 'good time' with a female. It's all been so calculated. You can't imagine how many women have told me they love to fish, but later I find out that they've 'researched' me and found out that I like fishing, so they . . ." He trailed off, then shrugged. "One woman I met had taken fishing lessons."

"So freedom would mean that we . . . ?" Madison asked, looking down at him.

"Have a good time. No strings attached. You seem to dislike the same things that I do, so I thought that maybe you like some of the same things too. I can see that you like to fish, so I thought that maybe we could walk and fish and, well, just be people. You forget that I'm rich and I'll not pay any attention to the fact that you're the most beautiful woman I have ever seen in my life."

In spite of herself, a little thrill at his words ran through her. She wanted to say, "Really? The *most* beautiful? Or just *one* of the most beautiful?" But Madison didn't say anything.

"How does that sound to you?" he asked.

Madison cleared her throat for fear that she'd squeak. "Fine," she said. "It sounds fine."

"Unless you'd rather stay at the cabin for the rest of your stay and read and go to parties with your husband. Or you could sit on the porch at night with Mom and Dad and—"

"No," Madison said quickly. "I'd rather spend time with—" She stopped herself from saying, "with you." She wasn't going to let him think that she was one of the many women who was chasing him. "With the outdoors," she said at last. "What exactly did you have in mind that we'd do?"

"Hiking. Unless you're one of those city women who's afraid of the wilderness."

At that Madison laughed. "I'm from Montana. What could you possibly have in these little New York mountains to rival my home state?"

Thomas smiled at her, and when he did, his face softened. "Good. I need a break from studies and school. We could do a little white water-rafting. Nothing danger-ous, so we wouldn't need a guide, just the two of us. We could float down the river and camp out if you . . . Well, if you wouldn't be afraid to be alone with me, that is. And if your husband gave his permission."

After what I've done for Roger! was the first thought that entered Madison's mind, but she didn't say it. "I'm sure it will be all right. Roger and I have a very adult relationship." She almost choked on that lie.

"That's wonderful," Thomas said, then got up to stand over her and stretch.

Madison, still sitting on the rock, looked up at him, the early morning sun behind him, outlining his big, strong body, showing the way the muscles moved under his clothes. How long had it been since she'd touched a body that wasn't in need of doc-toring? How long—

When he looked back down at her, Madison put her empty cup to her lips and looked down at the ground. She'd better hide what she'd just been thinking and feeling.

"Have some more chocolate," he said cheerfully as he took her cup, then poured more liquid out of the big thermos. "I think this is going to be a great vacation for both of us. No strings attached. No worries about any physical relationship coming between us. I know that things aren't great between you and your husband, but I think that you're the kind of woman who would respect her marriage vows."

When he didn't say any more, she looked up at him and saw that he seemed to be expecting her to answer.

"Oh, yes," Madison said. "Great respect." As she drank the chocolate, she wondered if Roger and little Terri were also respecting his marriage vows.

"Perfect," Thomas said. "Absolutely perfect. Now, what would you like to do first? Any suggestions?"

"You know what there is to do better than I do," she said, looking up at him.

"I'm sure it was presumptuous of me,

but I thought you might like this idea, so I did a little preplanning. In about two hours Pretty will meet us on the other side of that mountain—or maybe to you it's just a hill—with a pickup full of supplies and a rubber raft. We'll set off from there and take a little trip. Not too long. Three or four days. Think you can handle that?"

All Madison could do was blink at him. Three or four days alone in beautiful wilderness with a man she found extremely attractive? Days away from constantly having to encourage a man to do his exercises? "I can't," Roger would whine, then Madison would have to tell him he could. Then when he did it, she'd have to praise him. And praise him and praise him.

"Who cooks?" she asked, squinting up at Thomas.

"We'll split it. But most everything has been made by Adelia and put into little bags. She dries her own fruit, smokes the meat herself. She even makes the granola from scratch."

Part of Madison knew she should say no. A big part of her knew she should return to the cabin and discuss this with Roger. After all, he was still her husband. He didn't act as if he was and he'd made it publicly clear that he—

"Yes," Madison said. "I would like that very, very much."

Nine

"So what happened?!" Ellie demanded as she held her glass out for Leslie to refill.

Madison lit another cigarette, then exhaled before speaking. "I had the most wonderful time of my life."

When she didn't say any more, Ellie looked as though she were going to strangle Madison. "Details! I want details. You were there with that lazy, no-good husband of yours; then you went off into the wilderness for days with a man who wanted a platonic relationship with you, and—" She broke off when Madison started laughing. "What?!"

"Thomas was lying. Every word about his 'proposition' was a lie. Later he told me that he was so hot for me that I made his palms sweat. But when he saw that all men everywhere had that reaction to me, he knew he wouldn't have a chance if he made a play for me."

"I see," Ellie said. "That makes sense. From a writer's point of view, that is. So he wanted to give you time to *like* him."

"Yes," Madison said softly. "That's just what he wanted. He wanted me to get to know him, away from his family, away from every outside influence. And he wanted to get to know me, the me inside, not just the outside of me."

"Yeah, I have that problem too," Ellie said. "You too, Leslie?"

When Leslie was silent, Ellie turned to look at her. "Believe it or not, I did at one time. Not my face so much as my body. But now it's hard to remember back that far."

Madison squinted through the smoke at Ellie. "Don't you start acting like you're not pretty enough to set men on their ears."

"Maybe. But I've never inspired men to great heights of lust the way you two have. You know what men like to do with me?"

Madison lifted her eyebrows. "Sure you want to reveal that?"

"Maybe your secrets are private, but all mine have been printed and published.

Anyway, men have always liked to *talk* to me. No, it's true. Give me ten minutes with a man and he's telling me things he wouldn't tell an analyst."

"With me, men wanted acrobatic sex," Leslie said with a sigh. "You wouldn't believe the things that the boys in college proposed to me."

When both Madison and Ellie looked at her expectantly, Leslie smiled. "Ellie may write all her secrets down, but I'm keeping mine to myself. So go on with your story."

But Madison didn't speak for a moment. "If men only understood that one thing, they could win any woman in the world. The ugliest man could have the most beautiful woman."

"Did I miss something?" Ellie said. "What 'one thing' do men need to understand?"

"To give a woman what she *wants*, not what he thinks she wants," Madison said in a faraway voice; then she looked at the other two women and smiled. "What Thomas realized is that, all my life, men had been making passes at me because of my looks. So of course what I hungered for was someone to *talk* to me. I used to fantasize about falling in love with a blind man, a man who couldn't see me, so he'd treat me like other women."

Ellie gave a snort of derision. "And I'm just the opposite. I was in a gifted program all through high school, so everyone thought I was a 'brain.' What I wanted was *physical*. And now my life is spent thinking. If I had a romance—not that I will—but if I did, I'd just want feeling, emotion. *Thunderous* romance."

The way she said the last words made the others laugh.

"Not me," Leslie said. "I'd want hearts and flowers. Champagne. Tea in porcelain cups. Picnics while I wear lace. Hand kissing. And *no* groping. And absolutely nothing that *thunders!*"

At that the three of them laughed together.

"But at least you got what you wanted," Ellie said to Madison. "You got a man to talk to you, but I'm still waiting for my thunder."

"And I can tell you that Alan isn't the hearts-and-flowers type," Leslie said. "For our tenth anniversary, he bought me an annuity." When the other two looked at her in question, she shrugged. "It's a very sensible thing. I'll have it long after the flowers that I wanted died."

"On the other hand," Madison said, "diamonds last longer than companies that hold annuities."

Again the three of them laughed; then Leslie's face suddenly grew serious as she looked at Madison. "Pardon me for asking something so personal, but why didn't you divorce Roger and marry Thomas?"

For a moment, Madison turned away, and there looked to be tears in her eyes.

"Okay," Ellie said, lying back down. "Go back to the story. Tell us as it happened. Tell us every detail. Lead up to the punch line. If you didn't marry him, I trust that you had a good reason."

"Yeah," Madison said softly. "I had a good reason. He—"

"No!" Ellie said. "You're in my domain now. You have to tell a story in the proper order. You don't tell the punch line before you tell the joke. Go back to that beautiful wilderness in Upstate New York and tell us about—" Ellie sat up abruptly. "Tell us why that woman was named Pretty."

The tears went away and Madison smiled again. "Any more of that wine? Do you think they have a pizza parlor in this tiny town? One that delivers?"

"They have pizza parlors that deliver even in Egypt," Ellie said, and when the others looked at her in question, she smiled. "You can read all about that in my third book, but now let's look for a phone book and order. And can we get something besides pepperoni? And you—" She pointed at Madison. "You sit and talk. So, tell me, did Thomas have really great legs?"

"Beautiful," Madison said, leaning back against the leg of the couch. "Every part of him was beautiful."

Ten

"And you're how old?" Thomas said with a deep scowl as he held Madison's foot in his palm and turned it to look at the bloody blisters. "You couldn't be more than six if you did something this dumb."

For all that his words were harsh, Madison felt nothing but caring concern coming from him. It had taken them three hours to walk over the hill that Thomas called a mountain to reach the pickup where Pretty waited for them.

And during the walk, Thomas had encouraged Madison to talk. He told her that his mother had said she'd rehabilitated Roger, so he wanted to know, in detail, what she'd done.

At first, Madison was reluctant to talk about the matter. For one thing, she'd had no experience with talking with a man. She'd tried it, but as men looked at her, they became "distracted." And since she'd been married, she'd tried to interest Roger in what she was reading about, but he'd said that it was enough that he had to *do* what she read about, he didn't want to have to listen to it too.

But Thomas, walking ahead of her on the trail, had persisted. "I'm about ready to choose my specialty in medicine, so maybe I'll become a physiatrist."

She knew that he was testing her on this obscure word for a doctor who specializes in physical medicine and rehabilitation. "Do you have the personality?" Madison teased, but Thomas glanced back at her with his usual frown.

"What do you mean?"

"If I had to put it into one word, it's 'Encouragement.' Rehabilitation is nonstop encouragement. The patient isn't just a doll you can manipulate. You have to deal with his personality and make him want to do all the work involved. It's easier to lie in bed and watch football than it is to try to lift a leg three inches off the bed, then repeat the process twenty times."

"I see," Thomas said, turning back to the trail. "So what did you do to encourage your patient?"

Not "Roger," Madison thought, but "your patient." She liked that. It made her feel as though she were actually in the medical profession, rather than just Roger's wife who wasn't sure what she was doing half the time.

When she didn't say anything, Thomas said, "Start at the beginning."

Madison made a sound of disgust. "The beginning is difficult. With Roger it was especially difficult because he'd been told by the neurosurgeon that his spinal cord had been severed and that he'd never walk again. When I got back to Montana, Roger was suicidal."

"But you gave him hope," Thomas said softly. "And, more important, you made him walk again. So tell me how you did it."

The way he said that made Madison feel wonderful, but she didn't want him to think she was an egomaniac, so she passed the buck. "I had a lot of help from your aunt. She'd told Roger's parents that the X-rays seemed to show a complete lesion, but there was so much swelling that she couldn't be sure. I called her. I was very nervous about doing so, and I didn't know if Roger's parents would pay her bill if she sent one but I wanted to learn all that I could. She was very nice and she told me to put towels under Roger's knees then push down on his legs. If his feet came up and seemed to show signs of movement, then there was hope."

"And you did it," Thomas said, encouraging her to go on.

"Yes," Madison said. "And when we saw that there was a possibility that he might walk again, I had to start reading and figuring out what to do next." With Thomas's intense listening, Madison began talking about what she'd done over the last two and a half years. At first she tried to be scientific and talk about drugs and pain and specific exercises. But after about twenty minutes, her personal feelings crept in and she started mentioning the troubles she'd had with Roger's parents and how they wouldn't give her the money for equipment.

"It was as though they wanted the neurosurgeon to be right; they didn't want Roger to walk again. His father said, 'What does it matter? He'll never again be able to play sports, so he might as well be in a wheel-chair.' "

As he listened, Thomas made no comment except to now and then look back at her with a sharp glance.

She told Thomas about the nerve damage to Roger's right hip. "He'll never feel much with that leg," she said. She told about the bone grafts, the skin grafts. She told about having to roll Roger about when he still had on a hip cast, having to lift him and move him in the many months before he could pull himself up by the triangular bar that hung above his bed.

"And what did you do for the depression?" Thomas asked.

At that Madison looked away because she didn't want to tell him about a long conversation she'd had with Dr. Oliver. It was three months after the accident and Roger wasn't cooperating; all he could think about were the things he could no longer do. Once again, Madison had called the woman who was becoming her friend, and to Madison's horror, Madison had burst into tears on the phone. "I can lift his legs, but I can't lift his spirits," she'd cried, "so nothing I do is making him progress."

"It's a common problem," Dorothy had said. "Not many years ago hospitals had spinal cord injury wings, and the men and women smoked grass and had sex with each other and outsiders."

It took Madison a moment to clear her tears away enough to hear. "What?" she asked.

"Sex, Madison," Dorothy said. "After injuries like this the first question is, 'Will I walk?' The second question is, 'Can I have sex?' or, in women, it's, "Can I have children?' I believe that Roger's genitalia are intact, so you could probably have sex."

"A baby?" Madison asked, stunned at the doctor's words. She'd expected the doctor to tell her about some new exercises or—

"Actually, I doubt very much if you would get pregnant. Due to his inactivity, the drugs, and the hormone interruptions of the HPAC axis, I doubt if his testosterone levels are high enough to make you pregnant. But try sex. It gives men something to live for."

"Oh," Madison had said. "I . . . never thought about that."

"Madison, dear, don't forget to *live*."

So now Thomas was asking her how

she'd given his spirit back to Roger. "As he saw improvement, he was better," she'd mumbled at last.

Thomas nodded, seeming to accept her answer. "Tell me about drugs," he said.

"Blood thinners," she replied, once again on safe ground, glad she hadn't been asked to go into what had become something quite unpleasant between her and Roger. It wasn't good to be a man's nurse as well as his sex partner, as the two seemed to get mixed up. Roger had wanted every exercise session to turn into sex. He'd wanted Madison to play out fantasies about being his nurse. "But I *am* your nurse," she'd say, exasperated. She found it impossible to reconcile the two roles: love words one moment, fierce orders of, "You *must* do this!" the next moment. Nurses don't usually give two-and-a-quarter-inch intramuscular shots one minute and kisses the next.

Madison skipped all that part of Roger's rehabilitation and went on to talk about the drugs used in Roger's recovery.

By the time they got to the truck, she realized that she had talked nonstop and she felt embarrassed. Truthfully, she didn't think she'd talked so much in all the last two and a half years combined. Neither Roger nor his parents were much for talking.

There was no one at the truck, just the big orange raft, ready to inflate, and a couple of heavy-looking backpacks.

"Where's . . . Pretty, is it?" Madison asked, looking around. They were by a wide, shallow stream, the truck parked on gravel. The narrow road was overgrown, and tall, drooping trees nearly obscured it.

Thomas was leaning over the side of the truck checking the supplies. "She's around, but you probably won't see her. She's shy."

Madison moved closer to him. "So why's she called Pretty?" she whispered.

He didn't look up from the truck bed where he was rummaging, and his answer was so smooth that he'd obviously repeated it many times. "Pretty shy. Pretty useful. Pretty-much-not-seen. Take your pick." He looked up at her. "Looks like everything is here. Can you carry a pack?"

Tilting her head, Madison smiled at him. "If I said no, would you carry it for me?"

She was teasing, but Thomas didn't treat her words as though she were. "Yes," he said simply.

For a moment, they locked eyes and

Madison began to feel her heart rate speed up. Nervously, she looked away from him. "I can carry it," she said at last.

So she had carried a pack. Thomas had carried his pack plus the big raft for about a mile before he reached a place where he put it down and inflated it. "And what else?" he asked as he helped her off with her pack. As before, he had questioned her about every detail of her rehabilitation of Roger.

"I can't think of anything else," she said honestly; then, as she looked around them, she realized that she felt lighter. To her left was a rock wall that went straight up for about fifty feet. To the right was the stream, much deeper here than it had been where the pickup was. And between the water and the rock, in the deep shade of the over-hanging cliff face, it was quiet and private and Madison was suddenly aware of being alone with this attractive man.

She watched Thomas strap everything down into the rubber raft. If it had been Roger, he would have been complaining that Madison wasn't doing her share. But of course that thought was absurd. Roger would never think of taking a female into the woods with him. No, Roger was a "man's man." He did the interesting things in his life with other men. With Roger—

"And what have you done about your beauty?" Thomas asked, breaking into Madison's reverie.

"My what?" she asked, taken off guard.

Thomas didn't smile. "Your beauty. What have you done with it?"

She blinked at him. "Fed it a lot of mois-turizer?" she said, having no idea how to reply to his question. "Dry skin."

He motioned for her to get into the raft; then as he pushed it into the water, he said, "Beauty like yours is like having a talent, like being able to play the piano or to paint. So what have you done with this talent?"

Holding on to the safety straps of the raft as he jumped inside, Madison could only look at him. She'd never thought of her looks as a "talent."

Picking up the oars, Thomas began to manipulate the raft about in the water. The sun filtered through the trees and it was very quiet. She'd never been in a raft before and she liked it.

Once he had the boat straight, he looked at her. "Well?"

"My hometown sent me to New York to become a model," she blurted out.

"And what happened? Other than Roger, that is?"

At that Madison again blinked at him, for his words showed great perception. Since she'd married Roger, she'd been living away from her hometown, but whenever she met anyone from Erskine, she told them that she'd had to give up modeling to nurse the man she loved.

"What makes you think that I didn't abandon a potentially fabulous career to nurse the man I love back to health?"

As Thomas muscled the raft around some rocks sticking up out of the water, he said, "Your enthusiasm for what you did tells me that you love nursing. But I've not heard or seen you show any enthusiasm for Roger. Based on those two things, it's my guess that you love nursing more than you loved modeling."

She couldn't help but laugh; then she leaned back against the back of the raft and let her hand dangle over the side. "You're exactly right. I know that many little girls dream of the glamorous life of modeling, but I hated it. I don't mean that I disliked it. I mean that I really and truly *hated* it. And, besides, they made me feel ugly."

At that Thomas stopped rowing and looked at her. And his expression made Madison feel very good. His face said that her being less than beautiful was impossible.

"Modeling is a science," she said. "Well, sort of, anyway. It was enough of a science that I wanted nothing to do with it."

He was still staring at her in that way that told her that he didn't believe a word she was saying. "Isn't nursing a science?" he asked.

"All right," she said with a sigh. "My ego was crushed. Really. It was trampled into the ground and smashed beneath the feet of those . . . those prissy little men in their—" She broke off because she was becoming angry.

After a moment of staring at the water, she turned back at him. He had a way of looking at a person that *forced* you to tell the truth. "I can't get you to buy my story that I'm a martyr to the cause of love?"

"No. Roger's a jerk and you don't love him. Truthfully, I doubt if you ever did. But when you talk about rehabilitating him, your face glows. You went to him because you *wanted* to. But then we all do what we want to, don't we? So why didn't you *want* to model?"

"You're tough," she said, then looked away for a moment, then back at him. "Okay, so the truth was, I liked being the most beautiful girl in my hometown. I liked people stopping their cars to talk to me; then I'd pretend that I didn't know why they'd stopped."

She looked at him to see how he'd take this confession. Madison wasn't used to talking about her beauty. She'd worked hard to perfect her modest smile when someone told her she was beautiful. She liked to act as though she'd never heard that before.

"In New York girls like me are everywhere. I was nothing special."

"I don't believe that," Thomas said flatly. "I live in New York and I don't see women like you every day."

"Maybe not, but they're there. They get up early and go to bed late. And in between they're pushed around and told to stand and to sit and to look and to . . . Well, to do whatever anyone can think up for them to do." She grimaced. "And they are criticized. That's what my ego couldn't take."

For a moment, Thomas rowed and didn't say anything. "How could they criticize you?"

"I have one eye that is slightly smaller than the other. See?" she said, leaning toward him. "And I'm a bit heavy in the seat."

"Ha!" Thomas said. "You are perfect."

"But *you* are not a photographer."

"If you have flaws, then all those other women you see on magazine covers must also have flaws," he said, looking at her hard.

Madison smiled. "True. They do, and they learn how to cover them. Lighting helps a lot. Ever see the sixties model Jean Shrimpton? She had big bags under her eyes, but when she was lit properly . . ." Madison trailed off and looked at the river-bank they were passing. Thomas was right: She left modeling because she had *wanted* to, not for Roger.

She turned back to him. "Why don't we talk about you?" she said. "What made you choose medicine?"

"When I was a kid I saw a cousin of mine

drown. I was only nine at the time, but I decided at that moment that I wanted to learn how to keep people alive."

"I'm sorry," she said. "Before Roger, I had to watch my mother die. It took her four long years."

Thomas was silent a moment as he rowed. The water was calm and the sunlight made everything sparkle. "Is that what you did during your college years?"

Madison shook her head at him. "I'm beginning to think that you're clairvoyant."

"Naw," he said with a one-sided grin. "Just years of reading mystery stories. I like to watch people and figure them out. I like to look at clues and see what they add up to."

"Oh? The first time you met me you thought I was going to try to extort money from you. Or was it your sister I was going to blackmail?"

Thomas ducked his head to one side, and she thought maybe he was hiding a blush. "I was distracted by the look of you." Before she could say anything in reply to that, he said, "So what else do you want to know about me? I'm a very interesting fellow. I've been everywhere and seen a lot."

She thought he was teasing her. "In medical school? Isn't that the place where you're not allowed to sleep for years at a time?"

"I'm thirty-one, so I've done some things other than sit in a classroom."

At Madison's age of twenty-three, thirty-one seemed old. Very mature. "Tell me," she said, and there was a little catch in her breath, "I've been in Montana and New York and that's it. But I'd like to go to . . . to . . ."

"Name a place," he said as he moved the boat around a tree that had fallen halfway across the river.

"Tibet. Petra. Morocco. Some tropical island somewhere. The Galapagos to see the turtles."

Thomas didn't so much as smile. "So give them to me in order of preference and I'll tell you all about them."

"You've been to *all* those places?" she asked, one eyebrow arched in disbelief.

"All of them that you named. So where do you want to start?"

She thought for a moment. "Australia."

"The wet part or the dry part? City or outback? Where the orchids grow or where they mine opals?"

"Anywhere," she said breathlessly, eyes wide.

So for the rest of the day, Madison listened to Thomas talk about where he'd been in the world and what he'd seen. And she never gave her feet a thought. But as the sun set, Thomas pulled the raft to the side of the river, saying that they could camp there, and when Madison stepped out, pain shot up her legs.

Thomas saw her wince, and saw her limp. He told her to sit down on a flat rock, pulled her foot onto his lap and untied her shoe. "I should have noticed that your hiking boots were really worn out," he said, his scowl more pronounced than usual. "Look at that!" Holding up her foot, he showed her the blisters on her heel and her toes. "Do you know that these could become infected?"

"They're just blisters," she said.

"A former president's son died from a blister he got while playing tennis," was Thomas's answer as he put her foot down, then opened his pack to remove a first aid package in a plastic bag.

Madison couldn't help but laugh.

"Haven't we made some medical advances in the last few years?"

Thomas didn't laugh as he poured clean water on sterile gauze, then cleaned the blood from the ruptured blisters. "Not really. In fact, I've just seen in England that they're going back to using leeches."

"Tell me," Madison said eagerly, then listened intently as Thomas described how leeches were being used to drain the excess blood from such things as amputated fingers that had been reattached.

When he'd finished his description, which Madison found to be fascinating, Thomas said, "Have you ever thought of doing something in the medical world?"

"You mean like becoming a nurse?"

"I was thinking more along the lines of your becoming a doctor," he said quietly as he began to bandage her foot.

"Me? A doctor?" she said, her voice telling him what she thought of that idea.

Thomas frowned. "You've doctored two people. Why not more?"

"One of my patients died, and the other . . ." She lowered her voice. "Roger hates me for what I did to him. He says my nursing skills are as subtle as a stone baseball bat."

Thomas snorted. "Roger is jealous of you."

"Of me?" Madison said, laughter in her voice.

"Of course. He reeks with it, like a fish left out in the sun for a week."

Madison smiled. "You make me feel good. Smart, I mean."

"You don't need that from me. Roger knows that you're smarter than he is, as well as better looking and a better person. How can he compete with someone like you?"

"Someone like me," she said softly. " 'A Montana cowgirl.' "

Thomas didn't respond to what she'd said, nor did he apologize for having called her that before he'd met her. Instead, when she looked down at the top of his head, at his thick, black hair, she thought that he was taking an extraordinarily long time bandaging her second foot. As for her, she thought that he could go on holding her foot—or touching any part of her—forever.

It was growing darker by the minute, and they were so very alone, with nothing but the water to one side of them, high rocks to the other.

She was looking down at him hard. What would she do if he made a movement toward her? If he, say, ran his hand up her leg under her trousers? She'd never been touched in that way by any man except Roger, and she had never felt with him as she did with this man right now. Every pore in her body seemed to be alive.

It was Thomas who broke the spell. Abruptly, he dropped her foot, stood up, then looked down at her. "We only have one tent for the two of us. Two sleeping bags but one tent. If we sleep in the same room, so to speak, are you going to try to take my virtue?"

The way he said it made her laugh. "Depends on what color your underwear is," she said as she stood up.

"Red," he said instantly.

"Nope, does nothing for me."

"Sorry. I forgot. It's black."

Madison laughed again. "No. Nothing."

"Green?" he asked hopefully.

She smiled. "So what are you serving me for dinner? I could eat a horse."

"Ah, now I remember. My underwear is

made of that pony fabric. You know, white with big brown spots. Makes me look like a horse. Dead ringer."

Madison laughed hard. "Go away. Get me something to eat. And where can I . . . You know?"

"I'll take you," he said, wiggling his eyebrows.

"What happened to 'No romance'?"

"That was before I liked you so much," he said, smiling at her.

For a moment she looked at him. "I bet you had some interesting encounters with women while you were traveling. All you had to do was look at them without your scowl and they'd—" She broke off because Thomas was looking at her with a wide smile. His scowl was gone, so his eyes were round, not narrow slits, and his lips were soft and full.

It was in that moment that Madison knew that if—a big, big if—there was ever to be anything between them in the future, then she must, absolutely, positively, *must* not allow anything to happen on *this* trip. For all his leering and teasing, her intuition told her that she had to keep this whole trip light.

"Well, I like you too," she said as though

to a little boy, "but there's a matter of previous ownership." With that, she headed for the bushes.

"Sharing," Thomas called after her. "People should share. The world would be a better place if people shared their toys."

Madison's laugh echoed off the overhanging rocks.

Eleven

"I like him," Leslie said as she finished the last of the pizza.

Ellie was staring at the ceiling and thinking. "I could see how it would have been easier after the two of you acknowledged that you had the hots for each other," she said thoughtfully.

"Yes," Madison agreed as she lit another cigarette. "It did. But we also seemed to have made a rule between us that we weren't to act on our inclinations."

"That must have been difficult," Leslie said, looking over her glass of cola at Madison. "I'd think that in a setting like that, alone as you were, that it would have been nearly impossible to keep your hands off each other."

"Probably," Madison said. "Actually, I

don't think we could have. If we'd stayed alone, that is. We spent that first night in the tent together, and I'm not sure what would have happened if I hadn't fallen asleep as soon as I closed my eyes. I'm sure I would have stayed awake all night lusting after Thomas."

"I would have," Ellie said. "But you fell *asleep*? What kind of heroine are you?"

"At that time I was a very tired one," Madison said. "You can't imagine what it was like nursing Roger around-the-clock."

"I've had two kids," Leslie said. "And my daughter—" She cut herself off. "Trust me, Roger couldn't have been more demanding than Rebecca was—and is."

"You said 'if we'd stayed alone.' " Ellie said. "You didn't?"

"No. The next morning we met some friends of Thomas's on the river. His family had lived in the area for generations, so I should have expected that he knew everyone." Madison stubbed out her cigarette. "But, you know, I think I had a better time when the others were around than Thomas and I would have had alone."

"Right," Ellie said.

"No, I mean it. What were Thomas and I

to do? After just a few hours alone together we had trouble keeping our hands off each other, so did we go to bed together and later—if something emotional did happen between us—did we have adultery hanging over our heads?"

"Montana *is* in the U.S., isn't it?" Ellie asked Leslie. "This whole country is in bed with everyone else, but you had a husband you couldn't stand, you were alone with a man you were mad about, yet you worried about having sex with him."

Looking at Ellie through a cloud of smoke, Madison said, "Now, tell me again how many times you were unfaithful to *your* husband? The one you couldn't stand?"

Ellie gave her a one-sided grin. "Okay. But I never—"

"If you say that you never looked like me, I'll hit you with this ashtray," Madison said seriously.

"Okay, point taken."

"So what happened after you met Thomas's friends?" Leslie asked, getting the two of them back on the story.

Madison took a while to answer as she thought back to those many years before. "Thomas and I sort of . . . well, we lied.

When we saw the people in the other raft, they assumed that Thomas and I were 'together,' you know, a couple. I started to tell them that we weren't, but Thomas stopped me. Later I thought about how it would have sounded if he'd told them that he was in the woods alone with another man's wife. There would have been questions about my husband, and if I'd told them that Roger was recovering from having been run over by a car . . . well, it could have made Thomas and me look quite bad."

"And Roger look great. I've been there," Ellie said bitterly. "My ex-husband was a master at getting sympathy from people. I was working day and night to support him while he was out having lunch—at my expense, of course—whining that all he wanted was 'a wife.'"

After Ellie finished this little tirade, the other two were looking at her in silence. "Sorry," Ellie said. "Go on with *your* story."

"But you're next," Madison said, pointing her cigarette at Ellie.

"No, I know my story. Leslie is next."

"Would you two mind!" Leslie said. "What happened, Madison?"

"In a way, I guess you could say that for

two days Thomas and I played house. Or at least we played at being part of the real world." Madison took a breath, closed her eyes in memory for a moment, then opened them again. "My mother always said that I had no idea what a 'normal' relationship between a man and a woman was. She said that since she'd been a single mother, I hadn't learned anything at home about men and women. Then Roger . . . Well, my mother never really liked him."

"I can't understand that, can you, Leslie?" Ellie asked sarcastically. "Tell me, Madison, if you had a daughter and she was dating a guy like Roger, the man you can see him as now that you've had some experience in the world, would *you* like him?"

"Actually, I can't imagine having a daughter," Madison said softly.

Ellie started to say something, but Leslie cut her off. "So you got to see a 'normal' relationship. Why don't you tell Ellie and me what that's like? I'm sure I've never seen one."

"I've not only not *seen* one," Ellie said, "I've not even *written* about one."

Smiling, Madison lit another cigarette. "Thomas's friends assumed that Thomas and I were a couple and they treated us as though we were. It was . . . a . . . revelation to me. You see, Roger was the only man I'd ever even been out on a date with, and his parents thought I was trash. They were rich and I was . . ."

"A bastard," Ellie said angrily.

"Exactly. I think that Roger's mother knew who my father was—is, for all I know. I overheard her once on the telephone saying, 'Imagine the gall of the woman naming her child after him! What must his lovely wife feel?' "

"You never tried to find out more about your father?" Ellie asked. "At least who he was?"

"He always knew where I was, but he didn't make any effort to contact me, so why should I bother him?" Madison said.

Ellie frowned. She didn't like the way Madison said, "bother him," as though Madison weren't worthy to contact her own father, a man who had abandoned a woman he'd impregnated.

"I want to hear the rest of this story," Leslie said impatiently.

Ellie grinned. "I love people who love stories."

"And I love people who *listen* to stories," Leslie said sharply.

"Okay, no fights," Madison said. "Thomas and I spent the night at his friends' 'cabin,' if you can call it that. It wasn't as big as Thomas's place, but it wasn't what I think of when I imagine a cabin. Thomas's friend's name was Alex and he was there with his fiancée, Carol. They were getting married in about six weeks, and all Carol could talk about was the coming wedding. Alex's parents were there and his young sister, Paulette, who everyone called Pauli."

Twelve

"You're not like Thomas's usual girlfriends," Pauli said as she flopped down on the grass beside Madison. She was thirteen and still trying to decide if she wanted to remain a child or grow up.

"Pauli!" her mother, Mrs. Barnett, said sternly. "That's not a polite thing to say."

They were sitting outside the big log house under an oak tree that George Washington had probably sat under and drinking lemonade.

"It's all right," Madison said in what she hoped was a demure way. At least she hoped that none of the eagerness she felt was in her voice. "And what were his other girlfriends like?"

"Boring," Carol said without looking up from an issue of *Bride's* magazine that was

three years old. She'd been collecting issues ever since she'd met Alex, and according to Pauli, she carried them with her
wherever she went. "If my brother hadn't
asked her to marry him, Carol would have
committed suicide," Pauli had confided to
Madison on the first evening she and
Thomas had arrived. Truthfully, Madison
doubted that, as Carol was pretty and smart
and educated.

"Really, Carol," Pauli's mother said,
"we're going to give Madison the wrong
idea. Thomas's other girlfriends weren't exactly boring; they were—" She broke off as
she looked at the three pairs of eyes looking
at her in question. Mrs. Barnett looked
down at her lemonade. "All right, so maybe
they were a tad . . . well, uninteresting."

"*Hmph*!" Carol said, then looked back at
her magazine.

"You know all those girls with the thick
glasses and the big noses who can't get a
date to the prom? *They* are the girls Thomas
dates," Pauli said.

"Why?" Madison blurted out before she
thought, then tried to retreat. "I mean, why
would someone like Thomas want . . . ?"
She trailed off. She was trying hard to re-

mind herself that she didn't belong with these people, but she wasn't having much success. Both Thomas's family and this one had been born to wealth and privilege such as Madison had seen only in the movies. And, like most people who had to struggle to pay the utility bills, she'd assumed that these rich people were snobs, that they were only interested in "their own kind."

But, inadvertently, on the first night, Madison had said something to that effect to Mrs. Barnett. For all the deception about her "involvement" with Thomas and about her marital status, Madison had been brutally truthful about her origins. At the time, Mrs. Barnett and she had been alone in the kitchen, breaking green beans that Mrs. Barnett had grown in a little plot at the back of the cabin. Unlike Mrs. Randall, she had no full-time cook.

Mrs. Barnett had listened to Madison's words, but she'd listened harder to her tone. "We're not the British royal family, dear," Mrs. Barnett had said calmly. "Our children don't have to find virgins to marry, or even someone 'suitable.' And our children have trust funds, so they don't need to marry for money. If you think about it, it gives them great freedom of choice."

Madison had stood there gaping at the woman, both for what she'd said and for her insight.

"So you nursed your mother?" Mrs. Barnett had continued when Madison said nothing. "I've always had a great sympathy for single mothers, especially since, when my children were young, my husband was gone so often that I was too often alone. So tell me how you met Thomas."

Madison picked up another handful of beans. Mrs. Barnett's words had relaxed her so much that she told the truth about her first meeting with Thomas. However, she left out any mention of her husband, Roger. Madison told of her friendship with Thomas's aunt, Dr. Dorothy Oliver, being vague about how she'd met the prominent physician. Then, with her breath held, Madison told how Thomas had caught her hiding in the kitchen and later how he'd accused her of blackmail.

Mrs. Barnett smiled. "That sounds just like Thomas. He's a throwback to his great-grandfather. It was said that the man never laughed, except when he made some brilliant business deal and had earned a fortune, that is. I sometimes think that Thomas went into medicine because he wanted to be the opposite of what his grandfather was. There now, that should be enough for dinner. Do you cook, dear?"

"I can thaw anything," Madison said with a smile.

"All right, then, stay and talk to me while I cook. The boys won't be back for a while, so we might as well get to know each other." Mrs. Barnett gave Madison a steady, penetrating look. "I think that Thomas may be serious about you."

"I don't think so," Madison said as she ducked her head to hide her blush. "He and I are worlds apart."

"Not so far apart," Mrs. Barnett said softly. "I think that there's a very serious side to you that you hide from the world. That beautiful face of yours is a mask, isn't it?"

Madison didn't know how to reply to that, and since the door opened and two men, Thomas and Mr. Barnett, entered at that moment, she didn't have to answer.

Thomas caught Madison off guard when he exuberantly threw his arms around her waist and lifted her off the floor. "What's for dinner, woman? I could eat a bear," Thomas said as he let her back down, then nuzzled her neck.

Madison knew she should push Thomas away, but his light play was new to her and startling. Roger was aware of his dignity when others were around, and when they were alone, Roger was aware of sports on TV or on a field or—

"Green beans," Madison said when she realized that everyone in the kitchen was looking at them. She had no idea that they'd never seen Thomas act so lighthearted. He had been serious even as a child.

"That it?" Thomas asked, smiling at her. "Just green beans? I'm sure they'll take hours to cook, so let's go outside and catch fireflies until the food's ready," Thomas said in such a leering voice that they all laughed.

Madison lifted herself on her toes and looked over Thomas's head. "Isn't someone going to save me from this satyr?"

"We're all much too fascinated to move a muscle," Mrs. Barnett said with what Madison had come to see was her usual honesty. "Go on, Thomas, take her outside and ravish her in the moonlight."

"You've been reading romantic novels again, haven't you, my love?" Mr. Barnett said with a smile at his plump, soft wife. "In case you haven't noticed, it's only six o'clock and it's summer, so there is a great deal of daylight outside."

"It's always moonlight to lovers," Mrs. Barnett said, her eyes on her husband.

"Go!" Mr. Barnett said to Thomas, then walked toward his wife.

Thomas grabbed Madison's hand and pulled her from the kitchen onto the porch.

"Aren't you overplaying it a bit?" Madison said nervously once they were alone. Pulling her hand from his, she stepped to the porch rail, her back to him.

"I'm not playing at all," he said softly.

Madison didn't dare look at him. "I don't think that we should—"

She didn't say any more because Thomas pulled her into his arms and kissed her. And it was a kiss such as Madison had never received before. It was deep and thorough and altogether wonderful.

When he broke away, her first thought was, How very much I've missed in my life!

Her inclination was to fling her arms around him and kiss him more, but she forced herself to move away. "What was that for?" she asked, trying to make her voice sound angry. But if there was anger, it was at herself, not at him.

"Just to see," Thomas said as he put his hands in his pockets.

If he starts whistling, I'll pick up a chair and hit him, she thought. "To see what?" she snapped, this time the anger genuine.

"If you like me as much as I like you," he said.

There was such innocent sincerity in his voice that her anger dissipated. "And what did you find out?" she asked.

"Yeah, you do."

She couldn't look in his eyes for fear that she'd give too much away. She wasn't going to be the country girl who oohed and aahed and told him that no man had ever before been as nice to her as he was being. No, that would make her sound as though she were from a class where the men dragged women about by their hair.

Instead, she turned back around, put her hands on the porch rail, and looked out at the forest. There was about fifty feet of mowed grass between them and the dense trees, then beyond that was pristine forest.

"So what do we do about it?" Madison asked softly.

"Anything we want," he answered, and she could hear the intensity in his voice.

She took a deep breath. "You don't know me. For all you know, I—"

He didn't let her finish the sentence. "I know all about you that I'll ever need to know. You have a great sense of humor. You're smart and you care more about other people than you do about yourself. That's rare in a person. Most people—"

He didn't finish that sentence, but took a breath and lowered his voice. "You like to fish and to walk over mountains. Although I do plan to buy you some proper hiking boots and—"

She turned to look at him, a frown on her face. "And when do you plan to do this? Before or after I go back to my husband?"

"After," Thomas said, not in the least perturbed by her outburst. "After you tell him that you want out."

"You presume a lot," she said, drawing herself up to her full height and doing her best to look intimidating.

"Yes, I do," Thomas said softly, then he picked up her hand and kissed the palm.

"Oh, damnation!" Madison said under her breath; then she gave a great sigh as she pulled her hand away and put it back on the porch rail. "We can't do this. This isn't right. You're—"

"If you start that speech about our being from two different worlds, I'll walk away now," Thomas said, and it was his turn to sound angry. He, too, put his hands on the porch rail, then looked out at the forest. "Look, I apologize if I'm going too fast, it's just that I've always been a person who makes quick decisions. I decided in an instant that I wanted to be a doctor, and in the many years since then, I've never once wavered in my decision."

"Your first impression of me was that I was a criminal, a person from a very different world than the one you live in."

"Your beauty blinded me," Thomas answered. "I couldn't see you for the façade. And, for the record, criminality isn't determined by the amount of money a person was born with or their education."

"Shall we check statistics on the number of poor people in prison versus the number of wealthy ones?"

"How did we get onto this?" Thomas

asked, turning to look at her. "Or are you just trying to get me off track?"

Madison looked away from him, then glanced down the length of the porch. "Too much is happening too fast," she said as she turned back, but she still didn't look at him. "Give me some time. I go for years with no excitement, then in a few days, I . . ."

"Meet the man of your dreams?" Thomas asked with hope in his voice.

Madison laughed. "I just need time."

"Take all you need," Thomas said, then glanced at his watch. "Is an hour enough? How about forty-five minutes?"

Madison opened her mouth to speak, but Pauli pushed open the screen door and walked onto the porch, and when Madison turned to look at her, Pauli moved to stand between them; then she gave a dramatic sigh.

"If you two also run off to bed together, I'll jump into one of the canoes and run away and you'll all have to spend all night trying to find me."

Madison was sure it was her middle-class mores showing, but she was shocked at the words of this child.

Not so Thomas. "So who else is in bed together?" he asked casually.

"Everyone. Mom and Dad. Carol and Alex. And you two look like you want to."

At that Thomas laughed, but Madison felt herself blush. "I really think that this is a subject that—"

"Is too old for me?" Pauli said with a sigh. "I know. I'm cursed with being wise beyond my years."

"Cursed with an ego that's too big for the world," Thomas said easily, then looked over her head to Madison. "I used to change her diapers."

"That was when I was a boy," Pauli said, making Madison blink at her.

Thomas snorted. "Still are from what I can see," he said, looking at the girl's flat chest.

Pauli looked down the front of her. "I know. It's a tragedy, isn't it? Do you think they'll ever grow? You're a doctor, what do you think?"

"I'm not a doctor yet, and when I am, I'm not going into female medicine. Why don't you ask Madison? She's had some experience in this area."

Madison had to work to keep from clasping her arms across her breasts. "I think I should check on dinner."

"It won't be for a while," Pauli said. "When Mother and Dad go at it, it takes them a while."

Madison decided that she wasn't going to continue to be a prude. "How lucky for your mother. She must tell me her secret."

Turning, Pauli looked at her. "So what's Thomas like in bed?"

But Pauli never got to hear Madison's reply because he grabbed the girl by the ear and pulled while holding the screen door open. "Get inside and try to mind your manners."

"How am I going to learn if I don't ask?" Pauli whined after Thomas had closed the screen door, with her inside the house.

"There are some things that you have to learn from experience, not from what others tell you. Now go find your mother and tell her that we're ready to eat."

"Some doctor you'll make," Pauli muttered as she disappeared into the house.

"What an extraordinary child," Madison said as she turned back to Thomas.

"Spoiled. A late-in-life child and spoiled without mercy. Poor Alex got nothing but discipline, but that child has never had *any* discipline."

"You love her madly, don't you?" Madison said with a smile.

"Quite daffy about her," Thomas said. "Now, back to you and me. I was saying that—"

But the door to the cabin opened and Mr. Barnett came out onto the porch, a beer in his hand, and soon afterward Alex came outside, and minutes later they all went in to dinner. After that she wasn't alone with Thomas again. Even when they said good night and went to their separate rooms, there wasn't a private moment between them. At one point during the evening, Madison thought that maybe Thomas was trying to convey a message to her to meet him outside later. But she looked through the windows at the moonlight and pretended that she had no idea that Thomas was trying to get her attention.

Thirteen

"Madison!" Ellie said in exasperation, "you're driving me crazy! This all happened, what, fifteen, sixteen years ago and I know that you didn't marry him, but *why*?! Whenever a man's friends and relatives tell you, 'You're not like the other girls he dates,' then you know you're in. What *happened*?"

Looking down at her cigarette, Madison said nothing.

"Children," Leslie said into the silence. "That was it, wasn't it?"

When Madison looked up at Leslie, there was such pain in her eyes that Ellie had to turn away. To be a writer it helped to feel things deeply, and Ellie did. And what she was feeling now was Madison's pain, still raw and bleeding after all these years.

"I see," Ellie said after a while. "I thought maybe Roger had a relapse and begged you to stay. Or . . ." She trailed off, as the reality was worse than what she'd made up.

"What did you tell Thomas?" Leslie asked softly.

When Madison put her cigarette to her lips, her hand was trembling. "It was Pauli who brought up the subject of children. She said that she wasn't going to have any, that she was going to be a free spirit and spend her life breaking men's hearts. Then Mrs. Barnett said—"

Madison took another deep drag on her cigarette, then stubbed it out and lit another. "The consensus among Carol and Alex, Mr. and Mrs. Barnett, and . . . Thomas, was that there was nothing else in life, that only children really mattered. Thomas said something to the effect that a man could work all his life and achieve everything, but if he didn't have children to pass it on to, then his life was without meaning. While he said this, he was giving me looks that said he wanted to have children with me."

Neither Leslie nor Ellie could think of anything to say as they looked at Madison and thought of what she'd lost and how she'd lost it. If she hadn't returned to Roger . . . If she'd stayed in New York . . . If . . .

"Now do I have the two of you feeling sorry for me?" Madison asked, trying to make light of what she'd just told.

But Leslie didn't so much as smile. "What did you do? I mean, after you heard what they said, how did you hold it together?"

"Alex and Carol drove us back to Thomas's house. I was trying to pretend that nothing had happened, but I didn't do a very good job of it. Thomas knew that something was wrong. I told him it was difficult for me to think of breaking marriage vows. Of course it didn't help that when we got back, it was about nine at night and Roger and Terri were skinny-dipping in the pool together."

"Did you tell Alex and Carol that you were married?" Ellie asked.

"Thomas did. He was quite nonchalant about it as he stood by the pool and introduced Roger as my husband. I must say that neither Alex nor Carol so much as blinked. All of them had wonderful manners. Afterward, we walked back to the house and Carol took my arm and said she'd lend me all her bridal magazines so I could choose my dress to wear when I married Thomas."

"*Yeow!*" Ellie said. "I can't imagine how you must have felt, knowing what you did. Did you ever think of talking to Thomas about—"

"No!" Madison half shouted. "I did *not* consider talking to Thomas about my . . . my lack of a uterus. I couldn't put him in the position of having to make a choice like that! Nor did I think of telling him that we could adopt. He was a whole man and I was only half of a woman. I wasn't going to punish him for what had happened to me. He was a wonderful man, and I knew that he could—"

Madison broke off and calmed herself down. "It's amazing how fresh this seems. It's as though all these intervening years didn't happen. But they did and it was all done a long, long time ago."

There was silence for a moment as Madison drew on her cigarette and looked down at her hands. "Thomas had to leave the next morning, and I . . . I hid so I wouldn't have to say good-bye to him. For the rest of our stay, I walked. Miles and miles I walked, and Roger . . ." She drew on her cigarette. "I really don't know what Roger did."

After Madison stopped talking, Leslie asked softly, "What happened between you and Roger?"

"He divorced me about four months later. The first step he took without his canes, he walked straight to a lawyer. He married Terri, but it lasted only about three years. I think he was sick of getting money from his parents, so he thought he'd get himself a rich wife. But all Terri's money was tied up in trust funds, so Roger couldn't get his hands on a penny of it."

Madison gave a little smile. "I don't know if it's true, but I heard that the minute Terri's family told him he had to get a job, he filed for a divorce."

For a moment she looked away, then back again. "But in the end, it all worked out all right, as two years later, his parents drowned in a boating accident and left him everything. Roger sold the house, sent his parents' art collection to Sotheby's, where it was called 'important,' and so it sold for over a million. Roger turned the money over to one of his college buddies, who invested it, and, the last I heard, Roger was a multimillionaire and—" She took a deep breath. "And he married well and has three children. The youngest is only five."

"Bastard!" Ellie said under her breath.

"Ditto," Leslie echoed, and the room filled with their unspoken thoughts of the injustice of what had been done to Madison.

"And Thomas?" Ellie asked. "What happened to him?"

Madison had just lit a cigarette, but now she turned the pack over and shook out a new one, then lit it. She now had two of them going at once, but she didn't seem to be aware of this.

"Thomas . . ." Madison said slowly, "didn't fare as well. Years later, after Roger and Terri had divorced, I saw Dr. Oliver again. She and I hadn't had much contact after Roger and I split up, but I was up at the ski basin with my veterinarian boss and there she was. My first inclination was to run the other way, but she insisted that I stay and have dinner with her, just her, without her husband or children."

Madison picked up the second cigarette. She now had one in her mouth and one in her hand. "I tried to stop myself, but I wanted to hear about Thomas, so I asked.

She told me that he finished medical school, but he didn't go into rehabilitation medicine as he'd talked about. Instead, he studied tropical diseases. She said he'd decided to go into research rather than hands-on care."

Madison stubbed out one of the cigarettes. "I'm not sure if anyone in Thomas's family knew about Thomas and me—not that anything had actually happened for them to know about—but Dorothy told me that that summer at the cabin had changed Thomas. After that he'd become even more reclusive than he had been in the past. 'More morose,' is what she said."

For a few moments Madison concentrated on smoking, not looking at either of the two women across from her. But they were waiting and she knew it.

"It was a long time ago," Madison said so quietly that they could barely hear her. "But I don't think that any amount of time can lessen the pain."

She lifted her head and looked at them, and when she did, Ellie gasped. Madison, beautiful woman that she'd once been, looked as though she were a hundred years old. She looked as though she were a corpse that by some freak of nature just happened to be still moving.

"Thomas was in a small plane that was taking medicines into the rain forest in Brazil when the plane went down. They think it might have been struck by lightning. All three passengers died instantly."

There was nothing either of the two women could reply to that.

"What a waste!" Ellie said after a few minutes. "What a horrible, horrible waste of lives. And that a low-life like Roger came out on top makes me . . ." She couldn't think of a word that was strong enough to describe what she was feeling.

Abruptly, Madison stood up. "Do you mind if we go to bed? It's been a long day and I'd like to get some sleep."

Ellie wanted to stay up and talk. After three years of living alone and having no stories in her head, she was starving for stories. Famished. But Leslie also stood, so Ellie knew that she had to quit listening.

"Beds?" Ellie said as she got off the couch. "Who sleeps where?"

It was Leslie, the peacemaker, who came up with a schedule so they alternated beds and couch. Leslie took the couch for the first night, and fifteen minutes later, the three women were asleep. And Madison slept the most soundly that she had in years. It was as though, by telling her story to sympathetic listeners, she had released something inside of her.

Fourteen

Ellie woke to a heavenly smell, and for a moment she didn't know where she was. Had the deli delivered early? she wondered, in her half-awake state. But then, nothing from the deli had *ever* smelled that good.

Grabbing her clothes off the back of a chair, she left the bedroom and went to the bathroom, where she made a token application of makeup and pulled on black sweatpants and a huge, concealing shirt. With every pound she had gained, her clothes had become bigger, until now she could hardly keep them on her body. She knew it was an illusion, but she hoped that if she covered herself completely, no one could see how big she had become.

The kitchen was sunny and bright, the table was set with pretty green and yellow linens, and in the middle there was a platter with a heap of pancakes and strawberries. Leslie was at the stove wearing a bright yellow apron with cherries on it.

Ellie took one look at the table, then up at Leslie. "Will you marry me?" she asked, eyes wide.

"I've already asked," Madison said as she stepped inside the house. She'd been outside, Ellie assumed for a smoke.

Smiling, Leslie put a plate of blueberry pancakes in front of Ellie. "I can't tell you how good it is to cook for people who like to eat," she said, motioning toward Madison.

"Don't tell me," Ellie said with a groan, as she nodded toward Madison. "She ate half a dozen of these things."

"Closer to a dozen," Leslie said, then leaned closer to Ellie. "Don't let her kid you; she's skinny because she never eats. This weekend's gluttony is unusual for her."

"I heard that," Madison said. "I don't eat much because I never have time and I have no idea how to cook." As she said this, she sat down on the chair across from Ellie, and immediately, Leslie set in front of her a bowl of out-of-season strawberries piled high with freshly whipped cream.

Ellie groaned again.

Madison, with a smug smile, lifted a fat, red strawberry and licked the cream off it.

"I hope you get fat," Ellie muttered as she dug into the pancakes.

"So why did you?" Madison asked as she crunched the berry.

"Really, Madison!" Leslie said. "That wasn't polite." She sounded as though she were talking to her teenage daughter.

Madison was unperturbed by the chastisement. "Last night I told what had happened to me to make me ugly, so now it's her turn to tell why she's fat."

Ellie had to blink a few times at Madison's bluntness, but then she smiled. Truthfully, Madison's question was easier to reply to than other women's not-so-subtle hints about salads and gymnasiums and personal trainers. "It's the most marvelous gym and he's the best trainer in the world" had been said to her more than once, as though Ellie didn't know that there were ways to get rid of her extra pounds.

"I got screwed by the legal system and I got depressed," Ellie said, her mouth full. "I am now a washout. A has-been. I haven't written a word in three years. I don't even hear stories in my head any longer."

"You were listening pretty hard to me last night," Madison said.

"I keep trying, but . . ." Ellie looked up. Leslie had her back to them as she washed glasses at the sink, but she was listening intently. "I don't know . . . I think I had the heart taken out of me, and I can't seem to find my confidence again."

Turning, Leslie put a glass of freshly squeezed orange juice in front of Ellie. "I thought you were going to be an artist."

Ellie laughed. "That seems so long ago that I can hardly remember it. I met this man who—"

At that both Leslie and Madison gave a loud groan in unison.

"Why do *all* the stories of *all* women start with, 'I met this man'?" Leslie asked. She at last put a plate of pancakes down on the table between Ellie and Madison and began to eat. Not until everyone else was served had Leslie taken a seat.

Ellie smiled. "He was a musician, twice as talented as I was, and from the beginning I knew that I was in the presence of genius," she said simply.

"I see," Madison said. "So you gave up *your* career as an artist to help him with his, but he never did anything with his prodigious talent. Instead, you found yourself supporting him, doing his laundry, cooking his meals—"

Laughing, Ellie put up her hands in front of her face as though to protect herself. "So my life is a country-and-western song. I admit it. But he really was brilliant."

"Brilliant in finding someone to worship him," Madison said, looking Ellie hard in the eyes.

Ellie wanted to protest that she hadn't been as stupid as Madison made it sound, but she had no defense. "How do you know so much about this?"

"One of the women who works with me has the same story. She married a man who welded hubcaps together into these huge structures. He was going to become Someone Famous. That's with capital letters: Someone Famous. But while he was making his way in the world, all he asked was that she 'help' him a bit. She now has three kids, and he hasn't had a job in four years. She used to say that someone as talented as he is can't just go out and get an ordinary job."

"Exactly," Ellie said, pushing away her half-empty plate of pancakes. "That's just what happened. Over these last years I've looked back on it all a thousand times, and I still don't know *how* it all happened, just that it *did* happen. One minute I was in New York planning to make a name for myself, and the next I was living with this man and I was taking any job I could get to make money to give *him* a chance in the music world."

"Love," Leslie said with a sigh as she took the plates to the sink.

"That's just it," Ellie said quickly. "I'm not sure that I ever did love this guy. I'm not sure that I ever—" She looked up at Madison. "Would it make me sound stupid to say that I'm not sure that I ever had a *choice*?"

"My friend told me how her husband courted her," Madison said. "He went after her night and day. There were roses on her doorstep every morning for months. He wrote her poems and letters. There were sexy telephone calls that went on all night.

He bought her gifts, talked to her endlessly, *listened* to her, cared about her. There was nothing about her that he didn't want to know."

"So he could use it later to control her," Ellie said as she turned her head away, not looking at either woman.

"Exactly," Madison said. "A master controller. He saw something in my friend that he wanted, so he went after her."

"Right," Ellie said.

"What I want to know is how you became a writer," Leslie said, tactfully steering the conversation away from the bad to the good.

"I wrote my way out of misery," Ellie said. "At least that's what my therapist, Jeanne, said. This is her house, by the way. She's helped me to see what—"

Halting, Ellie drew in a deep breath. "Are you sure you want to hear all this?"

"Every word in chronological order," Madison said with a smile.

For a moment Ellie looked out the window over the sink. No, she wasn't ready to tell anyone the "whole" story. Not yet.

She looked back at the other two women. "Why don't I make us some coffee?"

Leslie said. "Or would anyone like some strong tea?"

"I'll have tea," Ellie said, while Madison wanted coffee. And while Leslie waited on them, Ellie said, "Would anyone believe me if I said that I was working so hard that I didn't notice what was going on in my marriage? I got up at four A.M. and hit the floor running."

Neither woman answered Ellie's question, and she was glad of that. Here in this house with these women who were at once strangers and her oldest friends, she knew that she didn't have to make excuses, didn't have to apologize.

"Anyway," Ellie said, "Martin, that was—is—my ex's name, Martin Gilmore, was brilliantly talented as a musician. He played a guitar, and he could make you weep at the sound. Or laugh. Whatever emotion he wanted from his audience, he could get." Ellie's head came up. "Anyway, I thought I was going to be the person who gave the world the opportunity to hear him; then, after he was internationally successful—"

"It was going to be your turn," Leslie said. "There's always the promise that the woman is going to get 'her turn.'"

"Right," Ellie said with a grimace. "When he asked me to leave New York and go live in a small town outside L.A., I agreed readily. Martin said that only in L.A. would he have a chance to become known. So I—" Ellie took a deep breath. "I sold my art supplies and all the work I'd done, and flew out to L.A. with him.

"And at first it was great. He got some wonderful jobs with some excellent bands and it was all so exciting. I was working as a receptionist in a used car office and I was bored out of my mind, but at night there was Martin with his fascinating stories about who he'd seen and what he'd done that day."

Ellie looked down at her hands. "But slowly, things began to go wrong. He quit one job after another, and with every job he quit, he seemed to pull back within himself more. At first he was making good money, but as the years went by, earning money didn't seem to be something that he thought he needed to do. He said that life wasn't giving anything to him, so he didn't feel he needed to give anything back."

Smiling, Ellie looked up at the other women. "So I decided to help him. I decided to *make* him into a success. I began to make appointments for him with the biggest names in L.A. I must say that I had no pride at all. I begged and I cried. I made up outrageous stories to get people to listen to Martin, either on tape or in person. But—" Ellie threw up her hands in frustration. "He wouldn't pursue the opportunities I got for him," she said, then had to unclench her hand, as her nails were cutting into her palm. Leslie handed her a cup of tea, and for a moment Ellie sipped the tea while she worked to calm herself.

She put the cup down. "I've learned that talent alone isn't enough to make a person successful. You can write a great software program, but unless you make an effort to market it, it might as well lie in your desk unseen. That's what happened with my ex. I don't think he could have stood the competition or the criticism that goes with trying to make it to the top of any field, so he sabotaged himself at every opportunity. I'd get him an appointment with a DJ to hear his tape or for him to meet someone who could give him a start. Martin would be wildly excited about the opportunity, and he'd make mad, passionate love to me the night before, telling me how grateful he was and what a great wife I was, et cetera."

"Let me guess," Madison said. "Then he wouldn't show up for the appointment."

"Exactly!" Ellie answered. "But he always had these heavenly excuses. And I mean that literally: heavenly. Always, he didn't take an opportunity because he was *helping* someone."

"So you couldn't get angry with him," Leslie said. "Not with a saint like him."

"Of course not. He'd say, 'What could I do? Joe *needed* me. Could I have said, "Sorry, Joe, but I have to leave you in pain because I have to go play music to some rich dude who cares about nobody on earth"?'" Ellie said.

"So how long before you gave up living for him and rediscovered your own talents?" Madison asked as she drank of her strong black coffee. So far this morning, Ellie hadn't seen her smoke one cigarette, but now she opened a new pack and took one out. Leslie got up to open the window over the kitchen sink.

"I don't think that I did, actually," Ellie said. "I think it just sort of happened. No preplanning; it just happened. Martin was away visiting one of his many friends and . . ." For a moment Ellie didn't say anything.

"Woman?" Madison asked.

"I know I'm going to sound naive, but back then it never crossed my mind that his many trips to 'help' some old friend or play music with some guys were actually rendezvous with about a dozen . . . mistresses, I guess you'd call them."

"So you were alone," Leslie said, encouraging her to continue. She'd put a bowl of strawberries in front of Ellie, but when she didn't eat them, Leslie did. "Did you start painting again?"

"No," Ellie said. "I know that this is one of those stupid women-things, but I think that because I knew that the man I was married to was more talented than I was, I gave up art. After I met Martin and heard his music, I never so much as did a watercolor again."

Ellie's head came up. "Jeanne, my therapist, thinks that I didn't paint, not because of who had the most talent, but because I was deeply unhappy and I was suppressing it. I really had no life, either when Martin was home or when he was gone. When he was home, we lived in . . . How can I say this?"

She looked at Madison. "You said that your marriage was hell, but mine was . . . I guess you would call it sadness. We lived in sadness because Martin was *sooooo* brilliantly talented, but no one would give him a chance."

"Does this include the people he stood up?" Madison asked as she drew on her cigarette.

"Oh, yes," Ellie said, smiling. "Them most of all."

"So you were alone and you started writing," Leslie said as she finished the bowl of strawberries.

"More or less, yes. While Martin was away, I began to write down the stories that were going around in my head," Ellie said. "I had a whole imaginary life going, one about a man named Max and—"

"And you were Jordan Neale," Leslie said, smiling. "I've read every one of your books."

"I haven't read any of them," Madison said. "So tell me about them."

Ellie started to reply, but Leslie beat her to it. "They're funny, sexy, complicated romantic murder mysteries about this married couple who—" She turned to Ellie with wide eyes. "In the last book you hinted that Jordan might be pregnant. Is she?"

"Beats me," Ellie said.

"But you're the writer," Leslie said in disbelief.

"If I knew what was going to happen, why would I bother to write the story? In fact, when I get two-thirds the way through a book and can see the ending, I'd like to stop writing it and start something new."

At this, Leslie opened and closed her mouth a couple of times. Like most people, she thought that the author knew everything there was to know about the characters in her books.

"So the books were your fantasy about you and your husband," Madison said, then looked around the kitchen.

"More strawberries?" Leslie asked, her radar up when anyone needed something in the kitchen.

"I'll get them—" Madison began, but Leslie was on her feet before Madison could move.

"I guess they were," Ellie said. "I didn't think about it while I was writing them. I was just filling up my evenings with something besides TV. And my weekends. They were the worst."

Leslie put a huge bowl of strawberries in front of Madison, then another pile of pancakes beside it.

"So how did you get published?" Leslie asked. "I don't know much about the business, but a friend of mine told me that to get published you have to get an agent and the better the agent, the better your contract."

At that Ellie said a very rude word and made an even ruder sound. "Agents put out that rumor. My editor does a hilarious skit in which she shows the training of a person becoming an agent. She picks up a piece of paper, writes 'I am an agent' on it, then puts the paper on her chest."

When neither Leslie or Madison seemed to get this, Ellie took a drink of her tea. "Let's just say that it is *not* necessary to have an agent to get a book published, nor do you have to have an agent to continue to be published. I don't have one and never will."

There was so much passion in Ellie's voice that when she stopped speaking, it left the others in silence.

"Sorry," Ellie said. "Pet peeve of mine. Now, where was I?"

"Too bad you didn't use that tone with your husband," Madison said under her breath.

"Isn't it?!" Ellie said. "When I look back and think of the things that I'd do differently . . . Oh, well, that won't happen. Anyway—"

"What did your husband think of your writing?" Leslie asked.

"I didn't say a word about it to him," Ellie said. "You have to understand that there wasn't room in our lives for much more than Martin's sadness. We lived and breathed his suffering. Our 'conversations'—if you can call them that—were about how rotten the world was because it didn't give brilliantly talented men like him a chance. I couldn't very well tell him that while he was suffering so much, I was having the best time of my life writing funny little mysteries."

"And all the while *you* were supporting the two of you?" Leslie snapped so sharply that the other two women looked at her. "Sorry. It's just that I believe that you put up with a lot about a man, but he *does* earn money. And that money is used for family expenses."

"You would have been better with Martin than I was," Ellie said. "But then, according to him, he *was* paying 'family' expenses. Now and then he'd get a job with a band and he'd fly off to some state I'd barely heard of and stay there for months at a time. The only problem was that what he earned he spent on electronic equipment. We had four speakers in our living room that you could set up house in. We had three beat-up old chairs, no coffee table because there wasn't room, but we had speakers that the Rolling Stones would have envied. Martin said that everything he bought was an 'investment' in our future."

"I can't stand this!" Madison said. "What is wrong with us women that we get men like these guys? Last night I told you of Roger, and now this guy . . ." She trailed off, as though she couldn't think of a description bad enough for Martin Gilmore.

Ellie shrugged. "When you're out of an intolerable situation, you can never make anyone understand why you remained in that situation. I don't understand it myself.

When I was in it, I didn't question it. It's just the way it was."

"But you knew that it was bad, so you wrote yourself into a whole different life," Leslie said.

Ellie smiled at her warmly. "Exactly! That's just what I did, only I didn't know then that that's what I was doing. I wrote just for the pleasure of doing it. Five books in all."

"Then what did you do?"

Ellie smiled. "You know how your life can change in an instant?"

"Oh, yeah," Madison said. "Roger called and said he needed me, so I left New York and went to him. One phone call."

Ellie smiled. "For me it was going to the dentist and picking up a copy of a local magazine off his table. In the back was an ad about a writers' conference that was being held in a town about sixty miles south of us. At the bottom of the ad was a sentence that said that editors would be available for conferences to talk about the writer's work."

"So you went, and they fell in love with Jordan Neale," Leslie said, smiling as though she'd heard the happy ending of a fairy tale.

Ellie laughed. "Not quite like that. Did I mention that I didn't learn to type until after I was published?"

"So you hire someone to type the books for you," Leslie said, puzzled.

"And how was I going to pay for that?" Ellie said. "If Martin had found out . . ."

"He would have cut you down until you burned everything you'd written," Madison said softly. "But in a 'loving' way, of course. 'Are you *sure* you want to have someone else read what you've written, sweetheart?' he'd say."

"Yes," Ellie answered. "Exactly. Verbal abuse. Of course at the time, I didn't think that consciously. Jeanne said that women in my situation must make themselves believe that the man they're with is good. If they begin to see the truth about him, then . . ."

"Then they have to do something and they're too terrified to try anything. After all, the man has spent all his energy on making her feel incompetent and inadequate," Madison finished for her.

"Yes," Ellie answered, saying everything in that one word.

"So how *did* you get published?" Leslie asked in exasperation.

Ellie laughed as she looked down at her empty cup. "Innocence, for one thing. If I'd known anything at all, I wouldn't have tried. I wouldn't even have made that appointment with the editor. Later, people told me that I couldn't do what I did, that I *had* to have an agent, that my manuscript *had* to be this and that. I was told that there were rules and that I had broken *all* of them."

Ellie looked up, smiling. "But you know what? The publishing world is just as hungry as we readers are for good stories. My editor would kill me for saying this, but if your story is fabulous, you can turn it in written in charcoal on bark and the publishing house will take care of the rest."

"Yeah, but how did you get anyone to read those manuscripts in the first place?" Madison said. "I hate handwritten insurance forms, so I can't imagine a whole book done in pen and ink."

"You're exactly right. If my editor had known what she was asking for, she wouldn't have asked me to send my books to her. You see, Daria was late. She's usually late, but not through any reason except that she has a thousand things to do and ten minutes to do them in." Ellie smiled. "I've often told her that my career started because she was late. In fact, I once gave her a pocket watch for a gift."

When Leslie and Madison looked blank, Ellie explained. "You know, like the White Rabbit in *Alice in Wonderland*. 'I'm late. I'm late,' the White Rabbit says."

The women smiled, but Ellie could see that they wanted her to tell them about her book.

"Okay, but I only know what happened because later Daria and I became friends and she told me the story."

For a moment Ellie was silent; then she smiled and started to speak. There was a faraway look in her eyes, a look of happiness the women hadn't seen before.

"I'm late," Daria said to her assistant, Cheryl, who had traveled to the writers' conference with her. "I have to go *now*!"

"But there's just one more and she looked so hopeful. She has this big box clutched to her chest and she looks scared to death, as though if she's caught she'll be punished."

For a moment Daria closed her eyes in exasperation. Cheryl was new, fresh out of a prestigious university with a degree in English lit, a minor in creative writing.

"They *all* look like that," Daria said in exasperation to her assistant, then thought, Until they get some money; then they—No, she wasn't going to complete that thought. This was the third day that she'd been at the conference, and she'd heard at least fifty authors pitch their work, but she'd heard nothing that was of any interest to her. One by one, she'd sent the authors to Cheryl to pick up standardized sheets with pointers on how to get a science fiction novel published, how to get a romance published, and so on.

Daria looked at her watch again. It wasn't as though she were late for a hairdresser's appointment. She was late for a *speech*. At the end of the hall was an auditorium, and there were about three hundred paying would-be writers sitting in there right now waiting to hear Daria tell them how to get their books published and on the best-seller lists.

Of course, what Daria wanted to do was get up there and say, "Write a good book and it'll sell," then sit down. But, no, that wouldn't do. No, she had to stand up there and talk for thirty minutes about margins and how much her publishing house was willing to pay for a book they hadn't seen to an author they'd never heard of.

Daria looked at her eager young assistant. Was she actually a nice person or was this some passive-aggressive action meant to make her boss do what *she* wanted her to do?

Whatever, Daria thought with a sigh. "Five minutes," she said to Cheryl, then tried to look stern and like a "real" boss.

With a radiant smile, Cheryl put her head around the door and said, "You can come in now," and in walked a short, thin young woman who did indeed look frightened.

"I don't mean to take up your time," the woman said hesitantly.

"That's all right," Daria said as patiently as she could manage. "You've written a book?"

"I . . . well, I guess so. I mean, I'm not really a writer, but I did have a few ideas, so I wrote them down. I'm sure they're not worth anything, but then, maybe, someone might like them. Or maybe one of them, I don't know."

Daria had to work hard to keep the smile on her face. One of those, she thought. Some writers hyped themselves up and came at you like a tsunami released on your face, telling you that they were going to put your publishing house on the map with this magnificent opus they had wrought.

Then there were people like this woman, this . . . Daria looked at the woman's name tag, but all she could see was the last name of Gilmore. The first name was hidden behind the blue typing-paper box that she was holding so tightly to her chest that her fingers were white.

"Ms. Gilmore," Daria said, "may I be honest with you? I'm late for giving a speech, and—"

Instantly, as though she were obeying orders, the woman stepped back and started apologizing. "I'm so sorry. I didn't know. They didn't tell me. I thought I had an appointment for one o'clock, and—"

Daria very well knew that it was now two-thirty, so that meant the woman had been sitting outside in the hall waiting for this moment for . . . Well, based on Daria's experience, the woman had probably been waiting all her life to hand her manuscript over to a New York editor.

Daria couldn't take the guilt anymore. As she gathered her things, she handed the woman her card. "Here, send what you have to New York. Mark it to my personal attention and I'll take care of it myself. How does that sound?"

"Very generous," the woman said, looking at the card as though it were the key to heaven.

As Daria left, to ease her guilt a bit, she gave the woman a little squeeze on the shoulder; then she practically ran from the room.

Cheryl walked into Daria's office, laughing. "You'll never guess what I just received in the mail."

"I can't imagine," Daria said absently as she searched through the pile on her desk to find the fifty pages of manuscript that she'd just edited. She had to get everything into her bag to take home. Unfortunately, she had to go to a dinner tonight with some of the bigwigs of the company, which meant that she'd be up until midnight trying to catch up on her workload. She had three—count 'em three—books that she was crashing, books that had been put in the schedule, then the authors, for one reason or another, hadn't turned their manuscripts in on time, so it was up to Daria to do a year's work in just weeks.

"You remember that writers' conference last week when you had that late author appointment? You told her that she should send what she'd written to you here, to your personal attention. Remember?"

Daria's head came up. She was stressed-out right now, so she had to bite her tongue to keep from saying that if there was anything wrong, then it was going to be on Cheryl's head, not hers. But Daria didn't say that. "I remember. What about her?"

"If I remember correctly, you said, 'Send me what you have.'"

"Yes," Daria said impatiently. She didn't have time to play guessing games. If she didn't rush, she was going to be late to dinner, something that one didn't do to the publisher and the CEO.

"She obeyed you to the letter," Cheryl

said, barely able to contain her mirth. "She's sent you a package that is—Oh, wait, here it is. I got Bobby from the mailroom to carry it for me. You *have* to see this!"

To Daria's great annoyance, a guy from the mailroom plopped what had to be a three-foot stack of paper on top of Daria's already overcrowded desk. She had to count to five to keep from snapping that she didn't have *time* for this!

"There are *five* novels, and they are all *handwritten!*" Cheryl said as though this were the greatest joke in the world.

Daria gave her assistant a tight little smile. Everything was new to Cheryl, including handwritten manuscripts. But Daria had been in publishing for a long time, and she'd seen a lot of them. "Send all of it back," she said. "Tell her our policy on handwritten—"

But before Daria could finish the sentence, the phone on the desk outside rang and Cheryl ran to answer it. Bobby from the mailroom, obviously afraid that he was going to be told to rewrap the huge package, disappeared as though he were a genie returning to his bottle.

"One. Two. Three," Daria counted in an

attempt to calm her already jangled nerves. The papers she desperately needed for her work tonight were *under* this monstrosity on her desk. And, looking at the thing, she was afraid that if she touched it, it would collapse and all three feet would go everywhere. Ten years from now, she'd still be finding handwritten pages scattered about her office.

"Cheryl!" Daria called through the open door, but there was no answer. Just then Daria looked down and she thought she saw a corner of the pages she'd been looking for sticking out from under the towering mass. Maybe . . . If she was very careful . . .

Leaning over the stack of papers, Daria reached, her nose practically on the top page of the manuscript. Actually, the handwriting on the pages was quite legible.

"Max turned to me and said, 'What's to eat?' so I knew that it was time to find another murder," Daria read.

At that Daria smiled. Bored housewife turned detective, she thought; then she read the next sentence.

Ten minutes later Cheryl returned to the office, still laughing, "I'll get Bobby to take this away. I just wanted to show you—"

"Go!" Daria said, her eyes on the tenth page of the manuscript.

"But—"

"Go!" Daria repeated louder as she turned the page. "And shut the door behind you."

Without a sound, Cheryl tiptoed out of the room, closing the door behind her.

Thirty minutes later, when the telephone rang, without glancing up, Daria pushed the button that cut off the caller, and when it rang again, she slid the lever on the side of the phone that silenced the ringer.

The next morning, at eight A.M., an irate publisher stormed into Daria's office. "You'd better have a damned good reason for last night!" the publisher said. "I spent the evening making excuses for you." The woman broke off when she saw Daria's face. She'd been in publishing for a long, long time and she knew *that* look. It's what she called The Holy Grail Look. It appeared when an editor got to do what she'd become an editor to do. That look didn't have to do with money or the latest demands of some spoiled author. No, that look meant that the editor had just read *a good book.*

That most holy of holies in the publishing world: *a good book.*

Immediately, the publisher stopped bawling out her editor. This was the best excuse, the only truly acceptable excuse there was.

"How many?" the publisher asked softly. You couldn't tell about editors. Sometimes they fell in love with books that had *no* commercial value.

"At least a million copies in hardback," the editor said, speaking of the print run. Daria's voice lowered to a whisper. "And there are five books completed, and three more outlined."

For a moment the publisher blinked. "You need anything? Bagel? Juice? Coffee? Bags of money to send to the writer?"

"A typist."

"I'll send you five of them," the publisher said, then left her editor's office. Halfway down the hall, she let out a loud whoop of sheer joy.

Fifteen

For a moment both Leslie and Madison were silent. For all that Madison hadn't read any of Ellie's books, she was alive, therefore she'd heard of them. The first one had come out about six or seven years after they'd met in New York, about 1987, and it had swept the country. Madison remembered that for months that first book was all that the women in her office had been able to talk about. They'd loved Max, the flawed hero, but, even more, they'd loved the dashing heroine, Jordan Neale, who was so clever at getting herself into and out of messes.

"When I read about her, I feel like I *am* her," one of the women at work had gushed to Madison.

Madison had always meant to read one

of the books, but she'd never had time. In spite of thinking that, after Roger, she never again wanted anything to do with the medical world, Madison still spent most of her evenings curled up with medical textbooks and trade journals. That the texts and magazines had changed to dealing with animals instead of people didn't bother Madison in the least.

However, she'd been aware of the growing popularity of the Jordan Neale romantic mysteries. When the second book came out, the women were reading it under their desks. One day a golden retriever had swallowed the staple puller off a woman's desk because she'd been so engrossed in Alexandria Farrell's latest novel that she hadn't even seen the dog. Dr. Parkhurst said that it was a good thing the dog hadn't been brought in for rabies. "It would have been worth it," the woman had said as she clutched the book to her bony chest.

Now, having heard about the man Ellie had been married to, Madison couldn't imagine what his reaction to his wife's success had been.

"What a great story," Leslie said.

Frowning, Madison drew deeply on her

cigarette. "So what did *he* think of your success?"

"He suffered," Ellie said, then threw up her hands in exasperation. "He said that he was glad that one of us had been 'given' success. I can't describe how guilty he made me feel. For years we'd talked of nothing but how *he* was going to set the world on fire, how *he* was going to achieve greatness, but, instead, *I* was going to get everything that he'd ever wanted. He made me feel terrible, really and truly *terrible.* I couldn't enjoy my success because I felt that anything I achieved was at his expense."

She took a deep breath to calm herself. "So I did everything in the world that I could think of to make him feel that my success was just as much his. I dedicated every book to him. At every interview I said that *he* was my inspiration. And of course I turned over every penny I earned to him to manage. But he wouldn't 'manage' the money. I negotiated all contracts, made all the decisions about investments. I set up the corporation. Everything. I had to do it all by myself. All Martin did was spend the money. But, between him and me, we pretended to each other—and to others—that *he* was the 'manager.' I didn't think about it consciously, but I think that I hoped that if he believed he controlled the money, he'd believe that it was his as well as mine. . . ." Trailing off, she looked at her hands.

"But nothing can please men like that," Madison said. "Nothing you do is enough for them. Roger was threatened by anything that I achieved. During the divorce several people, including Dr. Oliver, testified that he wouldn't be walking if it weren't for me, but Roger said that he would have been walking *sooner* if I hadn't dragged him down."

"Right," Ellie said, her head coming up. "The more success I had, the more Martin put me down. And he put me down in a way that he knew would get to me. He told me that I'd *prevented* him from becoming a musician, that if he hadn't left New York *for me,* he would have made himself into 'Somebody.' But instead, he'd given all his success to me and I'd *forced* him to give up the only dream he'd ever had. I used to talk for days, trying to make him remember that that's not how it was. I'd spend hours just on the fact that I'd given up my art and left New York because *he* wanted to go to L.A.

to become a musician. But no matter what I said, Martin remembered something different. He remembered that I quit painting because I wasn't very good, and he remembered that he'd left what would have been a fabulous future in New York and we moved to L.A. because I said I had to have more sunshine in my life."

Ellie took a deep breath to calm herself. "I stood it as long as I could. I got to the point where I didn't care whether what he remembered and what I did were the same. And I was sick unto death of all of my money he was spending. We bought a beautiful big house with a dedicated recording studio on the end of it. But after Martin filled the studio with music equipment, he then packed the house with speakers and lots of black boxes with flashing lights on them. And when the house was bursting at the seams, Martin said we had to buy a bigger house, this time with a recording studio four times as large as the one he had. And while he was buying and buying and buying, he was whining to me that I wasn't earning enough fast enough. When I couldn't take it anymore, I filed for divorce."

Here Ellie had to pause. "It was in the divorce courtroom in that small town that I found out that the judge agreed with my husband," she said softly. "Martin went into the courtroom with copies of my books and the interviews I'd given as 'proof' that he'd been deeply involved in my writing. And the judge believed every word he said. The judge told my attorney that it was a community property state, so Martin owned my books as much as I did, so why should *I* get control of them and not him? And by control, I mean that he could have added porno to them, could have let them lapse out of print, anything he wanted to do with them."

Ellie had to take another breath before she could go on. "In the end, to keep control of my books, I agreed to give Martin all the money I'd earned, everything that had been purchased with the money from the books, and I have to support him forever. *Lavishly* support him."

"You're kidding," Madison said.

"No. That is not something I joke about. He gets his first. I even have to carry a huge insurance policy on my life so that if I die— or go bankrupt—he gets paid."

When Ellie said no more, neither Leslie nor Madison could think of a reply. Didn't people who had made as much money as Ellie have all the power in a divorce? Wasn't it the money that always won?

It was Leslie who broke into the gloom that had descended on the three of them. "How about if we forget about our troubles for a couple of hours and go look at this town? Maybe we can buy each other birthday gifts. Anybody know what she'd like to have for the big four-o?"

"A new start?" Madison asked.

"*Hmph!*" Ellie said. "I'd just like revenge. No! I'd like to have *justice!*"

"I think I saw both those items in the little store on the corner. You know, the one by the fishmonger?"

For a second both Madison and Ellie blinked at her; then they smiled.

"Okay," Ellie said, "I know when I'm losing my audience. Actually, I think I saw a little lamp shaped like an alligator in one window. I'd like to investigate that because my editor collects alligator things."

"In that case, I met a guy from Fort Lauderdale she might like," Madison said, smiling as she got up, then pushed the chair back.

"Sounds like the plot of the last book my

editor *didn't buy*," Ellie said as she, too, got up. Then, as she turned and looked out the kitchen window, she thought that she felt oddly lighter. Maybe the telling of what had been done to her had released some of the bitterness that filled her because of the injustice of the court system. Of course she'd told every detail to Jeanne, but, somehow, telling someone you were paying a hundred and fifty bucks an hour wasn't as satisfying as telling these two old friends.

"I'll go shopping with you two, but on one condition," Leslie said. When Madison and Ellie turned to look at her, she was standing with her hands on her hips and glaring at them.

"What condition?" both Madison and Ellie asked.

"That no one—and I mean that, *no one*— asks me to make an intimate, soul-searching exposé of *my* marriage."

At that Ellie looked at Madison. "She always has to win, doesn't she?"

"*Mmmmm,*" Madison said, then smiled at Leslie. "So what did you say when your husband took over the summerhouse *you* had restored?"

"While she was pregnant," Ellie said to Madison. "Don't forget that part."

Leslie narrowed her eyes at them. "The next one to talk about me gets to wash dishes tonight."

"Alligators!" Ellie said. "That's the only thing that's going to be on my mind."

"Is there anything to *do* in this town?" Madison asked. "I mean, you've heard my story and now we've heard Ellie's and if Betty Crocker here won't reveal anything about her life, what are we going to do with these remaining two days?"

Smiling, Leslie took both women by the arm and led them toward the front door. "How about if we find three sea captains named Josiah and have mad affairs with them?"

"Count me in!" Ellie said instantly, then heard herself laugh. It was the first time she'd had a lighthearted thought about sex in three whole years.

"I'm with you!" Madison said, and they left the house laughing together.

Part Two

Sixteen

In the end, they decided to separate for a little exploring and to get together again for lunch. "That way, maybe we'll have something to talk about besides the rotten part of our lives," Leslie said.

Of course each woman agreed because she wanted to have time alone to buy birthday gifts for the other two. They decided to meet at one at The Wharf, and laughing, they challenged each other to eat some of the stranger types of seafood offered in Maine.

Leslie headed toward the used-book store that she'd seen down a tiny alleyway, and she hoped that Ellie hadn't seen it. So what gift did you buy for an internationally famous person? she thought with a sigh.

She was still wondering as she entered

the bookstore. As she closed the door behind her, she felt as though she'd entered another time and place. The walls were lined with packed bookcases, and books were everywhere else, on chairs, on the floor, on and under little tables. The shades had been pulled down to protect the books piled high in front of the windows. There were a few ceiling lights and a couple of wall lights that, unless Leslie's eye was wrong, were antiques and quite valuable.

"May I help you?" came a voice that sounded ancient.

It took Leslie's eyes a moment to adjust to the low light, and when they did, she saw a little old man, thin to the point of emaciation, but with thick white hair and such an erect carriage that Leslie knew that he'd once been a heart stopper. Something about him made her feel . . . well, pretty. And, compared to him, she was very young.

She gave him a radiant smile. "I'm looking for gifts for two women friends of mine. They both have birthdays tomorrow."

He was shorter than Leslie, but she had an idea that no woman had ever felt shorter than he. "Could you tell me something about the women? What do they like?"

"I don't really know them that—" She broke off. Was she going to say that she didn't know Madison and Ellie very well? After what she'd heard in the last twenty-four hours? Not quite.

"Healing," she said, the word popping out of her mouth. "One of them is interested in all things to do with medicine. And the other one . . ." Leslie hesitated. What *was* Ellie interested in? If it had been for someone other than Ellie, Leslie would have bought her a book on "meditations for women," something calming, something to take the anger out of her. But Leslie could imagine Ellie scoffing at such a book.

Leslie gave the man a small smile. "You don't have anything for someone who wants revenge, do you?"

The man smiled in return, as though her request weren't in the least unusual. "Perhaps," he said, then turned and walked through the stacks to the back of the store. When she reached him, he was standing in front of a small bookcase that Leslie was sure was Chippendale—real, not reproduction—and holding out a book to her.

Taking it, she looked down at the title. "*A Life of Romance*," the title read. Puzzled,

Leslie looked at the book. What did this have to do with either revenge or medicine? she wondered. But when she looked up, the man was gone and she was alone in the back corner of the bookshop.

"*A Life of Romance*," she read aloud as she held the little book in her hands. It had a green cover, no dust jacket, and it felt old. The shade on the window behind her had been lifted a bit, so there was a ray of sunshine coming through. She could see dust motes dancing in the air.

The title of the book made Leslie think about her own life and whether or not her husband was having an affair with his young assistant. And she thought about what she was going to be forced to do if she did face the issue of his affair. Was she going to have to leave him? Or was the proper thing to do to throw him out of the house he'd come to love as much as she did? Rebecca's words that the family was going to lose everything because Leslie wouldn't fight came back to her.

Right now Leslie wished she'd stayed with the other women. At least listening to their problems made her forget her own. Or, if not forget, then at least shelve them for a while.

Maybe it was selfish of her, but Leslie thought that her problems were worse than theirs. They weren't bound by the chains of *love*. They were haunted by what had been done to them by two truly horrible men, but they weren't still pinned to the men by that much-over-used word, *love*. Ellie certainly wasn't still in love with her ex, nor was Madison.

But Leslie was as much in love with Alan as she'd been the day she'd met him. Long ago, when she was a young woman, she'd known what awaited her if she married a man she loved as much as she did Alan. And, because of what she saw, she'd tried to break it off. She'd even tried to burn her bridges behind her by jilting him. She hadn't consciously made a plan, but, now, with the wisdom that age gives one, she knew that she'd publicly humiliated him with the thought that she wouldn't be able to return to him.

But she had returned. She'd gone to New York and discovered that she might be considered greatly talented in Columbus, but in New York, she didn't have what it took to be a professional dancer. She had neither the drive nor the talent.

So she'd gone home, home to Alan, and they had married as though nothing had happened. And she had to give it to him, in the years since, he'd never thrown it in her face about what she'd done to him.

But, just the same, Leslie had been eaten with guilt over the years. "*Why* don't you stand up to him?" her mother often said. "What is it that you're afraid of?"

Leslie had wanted to scream, "I'm afraid of losing him. I've seen what life is like without Alan and I don't want anything to do with it."

But now she was sure that her life with Alan was over. It was only a matter of time.

She had been standing in one place, holding the little book, for several minutes now. Opening the book to the first chapter, she read, "I never married because I knew that love would place chains on me, and, above all else, I wanted freedom."

Leslie snapped the book shut. The words she'd read were too close to her own life. Turning her head, she glanced toward the front of the store. She heard the tinkle of the little bell attached to the door, so she knew other customers had entered the shop. How had the man known? she wondered.

No, she told herself, he couldn't have known.

She could hear the people quietly talking in the other room. She couldn't very well march through the store and say to the man, "I told you I was interested in medicine and revenge, what *they* want. So why did you give me . . ." Why did he give me what *I* need? Leslie thought.

She waited a few moments for the other people to leave. She could hear them laughing, so they probably weren't the kind of people to want to spend very long in a dirty old used-book store. But after several minutes the people were still there, so Leslie looked about her. In the corner, under a foot-high stack of books, was an old wooden chair with a worn-out cushion on it. Removing the books, Leslie sat down. She wasn't sure why she just didn't walk through the store and exit, but, somehow, she couldn't leave. Not yet.

She opened the book and began to read.

"So what did you buy?" Ellie asked Leslie.

They were seated at a long wooden table at The Wharf, half a dozen containers of food in front of them. In the end, they had chickened out on trying sea urchins. "Fry it and it can't be too bad," Ellie had said, so in front of them now were three big, white paper containers full of fried seafood, plus three other containers full of slaw, potatoes, and corn.

Madison and Ellie had spent the time between ordering and the arrival of the food showing off their purchases. Madison had bought three sacks full of toys for the children of various friends. "I'm Erskine's godmother," she said, smiling. "It's a rule in town that if you have a baby, then maidenly Madison must be the godmother."

"They're probably hoping that you'll give the child a gift of beauty like yours," Leslie said, making Madison laugh in a dismissive way but also making her blush with pleasure.

Ellie had bought the alligator lamp and, "a couple of other things that no one can see until tomorrow," she said, smiling.

Only Leslie had no shopping bags full of purchases. She should have bought gifts for them and for her children and for Alan. And Bambi? she thought, then made herself look up at the others. They were waiting for her to show them what was inside her one little bag.

"Sorry," she said. "I went to a used-book store with the best of intentions, but I—"

"Found some interesting old book and spent all the time reading it," Ellie said.

Leslie laughed. "However did you know?" she asked facetiously.

"Occupational hazard. So? Did you buy the book?"

"Oh, yes," Leslie said. "I did."

When she didn't say any more, Ellie pushed. "Are you going to tell us about it?"

Leslie reached to the floor to retrieve the package. When she'd finally gone to the cash register, the shopkeeper hadn't said a word about the fact that she'd been sitting in the back of his store for about three hours. He obviously wasn't the type of man to post No Loitering signs.

He'd just smiled at her, taken the ridiculously low price of three dollars that was marked in the front of the book, and told her that he hoped she'd enjoy it.

Now, Leslie opened the little brown bag and put the book on the table. "It's about a Victorian woman who traveled around the world," Leslie said. "She had several affairs but one longtime love, a man she had been engaged to when she was eighteen, but she left him to travel the world alone."

"Sounds like you," Ellie said, reaching for the book.

"Not quite," Leslie said quickly, hoping she sounded as though she hadn't thought of that idea. "I left, but I returned."

"Would you do it again?" Madison asked as she popped something fried into her mouth. She really did eat more than Ellie and Leslie combined.

"You mean, leave Alan?"

"No. Go back to him. If you had to do it over again, would you leave New York and go back to your hometown boy?"

Leslie smiled. "Let's just say that New York wasn't going to throw open its doors for a dancer of my caliber. And I never had talent for anything else."

"That's what I thought while I was in art school," Ellie said. "I lived, breathed, ate art. It was everything to me, but look at me now." She had been about to bite into a fried clam, but instead she dropped it back into the paper container. "Maybe that was a bad choice of words. Don't look at me *now* but look at me four years ago."

"You mean when you were married to a man who was sick with jealousy over you?" Madison asked as she picked up the clam Ellie had put back.

Ellie looked at Leslie. "She has a streak of pure mean in her, doesn't she?"

Leslie avoided both questions, the personal one from Madison and the rhetorical one from Ellie. "What about you?" she asked Madison. "If you had to do it all over again, what would you do?"

Before she could answer, Ellie said, "With or without knowledge of what's happened since?"

"What do you mean?" Leslie asked.

"If you're suddenly—speaking as a writer, that is—transported back in time and asked the same question as you were then, you'd probably make the same decision. Unless you had different knowledge, that is."

Madison raised her eyebrows. "So you're asking me if, knowing how it all turned out, I would take Roger's call, listen to him beg me to return to Montana to nurse him back to health, then *do* it?"

"That's exactly what I'm asking," Ellie said. "Actually, it's what *you* were asking since you started this."

"Let me think about that," Madison said sarcastically. "Roger or a life." She lifted her hands as though they were a balance scale. "Roger. Life. *Hmmm*. Which way should I go?"

Leslie laughed. "You two have it easy. You *know* which way you'd go. Madison would stay in New York and become a supermodel before supermodels were invented. And, Ellie, you'd start writing because you'd know that's where your real talent is. But with me . . . What choices did I have?"

"To meet men other than Alan," Ellie answered instantly. "You don't even know what's out there."

"Roger and Martin," Leslie shot back at her.

Ellie laughed. "You do have a point."

Madison twirled her fork in a pile of coleslaw on her plate. "But the men out there aren't all bad," she said quietly. "Thomas was out there."

The way she said "was" made the other two women unable to say anything as they remembered his death.

Madison looked up at Leslie. "I'd go find Thomas," she said. When the other two looked shocked, she gave them a look of disgust. "No, not like *that*. Not a séance! I thought we were talking about having a second chance. If I could go back to say, that day the three of us first met, and I knew what I do now, I'd do what I could to find Thomas. I don't think he was in medical school, then but maybe . . ." Trailing off, she looked down at her plate.

The story she'd told, of how she'd dedicated her life to one despicable man and, as a result, had lost the man she loved, floated around the table like a vile smell. By Madison's plate was a little wooden frog that clacked when you pulled it along by its string. The toy was a reminder of the children that Madison would never have.

Leslie broke the silence. Picking up the book she'd bought from where Ellie had put it down on the table, she said, "I think I *would* like to investigate some other choices," she said softly.

"You'd like to spend spring break with the rich kid," Ellie said. "Mr. Maybe-Going-to-be-President-Someday, wouldn't you?"

"Yes," Leslie said firmly, "I would."

"What's that?" Madison asked abruptly.

Leslie looked at the book, which Madison

seemed to be motioning toward. Puzzled, she said, "It's the book I bought."

"No. What's that sticking out of it?"

Turning the book on end, Leslie looked at the top edge. There was a small piece of paper barely protruding from the pages. Opening to the marker, Leslie took it out. It was a business card, cream-colored, and Leslie could see that it was in old-fashioned engraving, the kind where someone painstakingly engraves a copper plate.

Futures, Inc.
"Have you ever wanted to
rewrite your past?"
Madame Zoya can help
333 Everlasting Street

Leslie read the card, frowned, then handed it to Madison. "I have no idea what it is. I didn't notice it when I was reading the book."

Madison looked at the card for a moment, then put it down on the table. Opening her handbag, she withdrew another card and placed it beside Leslie's. They were identical.

"That's odd that we both have the same

card," Leslie said, "but then I guess the lady is just trying to drum up business. It must be difficult to earn a living in a small town like this. Maybe—"

She broke off because Ellie had rummaged inside her shopping bags and had placed a third identical card on the table by the other two.

Seventeen

"Palm reader," Madison said as she ate another piece of fried food.

"Tarot," Ellie said. "Or, actually, she could be regressionist."

"Past lives?" Madison asked, eyebrows raised. "Gee, I'd sure love to find out that I've done stupid things for centuries."

"You were probably a great beauty then too. Maybe you were some king's favorite courtesan," Ellie said.

"So why do I get courtesan and not queen?" Madison asked. "Why do I have to be illegal as well as immoral?"

"In real life queens are never actually beautiful. They're chosen for their lineage, not their looks."

"Does this include Princess Diana?" Madison shot back.

"She didn't make it to queen, did she?" Ellie said, one eyebrow raised.

"But that doesn't mean—"

"Let's go," Leslie said, and, without waiting for a reply, she began to gather her things.

"Back to the house?" Ellie asked, puzzled by Leslie's abruptness.

Madison leaned over. "I think she means for us to go to Madame Zoya."

"You're kidding," Ellie said as the waitress came up to their table.

"Is there anything else I can get for you ladies?" she said, but she looked directly at Ellie.

Before Ellie could make a reply to the skinny waitress's look, Leslie said, "Do you know where Everlasting Street is?"

The girl began to clear the containers from the table. "I don't get out of here very often, but they sell maps at the bookstore."

For a moment all three women looked at the girl in puzzlement.

"How long have you lived here?" Leslie asked quietly.

"All my life," the girl answered. "You sure you don't want dessert?" She looked at Ellie. "We have chocolate cake."

Madison put out her arm to prevent Ellie from physically attacking the girl, but the waitress just smiled and turned away, leaving the check on the table.

"Anyone leaves her a tip over five cents and she's dead meat," Ellie muttered, but the girl had brought her back to reality. Being with Leslie and Madison for these last two days had made her forget why she'd been hiding for the last three years.

Leslie was standing on the opposite side of the table, her cardigan and her handbag over her arm, the book in one hand and the card in the other. She was looking at it in concentration.

Reaching across the table, Ellie took the card from her. "Rewrite the past," she said. "I'd like to go back to the time before I was *fat*," she said with vehemence; then she handed the card back to Leslie. "Let's find this place."

The two women looked at Madison.

"You two don't believe this thing, do you? This has to be a hoax. If anyone could send anyone back to the past, she would have been on *60 Minutes,* and since I rarely miss an episode . . ." She trailed off, hoping to elicit a smile from Leslie and Ellie. She didn't like fortune-tellers. When she was a teenager, one of them had read her palm and told her of the wonderful future in store for her, complete with four children. Since her divorce, she'd thought of that charlatan several times.

"Why don't you two go, and I'll . . ." Madison began, but the looks on the faces of Leslie and Ellie made her retreat. "All right. What do I have to lose? My future couldn't be much worse than my past."

"Sure it could," Ellie said. "You could become rich and famous and have every person you've ever known drop you because they've decided that you're now a snob."

"Or you could be elected chairman of your town's Winter Carnival and be expected to raise the money as well as spend it," Leslie said.

"Or—" Ellie began.

Madison put up her hand. "I give up. You win. So how do we find Everlasting Street?"

"I think I saw a newspaper office somewhere," Leslie said.

"It's over the drugstore. I wonder what their subscriber rate is."

"At least twenty-five," Madison said,

smiling. "Which is about two more than the Erskine paper has."

"Shall we go?" Leslie asked, and there was impatience in her voice.

"Let *me* take care of the check," Ellie said with a malicious little smile on her face. Five minutes later the three of them were walking down the main street of the tiny town on their way to the newspaper office. But they hadn't gone four blocks when they saw a street sign that said, "Everlasting Street." It was true that the sign was smaller than the others, and it was almost hidden behind the leaves of a magnificent copper beech tree, but, still, it was there.

"Lived here all her life and she's never heard of the street," Ellie muttered, looking up at the sign.

"Well, ladies," Leslie said, "shall we?"

Leslie didn't wait for an answer as she trudged ahead, Ellie behind her, a reluctant Madison trailing in the rear.

"This really is absurd," Madison said. "I don't know what you two hope to find out. Fortune-tellers are out to get what they can. I saw a special once on TLC that showed how they see clues about your life from your clothes, your jewelry, even the way you carry yourself. Then, no matter how little you tell them, they pick up these clues. It was all just an act. The commentator took a couple of lessons, and at the end he told someone's fortune. He did quite well at guessing, but—"

All the time Madison had been talking they had been walking. As far as they could see, the narrow road was deserted. There were no houses on either side, just what looked to be virgin forest right up to the edges of the road. But then the road turned to the right, and they were suddenly staring at a big Victorian house, and the sight of it made Madison halt her speech.

The house wasn't huge, but it was exquisite. It had been painted in an intricate manner that one usually saw only on brochures put out by paint companies. This one was done in a sort of taupe green, with accents of dark brown and dark green. There were spindles on a little balcony, and they had been meticulously painted in all three shades.

"I wish Alan could see this," Leslie said under her breath. "He loves Victorian houses."

"Probably fake," Madison muttered.

"No," Leslie said. "I know something about building, and this one is old. See the way the windows are uneven? It takes years for a house to settle that way."

"Look at her lilacs," Ellie said, nodding toward a ten-foot-tall hedge along the right side of the house.

Leslie turned to Ellie. "Don't lilacs bloom in the spring? This is October."

For a moment, the two women looked at each other with wide eyes.

"Are you two going to go into some sort of supernatural trance? They're plants. Plants bloom at different times. So what? She has October-blooming purple flowers, and you two have May-blooming purple flowers. Snap out of it!"

When neither Leslie nor Ellie moved, Madison grabbed their arms and pulled them toward the perfect little white picket fence that surrounded the house. "Really, you two! You dragged me here, now you're the ones chickening out."

There was no answer from either Ellie or Leslie as Madison pulled them onto the front porch. And when she dropped their arms, they just stood there looking about the place. Leslie was inspecting the ceiling of the porch, while Ellie was studying the swing. There wasn't so much as a dead leaf on the porch. It was as neat and as perfectly tidy as the garden was.

"I don't think her trees drop their leaves," Ellie whispered.

"I have the feeling that it would be in bloom just like this even if this were January," Leslie whispered back to her.

Madison threw up her hands in exasperation. "Right. Madame Zoya is Merlin's first cousin, and she—Oh, no, wait, she's his reincarnation, and—" When she saw that the other two weren't listening to her, she stopped talking and put her finger on the doorbell.

The woman who answered the door could have been someone's plump, pleasant grandmother, except that her hair had been dyed a flamboyant shade of orange. But then, Ellie thought, grandmothers today had introduced the world to LSD and other such questionable "enlightenments," so maybe a grandmother would have orange hair.

"Won't you come in," she said graciously, opening the door wide. Inside, the house was furnished in a sort of country French style, with pretty, bright-patterned fabrics and big, overstuffed chairs and sofas.

The woman laughed at the look on Leslie's face. "My late husband was the Victorian lover," she said. She had a nice voice, soft and warm; it made you trust her. How could anyone with such a sweet-sounding voice be harmful? "But I never cared much about Victorian, so we compromised. The outside is Victorian, the inside is comfortable. No horsehair sofas for me!"

She smiled at the three of them, as though expecting them to laugh with her, but Leslie and Ellie were looking around at every corner of the house. Only Madison was looking at the woman.

"Are you Madame Zoya?" Madison asked, and a sneer was in her voice.

But the woman didn't take offense. "My professional name. My real name is Bertie, short for Brutilda. It's a family name. Now, what can I do for you young ladies?"

The "young" appellation made Ellie and Leslie smile, and for a moment, none of them spoke. To say why they had come would be to admit that there was a possibility that they believed that she could . . .

Well, what exactly was she saying that she could do?

"We, uh, found your card," Ellie said, then had to clear her throat. "You, uh, tell fortunes?"

"Oh, my, no," Madame Zoya/Bertie/Brutilda said. "I send people back in time to change their lives. I have no idea what a person's future is. Or past, for that matter. I can only do the one thing."

The four of them were still standing in the foyer of the lovely house. To the left, through an archway, was the living room, to the right the dining room. In front of them was the main staircase leading up to a hallway where a couple of pretty little tables flanked an open doorway. Inside they could see the corner of what looked to be a four-poster bed.

"Just the one thing?" Ellie asked, eyebrows raised.

"That's it," Madame Zoya said happily. "Now, if one or all of you are interested, we can step into the sunroom and, after we get the financial details out of the way, we can begin."

"*Ahhhhhh,*" Madison said. "The financial details."

Madame Zoya whipped her head around and froze Madison with a look that would have terrified any schoolchild. "Yes, dear," she said firmly. "I have expenses just as you do, and so I charge for my services."

With a weak smile, Madison took a step backward.

"I'd like to know more about what you do before I make a commitment," Leslie said with a smile. "After all, I've never so much as heard of anyone who can do what you do."

Madame Zoya's pleasant smile returned as she looked at Leslie. She did not invite the women to sit down or even to go into her living room. "I do just what my card says I do, I help people rewrite their pasts."

It was Ellie's turn to step forward. "Okay, so shoot us for not understanding, but we have no idea what that means. Maybe you could start from the very beginning."

For a moment Madame Zoya looked hard at Ellie, as though searching inside her for signs that she was actually telling the truth. Did she really and truly *not* know what it meant to rewrite the past?

The woman's look made Ellie feel as though she'd asked her to explain what a car or a television was. Ellie felt as though she *should* know what "rewriting the past" meant. She had an impulse to grab a yellow pages and show the woman that she was the only person in there under "Past, Rewriting of."

But Ellie wasn't about to miss out on hearing a story, so she bit down on the side of her tongue to keep her remarks to herself and gave the woman a look of regret, No, sorry, but she didn't know what it meant to rewrite the past.

When Madame Zoya seemed satisfied that not one of the three knew what she could do, she spilled out words so quickly that they could hardly keep up with them. "I can send you back for three weeks, that's all. You, of course, will choose when and where you want to go. At the end of the time you will return here and not one second will have passed. You will then be given some choices. You may keep your lives as they are now, or you can go with the new future you've created. However, I must warn you that going with the new future carries risks of the unknown. In this life you could have escaped accidents and deaths of loved ones, but who knows what will happen in the new one? I had one man who chose the new future, then his arm fell off. Well, not really *fell*. It was more that it disappeared. One minute his arm was there; then the next it wasn't. In his old life he hadn't been at the place where the accident occurred in his new life, so he hadn't had the accident that removed his arm. But that's the risk you take. So, now, any more questions?"

Leslie and Madison stood there blinking at the woman, not fully comprehending what she'd just said. But Ellie was used to following stories, and when she talked to her editor about a new story idea, they talked in the shorthand style that this woman was now using. "So if they stay with what they have now, will they remember the new time, the way they *didn't* go? And do they take back current knowledge with them to the past?" Ellie fired off at her.

"Your decision," Madame Zoya said. "Remember or forget, as you wish. And, yes, you return with everything you know now. You can be eighteen with a woman's knowledge of the world. A lot of women choose that path."

Madison hadn't fully understood all that had been said, but she knew the word "forget." "I'd like to forget everything that's happened to me since the day the three of us met," she said under her breath.

Madame Zoya heard her. "Your choice. So what do you want to do? Any of you? All of you? None?"

"How much does this cost?" Ellie asked. She was her own agent, so she had no qualms about discussing money with anyone.

"One hundred dollars."

The three women blinked, with Leslie recovering first. "You mean that you'll send us back to the past for a mere one hundred dollars?"

Madame Zoya's eyes sparkled in merriment as she looked directly at Madison. "Didn't hear that on The Learning Channel, did you, dear? That show was all about money, wasn't it?"

Madison gave the woman a weak smile, then looked away, embarrassed. Did she have an intercom on her porch so she could snoop into everyone's private conversations?

"What the heck?" Ellie said as she reached into her handbag for her wallet. "This is my treat. Even if it doesn't work—"

With her back to Madame Zoya, she wiggled her eyebrows at Leslie and Madison, letting them know that she was sure the whole thing was a joke. "—I can write off the expense as research." Turning back, she handed three one-hundred-dollar bills to Madame Zoya.

Smiling, the woman took the money, slipped it into the pocket of her lavender print dress, then motioned toward a hallway past the dining room. "My office is this way," she said. "Follow me."

"Everyone's arms on tight?" Ellie whispered to Leslie and Madison, sounding as though they were about to get on a dangerous roller coaster.

Madame Zoya led them to a small room at a back corner of the house. There were windows on two sides and a view into a deeply shaded part of the garden. Thick vines hung over a tall fence; trees drooped down above them. There wasn't a flower in sight, not a bit of color to break the dark green.

The only objects in the room were three identical chairs—Queen Anne, upholstered in dark green, facing the windows—and on the floor, a large, lush rug patterned with entwined leaves. The walls were painted a somber golden yellow, without a picture on them.

All in all, it was a soothing room, and the three chairs made it seem almost as though the three woman had been expected.

Ellie tried to lighten the mood by making a joke. "What if only two of us had accepted?" she asked, smiling. "Would you have run ahead and removed a chair?"

Madame Zoya didn't smile. "I choose my prospective clients well. I knew that all three of you needed me."

At that, Madison almost turned around and left the room, but Ellie and Leslie caught her arms and pulled her back to them; then they led her to the middle chair and half pushed her onto it.

"Does this hurt?" Madison asked.

"No, of course not," Madame Zoya said. "The only pain is what you experience in life. I will cause you no pain at all. Now, each of you must tell me where you want to go."

"You mean in time?" Ellie said.

Madame Zoya, standing in front of them, looked at her as though she weren't too bright. "Of course I mean in time. I'm not a bus service, now am I?" At that Madame

Zoya laughed as though she'd made a wonderful joke. She didn't seem to notice, and certainly didn't mind, that the three women didn't share her laugh. "Oh! There's one requirement that I forgot to tell you about."

At that, Madison gave Leslie and Ellie an I-told-you-so look.

"I want to take your pictures. I keep a scrapbook of all my clients before and after. It helps me to remember."

"Could we see your scrapbook?" Ellie asked instantly.

"You're the writer, aren't you, dear?" Madame Zoya said, smiling. "You can always tell writers. They're always trying to turn every word into pages, which of course turns into money for them, doesn't it?"

The way she stated it made it sound as though Ellie's whole life were about money. As Ellie gave a weak smile, she could feel her face redden.

"I'll be back in a jiff, and I'll expect you three to have made up your minds by then."

The second Madame Zoya left the room, all three of them let out their pent-up breath.

"What the hell have you got us into?" Madison exploded.

"Ellie or me?" Leslie asked calmly.

"What does it matter?" Madison asked. "This whole thing is absurd. I'm leaving right—"

"If she's a charlatan, I'm out three hundred bucks, but if she's for real—not that I believe she is," Ellie said, her voice low, her eyes on the doorway. "But if she can do what she says, you can find Thomas."

"Before you miscarried," Leslie said so softly that they could barely hear her.

At that Madison sat back on her chair and looked straight ahead at the greenery outside the window. There was a look of shock on her face.

"What about you?" Leslie said to Ellie. "You want to go back to the day the three of us met? Before you met your ex-husband?"

"No!" Ellie said firmly. "Who knows what would have happened to me? Maybe I would have met some nice, normal guy and had five kids by now. If I did that, I never would've had enough time alone to find out that I could write. No, for all that he was a jerk—or maybe because he was a jerk and I wanted to escape him—I wrote. I wouldn't want to mess up that balance. No, I'd just like to change what was done to me in the divorce. He went into that fiasco prepared; I was caught off guard by the ruthless way he handled it. What about you?"

Smiling, Leslie started to answer, but Madame Zoya returned to the room holding a cheap Polaroid camera. "Now smile, dearies," she said, then snapped them one after another.

She didn't show them the photos that came out of the camera. In fact, she didn't look at them herself but set the camera and the photos on the windowsill, then looked back at the windows. "Have you made up your minds?" she asked as though they were trying to decide about lunch.

"Yes," Leslie answered, while Ellie and Madison merely nodded.

Madame Zoya looked at Madison. "You first, dear. I feel that you have lost the most."

"I thought you didn't read palms," Madison said before she thought. She'd already had one encounter with the woman's sharp tongue and didn't fancy another one.

But Madame Zoya kept smiling. "I don't. But I've lived long enough to see pain in a

person's eyes when it's there. Now, where
do you want to go?"

"To the day the three of us met," Madison
said firmly. "The ninth of October, 1981."

Madame Zoya didn't reply to that but
looked at Ellie. "And you?"

"To three years, seven months, and two
weeks ago," she said. "To three weeks before the court date for my divorce." She
would have liked to return earlier so she'd
have more time to gather evidence, but she
had to return to a time after she'd already
filed for divorce.

Madame Zoya looked at Leslie.

"I don't know the exact date," Leslie said,
"but it would have been April of 1980, the
year before I graduated from college." She
lowered her voice. "Spring break," she
said softly. It was embarrassing that
the others should hear this, as she thought
it was a foolish wish to want to meet a
boy she hadn't seen in twenty years. But
how could she explain the ties that love
put on her? No matter how she tried to
explain, she knew that, by comparison, her
problems wouldn't sound as serious as
theirs. How did one faithless husband hold
up against what Madison and Ellie had

been through? If—she refused to think "when"—she and Alan divorced, she was sure that Alan would be fair and honest and . . . "A cheat," she heard her mother's voice say.

"Are you sure, dear?" Madame Zoya asked Leslie. "Absolutely sure?"

"Yes!" Leslie said firmly. "Yes, I am. Very sure."

"All right then, girls, lean your heads back and close your eyes and think about the time where you want to go."

Obediently, with mixed feelings about the absurdity of what they were doing, the women leaned their heads back against the chairs and closed their eyes.

Instantly, the three of them felt as though they were floating. It was a lovely sensation, and they each smiled as they experienced it. After a moment, the floating stopped and they seemed to be moving toward something, as though they were being rushed through a tunnel.

Just before she reached the end of the tunnel, Madison remembered that they had been on the road when she was talking about the show she'd seen on TV, not standing on the porch. So how had

Madame Zoya heard what she'd said? She didn't come up with an answer before she opened her eyes and saw that she was sitting on a bench in the DMV in New York. And Ellie, a very young, very thin, Ellie, was walking toward her.

Eighteen

May 1997
Los Angeles, California

Ellie put down her pen and glanced at the door again. The sign on the private detective's door said, "Be back in ten minutes," but she'd been waiting for thirty-two minutes and he still hadn't returned. She looked down at her notebook again. She was making notes on a story about three women who go back in time and change their lives. The book would be a departure from her usual stories about the life and adventures of Jordan Neale, but if it was good, the readers would like it.

She looked down at her watch again, then her glance traveled up her arm, and from there she looked down at her legs showing beneath her short denim skirt. Putting her notebook down on the seat beside her, she put her hands around her waist. She'd measured it every one of the three days since she'd returned, and each time she felt a thrill when she saw that her waist was once again a teeny, tiny twenty-four inches. And every morning, she'd weighed herself. The first time she'd stepped on the scales and seen the needle stop at one hundred and one pounds, she'd burst into tears.

Three days ago had been the day before her fortieth birthday, but three days ago she'd been sent back to her old life, back into her former, slimmer body. But, more important, she'd been sent back to her own mind. For the first time in years, Ellie once again had stories running through her head. She had energy. She had a feeling that good things were going to happen to her, that they *could* happen to her. This happy feeling was odd because she knew of the horror that was going to happen very soon in the coming divorce, but since it hadn't actually happened yet, she didn't have the depression that she knew would come after the divorce.

"How much time is wasted in depression," she whispered aloud.

She was sitting on a wooden bench outside the office of Joe Montoya, the private eye she'd hired to investigate her soon-to-be ex-husband. She'd gone to the detective the first day she'd returned, and she'd had a lot to tell him. Most of the things she told him were what she'd found out after the divorce, but now, this time around, she knew what her ex was up to.

On her first visit to the detective, she'd sat on the other side of his desk, opened her notebook and started on her list of things that she knew were going to be important in the divorce. "He's going to say that he coauthored my books, so I need for you to document his daily activities to show that he was too busy socializing at my expense to have time to help me write. And you said you know a forensic accountant? I need help in finding out what my husband has done with all my money over the years," she told the private eye.

He was writing quickly, only now and then looking up at Ellie in speculation. She knew what he was thinking, that most women on the verge of divorce were a basket case of tears and misery. But Ellie had done that—and as a result, she'd lost everything.

"He's going to say that he did all the research for my books, that he contributed at least half of their development," she continued. "And he's going to say that he was a brilliant manager of the money I earned, so I need an accountant to look at the discrepancy between what I earned and what was left after he finished with it. And I need someone who can be a down-and-out and get my ex to talk."

"What?" Montoya asked.

"My slimy ex-husband—almost ex, that is—is going to tell the court that he has no money hidden, but I know that he does because after the divorce I found out that—"

"What do you mean, 'after the divorce'?" the detective asked.

"Sorry. My mistake," she said, smiling. "It's just that I want to get away from him so much that I tend to think of it as a done deal."

She could see that he didn't accept her explanation, but she wasn't worried that he'd guess the truth. "*Do* you have someone who could get to know my ex . . . uh, my husband?" she persisted. "It has to be a man, preferably someone who looks like a drunk, or is a drunk; that would be even better."

The detective put down his pen. "Why don't you tell me what this drunk has to do with hidden money?"

"My ex—" Try as she might, she could *not* bring herself to call him her "husband." "Often goes out to bars in the evening. I believe he meets a woman there."

"I see," Montoya said, then bent over his desk and picked up his pen again.

"No, you don't see. This isn't about another woman" Taking a deep breath, she leaned back against the chair and tried to calm herself. "Mr. Montoya, may I be honest with you?"

"It would help," he said, also leaning back in his chair.

"The truth is that when you have as much money as I've earned in the last years, the courts and the lawyers couldn't care less about who's sleeping with whom. I could walk into that court with eight-by-ten glossies of my ex in bed with two men, three women, and a chimpanzee, and it wouldn't matter in the least.

"What matters to them is money and that's all. Money, money, and more money.

California is a community property state, and I don't mind giving him half of what I've earned in the past—not that he deserves a penny of it—but I can live with that. But I know him, and he's going to tell the courts that I couldn't have written the books without him. And, based solely on his word, the judge is going to decide that he deserves far more than what I have earned in the past. The judge is going to say that Martin Gilmore deserves *all* my past income and half my future income because he made me what I am. What I need to do, and do very quickly, is gather enough evidence to show the court that Martin Gilmore is not the upstanding, self-sacrificing person that he says he is. I want to show the court that he's been skimming money from me and that he now has it hidden. I just need to find out where it is."

For a moment the detective looked at her. He knew how successful she was, and he'd dealt with a couple of other writers, so he knew about royalty payments. "You're talking millions, aren't you?"

"Millions in money and an unimaginable amount lost in dignity and self-esteem," she said softly. "He's after money, but *I* am fighting for my sanity. For my future."

He continued to look at her for a moment; then he picked up his pen again. "So what makes you think he'll tell about this money to a stranger? A drunken stranger?"

She smiled at the top of his head. He was an ordinary-looking guy, and there were a couple of framed photos on the cabinet behind him of a woman, two kids, and a dog. "My ex has a big mouth and he loves drunks," she said. "The losers of the world make him feel better by comparison."

"And you want him to talk about money he's hidden?"

"Yes. Where is the money he's taken out of my bank accounts over the years? You see, I did a little accounting on my own and even though he spent—spends—a lot, I've earned more. But I don't know where it is. In the last three days I've searched through every piece of paper in our house, but I found nothing. My only hope is to get him to talk."

Looking at her, Montoya lifted his eyebrows in question. "And you think he's going to tell that to a stranger?"

"Yes," Ellie said firmly. "Martin loves to

brag, loves to tell people how clever he is. If you plant someone near him who has a mournful story about a wife who's ripping him off, Martin will reveal all his secrets of how to turn the tables and get back at the bitch."

The detective snorted, shook his head, then began to write again. "Okay, you got it. One drunk comin' up. I have an actor friend who—"

"What's he look like?"

"A two-headed green Martian in his last play, but I think he could easily manage being a drunk." The detective smiled at her, and she smiled back.

"What next?" he asked.

After that Ellie had given him all the details that she could think of that he'd need to help her prove that her ex had been hiding money from her for years. If she could find that money, he wouldn't be prosecuted for stealing; oh, no, taking money from his wife was purely legal. Most people would agree that it was immoral, but she'd seen that the law didn't care about immoral, only illegal. No, all Ellie could do, if she could prove that he had the money, was to force him to share it, to give half of it back to her, as the community property laws required money to be divided equally.

And, maybe, if she could show that Martin was the type of man to hide money, just maybe the judge wouldn't believe that Martin was being honest when he said he helped Ellie to write the books.

After her first meeting with the detective, she'd driven her red Range Rover back home, to the house that she shared with Martin. The first time around, the judge had said that Martin was to get the house, but Ellie had to pay the mortgage. The judge's "reasoning" was that Ellie was now "forcing" Martin to return to the profession he'd abandoned to manage her career, and since the house had a small recording studio in it, he had to have *that* house.

When Ellie first entered that house again, she was glad that Martin wasn't there; she didn't think she could bear to look at him. In fact, she wasn't able to look at the house because she knew she'd see all the personal possessions that last time became Martin's: her cookware, her photography equipment, years and years of photos, cookbooks, even some of her clothes. Instead, she ran through the house, out the back door, then down the hill to her studio. She knew that if history repeated itself, the judge was going to take away her beloved studio too. Take it from her and give it to him because they believed his lies. But Ellie also knew that just a few months after she signed the property settlement, Martin would rent the house and move to Florida, where he would live in comfort on the money that Ellie had to pay him.

During those first three days after Ellie returned to the past, she'd been so busy that she'd looked at nothing. It had felt so very, very good to work again! She'd had three long years of doing nothing but going over the horror of what had been done to her. She'd spent months asking herself *why* the judge had believed Martin.

Truthfully, she didn't think she'd ever understand *why* it had been done to her, but maybe, this time, she'd be able to head it off. The first time, she'd been unprepared for the accusations that had been hurled at her. All she'd done that first time was cry at the injustice of it all.

When she'd first reappeared in the small town outside of L.A. where she and Martin had lived for years, it had taken Ellie a while to remember that after she'd filed for divorce, she'd moved into a hotel to wait for the proceedings to take their course. During that time she had done little but cry and talk on the phone to her lawyer. Her pride hadn't let her dump on her friends or relatives, so she'd stayed alone in a room and waited.

But this time around she wasn't going to sit and wait. And, she reminded herself, she still had as much right to be inside the house as Martin did, and if she saw him, so be it. But so far, even though she'd returned to the house several times, had even spent hours inside it searching for papers, she hadn't seen him.

She'd spent a great deal of the three days writing letters and requesting documents. She wrote her publisher asking for an affidavit swearing that her husband had never negotiated a contract for her. She asked her money manager for a document swearing that her husband had never called or written her about a single investment.

For three days Ellie dug through documentation and put together all that she could. It was going to be said in court that she lied about her income, therefore she requested that her publishing house give her financial summaries for every year. These were faxed to her within minutes, so Ellie stapled them to copies of past tax returns.

So now, Ellie was sitting on the bench waiting for the PI to return so she could go over her list with him again. And she wanted to talk to him about her sanity. Or at least see if he had any ideas about how she could prove that she was sane. During the first divorce Martin had said that since Ellie had twice spent time with therapists during their marriage, this was proof that she was insane—and therefore incompetent to handle her own money. When Ellie had heard this, she'd laughed. It was too ridiculous to contemplate. But no one else had laughed.

She'd been told that she was going to have to get letters from those therapists swearing that Ellie was sane and therefore capable of managing her own money. Since Ellie had parted company with one of the therapists in anger, she knew that that letter would never be forthcoming.

Ellie had gasped at this. "This is not the Victorian era!" she'd said. "A man can't do that!" But she'd been told that in a community property state, all the property, in this case, the books, was considered as much his as hers, so, yes, the judge could indeed decide who was more competent to handle the money, she or her ex.

Even now, with her knowledge of what was going to happen, this sanity thing was a sticking point. How did one prove that one was sane?

She had been concentrating on this question so hard that she hadn't noticed that someone had walked up the carpeted stairs and down the hall. When she glanced at the doorway and saw the man leaning against it, she jumped. "Oh!" she said, then, "Sorry. I didn't see you come up."

He was a tall man, in his mid to late sixties, or maybe in his seventies and well preserved. As with many men in California, he was dressed in cleaned-up cowboy gear. Usually this was an affectation, but Ellie had an intuition that this man was real. This man probably spent most of the day on horseback and his favorite animal was, no doubt, the longhorn steer.

"Didn't mean to startle you," he said softly. He was one of those men who inspire jealousy in women because age looked good on him. Those sun creases radiating out from the corners of his eyes probably made him more handsome than he had been when he was a younger man. He wore Levi's, a cream colored cotton shirt with pearl inlaid silver buttons, cowboy boots with deep undercutting, and he held a tan cowboy hat in his hands. "But you were thinking so hard that I could have run a herd of cattle through here and you wouldn't have seen a thing."

She smiled at him. There was something about him that made her feel at ease, as though he were an old friend. "I was just thinking about how to prove that I'm not crazy. Any ideas on how to go about that?"

She'd meant the statement to be taken as a joke, the way she had always coped with serious subjects and intense emotion, but the man didn't smile. Instead, he looked at her with serious eyes. "If you're here to see Mr. Montoya, then I guess this is a court case, and if you're trying to prove you're sane, then you must have money. Nobody cares about the sanity of a poor person. So who's trying to get control of your money?"

For a moment Ellie just looked at him with her mouth hanging open. "Yes," she finally managed to say. "My ex-husband. Will be ex, anyway."

"Makes sense," the man said. "What's he doing? Saying that he's always 'managed' your money and since you're crazy, he has to keep on managing it even after you dump him? And since you're a woman and he's a man, the court is probably listening to him."

Maybe it was the way he said it, maybe it was the horrendous amount of work she'd done in the last three days, or maybe it was just being back into it all again, but Ellie put her hands over her face and burst into tears. Like a knight of old, the man sat down on the bench beside her, pulled out a clean, blue bandana handkerchief, and handed it to her. "I'm sorry," she said, still crying. "I don't usually cry in front of people, but it's all been so awful and no one *believes* me! People think that the courts of America are fair and just and that if someone goes to trial, she'll get a fair shake. And people think that because I've earned so much money that I have *power*. But I have no power because no one *believes* me. They all believe *him*. I don't understand it. Whatever I say, they think is a lie, but whatever he says, they believe. I told them he has a lot of money hidden somewhere, but neither my lawyer, his lawyer, nor the judge believed me. But he said he cowrote my books and they accept that as fact. The man couldn't name three *titles* of my books, much less tell the plots, but they believe that he wrote them with me. Yet I said that if I was sane enough to earn the money, then I was certainly sane enough to know how to put it in a bank, but they said no, that wasn't true. After all, writers are really just glorified liars, aren't they? And now I can't believe I'm saying all these things to someone I've never met!"

Ellie was trying to stop the tears as she wiped at her eyes with the handkerchief. It would be her luck that her ex had hired this man and he would testify against her in court. The first time she went through the divorce, it seemed that every person she'd ever met had been willing to testify against her.

"That's where I've seen you before," the cowboy said, leaning back to look at her.

Ellie sniffed. "What? Where?"

"On the cover of a book. My wife has them all over the house. You're that . . . What's the name? She says it all the time."

It had been years since anyone had recognized her from a book cover. For one thing, Ellie had gained so much weight that she no longer looked like her publicity photo, and for the other, if you don't have a book published for three years, the public forgets you. But now she wasn't fat and she had just had a book come out six weeks ago. It was still in the top five on the *New York Times* Best Sellers list.

She sniffed again. "Which name? Alexandria Farrell or Jordan Neale?"

"That's it!" the man said. "Both those names. My wife loves your books. Really loves them. She says she wants to be the woman in the book. Which one is that?"

"Jordan," Ellie said, her tears drying up.

He nodded toward her notebook beside her. "Don't tell me that you're writing another one?"

"Maybe not a Jordan Neale, but another book, anyway." The way he was looking at her was making Ellie feel much better. For years now she'd felt nothing but pity coming from people, pity because she'd become fat, pity because she wasn't writing, pity because she'd let some man beat her in a court case. "*I* wouldn't have let him win," she'd heard a thousand times. And the truth was that if it had happened to someone else, *Ellie* would have been the one saying that *she* would have fought until she won. But the women who said that hadn't been up against a judge who considered Ellie a liar and insane.

"This is amazing," the man said, then held out his hand to shake hers. "I'm Marcellus Woodward," he said, "but everyone calls me Woody."

She took his hand, warm, dry, brown from the sun. "Ellie Abbott," she said, then caught herself. "Gilmore. It's Gilmore until the divorce, but—"

"Well, Miss Abbott," he said, smiling at her, "I'm very pleased to meet you. You wouldn't want to come home with me, would you?"

She blinked at him. It had been a long time since a man had tried to pick her up.

"No, no," he said, smiling.

He had nice teeth, she thought. In fact, if he weren't thirty years older than she was . . .

"I live up north, on a ranch, and it's Friday, so maybe you'd like to fly up with me and spend the weekend with my wife and me and our little boy? And my brother will be there and about fifty ranch hands." When

Ellie didn't reply to this, he lowered his head and gave her a shy glance through his lashes. "But maybe you'd rather spend the weekend here digging up dirt about your husband."

At that Ellie laughed, *really* laughed. "You are a devil, aren't you?" she said, grinning. "You've seen something you want—a famous writer as a gift for your wife—so you're going after it, aren't you? I would sure hate to take *you* into a courtroom."

Lifting his chin, he grinned back at her. "Ain't lost a case yet," he said. "Here, hand me that notebook of yours."

She did so and he wrote down a few names, then handed the book back to her. The names were all of prominent people in and around Los Angeles. In fact, some of the names made her eyes widen.

"You know any of those people?" he asked.

One of the names was a banker whom she'd known for years. "Yes."

"Then call him or all of them and ask about me. They can probably even fax you a picture of me. I want you to check me out so you don't think I really am the devil."

Ellie looked down at the notebook. In all

the years she'd been married, she'd been absolutely faithful to her husband. She'd never so much as flirted with another man.

Three years ago, it would never have occurred to Ellie to accept an invitation to go away for the weekend, not with friends and certainly not with a stranger. If Ellie wanted to do anything that wasn't related to work and earning more money for Martin to spend, he would start whining that *he* never got to go anywhere, but then *he* wasn't a big-deal celebrity like she was.

"Well?" Woody asked. "You want to go or not?"

When Ellie looked up at him, her heart was pounding in her throat. This was a wild thing for her to do. Accept an invitation from a man she'd met in a hallway?

"Sure. Why not?" she said at last.

Woody smiled, then stood up. He was so tall that Ellie had to lift her chin straight up to look at him. "Meet me at the local airport at four. But I want you to call those people and ask about me so you aren't worried that I'm going to jump on you." He said this with a twinkle in his eye that said that he *wanted* to jump on her, but he'd restrain himself.

He made her laugh—and he made her

feel better than she had in years. "What clothes should I take?" she asked.

The twinkle in his eyes deepened. "Everything that you spend now you won't have to split with him later, so I suggest you buy yourself a whole new wardrobe and the luggage to carry it in. Just make sure you bring something you can ride in."

Ellie's eyes widened in horror. "Ride? As in, on a horse?"

Woody laughed. "We could arrange a steer for you, but I think . . ."

"Very funny," she said. "So, okay, I guess I'll be there." She still couldn't believe that she was doing this.

Woody pulled back his sleeve and looked at his watch, then at the detective's door that was still locked. "I have to go now, but if you see Montoya, tell him I was here and that he can't tell ten minutes from Shinola."

"Gladly," Ellie said, then watched as Woody turned and walked down the hallway, giving her a wave as he descended the stairs.

For a moment, Ellie sat on the bench. As soon as she reaffirmed her list with the detective, she'd—What? Do just what Woody had said and spend the weekend going over all that Martin had done to her?

Suddenly, Ellie was sick of giving her life over to Martin Gilmore. Since the day she'd filed for divorce, he had been her whole life. She'd spent the eight months after the divorce papers had been filed preparing to make a judge believe that she was a good person and not the crazy, neurotic liar Martin portrayed her as. But all she'd done to try to defend herself had failed. Since the divorce, she'd wallowed in such self-pity that her ex ruled her life more than he did when she was married to him.

She looked at the still-locked door of the detective's office, then at the stairs that led to the outside and to the road that led to downtown Los Angeles. Rodeo Drive. She had a lot of complaints about L.A., but the shopping wasn't one of them. Since she'd returned, she opened her handbag only to get her car keys in and out, but now she started rummaging inside. Her credit card holder held cards that she hadn't seen in years: local video stores, a public library card. And her platinum American Express.

Holding the silver card up, she looked at it. It had a pretty much unlimited credit line, and, as Woody had said, the more she spent, the less she'd have to divide with her ex-husband during the divorce. Smiling, Ellie stood up. Forget the detective, she thought. She was going *shopping!*

Nineteen

Smack on four P.M., Ellie drove into the parking lot of the local airport: small but big enough to handle the private jets that landed there. She was quite nervous about what she was planning to do in spite of the fact that she'd called Steven Bird at the bank and checked Woody out. "Very nice man," Steven had said. "I've known him for years." She asked a few questions and wasn't surprised to find out that Woody's "little boy" was just a toddler. She could believe that a man like Woody had a wife young enough to produce a baby just a couple of years ago and that Woody was "active" enough to have produced him.

After Ellie put down the phone, she decided to see what toys she could find for the child. And while she was at it, she might as well buy a gift or two for her hostess. Based on Woody's clothing, Ellie decided to take a chance and drove to a divine store full of Native American art and jewelry.

Five minutes after she pulled into the parking area at the airport, a man walked over to her. "You're Jordan Neale?" he asked.

He was a good-looking man, not flashy, but nice, about thirty, wearing all denim, top and bottom, just as Woody had been, but she could tell that this man's denim was for style, not for work. This man was no cowboy. Accountant, she'd guess. Or maybe even a lawyer. He looked intelligent and educated.

"Sort of," she said as she dismounted from the Range Rover. The step was so high off the ground that most of her women friends complained that they might as well be climbing onto a buckboard. But Ellie loved the car; by experience she knew that it could climb straight up a snow-covered mountain. "Jordan Neale is a character I write about, and my pen name is Alexandria Farrell. But my legal name is plain ol' Ellie Abbott."

The man smiled. "I see. Woody . . ."

Smiling, the man shrugged off the rest of the sentence. "I'm Lew McClelland and I work for Woody. Is your luggage in the back?"

At that question, she looked a bit guilty. "I hope you don't have one of those planes that can hold only about thirty pounds of luggage, because I, well, I did a little shopping."

The truth was that Ellie had made up for three years of buying nothing. When you are forty pounds overweight, mirrors are your enemy. But now, at a hundred and one, she'd loved trying on clothes—and she'd purchased nearly everything that she'd tried on. Thinking of the AmEx bill that she was going to receive made her smile.

"I'm sure we can handle what you have," the man said; then he opened the back of the Range Rover and saw the tightly packed mountain of leather luggage that Ellie had in the back. She'd had to fold the backseats down to hold all of it.

"Some of it is gifts for Woody's wife and son," she said weakly.

With his head cocked to one side, he looked at her. "You bought all of this in one afternoon?"

"Contents *and* luggage," she said with her chin raised defiantly.

"You and Valerie are going to become best friends," he muttered, then pulled the top case off the pile.

As it turned out, Woody wasn't going to be returning with them. She'd been told that something unexpected had come up and he would be arriving at the ranch later. Instead, two of Woody's employees, Lew and another man, were to take Ellie to the ranch.

As she mounted the steps into the plane, she looked back at Lew. "Will you have to fly back to pick up Woody later?"

From the outside, the plane was nice, but it wasn't an especially luxurious aircraft. Maybe she'd overdone it on clothes buying. But then, something that Steven Bird had said—no, maybe it was the *way* he'd said it—had made Ellie think that there was a lot of money around Woody.

At that Lew smiled in a way that said he had a secret. "No. He has another plane." Turning his head, Lew looked across the runway. Sitting there sparkling in the sun, was a big silver jet. Not one of those commercial jets, but a private one, the kind that are featured in *Architectural Digest* and have interiors clad in silk and wrapped in mahogany.

"His?" Ellie asked.

"His," Lew answered.

"I see," she said. "So when we're talking about Woody, are we talking the *m*-word or are we into the *b*-word?"

For a second Lew didn't catch her meaning, then he grinned. "*B*," he said. "With an *s* on the end of it."

"Well," Ellie said, then could think of nothing else to say, so she went up the remaining stairs. Lew was right behind her, and he motioned her toward a seat in the cabin. She was the only passenger. It didn't surprise her to see a box on the seat beside her, and when she opened it, she saw a packed lunch of small sandwiches with different fillings, a tin of smoked oysters, a box of petit fours, another box of Godiva chocolates, and a bottle of champagne. At first, Ellie started to dive right in, but instead, she pushed the food away. She'd found out where boxes of Godiva chocolates led—straight to her thighs.

The two men were checking the dials on the control panel in front, and Ellie leaned her head back against the seat and closed her eyes. A billionaire, she thought. *Billion* with an *s* on the end of it.

"How about this?" she heard, then opened her eyes to see Lew holding out a plate of food toward her. There was grilled chicken, salad, and some steamed vegetables. In his other hand, Lew held a bottle of water.

"Thank you!" Ellie said, then smiled at him. Wonder if he's married? she thought, then wanted to kick herself for thinking such a thing. She was still married. But not for long, she thought as she took the food he offered her.

"We'll be there in about an hour," Lew said, "so as soon as we're aloft, you can move around. There are books and magazines in the back, as well as the head. Anything you need, let us know." Smiling, he took his seat in the pilot's chair beside the other man, who turned, gave Ellie a smile and a salute, then both men gave their attention to the airplane's controls.

They landed before Ellie had time to finish all the articles in three *People* magazines. It was certainly odd to see stories about people and to know what was going to happen to them within the next three years. She knew which marriages were going to break up, who was going to die and who was going to be involved in a scandal. But, to Ellie's mind, by far the worst thing was knowing what was going to happen to Princess Diana in just a few months.

When the plane landed, she was almost grateful to have an excuse to close the magazines. She didn't like knowing the future. *People* magazine had once done an article on her and she was glad it wasn't in the magazines she'd just seen. She didn't want to see herself smiling and thin, but know that for the next few months she was going to go through the worst ordeal of her life.

"Ready?" Lew asked as he opened the door of the plane.

When Ellie looked out, she saw beautiful northern California landscape, rolling land in the foreground, snow topped mountains in the far distance. Between her and the mountains she could see little dots that she was sure were cattle.

"All his, I guess," Ellie said as she reached the bottom step.

"Every thousand acre," Lew answered, obviously enjoying Ellie's sense of awe.

"How far to the house?"

"About forty-five minutes. Valerie doesn't like the planes landing near the house and disturbing Mark."

"Let me guess," Ellie said. "Marcellus Woodward the Second, nicknamed Mark."

Lew cocked his head at her. "You're smart, aren't you?"

"Guilty," Ellie said, laughing. "But I don't think you're just the guy who flies the plane, now are you?"

"Harvard Business School, first in my class," he said, smiling at her. "Piloting is a hobby, and Woody lets me fly this thing but not the jet."

He's flirting with me! Ellie thought, then realized that she was flirting back. How long had it been since any man had looked at her in that way? How long had it been since she'd *wanted* a man to notice her?

As she followed Lew to the waiting Jeep, she thought, Maybe I should write a story about a billionaire who has an assistant who—

She thought about the story all the way to the house.

It was nearly six-thirty by the time they got to the house, and Lew drove past it. It was a long, low house made of logs, and it had been designed to look like a cabin out of the Old West, but it would never fool anyone. For one thing, it had to be the size of a football stadium.

"Wonder which forest was sacrificed for that?" Ellie couldn't prevent herself from muttering.

"One that Woody owns," Lew answered. "And he found oil under the trees, a little gold, and there might be some uranium there too."

"Right," Ellie said, nodding. "Figures."

Lew drove for a few minutes more, turned a corner around a stand of cottonwood trees, and they came into view of a perfect little house. It was small, set under mature trees, and it had the look that only age could give it.

"The original farmhouse?" Ellie asked.

Lew smiled at her perception. "That it is," he said. "But Valerie calls it the summerhouse."

At that Ellie smiled as she thought of

Leslie's summerhouse, and she wondered how the other two women were getting along with their job of changing their lives. If Madison would only hang up on Roger, then her life—

"I'm sorry, I was daydreaming," Ellie said when she realized that Lew had said something to her.

"Hazard of being a writer, I'd guess," he said as he opened his door.

She got out of the car and looked around as Lew began to pull her suitcases out of the back. She thought she should help him unload, but she wanted to see the inside of the house, wanted to explore the ranch; she wanted to . . .

That's it, isn't it? she thought. For the first time in years she wanted to *do* things. With a guilty glance back at Lew as he started pulling the second layer of suitcases out of the car, she stepped onto the porch of the summerhouse. It was wonderful! The porch had to be twenty feet deep, and the furniture on it was big and deep and covered with cushions of red-and-white check. She opened the screen door and went inside.

It was obvious that an interior decorator had done the inside, but it was a person with taste, as the inside had been kept simple and plain. The curtains were plain gingham, and the chairs were overstuffed and comfortable-looking.

"You like it?" Lew said from behind her.

When she turned to look at him, she could see that he was concerned that she would like the place. She had to look away to hide her smile. It had been a long time since a man had cared whether she liked anything or not.

"I love it," she said honestly.

He grinned. "Some people don't like it. They think that with Woody's money he should have a guesthouse more befitting his status."

"Marble Jacuzzis, that sort of thing?" Ellie asked.

"Exactly. One guy was disgusted that the faucets weren't gold."

"I like this. Did Valerie decorate it?"

This time Lew's grin lit up his face. "Actually, my wife did. She'd like to be a decorator, so Valerie gave her this to do."

"Nice," Ellie said as again she looked away. Damn, damn, and double damn! she thought. Wife. "For my taste I think she has a career."

"She's trying for it, but there aren't too many houses to decorate up here."

He was standing in the midst of a sea of suitcases and he seemed to be waiting for something. It couldn't be a tip, could it? she wondered. Then she knew that he wanted permission to leave.

"I'll take care of these," she said. "Go home."

He smiled his thanks. "Dinner's in the house at eight. If you get hungry, the fridge is stocked. And feel free to wander."

"Will I see you at dinner?" she asked as he reached the door.

"No, that's just family and guests. But I'll be around in the morning."

After he left, Ellie looked around and felt a bit lonely. She'd never before done anything as daring as this, accepting an invitation from a stranger, boarding a private plane and flying to an unknown destination.

"New experiences," she said aloud to herself. That's what she'd wanted and that's what she was getting.

She spent a few minutes exploring the rest of the summerhouse. There was only one bedroom, with an adjoining bath, a little kitchen with a refrigerator stocked as though to feed a family of four for a couple of weeks. She went back through the living room, then out to the porch again, for that's what she really liked. The porch went around all four sides of the house, and she walked all the way around it, looking at the mountains, breathing deeply of the clean air.

From the back of the house she could see a barn, so she went back inside, put on a new pair of jeans, a fresh, crisp denim shirt, and new hiking boots—no cowboy boots for her! She also draped an antique concho belt about her hips and slipped on a couple of old silver bracelets.

It was amazing what new clothes could do for a person, she thought as she left the cabin and started for the barn. Of course it didn't hurt to have a "new" body to go with it.

As she reached the barn, her sense of loneliness left her and she thought of what she was doing as an adventure. Whom would she meet? What would she see?

She could hear horses inside the barn but no people. And there didn't seem to be any-one outside either. But then it was nearly seven and she doubted if cowboys waited until eight to have their dinner.

A man was in the barn, bent over a horse's hoof that he held between his thighs, and as the sun filtered through a high window, spotlighting him, Ellie knew that the man and the horse were the most erotic sight she'd ever seen.

He wasn't a tall man, not over about five feet ten, but then she liked shorter men. He was wearing blue jeans and heavy, scuffed boots—not cowboy boots with their pointed toes, but square-toed boots with thick soles. He wore no shirt, and from the golden color of his skin, shirtless was his normal attire. A leather apron, the kind worn by blacksmiths in days of old, covered the front of him.

He was in profile to her, and she started at his feet and looked up: The thick boots led up to strong calves, then to heavy thighs encased in worn, faded denim, the seams straining against the man's muscle. His tight, round buttocks curved up into the small of his back, his waist cinched by a wide black leather belt.

His back was one long muscle that flared out toward arms that were straining against the horse's hoof he was holding between his thighs.

The horse was a heavy horse, a draft horse, and Ellie knew from research for one of her books that this horse was a Frisian. From the knee down the horse had long, silky hair called feathering. The massive muscle of the enormous horse matched the muscle and power that came from the man.

She looked up at the profile of his face: a mouth of sculptured lips, full, abundant. He held two horseshoe nails between his lips. His long nose had slightly flared nostrils. His eyes were lowered as he looked down at the hoof, and their lashes were as thick and as black as butterfly wings. A high forehead, slightly wrinkled in concentration, was beneath short, deep dark black hair.

She stood there paralyzed as she looked at this scene. She could hear nothing else, see nothing else. This man was all her senses could comprehend. She was several feet away from him, but she was so attuned to him that she could smell his skin, warm from the sun, fragrant from the hay, sweaty from his work.

Slowly, oh, so exquisitely slowly, the man turned his head to look at her. He blinked, and since everything in her body seemed to have stopped, she could sense the move-

ment of air that those thick, lush lashes
caused.

When he turned and saw her, when his
eyes made contact with hers, Ellie drew in
her breath and held it. His eyes were as dark
as his hair and as intense as an electrical
shock.

As he looked at her, time stood still. Her
body ceased to function. She didn't
breathe, didn't think. It was as though those
eyes had frozen her where she stood.

Yet she could feel herself moving toward
him. It wasn't as though she were walking.
It was as though the man's eyes had fas-
tened onto her soul, onto what made her
who she was, and he was pulling her to him
by some magic power, by some unseen,
mystical, hypnotic power.

She wasn't sure how it happened, but
she was closer to him. Slowly, as though in
a slow-motion film, with the only sound in
her ears that of her heart and her blood
throbbing through her veins, he stood up,
the horse's hoof sliding down between his
thighs. Ellie blinked; she could *feel* the
horse's foot's progress as it moved down-
ward between his legs: down his thighs,
muscles thick and taunt, past calves

rounded and hard, to those heavy boots with their thick, hard soles.

Slowly, his eyes never breaking contact with hers, he removed the nails from between his lips. She was close enough now that she could see those lips, see the tiny lines in them, see the lower lip curved, so round, so succulent, a lip that called to her to touch it with her own.

With his lips parted, he touched the tip of his tongue to the center of his lower lip, and at the sight of that pink, moist tip, Ellie felt her knees weaken.

The man reached out a hand to steady her, and she knew that if his skin touched hers, all would be lost.

But in that next second, the huge, wide back doors of the barn were flung open, and the room suddenly filled with light and noise as men and animals entered what had been such a very private, intimate place.

The spell was broken, and Ellie shook her head to clear it. She was standing inches from a man she'd never seen before in her life, and, judging from the angle of his head, he had been about to kiss her.

Quickly, she turned to the left and saw three men standing there, horses behind them, and they were looking at the two of them in open curiosity.

"Horse," she said. "He was showing me how to shoe a horse."

The smirks the men's faces wore were identical.

Before she could say another word and definitely before she could look at the man again, she turned and ran out of the barn with the speed, if not the grace, of an Italian greyhound. And she only stopped running when she was back in her guesthouse and had shut and locked all the doors, then drawn the curtains to keep out even the daylight.

When she was at last safe, she sat down on a chair, grabbed the notebook and pen that was never far from her side, and like the writer she was, she wrote down everything she'd just felt and seen. Who knew when she could use this scene in a book?

Twenty

❧

By the time Ellie went into the house for dinner, she was vibrating too much to think about anything but The Man. Who was he? What had made her react as she had? For one of her books she'd done some research on the occult, and a couple of the psychics she'd interviewed had blamed most everything on past lives. So had she known this man in a past life?

Was there a story in that?

Ellie's mind wasn't on dressing, but she had a lot of new things to wear, so that wasn't a problem. She put on a cute little navy blue knit pantsuit that had cost more than she'd spent for clothes in the last three years, some tiny gold earrings set with lapis lazuli, and sauntered over to the big house at a few minutes before eight.

For all that she was thinking of little else except Him, she was swept away by Valerie. She was tall, beautiful, and from Texas. Was more needed to describe her?

What was it about Texas that produced women who seemed to have no fears, no doubts, no hesitations? Had a Texas woman ever met a stranger? Were shy women somehow detected at birth and sent to other states?

"There you are," Valerie said, swooping down from an opentread staircase that must have been twenty-feet tall. She wore black silk trousers over her long, long slim legs. Draped around the top of her was some hand-woven concoction that flowed as she moved. She had reddish blonde hair that fell down her back in big waves. Dazzling green eyes smiled at Ellie from under sooty black lashes. Valerie Woodward was like a light with a two-hundred-watt bulb in its socket.

"Wish I were Madison," Ellie muttered under her breath as she smiled up at her hostess. Madison was on a level with this beautiful creature, but Ellie felt like slinking out the back door.

But Valerie wasn't about to let anyone

she had her eye on escape. She took Ellie's arm, tucked it under her own, and led Ellie toward what she assumed was the dining room.

"I couldn't believe it when Woody said that he'd met Alexandria Farrell. You just don't know how much I love your books. All my friends read them. I do hope that you don't mind if I asked a few people to meet you."

At that announcement, Ellie turned pale. What was "a few people" to someone from Texas?

As Valerie walked her toward the door, it opened as though by magic, and Ellie saw a room with a table that could seat at least fifty people. And to Ellie's eye, most of northern California was inside the room. While Ellie'd been shopping all day, Valerie had been putting together a little impromptu party the size of a state banquet.

Once Ellie put her foot over the threshold, her life was no longer her own. Instantly, she was surrounded by women holding out books to be autographed and telling her how much they loved her stories. She didn't get to eat much at dinner because, one by one, every person at the table asked her

THE question: Where do you get your ideas? It was what she was always asked wherever she went, and she tried to be as honest as she could be.

But of course she held back the truth. She couldn't very well say that today she'd walked into a barn and seen some ranch hand in a leather apron, with nails sticking out of his mouth, and she'd almost torn his clothes off. And even if she never saw the man again, she was sure that this scene, which she had recorded on paper in its entirety, would someday be in one of her books.

Since she was the guest of honor, the people seated on either side of her changed with each new course of food that was served. Ellie had to hand it to Valerie, she might live in the middle of nowhere on a ranch, surrounded mostly by cows, but she did know how to live. The plates were French, the glassware Italian, the silver was English. But the food was American and plentiful.

Not that Ellie got to eat much before the next person sat down and said, "I've always wanted to ask a writer, Where do you get your ideas?"

While Ellie was answering this question for the fourth time, she glanced down the long, narrow dining table toward Valerie. Woody was sitting at the head, Valerie to his right. She hadn't put herself at the opposite end of the table but beside her husband.

While Ellie answered, she kept her eyes on Valerie and Woody, as Ellie loved trying to size up people to see what was really going on with them. She's mad about him, was the conclusion Ellie drew by the time she was on her sixth telling of where she got her ideas. When she'd first seen that Valerie was much younger than Woody, she'd assumed that he'd been married for his money. And Lew's crack about Valerie's shopping had solidified the idea in Ellie's head. But now she could see that it wasn't true. Unless Valerie was the world's greatest actress, she was madly in love with her husband.

Somehow, the sight of the two of them together, Valerie constantly touching Woody's hand and the way Woody kept his head turned toward his wife's, made Ellie feel very lonely. It wasn't fair that a man could become a mega-success and still find

someone to love him. But if a woman became successful . . .

Ellie didn't want to think of what had happened in her own marriage. She didn't want
to yet again go over everything and ask herself what she could have done to make it up
to Martin for her success. How could she
have kept him from being jealous?

The dinner seemed to take hours, and
Ellie had to stop herself from looking at her
watch (new, set with turquoise) every ten
minutes.

Finally, at nine-thirty, it was over and
everyone was invited to go outside for
drinks and moonlight swimming in a heated
pool.

"I do hope you brought a suit," Valerie
said as she came up behind Ellie. "Lew said
that you did some shopping."

"Yes," Ellie said, smiling. "And I brought
some gifts for your son."

At the mention of the child, Valerie's face
melted into a look of love that Ellie knew
couldn't be faked.

Valerie leaned closer and said softly,
"Tomorrow you and I'll get together and
talk. I had to invite all these people or they
never would have forgiven me. But tomor-

row it'll just be family and you can play with my son."

Valerie said this last sentence as though she were bestowing the greatest honor in the world on Ellie.

It was Ellie's turn to melt, because Valerie was talking about family, that thing that everyone wanted: a warm, loving group of people to be with, to live with, to share with. "I'd love that," Ellie said sincerely.

"Good!" Valerie said; then she greeted four people who had drinks and little platters of munchies in their hands. "Yes, I'm just coming," she called to someone else. "Leave any time you want," she whispered to Ellie. "Your performance is over." Then Valerie went toward the big French doors that Ellie assumed led to the pool, leaving Ellie alone with her reprieve.

Yet, for a moment, Ellie hesitated. A couple of people urged her to get some food and join them, but instead, Ellie stood where she was, not moving. She could follow Valerie and ask her who the blacksmith was in the barn. Was he like Lew, a Harvard man who happened to like to fly planes?

Or was he an itinerant farrier who had three wives in different places around the state? Did Valerie and Woody have masses of trouble with all the women visiting them and getting a serious case of the hots over the man? Was he one of those cowboy gigolos who made sure all the women guests had a great time?

Suddenly Ellie realized that every idea she'd come up with was *bad.* Was it Leslie or Madison who had said that not all men are bad? It was Madison. She'd said that Thomas had once been in the world and he was a very good man.

"Come join us," said someone as he looked back at Ellie. "Moonlight and warm water. What else do you want?" the man asked, and his eyes issued an invitation.

Ellie had to stop herself from saying, "Privacy." She was Alexandria Farrell the writer now, not Ellie Abbott, so she had to be on her best behavior. She smiled at the man and made a little motion with her hand as though to say that she wanted to go with him but she had prior commitments.

With a sigh and a shrug, he went through the doors onto the artfully lit patio.

And Ellie ran out the side door that she knew led to her dear little guesthouse, which right now seemed to be a haven of peace and refuge.

Once she was alone and away from the others, Ellie felt relieved, but she also had the feeling that something was going to happen. She was jittery inside, expectant. For a while she stood on the porch and looked out at the night. She could hear music from the house, and she was glad that she wasn't there with the crowd.

She walked all the way around the porch, straining her eyes to see into the darkness. Where was he? she wondered. Why hadn't he come to her?

After about thirty minutes had passed and the high mountain air grew cold, she rubbed her arms and went inside the house. The lights were soft and the furnishings inviting. She liked the little house.

For a while she tried to write in her journal, but she couldn't focus her mind. She was waiting for something.

"Or someone," she said, annoyed with herself. She was nearly forty years old, and—Smiling, she thought that she still had three more years before that birthday came, but if she was zapped forward as quickly as she'd been sent back . . .

Forty, she thought. She shouldn't be pacing the room like a caged tigress. She should be . . . What? Taking crochet lessons?

At eleven she took a shower and told herself to calm down, that she was acting like a teenager, and that she was married and past the age to be excited about anything except recipes and her approaching grandchildren—which she wasn't going to have because she'd never had any children.

By the time she got out of the shower, she was calmer. And she was back to being the fatalist that her therapist Jeanne would recognize. So she'd had a few moments with a guy in a barn. So a good-looking assistant to a billionaire had flirted with her. And a man at a party had issued an invitation that she'd chosen to take very personally . . .

She got into bed, tried to read one of the books she'd bought that day, but she couldn't. Instead, she turned off the light and closed her eyes.

To her disbelief, she felt sleepy, but a sound outside made her sit up instantly. It wasn't a quiet sound, but loud. One. Two. Three. Four. Four thumps on the wooden floor of the porch.

Ellie opened her eyes so wide that they hurt. A horse was walking very slowly around the deep porch that ran all the way around her little house. She could hear each hoof beat, hear the click of the shoes.

Ellie didn't think about what she was doing. If she'd been asked, she would have said that she was past the age of leaving the house without having eye makeup on, not with her pale lashes, but now she didn't give a thought to what she looked like. Or to the fact that all she had on was a thin cotton nightgown.

She tossed off the down duvet and took off running the instant her bare feet hit the floor.

There were no lights on on the outside of the little house, and there had been when she'd returned from the party. But now everything was dark, with only the lights from the big house barely visible through the trees.

At first she didn't see him. And for a horrible instant, she thought that maybe she'd imagined the sound of the horse. In her bare feet, she ran around the porch to the back of the house.

And there he was. The moonlight was behind him, so she saw him as a silhouette more than as substance. He was dressed in black on a black horse and it was dark.

But Ellie knew it was Him. She felt it.

The saddle leather creaked, and she saw the flash of something white, a button maybe, and she knew that he was putting his arm down for her.

She didn't hesitate. She didn't have a single thought of not going with him. Nor did she think of talking to him, of asking his name, about his life, where he went to school, nothing. No, right now all that she felt was . . . just that, feeling.

She took his hand, big, warm, calloused, the kind of hand she loved, the hand of a *useful* man, and vaulted onto the horse behind him. Her narrow nightgown wasn't made for horse riding. It rode up until it barely covered her bottom. Her legs were as bare as if she'd been wearing a high-cut bikini.

It was as though she knew what to do. Her arms slid around the back of him, clasping over his chest, and for a moment she put her head down on his back and breathed in the clean scent of him. He'd been working. He wasn't dirty sweaty, just very male sweaty, that kind of smell that made her know he was male and she was female.

His body moved as he rode, and she felt her breasts against his back. How long had it been since she'd felt anything like this? Since she was little more than a kid, she'd been with one man, her husband. When had her marriage become sexless? When had it become more about control and one-up-manship than about sharing? Sharing anything?

At first he rode sedately, as though he were making the horse tiptoe across the ranch. Ellie hadn't explored the place much, but in the moonlight she could see long, low buildings, and she imagined that there were people sleeping inside the buildings. The idea that the world was asleep and that they were the only ones awake appealed to her.

After a few minutes, she relaxed her grip around his chest and lifted her head from his back. Then she held her breath as he reached back and ran his hand over her bare thigh, stroking it, his hand roaming as far as he could reach up her bare buttocks. The sensation Ellie felt nearly made her fall off the horse.

She heard what could have been a chuckle from him; then he said softly, "Hold on tight." These were the first words spoken between them. She liked his voice. It was a whisper, but she liked the deepness of it.

In the next moment he turned the horse sharply and they were on a trail. There were fewer trees here and no buildings, so she could look around him and see the open trail in front of them. But she only had a glimpse because the next moment he snapped the reins, moved his legs backward, and the horse took off running at a speed that made Ellie dizzy.

She clasped the man hard, buried her face in his warm back, and held on with all her might.

He raced the horse for several minutes; then there was another turn and they slowed down. This time they started climbing. She could feel and hear the horse's hooves on stone. A couple of times she heard loose rock falling.

But even when they seemed to be going straight up and Ellie was holding on so tightly that she feared that she was cutting off his circulation, she was never, for even one second, afraid. She wasn't afraid that he didn't know how to handle the horse, nor was she afraid of where he was taking her.

After a while the ground flattened out, and Ellie loosened her hold on him. He guided the horse so it walked slowly and carefully, so she wasn't surprised when she lifted her head and saw that they were on a trail that didn't look to be as wide as the horse was.

She clung to him, but still she felt no fear. It was as though, as long as she touched him, she was safe. If he'd set her to the ground on this rocky, narrow trail in the dead of night, she would have been terrified.

He walked the horse for some distance; then he halted and sat still. Ellie didn't want to lift her head from his back. She had her cheek in the deep crevice of his backbone and she liked it there. Right now she felt as though she could stay there forever.

But she could feel that he was waiting for

something, so, slowly, she turned her head and looked to her right.

The view below was breathtaking. All the ranch was laid out below them. The big ranch house was in the center, and from this distance the lights were beautiful. She could even see the way the light sparkled on the swimming pool. And in the cool, quiet night, she could hear the sound of laughter and music floating up to them.

But for all that she could see and hear people, she felt removed from them. She wasn't part of them. She was someone from another time and place as she sat on the big horse wearing only a thin bit of cotton over her body, and holding on to this man she didn't know.

Surreptitiously, she stole a glance up at him.

He was looking at her. He was looking down at her in a way that made the inside of her feel shaky, and she knew that if he kissed her, she'd be lost to him. She'd have no more willpower than a teenage boy in the backseat of a car.

But he didn't kiss her. Instead, he smiled at her. Not a big, wide grin, but just a little smile, as though to say, "Thanks for coming with me."

Nor did he speak. Instead, he turned back around, clicked to the horse, and started them down the side of the hill. Ellie settled into her place against his back and watched as the ranch buildings came closer and closer into view.

The trip down took much longer than the trip up. No more wild running along the road. It was as though he didn't ever want this night or this ride to end.

But it did end. When he halted the horse, Ellie looked up to see that they were right where he'd picked her up, at the back of the little guesthouse.

Part of her wanted to invite him inside with her. Part of her wanted to spend the rest of the night in bed with him.

But another part wanted just what she'd had: and no words.

Smiling to herself, she threw her leg over the saddle and held on to his arm as he lowered her to the ground. As she walked up the steps to the porch, she knew that the moonlight was behind her and that, probably, her nightgown was as transparent as a spider web, and the thought made her heart beat faster.

Once she was on the porch, she turned back to him, but he was already turning away.

Smiling into the darkness, she turned and went inside the house.

Twenty-one

The next morning Ellie awoke feeling as though there was hope for the future. Her therapist had told her that all depression was really just a lack of hope. "Hope goes and everything else slides down the drain," Jeanne had said.

What was it about attention from a man that could make a woman decide that life wasn't so bad after all? When Ellie was twenty-one, she'd known that success was what was important in life. She'd left her hometown and run off to big, bad New York City in search of fame and fortune.

But what had happened? The first man to really go after her had made her forget all her dreams. She'd given up all she'd wanted in an attempt to try to make Martin a success. But in the end, she couldn't do it. She couldn't force him to go after what he said he wanted. She couldn't prevent him from sabotaging every effort she made to make him a success.

But when Ellie had been given a second chance at success, she'd taken it. She'd walked away from the opportunities given to her that could have made her career as an artist, but she wasn't going to close the door the second time. Instead, when Daria had called and said they wanted to publish all her books and send her heaps of money, Ellie had said, "What do you want me to do to help?"

In the flurry of excitement that followed, Ellie had tried to make Martin a part of her success, but he'd refused to participate. "If a person does nothing, he can't take the blame if there's a failure," Jeanne had said. "But he can't take credit for the success either," Ellie had shot back at her. "Except that he *did*!"

But in the end, all that success hadn't changed Ellie. She was still that same starry-eyed girl who could walk away from possible success to follow a man.

"You're an artist," Jeanne had said. "A true creator. Whether it's on canvas with paint or done on a computer, you're an artist."

At that Ellie had smiled.

"And, above all else, you're a romantic," Jeanne said. "You need romance. Art *is* romance to you. You couldn't care less about the money. *You* want the romance."

So now, stretching as she got out of bed, Ellie felt better than she had in years. And maybe better than she had in years and years. Last night had been the most romantic encounter she'd ever had in her life.

Yesterday she'd been dying to know who the man was, but not today. Today she thought that if she never saw him again, she'd be all right. In fact, maybe she didn't want to see him again. Maybe she wanted to crystallize last night in her head and keep it there forever, the way a photograph freezes time.

She took her time dressing in jeans and a cotton shirt with silver buttons, nothing flashy, but she knew that Valerie would know to the penny how much everything she wore cost. She pulled out the gifts for Mark but decided not to take them to the house. For all she knew, most of last night's guests were still in the house—and all awaiting her.

Ellie forced herself to keep her eyes straight ahead as she walked toward the big house. She wasn't going to start rubbernecking to search for Mr. Midnight Cowboy.

At the house she started to knock on the door, but it was ajar, so she went inside. Right away she thought that it was a better house during the day than at night. Thanks to some lighting designer, at night the house looked like a theater set. This morning it just looked like a nice country ranch house. Astonishingly *big* ranch house, but still a home.

As though she'd been beeped, Valerie appeared. She was wearing jeans that had to have been made for her—and if she gained an ounce, she wasn't going to be able to get into them. It was disgusting to see that she looked better in daylight, in her rich cowgirl clothes, than she did at night in her designer duds.

"We've all been waiting for you," Valerie said.

Ellie controlled her urge to groan. Was the entire weekend going to be like this?

"I promise that this is the last one," Valerie said, as though reading Ellie's mind. "All the ranch hands are here, and they have books for you to sign. Do this one last time, then you're free. I promise."

Ellie wanted to say something funny, something to make Valerie laugh. In other circumstances, she could have, but not after the mention of "ranch hands." Was *he* going to be there?

She was working hard to control the loud pounding of her heart, but she hoped that Valerie couldn't hear it. "I'm sure it'll be fine," she mumbled, then wanted to kick herself for her flat, boring repartee. She wasn't going to impress anyone as a sparkling wit this weekend, that was for sure.

Valerie had set up a stack of Ellie's latest books on a little table near a set of doors leading out to the patio. Standing just inside the door, his hat in his hands, was a cowboy. He smiled shyly when he saw Ellie. Years before, in Oklahoma, a couple of cowboys had come to her autographing. One asked her to sign a book for his wife, while the other had just stood there and stared at Ellie without blinking. The first man asked his friend if he wanted to buy a book. "No, I wanta buy *her*," the man had said with feeling.

Thinking about that time, Ellie smiled back at this man, then took her place at the table.

It was a big ranch, and there were a lot of men and women who worked on it. Valerie seemed to have bought out an entire printing of Ellie's latest book, so every employee had at least three and as many as ten books they wanted autographed by Ellie. After an hour, she was hungry, thirsty, and bored.

While Ellie had been signing, Valerie had had a buffet set up against one wall, and the room was filling up with hands and managers, real cowboys with manure on their boots (and on Valerie's Oriental carpet) and fake cowboys with degrees from back east. Everyone had his or her hands full of big platters of food—and the smell was making Ellie's mouth water.

"Last man comin' up," she heard the unmistakable sound of Woody's voice from behind her.

She was bent over a book she was signing for a young woman who had a long list of relatives she wanted to give books to, and Ellie smiled when she heard Woody's voice. She hadn't spoken to him since she'd seen him outside the detective's office.

"This one is the most worthless," Woody said in a teasing voice.

Ellie could hear the love in the man's voice, so she smiled wider. At last, she was going to get to meet Woody's son. Closing the book, Ellie handed it to the woman, who said thanks, then dropped all of the hardbacks into a big shopping bag with the name Neiman Marcus scrawled across it.

Turning, Ellie expected to see a little boy, so her eyes were down. What she saw was a pair of black, thick-soled boots. And, instantly, she knew who was standing in front of her.

"I want you to meet my little brother," Woody said above Ellie's head. "He's been around here, but he's kinda shy, hates parties, so we didn't see him last night."

Shy? Ellie thought. And exactly what is your definition of shy? she wanted to ask. Slowly, Ellie looked up, her eyes moving up the man's body, a body that she knew rather well after last night. Her legs had straddled his hips for a couple of hours. Her arms had hugged his chest, her hands now and then moving over most of his upper body. She'd spent so much time with her head on his back that she could have identified that curve blindfolded.

He was smiling at her. He was smiling in that infuriating way that men do when they know something that you don't. All along he'd known that he was the owner's brother, but she hadn't. She'd thought he was a blacksmith. But he'd always known who *she* was.

There are some advantages to age, Ellie thought. For one thing, you don't have to worry about reputation. And you don't have to worry about misconduct getting back to your mother.

What would her heroine, Jordan Neale, do in this situation? she wondered. That is, if Jordan weren't happily married to Max?

A scene from the movie *To Catch a Thief* came to her mind. Grace Kelly had sexily slipped an arm around Cary Grant's neck and . . .

Smiling as sweetly as she could, trying to let no one know that she was affected in any way by this man, Ellie stood up from the chair. Then, with as much poise as she could muster, she stood on tiptoe and slipped her hand around the neck of Woody's brother and kissed him. It wasn't a passionate kiss with frantic embracing, but a nice, long kiss that had a great deal of heat in it.

He kept his arms to his side, and when she pulled away from him, he was looking at her in amusement. And interest. Oh, yes. He was looking at her with *lots* of interest.

Stepping back, Ellie turned her head to look at Woody. He was standing there with his mouth open in shock. Behind him, even Valerie was staring with wide eyes. In fact, when Ellie looked around, she saw that the whole room had come to a standstill. Forks were paused on the way to mouths. One man was suspended in midair, his fanny six inches above a chair.

It was one of the ranch hands who broke the spell cast on the group. He was an older man, with the look that he'd been born in a saddle. He had a belly that hung down over his belt buckle, and when he stepped forward, he had that bowlegged walk of a true cowboy.

He stopped on the other side of Woody's

brother. "I'm next," he said, then bent over, puckered up, and closed his eyes.

It was what was needed to break the tension in the room, and everyone exploded with laughter. Laughing, the people began slapping Woody's brother on the back—she still didn't know his name—then they slapped Ellie's back too. At a couple of hard slaps, her head bent so far forward that she touched the man's chest.

As for him, he just stood there, smiling at all the jests that were being made at his expense, saying nothing, just watching Ellie.

"And here I was feeling sorry for you being out there all alone," Valerie said so only Ellie heard her. "Heavens! but I thought you were *bored*."

The man put out his hand and said loudly over the ruckus around them, "Jessie Woodward. Nice to meet you."

Laughing, Ellie took his hand in hers. All the tension had left the room. The people were no longer tiptoeing about in respect for "the writer," but were now enjoying a morning of free time, free food, and the companionship of people who'd been together for a long time.

"Go on," Woody said to his brother. "You two get out of here."

For Ellie, she couldn't speak because she'd just realized what she'd been told. Heaven help her, but the man's name was *Jessie*!

Twenty-two

Once they were outside, away from the others, alone, "awkward" didn't begin to describe how she felt. What was she supposed to say, "So how's your horse this morning?"?

A couple of times she glanced up at him and gave him a weak little smile, but she really didn't know what to say. They had experienced together . . . What? Lust? Something more?

For all that Ellie had written some sexy little books and in the last couple of days done some—for her—wild things, underneath it all, she was a woman who didn't fool around.

As they approached the door to the summerhouse, Ellie could feel her feet becoming heavy. What was he expecting of her now? A wild morning in bed together? Last night, in the moonlight, she could have done that. She would probably have regretted it, but she might have done it. But now it was daylight and she was with a man she'd exchanged but a few words with. She'd had her hands all over his body, but she'd not *talked* to him.

But Jessie solved everything.

He stepped up onto the porch and held the door open for her, ignoring the fact that Ellie stood rooted where she was, still several feet away from the stairs. "I bet you're hungry," Jessie said. "I heard that last night Valerie had you pinned to a table autographing, then you spent dinner answering questions, and now this morning all you've done is write. How about if I make you an omelet the size of that state Valerie loves so much?"

Ellie opened her mouth to protest that she wasn't hungry. For the last three years she'd been fat, and she'd learned that fat girls shouldn't eat in public. Even in restaurants they can receive looks of disgust from other women. But now she was no longer fat, so it was okay to eat truckloads. When her stomach let out a growl, Ellie looked up at Jessie with wide eyes. Then they both laughed and the tension between them was gone.

"Come on," he said, then went inside the house, leaving Ellie to follow on her own.

When she entered the little kitchen, he was already pulling dishes out of the cabinets and ingredients out of the refrigerator. "You seem familiar with this house," she said, making an attempt at conversation. Ellie thought he was a good-looking man, with the kind of looks that appealed to her. But Daria wouldn't like him, though. But then Daria said that Mel Gibson "did nothing" for her.

Ellie climbed onto a stool on the other side of the bar that separated the kitchen from the living room.

In what seemed like seconds, Jessie placed a tall glass of tomato juice in front of her. There was a stalk of celery in it and celery seeds floating on top.

"Alcohol?" she asked.

"Yeah," Jessie said as he gave her a one-sided smirk, then wiggled his eyebrows. "To loosen you up for later."

Since he was saying what she feared, as

though he were reading her mind, she laughed.

Turning his back to her, he pulled out cookware, then more things from the refrigerator, and began to move about as though he knew what he was doing. "So what do you want to know?" Jessie asked, his back to her.

The drink was strong, made with Snappy Tom, so it was hot, just the way she liked it. She was so empty of food that just one sip began to relax her.

"Know about what?" she asked.

Jessie turned his head just enough to give her a raised-eyebrow look that said she knew very well what he was talking about.

Ellie took another drink. "Everything about everybody," she said. "You first."

"Not much to tell about me," Jessie said. "My brother's the one. He—"

"No!" Ellie said in warning. "*You.*"

She couldn't see his face but she felt his smile.

"Okay, I'm forty-two. I've been married once, but it didn't work out. I was gone too much and she got lonesome, so she figured out how to get rid of the blues. Men, mostly. No kids, so we divorced."

He put a bowl full of tortilla chips in front of her and some red-hot salsa.

"What else?" she asked as he put scallions down on a cutting board and began to chop them. Judging from the way he handled the knife, he'd done this before.

"Not much. I've worked for my brother for a number of years now. Ten? Maybe it's only eight; I don't remember."

"What do you do?"

"Manage this place, for one thing."

She could tell that he didn't want to talk about himself, and for her, that was a point in his favor. Martin was a nonstop talker. Sometimes Ellie hid inside her clothes closet behind her long skirts so he couldn't find her, just so she could have a few minutes of silence.

"Okay," she said, deciding to let him off the hook. "What about Valerie and Woody?"

Ellie could see Jessie visibly relax when the questions stopped being about him.

"Okay," Jessie said, knife poised above the scallions. "Where do I start? Valerie was chosen for her beauty and her fertility. Woody was married for thirty years to a very nice woman, but they had no kids, so Woody spent his time making money.

Everything he touches seems to turn to money. If Woody stuck a pitchfork in the ground, he'd hit a gold mine."

Ellie was pretending that she was interested in the tortilla chip in her hand, but she was listening very hard to the *way* Jessie said this. She was glad that, as hard as she listened, she could detect no sound of jealousy about his brother's good fortune.

When Ellie said nothing, Jessie continued. "Unexpectedly, she fell ill and died over the course of about six weeks, and suddenly, Woody was alone. Truthfully, he'd had no experience with women."

Jessie put the scallions in a skillet, then began to chop tomatoes and green peppers. "And that's when Valerie showed up. She was from Texas, graduated from some expensive private college, and not married. Experienced, but unmarried."

At that Jessie looked up at Ellie, maybe to see how she was going to respond to that statement. But Ellie didn't say anything. She was listening too hard to want to interrupt.

"They met through one of those chance-in-a-million things. Her brother was in the hospital with a broken leg at the time that

Woody's wife was in the hospital—one of those small, private hospitals where 'only the best' is a norm, so Valerie didn't have to check to see that Woody was rich. She was pregnant by my brother almost before they closed the coffin on his wife."

Ellie wasn't going to fall for his poor-little-rich-man-seduced-by-the-younger-woman story. It was her feeling that, no matter how they'd met, or how much money was involved, Valerie and Woody were a love match. She kept her eyes on a chip as she spoke. "So I guess your big brother used to spend lots of time with you when his first wife was alive, but now he spends all his time with his beautiful young wife and his new son."

When Jessie was silent, she looked at him, and for a moment, she thought that he was going to be furious—and Ellie knew that if he was angry, she'd back down. Why, oh, why couldn't she keep her big mouth shut?

But Jessie looked at her in astonishment; then he roared with laughter. "You really call the shots as you see them, don't you?" he said. "You're the only person who hasn't believed my story about Valerie being a piranha and after my brother's money."

She didn't share his laughter. "Why would you want anyone to think that?" she asked.

He gave her a one-sided grin. "Every time I tell that story to a female, she wants to prove to me that *she* isn't a gold digger, so she falls right into my arms."

Ellie knew that she was supposed to laugh at what he'd just said, but she didn't. Instead, she was annoyed, and, when she thought about what he'd said, she was angry. He was using a line on her that he admitted to using on *all* women.

He was standing there, looking at her, waiting for her reply, but she couldn't think of what to say.

As luck would have it, the phone rang and saved her from having to answer. But when she picked it up, a male voice asked for Jessie. Obviously, everyone on the ranch knew where he was.

Wiping his hands on a towel, he walked around the bar, then took the phone from her and listened for quite a while. And it was easy to see from the look on his face that something bad had happened. Her first thought was that Woody had had a heart attack.

"I'll be right there," Jessie said softly, then put down the receiver. "I have to go," he said, and started for the door. "I'm sorry about breakfast and sorry about . . ." He trailed off.

"What is it?" she asked, her hand going to her mouth in fear. "Is it Woody?"

Jessie paused at the door. "No. One of the men committed suicide last night and he was just found."

At the word "suicide," Ellie halted. In the last three years that action had haunted her, followed her about.

Reaching out, Jessie put his hand on her cheek and smiled at her. "Look, you and I need to talk. There's something between us, and . . ." He didn't seem to understand it any more than she did. "After I take care of this with Lew, I'll come back and we'll spend some time together." With that, he opened the door and left the little house.

For a moment Ellie just stood there in a daze. As long as he didn't touch her, she was all right. But when he touched her, she didn't seem able to think straight. And when he—

"Lew!" she said out loud; then the next second she was out the door and running to catch up with Jessie. "Lew McClelland?" she asked him. "The man who flew me here? *He* committed *suicide*?"

"Yeah," Jessie said as he walked quickly. "Sorry you met him. Look, you're a guest, so why don't you go back—"

"*Why* did he kill himself?" Ellie asked. "He was a nice man. I liked him a lot."

At that Jessie gave her a sharp look, but he didn't slow his walking. "Lew was depressed, deeply depressed. I knew it and some other people did, but we couldn't do anything about it. Now it's too late."

In trying to keep up with him, Ellie was getting out of breath, and when she tripped over a rock, she caught herself with his arm.

Jessie steadied her, then gave a bit of a frown. "I think you should go back to the summerhouse. In fact, I think maybe this isn't a good time for a visit."

Ellie acted as though she hadn't heard him. "What were you told on the phone?" she asked.

For a moment Jessie blinked at her. "Is this writer curiosity or real interest?"

Talk about not pulling punches, she

thought, but didn't say that. "I liked him," she said, with her mouth set in a firm line. She wasn't going to give up.

"All right," Jessie said with a sigh. "His wife, Sharon, found him this morning. She says that last night they had a big fight. She's been wanting to leave the ranch for months now. She wants to move back east so she can have a career. But Lew refused to leave, so last night she asked him for a divorce. It looks like Lew shot himself in despair."

For a moment Ellie held on to Jessie's arm and looked up into his dark eyes. But she wasn't seeing him. Instead, she was seeing that nice man who'd met her at the airport. "Lew wasn't that much in love with his wife because he was flirting with me," Ellie said softly. "And, anyway, he was proud of her having a career. It was in the way he grinned when he told me that his wife had decorated the summerhouse."

Jessie frowned. "Just because a man flirts with one woman—" he began, then cut himself off. For a moment he was silent as a couple of men rode past them. From the looks on their faces, they'd learned about Lew.

When they were alone again, Jessie bent down closer to her and lowered his voice. "I know quite a bit more about this than others do. Truthfully, it's not coming as a great shock to me. Sharon's been confiding in me for a long time. There were two men inside Lew. He was good at his job, but in a personal way, he wasn't an easy man to live with. Sharon gave up a lot for him."

That overused phrase of "pushing your buttons" came into play. "Suicide," "depression," "gave up a lot," and, above all else, "for me" were phrases that pushed so many buttons in Ellie's head that she was close to exploding.

"Let me guess," Ellie said through her teeth. "His wife says that she gave up a lucrative career to move out here to the middle of nowhere to be with him. She lives her life *for him*."

Jessie had dropped her arm and was looking at her as though she were about to lose her mind, but Ellie couldn't seem to stop.

"Tell me," Ellie said, venom in her voice. "Did the woman act as though she were reluctant to tell you about how miserable her life was? Did she say that all she wanted was a husband, but Lew was more interested in money than he was in her? Did she hint that Lew might be . . . well, *insane*?"

Jessie stared at her in shock, and his horrified look made Ellie come back to herself.

"Sorry," she said, starting to back away from him. "I'm sure this isn't the truth. I'm sure she's a nice woman and I'm just talking from my own personal experience, but—"

Jessie was still looking at her as though she had escaped from the local loony bin. Ellie glanced at her watch. "I have to go. I have to . . . change clothes," she said, searching for some reason to leave instead of just turning tail and running. "I think Valerie wants me for . . . for something," she said, continuing to back away from him. He seemed frozen in place as he stared at her.

"I'm sorry about what I said," Ellie said, desperately wanting him to stop thinking she was crazy. The divorce court had required that she prove that she was sane, but she couldn't do it then and she couldn't do it now. "It's just that I liked Lew, liked him a lot." She was still backing up as she spoke, putting more and more distance between them. "But I didn't feel any depression coming from him, and I think that after what I've been through these last three years, I'd know when a person is depressed. Madison is depressed, but Lew wasn't."

"Who is Madison?" Jessie snapped, the first words he'd said in minutes.

Ellie waved her hand in dismissal. "Just a friend of mine."

Jessie was glaring at her, his eyebrows drawn into a deep frown. "What's he to you?"

It took Ellie a moment to know what Jessie was talking about, as her mind was on Lew. "She. Madison is a she," she said, then took a deep breath. "If you're asking me about men in my life, I have a husband who is probably at this moment having lunch with someone and telling him or her what a jerk I am because I ran off for the weekend, heaven only knows where, with heaven only knows who. But the difference is that this time it's true. And I'm sure that this weekend is going to cost me even more than he did cost me." She knew this didn't make sense, but how could she explain a future that hadn't happened yet but that she knew? "I really *do* have to go," she said lamely.

He was still standing there looking at her, so she glared at him, willing him to leave. He wasn't for her. This thing with Lew had reminded her that she was still married and she still had to go through a vicious divorce. And her lovely weekend had turned into a fiasco. There was Valerie hauling her around to show her off, and Jessie had already admitted that he was using lines on her that he used on *all* women when he was trying to get them into bed with him. So much for her fantasies about love and a future, et cetera. And now this . . . This death of a man she'd liked very much.

"I think you're right," she said softly. "I think that another time *would* be better for a visit. I think . . . Tell Valerie . . ." Ellie couldn't think of any more to say, so she did just what she'd been trying not to do: She turned tail and ran back into the guesthouse and shut the door firmly behind her.

Twenty-three

When Ellie made up her mind to do something, it didn't take her long to start moving. "My strongest point and my weakest," she'd told Daria. If the decision was good, then great, but if the decision was to leave behind a possible career in art and follow a man . . .

Anyway, an hour and a half later, she was packed, had made her apologies to Valerie, and was sitting on a bench on the front porch of the summerhouse waiting for a driver to pick up her and her luggage and take her back to L.A. Valerie had said that Woody was sending a plane to fetch some of Lew's relatives at the airport, so she wouldn't be causing anyone to make an extra trip. Valerie had been so upset at the news of Lew's death that she hadn't paid much attention to what else was going on around her.

So now Ellie was sitting and waiting. Her daring little escapade had turned into horror—and now she was going back to her own personal nightmare.

For three years she'd thought about what she'd like to do to that man if she could do it all over again. She'd loved imagining hiring a private eye to stalk her ex. She'd thought long and hard about how she'd hire someone to get close to him and find out where he'd hidden the money he'd stolen from her. She'd spent months, even years, imagining all the things she wanted to do to him.

But now she was sitting on a cushioned bench, the California mountains were in front of her, and she dreaded having to do any of it. She just plain dreaded it. Years ago when she'd been complaining about her husband to someone, the person had said, "If you don't like him, why don't you divorce him?" "Too much trouble," Ellie had answered instantly.

Martin loved chaos and confusion. He gained strength from causing misery to other people. But Ellie needed peace and quiet. Only in peace could she think and make up stories and daydream and—

"Get in."

Ellie looked up to see Jessie sitting in an open Jeep that had skidded to a halt in front of her. He was frowning at her as though she was doing something he didn't like.

She didn't obey him. "I'm returning to L.A."

"No," he said. "I need you."

At that Ellie blinked. Was this modern courtship? "Maybe you don't understand that I'm married, and, whether I want him or not, I *do* have a husband."

With a look of annoyance, Jessie leaned across the seat and threw open the passenger door. "Not that way," he said. "I mean, I do need you like that, but that can wait. Get your damned divorce before I take you if that's what you want to do, but right now I need your brain."

"You'd sure make Madison happy," Ellie muttered, but she still sat on the bench and didn't get into the car. "Someone is coming to pick me up. I *must* return to the city."

"No one is leaving the ranch today," he said. "Sheriff's orders. He thinks Lew may have been murdered." Jessie didn't blink as

he watched Ellie's reaction to his announcement.

"His wife?" Ellie asked softly.

Jessie didn't say anything, just sat there
in silence. And Ellie knew that he wasn't
going to tell her anything until she did what
he wanted her to do. She wanted to stand
her ground and not give in to him, but her
writer's curiosity was stronger than her
willpower. With a grimace, she got up, went
down the porch stairs, and got into the car.
He didn't speak until they were moving.

"No," he said at last. "Not his wife. She
was really broken up about his death."

Ellie kept her eyes straight ahead. "I see,"
she said. She felt Jessie glance at her, but
she didn't look at him. This wasn't her problem. She had major problems of her own
that were going to start very soon. And she
had only three weeks.

As Jessie drove, it occurred to her that
she should have asked him where he
planned to take her. But he didn't say and
she didn't ask as he drove down a dirt road.
At one point he stopped, got out, opened a
gate, then got back into the car and drove
through. When he stopped the car on the
opposite side of the gate, Ellie was out be-

fore he was and she closed the gate behind them.

"I like useful women," he said when she was back in the car; then he put the Jeep into gear and kept driving. And Ellie smiled because "useful" is just what she'd liked about him.

They rode together in silence for a while, and it occurred to Ellie that she should be annoyed with him: he was altogether too sure of himself. He'd known that he could get her to go with him, and he'd assumed—

Oh, the hell with it, she thought. She'd had too much therapy if she was finding something wrong with being driven down a lonely road by a beautiful man.

"Where are you taking me?" she asked. "To some secret place where you plan to ravish me?"

He had his eyes on the road, but she could see the tiny smile that came onto his lips. "I thought you wrote murder mysteries," he said.

"I do. But they're also love stories. So where are we going?"

"Away from everyone," he said; then he turned a sharp left and they were in the mountains, in the trees, and before them was a beautiful lake. Stopping the car, he looked at her. "I want to know what you know. Tell me everything," he said; then he got out of the car and walked toward the lake.

Ellie followed him to where he was now standing at the side of the lake on a wide boulder, throwing rocks and watching them skip across the surface of the water.

"I listened with my eyes," he said. "Not my mind. And maybe because of that a good man is now dead."

Ellie knew that he wanted to talk, so she sat down on a rock and waited.

"She's beautiful, really a knockout," he said, and Ellie knew that he was talking about Lew's wife, Sharon. "And I felt sorry for her. She was talented and she said that she was trapped."

Pausing, he picked up more pebbles. "She told me that—"

"She loved Lew so very, very much," Ellie said in spite of her intention to keep quiet. And she couldn't keep the bitterness out of her voice.

"Yes," Jessie said, then turned to look at her. "How do you know all of this?"

Now was not the time to go into her

own problems. Ellie shrugged. "I've been through something similar. Did Lew ever complain about her?"

"Never. He was proud of her. I wouldn't have known anything was wrong if Sharon hadn't told me."

"How many others did she bellyache to?"

"I don't know. I thought she told only me." This time it was Jessie who sounded bitter.

"So what's this about the sheriff?" Ellie asked.

For a moment Jessie's mouth tightened into a straight line. "Me. My big mouth. This morning you made me wonder if Lew really did kill himself, so I said as much to the sheriff. Two hours later he arrested Bowie." He looked at Ellie. "You remember the man who wanted to kiss you this morning?"

At first she didn't know what he meant; then she thought of the cowboy with the beer belly who had puckered up and made everyone laugh. The memory made her smile.

"That's Bowie, and he's been taken in for questioning about Lew's murder."

"What?" she asked. "He didn't seem like a killer to me."

"No, he's not. But he likes the ladies, and a few years ago there was an unfortunate incident with one of Valerie's drunken guests. When she sobered up and saw Bowie in daylight, she decided to press charges. Woody had to pull strings and call in a lot of favors to get Bowie off."

"So now it's happening again?" Ellie asked.

"Not if I can help it!" Jessie said as he threw a rock at the water's surface. Turning, he looked at her. "So if *she* murdered him, how do we find out?"

He was looking at her as though she knew this sort of thing. "Did you tell the sheriff what you know?" she asked.

"That's how Bowie got into this mess, isn't it? If I hadn't said that I doubted that Lew was as depressed as everyone thought he was, then maybe the sheriff wouldn't have asked so many questions and found out that Bowie lusts after Lew's wife in a big way."

"I see. And if I hadn't said anything in the first place . . ."

"Exactly," he said. "This is our joint fault. So how do we fix it?"

It was one thing to write a book about a

woman who got herself into jams as she investigated murders but quite another to try something like this in real life.

Ellie stood up. "Look, this woman may be a killer. I don't think that I want to stick around for that. I'm on borrowed time here, and I don't want to change my future so that I return dead."

Jessie blinked at her. "You know, sometimes you say really odd things. You talk about things that have yet to happen as though they already have happened. And as though you know the future."

"That's silly," Ellie said quickly. "How can anyone know the future? It's just that I—I mean, I—"

"Go on," he said. "I'm waiting."

"The truth is that I need to get back to L.A. as soon as possible. I have less than three weeks to stop my ex-husband—my soon-to-be ex-husband—from taking everything that I've earned in writing and giving me a burden of debt for eternity, not to mention taking away my dignity and my self-esteem."

"How can you be sure that he's *going* to do this?"

"I know him," she said.

"Yes. I can almost believe that's all there is behind this. You have a good perception of people. You didn't accept what other people assume to be true about Woody and Valerie. I can tell anyone that she's a gold digger and they'll believe me. But you didn't."

She narrowed her eyes at him. "Have you told that lie to many people?"

"Only women," he said without a trace of humor. "I want you to stay and help me find out—"

"You aren't going to ask me to stay and help you snoop around a murderer, are you?"

"You don't know that she is a murderer. And, besides, aren't your books about some woman who investigates murders?"

"Do you think that writers experience what they write about? Do you think that Stephen King has lived through everything that he's written about? *When* would he write?"

Jessie grinned. "Okay, it was worth a try. So how about if you have her to lunch, find out what she'll tell you, and give me time to look through some files? Maybe something was written down."

"No, he never wrote anything down," she said, but of course that had nothing to do with Lew's wife, Sharon. Ellie put her hands over her face for a second; then when she looked back up at Jessie, she tried to be calmer.

"Look," she said. "I'd like to help, but I can't. I don't have time. I have to change my own . . . destiny, I guess you'd say. I thought I could afford to take a weekend off and have some fun, but I can tell you that this weekend has turned out to be very much *not* fun."

"All of it?" Jessie asked softly.

He had *those* eyes. He had those male eyes that Ellie hadn't seen in a long, long time. When she'd first met Martin, his eyes were always like Jessie's were now. Those eyes made every female hormone inside you start to vibrate and . . . and . . . giggle, she thought. Like a silly little girl. Like . . . Well, certainly not like the nearly forty-year-old woman that she was. And not like the mega-successful writer who managed her own career that she was either.

With all the resolve that she could gather, Ellie turned on her heel and walked away from him. If need be, she'd walk all the way back to the ranch.

Instantly, Jessie was beside her. "Don't leave," he said; then he put his hand on her arm.

Ellie looked down at his hand. It was strong and brown from the sun, and she could feel the warmth of him through her shirt. Don't look at him, she told herself. Focus on his hand. Don't look at him.

But she did look at him. He still had those eyes, and in the next instant she was in his arms and he was holding her.

Part of her wanted him to make love to her right there by the lake. She wanted him to take off her clothes and touch her and—

She was crying! She didn't know when she started, but she was clinging to him as though he were her life-support system, and she was quietly, but deeply, sobbing. Maybe it was seeing those male eyes of his. Maybe it was being around a man again after all those years of being alone, but all the emptiness of the last years came flooding back to her. She didn't *want* to yet again go through that divorce. She didn't want to have to hear herself accused of cunning and treachery. She didn't want to hear her sanity questioned.

Jessie didn't seem surprised by her tears, and he certainly wasn't at a loss about what to do. Bending, he swept her into his arms and carried her back to the lake where he sat down on the ground, his back against a tree, and he held her while she cried.

She didn't know how long she cried, but it was enough. The shoulder of his shirt was soaked.

He handed her a clean handkerchief. "Better?" he said softly.

Blowing her nose, she nodded, and Jessie gently pushed a tendril of hair out of her eyes.

"Is he trying to kill you?" Jessie asked quietly. "Is that how you know about Lew?"

With her head bent, Ellie nodded. This was something that had taken her a long time to face. The jealousy and hatred Martin felt toward her was not something that Ellie could comprehend fully. "I don't know for sure, but I think that's what he was after. My therapist thinks he was trying to get me to commit suicide. He made me feel like a failure, as though nothing I accomplished meant anything. No matter what I did, according to him, it wasn't good enough. And he said I had taken away his chance at success. And he tells people that I'm selfish and money-hungry. He spends his life telling people bad things about me."

She blew her nose again and took a deep breath. "If I were gone, he'd have the money and his freedom."

Jessie pulled her back into his arms so her cheek was on his wet shoulder. She was beginning to recover herself. "I'm sorry I've made such a fool of myself, but—"

"Did anyone believe *you*?" he asked. "When you told them that he was trying to drive you to suicide, did anyone believe you?"

"I've never told anyone before. You're the first," Ellie said, wiping her nose. "People think that if they've met a person, he couldn't be evil. And since my ex spent most of his life telling people how much he loved me, they thought he did love me. Most people aren't the liar that he is; most people have never met anyone like him."

"So poor Lew got pushed past the final step, from suicide to being murdered."

When he didn't say any more, Ellie pulled

away from his shoulder to look at him. All in all, they had had a very strange relationship. In one way, they were as physically familiar with each other as longtime lovers, but in another way, they knew nothing about each other.

"You haven't given up, have you?" she asked. She was sitting on his lap and his face was inches from hers.

"Not in the least," he said matter-of-factly. "But I need your help. I think you know more than you think you do."

She moved her legs so she was no longer sitting on his lap; then she stood up, but Jessie continued leaning back against the tree.

"I don't know anything," she said. "Nothing at all. And neither do you. Maybe she drove him to suicide, or maybe she killed him. But then, maybe she's a very nice woman and everything happened just as she said it did."

"That Bowie went to her house last night and that Lew threatened him with a shotgun?" Jessie asked, his hands behind his head.

"That's probably what made her decide

to do it *now*," Ellie said before she thought, then she put her hand over her mouth.

But Jessie gave a little smile and closed his eyes. "I figure that with all the research that you must have done for those books of yours that you know a great deal about the criminal mind."

"I know enough to know that killers are very dangerous people!" she said, but he didn't open his eyes. In fact, he smiled a bit more.

And it was in that moment that something clicked in Ellie's mind. Maybe it was the crying in a man's strong arms. Maybe it was once again feeling that she was desirable and not just a money-producing machine that Martin had reduced her to.

Whatever it was, in that second, Ellie gave up her quest for revenge. For three years of her life she had been immobilized by the trauma of what had been done to her and by her ceaseless, never-ending desire for justice.

But now, she was getting what she wanted: a chance to do it all over again. And now she knew that she wasn't going to do what she'd planned during those long years of misery. She wasn't going to return to their home near Los Angeles and spend her every waking minute doing to Martin what he'd done to her. No, she wasn't going to lower herself to his level.

The truth was, that the worst had happened to her and she'd lived through it. Back then, everyone involved had agreed that they'd never seen a nastier divorce than hers, and they'd never seen a judge so personally vindictive as hers had been. But, still, Ellie had survived all that had been dumped on her.

But now she saw that later it hadn't been the events that had disabled her but her reaction to them. It hadn't been the loss of the money that she still had to pay to her lazy, lying, philandering ex-husband. It had been Ellie's self-esteem that had been damaged. Martin had accused her of caring only about herself—and the judge had agreed with him.

While she'd been thinking, Jessie had remained quiet, and when she turned to look at him, she saw that he'd been watching her.

"You have some heavy things going on inside you, don't you?" he asked softly.

"Yes," she answered. "I do. But, you

know something? I don't care anymore."
With that, she smiled. She really, really
smiled. And she looked about her at the
beauty of their surroundings, and she took a
deep breath. Maybe the divorce court system in this state was a travesty, but the air
was heavenly.

"I don't want to go home," she said.
"There's nothing there for me. And when do
you want me to have Lew's wife over for
lunch?"

When Jessie didn't answer, she looked
down at him. He was looking up at her with
those male eyes again. But this time Ellie
didn't run away. And she certainly didn't
start crying. No, instead, she bent down to
kiss him, and in the next moment she had
his shirt unbuttoned.

Twenty-four

1980
OHIO

One second Leslie was in the Victorian house of a woman named Madame Zoya and the next she was standing in the dormitory room of her university.

She stood there blinking, disoriented, not sure of what she was seeing. There were two beds in the room, hers, neat and tidy, with its often-washed spread that she'd had since she was a freshman, and the other, her roommate's bed. It was a jumble of covers that looked as though they'd never been washed.

Leslie's first thought was that she was going to have to get after Rebecca to make up her bed. And straighten up her desk and—

It was then that the realization of what she was seeing hit Leslie. And when she had the thought, she didn't believe it. She took a step backward.

And that's when the realization of her body hit her. She was at least fifteen pounds lighter than she had been ten minutes earlier.

Her mind was clearing now, and even though she didn't believe what she was seeing and feeling, it seemed to be real.

"Mirror," she said aloud, then tried to remember back to her college days. Where was the—Ah, back of the closet door.

Opening the door, she was hit with the sight of herself at twenty years old.

Staring back at her was a Leslie Aimes that she hadn't seen in a long, long time. It wasn't just the twenty-year-old body that had had a lifetime of twisting and twirling that had made it into this beautiful machine. No, Leslie remembered that body. Every morning when she awoke, she remembered that body—and missed it. She missed being able to bend and stretch and turn with ease and grace.

No, that wasn't what surprised her as she looked in the mirror. What astonished her was the look of hope on the face of the girl in the mirror.

"When did I lose that?" she asked aloud. "When did I change?"

The Leslie looking back at her had sparkling green eyes that seemed to be on the verge of laughing. This was a girl who believed in herself, was sure that she was going to go far in the world.

This was *not* a girl who thought she was going to end up a housewife who served on one committee after another. This wasn't a woman who was terrified that her husband was going to leave her for a girl half her age.

Leaning toward the mirror, Leslie turned her face this way and that. No lines, no wrinkles, just pure, smooth skin. Gone were twenty years of damage caused by playing tennis in the sun and sitting by the club pool with the children. Maybe this time around she'd have sense enough to slather on sunscreen.

"And this girl isn't afraid of anyone," she said as she looked at herself. And that thought was a shock to her. When had she become frightened? Had it been when she'd found out that she wasn't going to be a Great Dancer, in capital letters? Had she become frightened when she'd gone crawling back to Alan, feeling that she was a failure? What had happened to Leslie to change the look that was sparkling in this girl's eyes?

When the telephone rang, Leslie jumped and looked about for someone to answer it. But then she remembered that it was her phone and she should answer it.

"Hello?" she asked tentatively.

"Leslie? Is that you?"

It was Alan.

"Yes," was all she could manage to say. She'd spent her entire life with him so now the impulse to tell him what had happened to her was strong. But she couldn't do that. Would she start with how she'd dumped him ten days before the wedding and end with Bambi?

"You sound odd. You aren't getting sick, are you?"

Had he always been so cut-and-dried? Where was the romance? "No," she said softly as she held the receiver tightly. She was trying to remember exactly what Alan looked like the year before he graduated from college.

"Well, something's wrong with you," he said, sounding annoyed. "I just called to tell you that I'll pick you up at eight A.M. tomorrow and we'll drive home together."

Leslie knew that Alan's car was going to break down on the way to her college and that he was going to spend the whole week of spring break trying to get the parts to repair it. And she was going to end up alone at school for that week, dancing alone in the studio, eating alone.

"Are you there?" he asked, this time sounding almost angry.

"Yes, I'm here," Leslie said. "I was just thinking how much I'd like to see you again. What do you want us to do together next week?"

"Together? Are you kidding? With your mother and mine planning our every minute? We have to do those things that have to be done to get ready for a wedding. You know better than I do what they are."

And at thirty-nine years of age I know what a waste of time they are, she thought. It's what comes after marriage that's important. Maybe if she and Alan had spent more time with each other, had talked more, then Leslie wouldn't have run away to New York and—

"You're acting very strange," Alan said.

"So I hope you get over it by tomorrow. We have a lot to do this coming week. Mother's invited some important people to spend next weekend with us, and I think you and I should try to come to some agreement about where we're going to live."

Leslie opened her mouth to tell him that they were going to buy the old Belville place, but she closed it. One thing about Alan: He didn't change. At twenty he was as bossy as he was at forty.

On the desk beside the telephone was an envelope of heavy cream-colored paper. Putting the phone to her shoulder, Leslie opened the envelope. In it was an invitation from Halliwell J. Formund IV to spend the coming spring break with him and his family and their other guests at their estate. If she accepted, a car would pick her up tomorrow morning.

Part of her wanted to tell Alan that she had another invitation for the break, but why burn bridges? Why cause unnecessary hurt?

"I'll be ready," Leslie said into the phone, sounding as sweet as she could manage. "But call me if you have any problems."

"What does that mean?" Alan snapped.

"Nothing. I just meant—Never mind. Forget it. If you call and I'm not here, I'll be at the studio dancing."

"Aren't you always?" he asked.

At that Leslie dropped the phone into the cradle. All these years she'd beaten herself up for running away and leaving poor Alan nearly standing at the altar, but now she remembered why she'd done it: He'd been a prig. A full-of-himself, self-satisfied prig.

But the Alan she'd married was no longer a prig. Bossy, yes. And, yes, maybe even controlling at times. But that Alan had a humility about him . . .

With wide eyes, Leslie stared, unseeing, at the bulletin board behind the desk. Had *she* changed him? Had her running off to New York shaken the insufferable attitude she'd just seen but had forgotten about over the years?

What irony, she thought. All their years of marriage she'd been burdened by this dreadful, dishonorable thing that she believed she'd done to dear, sweet Alan, and now she was seeing that maybe her jilting him was the best thing she could have done.

"*Hmmm,*" she said, smiling as she picked

up the phone. If jilting him had made him into a better person, what would spending the week with another boy do?

At that thought she laughed aloud; then she picked up the telephone and dialed the number for the Formund residence and accepted the invitation.

"It's none of my business, dear, but aren't you in the wrong department?" The saleswoman had iron gray hair and a suit that wouldn't have wrinkled if she'd run a train over it.

Leslie had managed to find only one decent pair of trousers in her closet at the dorm, and a single shirt that was too frilly. What to wear had instantly become her number one concern, so now she was in the best department store in town looking through the racks of clothes.

"No, I don't think I am," Leslie said, annoyed with the woman for interfering. Leslie had never been extravagant, so most of the money her father sent her every month was in her bank account.

"If you were about to turn forty, this

would be the perfect place for you," the saleswoman said, laughter in her voice.

"But I—" Leslie began then stopped herself. There was a mirror to her left and she had to look at it to remind herself of what had happened. She wasn't forty now. The truth was, that even under the harsh store lights, she looked wonderful.

With a beautiful smile on her face, Leslie turned to the saleswoman. "Could you help me?" Leslie asked in her nicest voice. "I've been invited to spend the break at the Formunds' place, and—"

"The Halliwell Formunds?"

"Yes, that is their name," Leslie said as innocently as she could manage.

The saleswoman narrowed her eyes. "I do believe they have a son about your age."

"Could you help me with what to wear? I can't very well show up in leotards, can I?"

"No," the woman said slowly, and Leslie could almost hear the thoughts racing through the saleswoman's head: If she was nice to Leslie and Leslie married a Formund, she might have a lifelong customer, and the commissions would be . . . "I'd love to help you, dear," the saleswoman purred.

Twenty-five

Five minutes after she arrived, Leslie regretted her decision. What was she doing here?
She had been put into a two-bedroom
guesthouse with three other girls. At first
they had asked her to join them in their activities, but when Leslie didn't, they began
to whisper about her. It had been a long
time since Leslie had been this young, and
she'd completely forgotten the sense of
competition between young women.

It was on Leslie's tongue to lecture them
about how they didn't need to cut each
other to ribbons in their competition to get
the best man to mate with. There were
enough men to go around.

Leslie had given this lecture to her own
daughter when Rebecca had been in a to-
the-death fight with a girl who had once

been her best friend. Of course it had been over a boy. Three months later Leslie had been glad to see the girls back together and the boy put on the "dregs" list, but Leslie knew that it could as easily have gone the other way.

"And where are you from?" one of the girls had asked Leslie. "And your major is what?"

Her tone was unmistakable: Leslie was not considered part of "the" crowd who usually frequented Hal's parties.

The truth was, Leslie wondered why she'd been invited. But as she walked away from the girls and their insinuations, she knew what she would have told her daughter. Leslie had been invited for her dancer's figure. Didn't rich boys usually have flings with "unsuitable" girls before they settled down to marry some blue-blooded girl whose daddy owned Kansas or something?

"I'm too old for this," Leslie said to herself as she left the guesthouse. On her bed had been a card with a printed list of activities that would be going on during the week, and as Leslie read them, she wished she'd stayed on campus and danced. Wouldn't it be wonderful after all these years to once again have a body that could leap with ease? Pirouette without aching toes?

She left the guesthouse and began to wander about the estate. When she saw a Sussex trug on the ground and a pair of ladies' gardening gloves and some clippers, it seemed natural to pick them up and start deadheading roses.

"Bored already?" asked a voice behind her.

Leslie turned to see an older woman standing on the path. She wore a skirt that had been washed many times and a sweater set that had to be twenty years old. But Leslie was willing to bet that the half-inch-diameter crystal at the end of the gold chain around her neck was a diamond. This woman owned the place.

"I'm sorry," Leslie said, holding out the trug. "This must be yours. I didn't mean—"

"That's fine," the woman said, smiling. "Why don't I sit in the shade and let you do the work? Truthfully, I hate gardening. I only do it because my doctor said I have to have some form of exercise."

"And gardening is so genteel," Leslie said, laughing. "At least that's what men think. Personally, I never thought there was anything romantic about cow manure."

The woman laughed. "Nor do I. But I have been assigned the task, so I must make it look as though I've done it."

Her hint was clear, so, smiling back at her, Leslie took the cutters and began removing the dead rose heads.

Mrs. Formund sat on a little iron bench under a nearby oak tree. "And which one are you?" she asked. "No, wait, you must be the dancer. No one else could move as you are doing without years of training."

Leslie had to turn away to hide her blush. No one had said such a thing to her in a long while. "Do you have any idea why your son invited me?" she asked. She wasn't going to pretend not to know who this woman was.

"I think the important question would be why you accepted."

Leslie didn't turn around, but she could hear the skepticism in the woman's voice. No doubt she was inundated with girls who wanted to get near her rich son.

"To see the estate, of course," Leslie said. "I'd heard of the gardens and I wanted to see them." She paused with the cutters in midair. "And also, to get away from my boyfriend for a while. I wanted to see if there were any other men in the world besides him."

"That's wise of you," Mrs. Formund said. "I had half a dozen marriage proposals before I married my husband."

"And I've never even dated a man other than Alan," Leslie said softly.

"Oh, dear!" Mrs. Formund said. "At your age, you should—Uh-oh. Here comes my doctor. Give me those secateurs and sneak away. Don't let him see you. Oh, good! You've done an entire bed. He'll report to my husband that I've done masses."

Smiling, Leslie ducked down behind the bed, then waddled out along the path, her head well below the line of the roses.

She spent so much time wandering about the grounds that when she returned to the guesthouse, the other girls were just leaving for the main house and the first of several parties.

"Planning to make an entrance?" one of the girls asked snidely as she looked Leslie up and down in her tailored trousers and white cotton shirt. There was dirt on her cuff and sticktights were on her trousers.

"No, I was just so busy helping Hal's mother in the garden that I lost all track of time," Leslie said sweetly, then watched the girl nearly turn purple at being bested. Everyone knew that the way to get a marriage proposal was through the boy's mother.

As the three girls hurried to leave the guesthouse, Leslie thought, Shame on you! But she didn't feel particularly shameful for having won a cat fight. Instead, she felt rather good about it.

She didn't want to go to the party. She'd never liked parties unless they were at her house and she was the hostess, but she knew that she had to go. She had a perfect little black dress that she knew showed off every curve of her dancer's body, but she didn't want to wear it—nor did she want to go prowling with the other girls.

But she made herself shower and dress because, after all, she was a guest and Leslie had strict ideas about how guests should behave.

But the party bored her. They were kids and they were fascinated with booze and each other. And all Leslie felt was old. Her body might be young, but in her mind, she was past this. And now that she was here, she was wondering if maybe she shouldn't have been so curt with Alan. After all, if she did end up married to him again . . .

She left the party before nine and went back to the guesthouse, where she snuggled in bed and was asleep by nine-thirty. She woke only briefly to hear the other girls come in at three A.M. She was vaguely aware of hearing them say, "She's here. In bed. Alone." Then Leslie heard giggles that meant that the girls had had too much to drink. As she drifted back to sleep, Leslie remembered that she hadn't seen Hal at the party. And the truth was, she wasn't sure she'd recognize him if she did see him. After all, it had been nearly twenty years since she'd last seen him in person.

The snores of the other girls woke her. Leslie looked at the clock. It was just a few minutes after five A.M. Getting up, she went into the bathroom, prepared to do her hair, put on makeup and get dressed. But the face that greeted her in the mirror didn't need makeup. Her eyelashes weren't dull and faded as they were at forty. There were no brown spots to cover up, no enlarged pores by the side of her nose. There were no dark circles under her eyes. And her hair was soft and silky, not dry, as it was going to become no matter what expensive salon treatment she used.

Smiling, Leslie didn't even bother to comb her hair, but ran her fingers through it to pull out the worst tangles; then she went back to the bedroom to pull on jeans and a shirt. At forty messy hair in the morning was called "bed head." At twenty, messy hair was called "sexy."

The dew was on the grass and, if possible, the garden was even more beautiful this early. There were no lawn mowers going, no gardeners anywhere. It was as though it was just Leslie alone in God's creation.

There was a little path that she'd seen the day before, but she hadn't gone down it because it had looked private. But this morning there was no one about, so she walked on the little round stones, wishing they didn't make quite so much noise. But at the end, she looked through the trees to the most beautiful sight she'd ever seen. Nestled in the shade, dripping wisteria, was a summerhouse. It wasn't as big as hers— the one she would someday own—but it was more charming. It looked like something off the pages of a children's fairy tale, with its thatched roof and stucco walls painted a pale cream.

"Beautiful, isn't it?"

Somehow, she wasn't surprised when she turned and saw Hal standing behind her. What had made her think that she wouldn't recognize him? She hadn't wanted to admit it to Ellie and Madison, but over the years she'd followed his career quite closely. She'd even subscribed to some obscure magazines because they were likely to have stories about Hal in them.

Now she looked at him, knowing that he was going to get better looking as he grew older. At twenty, he was a nice-looking boy with brown hair and brown eyes, and the best teeth that money could straighten, but he was ordinary-looking, not nearly as handsome as Alan was at twenty. But Leslie knew that age lines and gray hair and a body that was kept taut and hard was going to make Hal a knockout at forty.

"Yes," she said. "Serene."

He smiled, making his eyes crinkle at the corners. "That's just the way my mother describes it. She designed it and had it built the first year after she married my father.

She says that building has saved her sanity."

Leslie laughed. "Your father is that bad, is he?" She'd read a couple of in-depth articles about Hal and she knew that his father was a horror.

"Worse. He's as forceful as my mother is—" He broke off, as though he weren't sure how to describe his mother.

"Strong," Leslie said. "I would guess that your mother is the solid foundation that your father has built himself on. A person can't push against the world without a good, solid foundation." This was her own opinion after having met the woman. If her husband was sending the doctor out to see her, he wanted her to stay healthy.

Hal looked at her with eyes that showed surprise and maybe even shock. "Yes, you're right. My mother *is* the strong one in the family, but not many people see that. My father is so—"

"Dynamic?"

"I was going to say, in-your-face, but 'dynamic' is a nice word."

She turned away to look back at the little summerhouse house nestled among the trees, and she could feel his eyes on her.

"Why did you invite *me* here?" she asked softly. It was a question that had haunted her for twenty years. "Did we meet somewhere and I don't remember it?"

"No," he said, "not really. But I've watched you for three years now, and—" He broke off because Leslie had turned to give him a sharp look.

She had to remind herself that it was only 1980 and that stalkers hadn't yet come under prosecution, but she didn't like the way he'd said that he'd been watching her.

"Whoa," Hal said, putting his hands up before his face as though to act as a shield. "I didn't mean anything bad. I'm male; I watch all the pretty girls, okay?"

Leslie let out her pent-up breath and smiled. "Sorry. It's just that with being a dancer you get some . . ." She waved her hand to finish the sentence.

"Yes, I would imagine that with a body like yours you get every pervert on campus following you."

Leslie knew that she should say something modest, but it had been a long time since anyone had paid her such a compliment—a long time since she'd been in good enough shape to *deserve* such a compliment. Turning away, she blushed all the way to her hair roots.

"Why did you leave the party so early last night?" he asked.

"I . . ." she began.

"Didn't know anyone, and it was too noisy and too busy?" he suggested.

Laughing, Leslie turned back to look at him. "Exactly. You're fairly perceptive, aren't you?"

"Fairly," he said, and she could tell that he was amused. No doubt he was used to girls who flattered him endlessly.

"So why *did* you invite me?" she asked again. "And don't you dare say anything about the shape of me."

"That will be difficult," he said.

Heavens! But it had been many years since Leslie had flirted with anyone. In fact, had she *ever* flirted with a man? Alan wasn't exactly the flirting type.

"Maybe I should ask you why you accepted," Hal said. "I hear you're engaged to be married the second you graduate."

"His car broke down and I was going to be spending the week alone, and I wanted to see this place. Maybe I'll tell my children that I visited the Formund estate and met

Halliwell J. Formund IV, who is now president of the U.S."

She had meant to make him laugh, but he didn't. Instead, he was staring at her as though she were a witch. "How did you know about me and politics?" he asked softly.

"Oh, just something I heard, I guess," Leslie said, trying to cover herself.

"There was nothing you could have heard," he said. "My entire family assumes I'm going into the banking business with my father and my uncles. The idea of politics is inside my head only."

"Maybe you look like a politician," she said, smiling. "In fact, I can easily envision your face on campaign posters. I can even imagine you in Congress and the press saying that you're a president-in-the-making."

He didn't return her smile but looked away at his mother's little house. "I think you see me the way I see myself. But my family isn't going to like it."

"Not like that their son wants to be president of the United States?" she asked, incredulous.

Turning, he looked at her for a while, as though he were considering something.

"Would you like to spend the day with me? I mean, just the two of us? We could take a basket of food and go rowing on the lake."

It was amazing how much the idea appealed to Leslie. She knew that inside her mind, she was nearly forty, but she was in the body of a twenty-year-old and raging inside her were hormones that she hadn't felt in many years. The thought of a lazy day on a lake with a handsome young man who thought she was beautiful was vastly appealing.

He misinterpreted her hesitation. "I won't lay a finger on you," he said. "I promise."

"Then I am definitely *not* going," she said before she thought. But in the next moment they were both laughing.

"If I must," Hal said, his eyes sparkling, then he held out his hand to her and in the next moment they were running across the lawn toward the back of the big house, but he stopped outside the door. "If you go in with me and we get the food together, it will be all over the place within seconds," he said. "Your decision."

Looking at him, Leslie marveled that he could be so thoughtful. He knew that she was engaged to another man, and now he was giving her a chance to keep what she was doing secret. How many other boys his age would think of such a thing? "You're going to make a good president," she said; then she opened the kitchen door and stepped inside. Let Alan find out. Let Alan feel what Leslie had been feeling in the last months over his assistant, Bambi.

With a chef and two helpers in it, the kitchen was a flurry of activity as they prepared breakfast, but from the way Hal slipped in and out of the quickly moving people, he was a familiar presence. He knew where the picnic baskets were kept, and he knew where the best foods were stored. Leslie saw two of the workers drop things into Hal's basket without his asking them to do so. Fifteen minutes later he opened the door and they left the kitchen together, the big basket over Hal's arm.

"Do that often?" she asked teasingly.

"Not with a girl," he said, "if that's what you're asking, but, yes, I often take a lunch and stay away for the entire day."

"I thought that young men like you liked parties and girls and . . . well, parties and girls."

They were walking quickly, but he gave

her a quizzical look. "'Young men like me,'" he said, turning the phrase over in his mind. "And what does that mean? Aren't you 'young' like me? Yet last night you slipped away from a wonderful party." Pausing, he smiled. "At least I was told that it was a great party."

"You weren't there?" she asked, wide-eyed.

"Hate them."

"But if you want to be a politician, you're going to have to go to lots of parties."

"But I assume that those parties will have a purpose, and there *is* work that will be done when one isn't at a party, right?"

"Right," she said, smiling. "So what will your guests think when they find out that their host isn't here? That he's run off with the dancer? More important, what will your family think?"

"That I'm lucky," Hal said. "And as for the others, they can entertain themselves. The girls are here because they want to marry my father's money."

"Ah," Leslie said.

"And what does that mean?"

She decided to be honest. "That I didn't know that you knew."

"Couldn't very well miss it, could I? You wouldn't believe the number of 'accidental' encounters I have with girls. If one more fakes a drowning in the swimming pool, I'll—"

"With or without her top on?" Leslie asked.

"Two with, one without," Hal said; then they laughed together.

They'd walked down a pretty little path until they reached a stream. A green canoe was tied to a wooden dock. "This joins a river about half a mile from here," Hal said as he put the basket in the canoe. "This is your last chance to back out."

"And miss an opportunity to put the noses of those girls out of joint? No, thank you. Do you know how to row this thing?"

Hal smiled. "Yes. You're sure you want to spend the day with me?" he asked again as Leslie prepared to step into the little canoe.

She looked into his eyes. They were soft brown and gentle. But under it she could see that rocklike foundation that he spoke of in his mother. "You're like your mother, aren't you?" she said softly.

"Yes," he answered simply. "Her family isn't flashy like my father's, no great heaps of money made. But my mother's people know what they want when they see it and they go after it. They don't give up."

The way he said it and the way he looked into her eyes made the hairs on the back of her neck stand up. It was almost as though he were saying that he wanted *her*. It was absurd, of course, but it was a feeling she had. Truthfully, she didn't want to see this. She didn't want to have to make up her mind about her future right now. Right now it was a beautiful day and she wanted to have a ride in a canoe with a handsome boy who flirted with her.

"If you ask me to marry you, I'll tell Alan and he'll beat you up," she said in mock seriousness.

When Hal's eyes lit up and he laughed, she knew that she'd caught him off guard, but the laughter lightened the mood.

As he handed her into the canoe, Hal said, "I've seen him and I could take him."

"When did you see him?" Leslie asked as Hal jumped into the canoe and pushed off.

"Around. I told you that I've been watching you."

"Is that like being a Peeping Tom? That won't look good when they dig up dirt on you when you run for president." She'd meant it as a joke, but he was serious as he maneuvered the oars to steer them into the middle of the placid stream.

"There it is again," he said. "It's as though you *know* what's going to happen. Not that I believe in such things, but are you clairvoyant?"

Leaning over the side of the canoe, Leslie trailed her hand in the water. "No, not at all. It's just that—" There wasn't anything that she could say that would satisfactorily explain what she'd already lived through. Could she tell him that in spite of how she looked, she was one day away from being forty years old and that she was married with two almost-grown children?

"Are you still with me?" he asked.

"Yes," she answered, smiling. "I'm here for at least another three weeks."

He opened his mouth to reply to that, but then he closed it. "I like a girl who's a mystery," he said. "And you're about as mysterious as they come."

"As mysterious as Cynthia Weller?" she couldn't resist asking as she trailed her hand in the water. She knew that he married Cynthia and they had three daughters.

"Don't believe I know the name," he said. "Should I?"

"No, not yet."

Hal maneuvered the boat around a tree that had fallen into the stream. "I want you to tell me everything about yourself."

"To see if I'm suitable?" she asked, smiling.

At first Hal frowned; then he smiled. "I get the feeling that you know me, as though you know more about me than I know about myself. And, in answer to your question, yes, I want to know if you're suitable."

When she looked at him, she saw that ambition in his eyes. Every article she'd ever read about Halliwell J. Formund IV had talked about his eyes. The writers said that you could mistake Hal for the boy-next-door—as long as you didn't look directly into his eyes, that is. Once you looked into those eyes, you saw what was propelling him on the journey toward the Oval Office. "Eye on the Future," had been the title of one long in-depth article.

"He doesn't make mistakes," the article had said.

This isn't a man who will later have pictures surface showing some bikini-clad bimbette sitting on his knee. It was as though Hal decided when he was eighteen years old that he wanted to be president and since then he has conducted his life with that goal in mind. His wife, Cynthia Weller, is eminently suitable, the perfect helpmate for a future president. She's pretty, but not too pretty. Educated but not so much as to be formidable. She has a quiet sense of humor, a conservative sense of dress, and a background without a hint of scandal. No doubt she will make a perfect First Lady.

Now Leslie thought about the description of Hal's wife, and she realized that it described her as well. She was not someone who would cause controversy or engender anger among the American people. She wasn't elegant like Jacqueline Kennedy, but she wasn't Hillary Clinton, either.

"All right," she said, looking back at Hal. "My father is a building contractor, and . . ."

Twenty-six

"What have you done to my son?" Millicent Formund asked Leslie, her eyes narrowed at her. "Do you have any idea how many young women we parade before him, but he isn't interested? Yet he's spent every minute of the last two days with you, ignoring all his other guests."

Leslie liked this woman a great deal. She reminded her of a woman on her church fund-raising committee. When Lillian Beasley called and asked for a donation, no one ever said no. "You're wondering how a middle-class girl like *me* can interest him over these long-legged thoroughbreds, aren't you?" Leslie asked, an eyebrow raised.

"Dear, if you're trying to cast me as a

snob, it's not going to happen. My father drove a truck."

Leslie smiled. "Oh? And how many trucks did he have to drive?"

At that Millie laughed. "All right, so he owned them as well as drove them, and he owned more than a few. I can see what my son likes about you."

"He's a very serious young man, and he wants to do serious things with his life," Leslie said. "Who he marries is of great importance to his future."

Millie didn't say anything for a moment, but she looked at Leslie with interest. "You have an old head on your shoulders, don't you?" she said; then she slipped her arm through Leslie's. "Is it possible that you paint?"

"Houses?" Leslie asked. "I painted our summerhouse when I was—" She'd been about to say, "when I was pregnant." "When I was a teenager," she finished.

"No, I mean watercolors." Millie gave a grimace. "This was my doctor's idea. He said that my life was so stressful that I *must* slow down, so he got together with my family and they persuaded me to take private watercolor lessons. I'm really quite awful," she said. "But it is relaxing. But now, with all the guests, I'm weeks behind in my lessons."

Leslie squeezed Millie's hand on her arm. "Someone cares a great deal about you, don't they? Gardening for exercise and watercolors for relaxation. And house visits by the doctor."

"I'm very lucky in my life," Millie said softly, then smiled. "Do you think you could try painting?"

"I would love to," Leslie said, "but I know nothing about painting, other than houses, that is. But, truthfully, you don't have to spend the day with me. I can occupy myself easily."

"Actually, I think I'd rather like to have your company. And, besides, it seems that I've been elected to chaperone all the young people today."

The way she said this made Leslie laugh. "It couldn't be as bad as that. If you give them enough food and keep them out of the bushes, they should do all right."

"You *are* an old soul, aren't you? Well, come along and help me carry things. We'll set up by the pool, so I can see everything that goes on."

Actually, Leslie was glad for some quiet time so she could think. She'd spent two days with Hal and she liked him a great deal. In fact, she liked him more than a lot.

They reached the pool area, and set up under a big umbrella were two easels. It looked as though Millie had assumed that Leslie would spend the day with her, and that she would join her in painting. As a mother herself, Leslie knew that Millie wanted to get to know this young woman who might become part of her life.

"What do I do?" Leslie asked as Millie handed her a wooden paint box. Inside was a thick pad of paper, brushes, and a couple of dozen different colors of paint in tiny ceramic pots.

"This week my lesson is . . ." Millie picked up a piece of paper and looked at it. "'Capturing action with a brush.'" Smiling, she looked up at Leslie. "That means that we paint what we see as quickly as possible."

"Sounds easy enough," Leslie said, "as long as no one will be judging me."

"No one," Millie said, smiling. "Unless you enjoy it enough that you want to share lessons with me. It would be nice to have someone to encourage me."

"I think it might have to be the other way around," Leslie said; then taking the pad of paper, Leslie put it on her lap, eschewing the easel, dipped her brush into the water, then dabbed it into the red paint. In front of them was a girl in a red bikini, and a boy in baggy blue trunks was trying to grab her to throw her into the pool.

In spite of Millie's statement that she wanted to spend time with Leslie to get to know her, once the paints were wet, she gave her attention to the paper. And Leslie saw immediately that for all Millie's protests that she wasn't any good, she was able to capture the bathers in a few quick brush-strokes. And while she was working, Millie didn't say a word.

Following her lead, Leslie gave her hands over to the paints and her mind over to the thoughts that raced through her head. She liked Hal, liked him much more than she'd ever thought she would. In the many articles that she'd read over the years she'd guessed that he was good at keeping his inner core hidden from the world.

She could love him, she thought as she

whipped her brush across the page, trying to copy what she saw as the boys and girls—as she thought of them—splashed about in the pool.

She could love him, and she felt that he was already half in love with her. And with that age-old instinct that women have, she knew that, if she wanted him, she could have him. But what would her life with him be like? It's one thing to joke about being First Lady, but she knew that in twenty years he would be close to attaining the presidency. She didn't know if he'd get it or not, but he had a good chance.

And if she took that road, then she wouldn't have her life with Alan and Rebecca and Joe. She'd have different children, as well as a different husband.

But the psychic had said that they could choose to forget their lives that they'd had. Leslie could choose to have a life with Hal and not remember the family she had now. She could forget all about having gone to New York to try to be a dancer and having failed, that thing that had hung over her all her life. She could forget that she'd spent a lifetime feeling guilty about having run away from a wedding with her childhood sweetheart. And she could forget her daughter, Rebecca, who was always complaining that her mother was a wimp. And Leslie could forget her son, Joe, who hid from any controversy, who was like his mother and would do most anything for peace and quiet.

But what kind of life would Leslie have with Hal? Riches beyond her wildest imagination. She wouldn't have to paint a house herself. And she wouldn't have to put up with Hal filling her house with untouchable antiques. No, they'd hire a decorator who would . . .

"Fill the house with untouchable antiques," Leslie muttered to herself as she cut the brush across the paper, then tore the sheet off and dropped it onto the stone terrace; then she started on a clean sheet. She was unaware that Millie was watching her with interest. No, Leslie was in her own world, trying to make the biggest decision of her life—and the paintbrush in her hand was an extension of what was in her mind.

"There he is now," Millie said, at last breaking Leslie's trance.

When Leslie looked up, she was surprised to see that Millie had closed her paint box and was now sipping iced tea and munching one of the little sandwiches from a tray sitting next to her. When had someone brought the food? Also, there were half a dozen girls standing around in their swimsuits, giving glances at Leslie and whispering.

When she looked at her watch, she saw that she'd been sitting in one spot for three hours. Beside her, on the stone terrace, was a wide spread of her watercolors. Someone had moved them from being piled on top of each other and had fanned them out across the stones and the surrounding lawn.

Leslie was embarrassed at having been in such deep thought that she had forgotten where she was. "I lost track of time," she said, smiling a bit. Why in the world were those girls whispering and looking at her? It was on the tip of her tongue to tell them that they were being rude, but she didn't want to sound like the mother she was.

"That's quite all right," Millie said. "In fact, here's someone I want you to meet."

Leslie looked up to see a tall man with gray hair and dark blue eyes approach them, and, judging from the way he looked at Millie, Leslie thought that he was in love with her. Was some family secret about to be revealed to her?

"Leslie, dear," Millie said, "I want you to meet an old friend of mine, Geoffrey Marsdon."

Politely, Leslie held out her hand to shake his, but he didn't shake her hand. Instead, he walked behind Leslie and picked up one of the watercolors she'd just done.

"Where have you studied?" he asked.

These people are so polite, Leslie thought. "At my father's construction business," she said, joking.

But Mr. Marsdon didn't smile in return. "Give me three days of your life and I'll tell you what you have."

At first Leslie had no idea what he was talking about, but Millie was smiling at her. "He knows what he's talking about. Those paintings of yours are quite good."

Leslie looked at Mr. Marsdon. "Raw. Crude, of course, but there's talent there," he said, picking up another painting and squinting at it.

"Raw?" Millie said. "Come on, Geoffrey, dear, you just asked where she'd trained."

"Do you think that I could . . . do something with . . . that I have . . ." Leslie said hesitantly.

Before Mr. Marsdon could reply, Millie said, "Geoffrey, dear, why don't you stay in the blue room, I know how you love it, and why don't you spend the rest of the week here with us? Maybe you and Leslie could work together and she could find out if she actually has talent or if today's paintings are just a fluke."

"What a gracious offer, Millicent," Geoffrey said. "And I accept."

They then both turned to look at Leslie.

"If you agree, that is," Millie said.

Leslie took a deep breath because she had an idea that the answer to this question was going to change her life forever. "Yes, I'd like that," she said at last. "I think I'd like to find out if there's more to me than just joining committees."

This answer seemed to puzzle Millie, but she smiled anyway. "And what about your dancing?"

"My jumps aren't high enough, and my— Well, let's just say that Broadway is safe."

Millie took Leslie's arm in hers. "Painting is much more . . . well, usable anyway."

Leslie knew that she meant that in a

woman's true profession of being a wife and mother, painting was more "genteel" than leaping about in front of people wearing little clothing. And privately, Leslie thought that painting would be something she could do while spending her days on the campaign trail.

"All right," Leslie said, "when do I start?"

Part Three

Twenty-seven

The three women were standing in Madame Zoya's little room, and each of them was dizzy from the quick change in time. But Madame Zoya's smiling face steadied them as they looked at her.

"And what have you decided?" she asked, looking at Leslie.

But Leslie was too disoriented to reply; she could only blink at the woman.

"I want the new life," Ellie said because her writer's mind knew what the psychic was asking. It was a question that she'd thought about a great deal in the last weeks. "But I want to remember everything. I don't want to forget what happened to me in the past." Her voice lowered and she gave a bit of a smile. "Or what was done *for* me."

Madame Zoya nodded, then looked at Leslie again. "And you?"

"I want the life I have," she said softly, "but I, too, want to remember it all. There is something I need to remember."

"A man," Ellie said, smiling.

"Oh, no," Leslie answered quickly. "Not a man. Me. I want to remember myself."

"What does that—" Ellie began eagerly.

But Madame Zoya interrupted her. "And you, dear?" she asked softly as she turned to Madison; then the other two looked at her also.

Madison didn't look well. She looked as though she'd just been through hell and hadn't yet returned. For a moment Madison swayed on her feet, as though she were going to faint, but then she lifted her head and looked at the psychic. "The new life," she whispered. "And I want to forget the old one. I don't want to remember anything about that life," she said with no hint of hesitation in her voice.

"Done," Madame Zoya said. "Now, dears, run along. I have other people to help."

Part of Ellie wanted to shout, "That's it?! You don't want to hear what happened to us?" But she didn't say anything. For one thing, she was confused. Right now she had two lives in her head—and she had a thousand memories, memories that contradicted one another. Which were real and which weren't?

Slowly, and awkwardly, the three of them made their way out of Madame Zoya's house. It wasn't easy, as it had been weeks since they'd been down those corridors. Twice they opened wrong doors, then stood and stared into rooms without having any idea what they were seeing.

At long last they were outside and standing on Madame Zoya's little porch, and the sunlight nearly blinded them.

It was Madison who recovered first, because her mind wasn't taken over by conflicting memories.

While Ellie and Leslie were blinking at the brightness and trying to sort out what was in their minds, Madison began to rummage in her big tote bag that was slung over her shoulder.

"Do either of you know what happened to my cell phone?" Madison asked. "I'm sure I had it a minute ago."

"Cell phone?" Ellie said, sounding as though she'd never heard of one.

"I must say that that was certainly a bust," Madison said, still digging inside her bag.

"A bust?" Leslie asked, looking at her hands. She had paint under her nails.

"Yes." Madison sounded impatient. "We went there to have our fortunes told, and we got zip. Really, the woman ought to be stopped."

Ellie and Leslie were looking at Madison as though she'd lost her mind, but Madison didn't see them. She was still rummaging in her bag. "Good heavens!" Madison said. "Where did these filthy things come from?" She was holding up a pack of cigarettes between her thumb and forefinger, and holding them away from her body as though she might be contaminated by them.

It was that gesture that brought Ellie and Leslie out of their own thoughts. Both of them were now looking at Madison—really, really *looking* at her.

Was it their imagination that she didn't seem as thin as she had been a day ago? Or was it just that there was now a look of health about her? She wasn't gray-looking, as she had been. And there was something about her eyes . . .

"You're pretty again," Ellie said.

Madison laughed. "Thank you," she said. "You're not bad yourself."

"No, I'm—" Ellie had been about to say that she was fat, but as she looked down at herself, her clothes seemed to be looser on her.

"Look at this thing?!" Madison said, holding up the bag. "I can't find anything I own in it, and it must have cost all of five dollars, and—" She broke off as she looked down at her clothes. "Could someone please tell me what is going on? Why am I wearing these cheap clothes and where is my cell phone? Ellie, could I borrow yours?"

Ellie was watching Madison with wide eyes because it was as though she were seeing movie special effects take place in front of her. Only this was no movie, this was real life. Years seemed to be sliding off Madison. She looked older than she did when they'd met each other nineteen years ago, but now she no longer looked beat-up by life. Now there was a light that shone in Madison's eyes, and light seemed to illuminate her skin from beneath it.

"I don't have a cell phone," Ellie said softly. "I've never liked telephones."

"I know," Madison said, looking at Ellie with exaggerated patience. "You told us you'd always hated them. But you said that after you had a child, you wanted to be in contact with him at all hours of the day."

"Child?" Ellie said, her eyes blinking blankly.

Madison looked from Ellie to Leslie, then back again. "What is wrong with you two? Did that charlatan tell you something dreadful? Is that why the two of you are acting like zombies?"

"Child," Ellie said again.

Madison bent down so her nose was close to Ellie's. "Yes, child. You have a two-year-old son. You and your second husband, Jessie, had a baby."

"Jessie," Ellie said, her eyes wide. At the moment, the memory of her life with Martin was so clear in her mind that she could hardly remember her time with Jessie. But the mention of his name was making her remember. "Nate," she said. "Nathaniel." She looked at Leslie in wonder. "I have a son named Nathaniel and I am married to Jessie Woodward."

"I'm so happy for you," Leslie whispered; then she put her arms around Ellie and hugged her. "So very, very happy for you."

"What is it that I'm missing?" Madison asked impatiently. "And could we go somewhere and get something to eat? I'm starving. I feel like treating myself to some rich, gooey dessert." She narrowed her eyes at both of them. "But if either of you tell Thomas, I'll deny it. He is fed up with hearing me complain about every pound I gain."

"Weight?" Ellie said. "*You* gain weight?"

"We can't all be like you and forget to eat."

With wide eyes, Ellie looked down at herself. It couldn't be possible, but her clothes seemed to be even more loose on her than they had been a few minutes ago.

But Madison wasn't aware of having said anything unusual. "I don't know why you don't remember this. We had this conversation only last night. You said that you and I have opposite metabolisms. You said that the happier you are the thinner you are. You said that if you ever got really depressed, you'd probably be the size of a house. Then I said that I was the opposite, that happiness makes me eat. I said that if I were ever unhappy, I'd probably weigh eighty pounds."

"That's right," Ellie said. "I would and you would. And we did."

Madison looked at Leslie as though to ask if Ellie were losing her marbles.

"I think we should all sit down and have something to eat," Leslie said. "And I think we should hear Madison's life story."

"But I told you two everything the first night we were here," Madison said. "I distinctly remember telling you about modeling in New York, about meeting Thomas at Columbia, and about getting my degree in—"

"No!" Ellie said loudly. "You must tell a story in the correct order."

"Yes," Madison said, smiling, obviously glad that Ellie remembered *something*. "You told us that you can't tell the punch line before you tell the joke. If you remember that, why don't you remember the other things you said?"

"Dumb," Ellie said as she took Madison's arm. "That's all it is: stupidity."

"Right," Leslie said, taking Madison's other arm as the three of them left the porch and began to walk down the street.

"Actually, Ellie liked your story so much that she wants to use it in her next book, so she wants to hear it all over again. She doesn't want to miss even one of the details."

"Good thinking," Ellie said. "I wish I'd thought of—I mean, Leslie is one hundred percent right. So let's go in here and you can tell us everything in detail. Start where you met us in New York." She looked around Madison's back to Leslie. "That's where she went back to, isn't it?"

"Yes," Leslie said as she opened the restaurant door.

"What does that mean?" Madison asked. " 'Back to'? You two are certainly acting strangely."

"Leftover hormones from childbearing," Ellie said quickly.

"Ridiculous!" Madison answered as she followed the hostess toward a table. "I've had four kids and the hormones are *not* left over."

At that statement, both Ellie and Leslie stopped in their tracks and looked at each other.

Leslie spoke first. "Four," she whispered.

"And Thomas," Ellie replied; then the next

second they were practically running to get to the table to sit across from Madison.

Ten minutes later they had placed their orders. Ellie leaned across the table and said, "Every word. I want to hear every word about your life from the moment you left the DMV."

"But you already know most of it, so why—"

"I'll dedicate my next book to you," Ellie said quickly.

"Will you put the names of my children in there?" Madison asked, smiling, her face softening.

Ellie looked about her, and as she'd suspected, most of the diners were looking at Madison. At forty, Madison was still so beautiful that she mesmerized people. But Ellie knew that just yesterday, this same woman had walked into shops and restaurants and no one had paid any particular attention to her.

"All right," Madison said. "I distinctly remember telling you two all of this, but if you want to hear it again, well . . . Let's see, where do I begin? After I left you two at the DMV, nineteen long years ago, I came up with a plan to distinguish myself at the modeling agency. After all," Madison said, "tall, gorgeous girls from Montana are a dime a dozen in New York, so I had to do something to stand out."

Madison saw the way Ellie looked at Leslie at that statement. "Are you two sure you want to hear this?"

"More than I want to call my . . . husband," Ellie said; then she took a deep breath. "And my son. So get on with it. You're holding me up."

"All right," Madison said, smiling. "I want to call my kids too, and, truthfully, maybe I did leave out some of the more colorful details when I told you about me. So, now, where was I? The first thing I did after I left you two was throw away that dreadful portfolio that my hometown photographer made for me. Poor thing. He meant well, but the pictures really had no pizzazz. Then . . ."

She looked at the other two women with a puzzled expression on her face. "Sometimes you look back at your life and you see things that you did and you wonder why you did them and, even, how you knew to do them. To this day I can't figure out how I knew to do this, but I looked in a phone book and found the name of a photographer and asked *him* to photograph me."

For a moment she paused for effect. "But he wasn't just *a* photographer, he was Cordova."

At this Ellie sucked in her breath; then she looked at Leslie, who was also impressed. Neither woman was involved in the world of photography or high fashion, but they knew this name. It was said that Cordova had single-handedly made modeling into an art form. There were galleries full of his work.

"Anyway," Madison continued, "maybe I'd read his name somewhere; I don't know. He was very young, he'd just graduated from some Midwestern university with a degree in photography, and he planned to spend his life taking pictures of fruit. Can you imagine? A talent like his, and on the day I met him, he was taking pictures of oranges to be put in some trade magazine that only buyers for grocery stores would see. But I went to his studio and I persuaded him to take a picture of me wearing only a snake."

At that Ellie blinked a couple of times; then she said, "Poor Nastassja Kinski."

"Why would you feel sorry for the actress?" Madison asked as her plate was put in front of her. It was heaped with three kinds of fried seafood on top of a bed of french fries, while Ellie and Leslie were having cold lobster salads.

"Never mind," Ellie said. "Go on with your story."

Madison smiled as she picked up her fork. "I remember that day as though it happened last week. And I remember the man who got the snake." She looked up at Ellie and Leslie. "It was a big snake. A really, really *big* snake."

Twenty-eight

1981
NEW YORK

Madison was standing outside the door of the DMV in New York, and for a few seconds she was so disoriented that she didn't know where she was. But when she turned her head and saw her own reflection in the window of a bakery, she gasped. It had been a long time since she'd seen *that* face.

She kept staring at herself, seeing her face as others saw it. When she'd been twenty-one and had lived with that reflection all her life, Madison hadn't paid much attention to it. In fact, most of the time, she regretted her looks, as they stood in the way of her achieving anything beyond the beauty that so interested other people.

But now, at nearly forty, Madison had had enough time to know what a gift she'd been given. And she knew that she should have valued that gift.

Part of her was still that girl, fresh from Montana and feeling homesick and alone. Part of her wanted to go home and wanted an excuse to do so.

But now, years later, Madison also knew what was out there. She knew what awaited her at home.

And this time, she was going to change her life.

There was a wire trash basket on the sidewalk, and propping her heavy tote bag on it, Madison began to look inside the bag. There were candy bars, two little plastic bags filled with cheap makeup, a hospital magazine, a tiny box that she knew contained a necklace her mother had given her when she was five, and there was the portfolio of pictures that had been taken in Montana.

Opening the portfolio, Madison looked at the photos in disbelief. Nineteen years ago the world at large knew a great deal less about modeling than it did now. Was that good or bad? she wondered, then decided that she didn't have time to ponder philosophical issues. However she came by the knowledge, she knew that these were not photos that would get her inside the inner sanctum of the people who could get her bookings.

Thinking back to the first time she'd been here, she remembered the horrible time she'd had in the modeling agency's office. The receptionist was a little snit of a thing, ugly inside and out, and she took pleasure in making the beautiful girls in the office wait. After she'd looked at Madison, wearing her summer dress with its ruffles down the front, she'd flipped through the book of photos of Madison posing picturesquely by a tree; then she'd made a snort that could be heard three floors away. Every hopeful girl in the office had smiled, for they knew that Madison had probably just lost her chance in the modeling world.

And now, Madison remembered how angry she'd been at that receptionist. How dare she set herself up as a judge? Madison had thought. Madison's anger had made her look down her nose at the woman and let her know what she thought of her.

Big mistake. Later Madison had been told that the receptionists were the first lookers and the agency heads trusted their judgment.

"You don't photograph well, do you?" the woman had said, then handed the portfolio back to Madison with a little smirk on her face.

Now Madison was embarrassed to remember her arrogance, ashamed to remember how she'd stormed out of the office in a rage.

The same sort of thing happened at two other agencies, but by that time Madison had a chip on her shoulder that was as big as a Montana mountain. All her life she'd been told that she was smashingly beautiful, but to have her features taken apart and commented on . . . It had been too much for her. So when Roger had called, she was glad for the excuse to get out of the city and go back home.

But *this time* she was going to do things differently, because now she knew what awaited her at home.

Looking back in her bag, Madison removed the box that held the necklace from her mother; then she tossed the candy, the makeup and the portfolio into the trash bin. She took out a little bank book that showed how much money she had. There was almost seventeen thousand dollars in the account, and she knew that more than half of it was from her father.

Looking at the little book, Madison smiled. Nineteen years ago, the fact that her father had handed over ten grand to his illegitimate daughter had made her furious. He didn't acknowledge her as his, but he *did* send her his dirty ol' money.

But Madison was older and wiser now, and she understood a great deal more about the world. She understood about passion and how you could do things in a moment that you could spend the rest of your life regretting. And Madison knew that there were fathers who wouldn't have sent money no matter how much they had.

Now, she looked at the money her father had given her and thought of it as a gift. And she thought about what her hometown had done for her too. Years ago she'd been angered that they had "made" her go somewhere she didn't want to go and had tried to "force" her to become something that she didn't want to become.

All these things had become rage inside Madison, and she'd made sure that she'd repaid everyone by *not* doing what they wanted her to. She'd spent the town's money and her father's money on Roger. And while she was in New York, she made sure that she got no bookings for modeling. Later she'd returned to Montana and she'd told her old high school friends that New York had been a cold, hard place and that she hadn't wanted to live there. Her friends had wanted to hear that, but the merchants who'd paid her way had sighed and looked away from her. It was no wonder that until after the divorce, Madison rarely visited her hometown. But by the time of the divorce, all the things that had happened to Madison showed on her face and her body, so no one ever again talked to her about modeling.

So now she had a chance to change things. Now she was a different woman. Now she'd learned the value of an opportunity.

There was a telephone booth nearby, and there was a battered yellow pages hanging on a chain below it. Quickly thumbing through the pages, Madison found the listings for photographers—and there it was. "Michael Cordova."

Years ago someone had asked Madison if she'd ever been photographed by Cordova. Madison had smiled and said that when she'd been in New York, no one had heard of Cordova. It had been a young girl who'd asked—her mother was a high school friend of Madison's—and she'd looked at Madison as though to say that she was very old.

Later, while sitting at her lunch of a carton of yogurt, Madison had thought about that. Wouldn't it have been ironic if she had met Cordova and they could have started their careers together?

She put money in the telephone to call him, but changed her mind and put down the receiver. No, she was going to go see the man. And she was going to do whatever she could to persuade him to photograph her.

"I don't do models," he said as he looked down the viewfinder of his Hasselblad. In front of him was a table piled full of oranges that had been dyed to be more orange. He was a little man, the top of his head hardly coming up to Madison's shoulder. He had a hooked nose, a lipless mouth, and eyes that were as intense as an eagle's.

"I've heard of you all the way in Montana," she said in her most innocent, but most seductive voice. His studio was in an old warehouse, dirty, probably unheated.

Quickly, he turned and gave her an up-and-down look. "You wanta cut the crap and tell me what you're after?"

I could never have done this at twenty-one, Madison thought, but now his tone and attitude were a relief to her. She was having difficulty trying to pretend to be a young girl. "I want you to take pictures of me."

"I don't do fashion," he said, not bothering to look at her. "Look in the yellow pages. You can find a hundred photographers who'd love to shoot you."

Madison wanted to say that she only had three weeks in which to change her entire future, so she didn't have time to beg. "If you can push the button on a camera, you can take fashion photos," she said, and more annoyance than she meant to show came out in her voice.

"You've got b—"

"Determination," she said quickly. "And obviously more belief in you than you have in yourself. What do you lose if you fail? You go back to taking pictures of fruit? But if you make a star of me, what can happen to *you*? Did you buy that camera *used*?"

For a moment she held her breath. Would he throw her out? He turned the crank on the camera, shot again, then turned the crank again. He didn't look up at her. "You pay the costs of film and developing."

"Deal," she said instantly.

She'd taken a cab to his studio so she wouldn't arrive sweaty, and while in the cab she'd made a sketch. She felt bad that she was copying something that someone more original than she was going to do, but she'd made a simple drawing of a woman lying on her side, with an enormous snake wrapped around her.

"Someone once told me that he'd like to see a girl wearing nothing but a snake."

The photographer didn't respond to that, just kept on shooting pictures of his oranges. He had an assistant, a mousy little man, who stood on the sidelines and loaded the cameras.

"A big snake," Madison said into the silence.

Turning, he looked at her. "I don't do porn."

At that Madison drew in her breath. "Give me a break, will you? I'm a tall beautiful girl from Montana, but tall, beautiful girls from Montana are on every corner in the modeling world. I need something to make me different. No porn, but art. Shocking art. Can you do it or not? If you can't, tell me so I can stop wasting my time."

For the first time, she saw interest in his eyes, and she held her breath to see what he was going to say. "You have a head on your shoulders, don't you?"

"Old head in a young body, but I'm marketing the young part. Nobody pays to look at the old part."

When she saw his smile, she knew that she had him. She wanted to dance around in triumph, but she made herself stand still and wait. It was his turn to act now.

She handed him the sketch she'd made. He looked at it for quite some time, then he took his wallet out of his back pocket, removed a credit card, and handed it to his assistant. "Get me a snake."

The young man looked at the plastic card

in horror. "Where do I . . . ?" he whispered, unable to finish the sentence.

"It's New York, so find me a snake, a big snake. Have it here at nine tomorrow morning."

Ccrdova then turned his attention to Madison and looked at her as though she were a piece of merchandise. "You have fat hips and one eye is larger than the other."

Madison smiled. She'd been told this before, but that time it had made her furious. "Then you'll just have to light me so the flaws don't show, won't you?" she said.

He didn't answer, but she could see that his eyes were twinkling. I think he likes me, she thought.

"Who does your makeup?" he asked.

"Have any friends?" she asked, hope in her voice.

"Actually, I do. Be here at six tomorrow morning. You're going to take some work."

Again, in the past, a remark like that would have insulted her, but now she just smiled. "Right. Better tell your friend to bring a trowel and a bag of cement. It's going to take a lot to make me look as good as your oranges."

He tried to keep one corner of his mouth

from turning upward, but he couldn't. "Go. Get out of here. Get some sleep. Maybe your eyes will even out. And do something about that dress. It makes me sick just to look at it."

Madison turned toward the door and by the time she reached it, he was already back at his camera. "Thanks," she said, but he didn't look up at her.

Once she was outside, she looked in her bag and saw that she had a key and, thankfully, the address of the cheap downtown hotel where she was staying. If she hadn't written it down, she knew she wouldn't have remembered the address after all these years.

When she reached her little hotel room, she pulled all the clothes she'd brought with her out of the closet and the rickety chest of drawers. Mrs. Welch, who owned the only clothing store in Erskine, had donated an entire wardrobe to Madison to take with her to New York. "It's difficult to get things in your size, but I did it," she'd told Madison the day before she was to board the plane.

Now, looking at the clothes, Madison was horrified. Frills and little gold buttons, plaids and flowery prints, were spread out in front of her. If she'd worn any of these clothes to the modeling agency, no wonder the receptionist had smirked at her. But then, Madison seemed to remember that the other hopefuls had been wearing clothes just like hers.

Leaving the clothes on the bed, Madison walked uptown to Saks.

Three hours later she returned, exhausted, and flopped down on the bed on top of her clothes-from-home, dropping her heavy shopping bags to the floor.

In the bags she had nothing but black and white. She'd bought nothing that wasn't perfect in 1981 as well as the year 2000. Classic. Plain. Simple.

And unbelievably expensive. She'd bought a pair of black wool trousers that cost twelve hundred dollars new, but she'd purchased them on sale for a "mere" six hundred. A white cotton blouse, from Italy, had cost her, on sale, two hundred and fifty. She'd bought a Hermes belt, with a matching bag and shoes.

On the way back from the stores, she'd stopped in a shop and had her eyelashes dyed. When she did show up at the modeling agency, she planned to go with a face devoid of makeup. She planned to show off her skin, not hide it under foundation makeup. She would have just the deep black lashes, unclumped by mascara, and her hair would be streaked and in a perfect cut.

The next morning, Madison was at Cordova's studio at five-thirty A.M. She'd eaten nothing since noon the day before, and she hoped she lasted the day without food. She had to drop about fifteen pounds as soon as possible.

To Madison's surprise—and delight—the photographer seemed to have decided to make a serious try at the shoot, because there were two young men waiting for her. They were young and inexperienced, but eager. And when Madison heard their names, she had to keep from swooning. She knew that one of the young men was going to go to Hollywood and on a future Oscar night his name would be mentioned in answer to the question, "Who did your makeup?" Now he was staring at Madison, a pair of tweezers in his hand, and frowning. "Honey, with those eyebrows I should have brought a lawn mower."

The other man was a hairdresser, and

Madison knew that someday he'd have not only his own salon but also his own line of extremely expensive hair products. "And what am I to do with *this*?" the hairdresser said as he picked up a handful of Madison's hair.

Madison smiled down at the two of them and said, "I hope you boys brought a ladder with you."

She made them laugh and, as a result, she made them her friends. She was able to direct the hairdresser to cut her hair in the style of Jennifer Aniston on *Friends,* a cut that would sweep the country years later, but in 1981 was absolutely new. "Sorry, Jennifer," Madison mumbled as she looked in the portable mirror that was in front of her.

At precisely nine A.M., the door to the studio opened and in walked two huge, sweaty men wearing sleeveless T-shirts and carrying a snake that was as big around as Madison was.

What the hell have I done? she thought; then Cordova whispered in her ear, "Turning coward?"

Madison swallowed.

The two sweaty men were looking at Madison as they put the snake on the floor.

She was made up, her hair was soft and framing her face, and she was wearing only a thin kimono.

"I want fifty copies of the picture," one of the men said, leering at Madison.

Turning away, Madison grimaced. It was one thing to disrobe in front of the photographer and the other men—they certainly weren't interested in *her*—but these men . . .

"I hope he puts the pictures on the Internet," she mumbled.

"The what?" the hairdresser asked.

"Never mind," Madison said; then she took a deep breath and untied her robe, but held it closed.

But then she smiled. What the hell? she thought. When you're twenty, you want to keep covered, but when you're forty, you're glad when someone asks. Naked, she turned around and looked at the snake. "Let's *do* it," she said.

When Madison walked into the office of the top modeling agency in New York, her first thought was that she felt old. The office was full of girls young enough to be her daughter.

But there was a mirror by the door and a brief glance showed that her body was as young as these girls'. But she was happy to see that age was the only thing that they had in common.

The girls were dressed as she had been the first time she'd walked through those doors. They had on their "Sunday best," which meant little suits and lots of jewelry. And their makeup was in the style that was taught in "charm schools" all over the U.S.: too much and too obvious.

Standing amid the other girls, Madison, with her plain white blouse and her plain black trousers, with her glowing skin without any makeup, looked like a perfect pearl beside a bed of aquarium gravel.

Sitting behind the desk was the same squat, ugly, bad-tempered receptionist she remembered so well. "Yeah?" she said as she looked up at Madison.

The first time around that sullen glare and the hostility of the woman had enraged Madison. But this time, she smiled sweetly at her. "I'd like to present my portfolio and possibly see Mrs. Vanderpool," Madison said.

The receptionist tried to cover it, but she

was impressed by the look of Madison. Obviously, the woman recognized the quality—and cost—of the clothes she had on. "You got an appointment?"

"Actually, I do," Madison said. She'd been caught in this trap the last time. "It's for eleven, and I believe it's that now."

"I've been waiting for three hours!" said a girl from behind Madison.

"We didn't even open until an hour ago," the receptionist snapped; then she looked down at her appointment book. "I don't see you in here."

Madison pointed to the eleven A.M. slot. "That's me."

"What kind of name is 'Madison'?" the receptionist snapped again.

Madison resisted the urge to snap back. "The one my mother gave me," she said, still smiling. "Perhaps you'd like to look over my portfolio while I wait," she said, then she put the big black book on top of the woman's desk. This time the portfolio was leather, not plastic.

More than anything in the world, Madison wanted to stand there and watch the face of the woman when she first opened the book and saw the pictures that Cordova had taken. In the end, she'd spent three days with the man. Once his creativity was unleashed, there was no holding him back. When a crate of peaches had been delivered to him to shoot, he'd sent the hairdresser out to buy a cheap black wig and he'd sent his assistant out to find clothes "like a gypsy would wear." After the snake, the assistant wasn't protesting any assignment.

Cordova had photographed Madison dressed as a gypsy sitting in the middle of a thousand peaches. Well, it looked like a thousand when Cordova got through arranging them around an artificial hill.

It was Madison who suggested that he drop the "Michael" from his name and just go by Cordova. He'd liked the idea instantly, but he kept looking at her out of the corner of his eye, as though he were afraid that any minute she might change into a creature from outer space.

But now, in the agency office, Madison made herself keep her back to the receptionist as she walked to the end of the room to the only vacant chair. But when she turned around, she had the deep satisfaction of seeing that dreadful little woman looking at the photos with her mouth hanging open in shock.

When she looked up and saw Madison watching her, she closed her mouth and the book. Then, as though it were something she did every day, she got up from her desk, pulled her too-tight blouse down, then picked up the stack of portfolios off her desk. Acting as though taking Madison's were only an afterthought, she dropped it on top of the stack, then went to the door of the office where Mrs. Vanderpool decided the fates of hundreds of young women.

The receptionist gave a quick knock; then when she opened the door, they heard, "This better be good," from inside the office. Obviously, Mrs. Vanderpool didn't like interruptions.

When the door closed behind the woman, Madison realized that her heart was pounding. Had she been too aggressive? Maybe she should have just had her photo taken by a good New York photographer. Something plain. Ordinary. *Not* with a snake.

It was probably only minutes later that the door opened, but to Madison, it seemed hours. And when the door swung wide, it wasn't the snotty little receptionist standing there but Mrs. Vanderpool herself. Or, in the modeling world, that would be, Herself.

Madison held her breath as the woman, with her iron gray hair, in her ordinary little dress, scanned the room. When she saw Madison, she halted. "Are you Madison Appleby?"

Madison gave the woman a polite smile and nodded. Truth was, there was a lump in her throat too big for her to speak.

"Would you like to come into my office?"

"Yes, thank you," Madison managed to get out; then she had to make her feet move forward.

She followed Mrs. Vanderpool into her inner office, and the door closed behind them.

Twenty-nine

"That is, without a doubt, the most wonderful story I have ever heard," Leslie said.

"Even the second time around?" Madison asked, smiling.

"I could hear that story a thousand times and it would get better with each telling," Ellie said. "So what happened next?"

"But you know the rest," Madison answered, looking about for the waitress. "Do you think they have a dessert menu?"

"It's Maine, ask for blueberries," Ellie said impatiently. "I want to know what happened next."

Leslie put her hand on Ellie's arm. "But we know the rest, don't we? Haven't we been seeing your picture in magazines for years?"

"Have we?" Ellie asked eagerly.

"Here and there," Madison said, smiling, "but I've had other things to do besides stand in front of a camera. But then, you two know that story. Oh, good, here comes the dessert cart."

"Madison," Ellie said slowly, "I will buy you everything on that cart if you'll just tell the rest of the story."

Laughing, Madison pointed to a large slice of chocolate cake with chocolate icing. "I behaved myself," she said simply as the waitress placed the dessert in front of her.

Ellie and Leslie waved the cart away.

"And that means?" Ellie encouraged her.

"I showed up on time for bookings, and I took all the work I could get. I don't mean to brag, but the result was that I was on the cover of three fashion magazines and was offered a lucrative cosmetics contract at the end of just eight weeks."

Madison paused to take a bite of her cake. "But when I held the checks I'd received for the work, I thought, I could send two kids to college on this. And that's what gave me the idea, and you know the rest."

"No we don't!!!" the other two said in unison.

Madison looked at them in disbelief that

they could have forgotten something so big. "I used the money to start working on getting my degree," she said.

"Your degree in what?" Ellie asked, her breath held.

Madison narrowed her eyes at her. "You know as well as I do that I'm a doctor."

"Of medicine?" Leslie asked, her eyes wide.

"Yes. I'm a physiatrist," Madison said, shaking her head at them. "I'm glad I chose that specialty because I had a wonderful teacher at Columbia, Dr. Dorothy Oliver. It was as though she and I had known each other forever."

Ellie looked at Leslie; then Leslie looked at Ellie. At first they smiled at each other; then they grinned. Then, in a spontaneous gesture, they began to laugh. Then they threw back their heads and laughed some more. Then they pushed their chairs back and got up and linked arms and began to dance around, laughing happily.

The other patrons looked up, at first frowning, but when they saw the unabashed happiness of the two women, they smiled.

There was music playing in the restaurant, something soothing, but Ellie and

Leslie seemed to find a beat as they whirled each other about in what looked like fifties swing. "Doctor!" Ellie said. "She's a doctor."

"Of medicine," Leslie answered, laughing, as she twirled about with Ellie.

When it came to dancing, Ellie was outclassed by Leslie, so she stepped back, and in the next second Leslie was on her toes. In a way, it had been about eighteen years since Leslie had danced, but in another way, for the last two weeks, she'd spent two hours a day dancing. Now, she put her hands above her head in a graceful arc and began to twirl her body in a tight little circle; then, still twirling, she made her way between the tables.

The diners knew talent and experience when they saw it. They put down their forks and gave their attention to Leslie, and when Ellie began to clap to the rhythm of the music, so did they. Leslie twirled through the entire restaurant, never losing her balance, or her momentum.

When she returned to their table, she stopped. And when she stopped, the restaurant burst into applause. Smiling, her face red with embarrassment, but pleasure also, Leslie dropped into a deep curtsy, as though she were a ballerina at the end of a bravura performance.

Moments later, they were again seated at the table, both Ellie and Leslie looking at Madison with shining eyes.

"You still have it," Madison said to Leslie.

"No, not really," she answered, but this time there was no sound of "failure" in her voice. "The truth was that I never did have it."

"But I just saw—"

Leslie had to take a deep drink of water. Yesterday she may have been twenty, but today she was forty, and the body she'd just used was not in shape. "I'm a better dancer than the average person, but I'm not as good as the best dancers. And that's what I always wanted to be: the best."

"But—" Madison began, but Ellie cut her off.

"So how did you meet Thomas?" Ellie asked.

Looking down at her empty dessert plate, Madison smiled. "Do you two remember that when I met you, I said that I'd been jilted by a boy back home?"

"We remember," Leslie said quietly. "What happened to him?"

"Don't tell the punch line before the story, remember?" Madison said, smiling. "The boy who jilted me, Roger, that was his name, wrote me a couple of letters while I was in New York, and it was through him that all the best things in my life have happened."

Pausing for a moment, Madison waited for Leslie or Ellie to make a reply to this, but both women wore identical expressions: both women had curled upper lips, as though the mention of Roger's name disgusted them.

"Roger wrote me that the brother of a college friend of his was going to Columbia University. With my background, I didn't know one college from another, but that school was in New York, so I applied there."

Looking down at her water glass, she gave a secretive little smile. "At the time, I didn't know what a prestigious school Columbia was and how difficult it was to get into. But all through high school, I'd done my own schoolwork and Roger's as well. So, in essence, I'd had two educations. I'd studied English and history, but Roger wanted to impress people, so he'd taken physics and chemistry courses." Still smiling, she looked up at Leslie and Ellie. "Let's just say that Roger made straight As in all his courses. So, any test they gave me, I passed with high marks. I was told that I should apply for a scholarship, but I wanted to pay my own way."

"So you went to Columbia thanks to Roger," Ellie said, smiling; then she exchanged looks with Leslie.

"Yes," Madison answered. "But when I got there, I was much too shy to introduce myself to Roger's friend's brother." Smiling, Madison looked down for a moment. "I'm not sure either of you saw it in our one brief meeting so long ago, but I used to believe that I wasn't . . . Well, I guess you'd say that I didn't believe that I was of the class of people who went to medical school."

"I never noticed that, did you, Leslie?" Ellie said, with her eyes wide in feigned innocence.

"*I* certainly never thought you were less than brilliant," Leslie said, smiling.

"You two are great for my ego," Madison said. "But, anyway, I think it was Roger's letters telling me about something that had happened to him that made me choose my specialty, and because of that, I met my wonderful teacher, Dr. Dorothy Oliver. And, by some one-in-a-million chance, it turned out that her nephew was the friend's brother who Roger had written me about."

Madison waited for a moment as though she expected this extraordinary coincidence to garner exclamations from Leslie and Ellie, but, instead, they sat there silently, waiting for her to continue.

"So I finally met Thomas in my second year in med school," Madison continued, "and we hit it off immediately. He helped me every step of the way through school and we were married the day after I graduated."

Ellie and Leslie leaned back in their chairs, smiling in satisfaction.

"And you have children," Leslie said, not as a question but a statement. Happiness sounded in her words.

"Yes, four of them," Madison said, still smiling. "Both Thomas and I would have a dozen if we could. We love kids. They make life worth living. If I didn't have them . . ." She looked up. "Well, anyway, I can't imagine what my life would be like if I didn't have Thomas and the children. Sometimes I think that we were all made for each other, that if we didn't have one another, that there wouldn't be anyone else for us. Does that make sense?"

"More sense than you can possibly imagine," Leslie said.

"So now all of you live in New York?" Ellie asked.

"No," Madison said. "Didn't I tell you— Oh, right. You don't remember anything. The lot of us live in Montana, in Erskine. We have a clinic there."

Ellie had once researched clinics in small towns, and she knew that they made little money. Without thinking, she said under her breath, "That's right. Thomas was wealthy."

"Oh, no," Madison said quickly. "It was *my* money that we used for the clinic. What money Thomas has is tied up in trust for the children."

"From modeling," Leslie said pointedly to Ellie. "She earned the money from modeling."

"No," Madison said; then she looked down at her cup of coffee for a moment. The waitress had taken their plates and refilled their coffee cups. "You two are going to think this is strange, but I made the money in the stock market. It was weird, but I could look at a list of companies that were on the stock exchange and I seemed to *know* which stocks were going to go up."

For a moment she looked at the other two women, as though waiting for them to express surprise at this, but when neither of them said anything, Madison continued. "It started out innocently enough. One day one of my fellow medical students was reading aloud about the stock market and I told him which stocks were going to go up. It was as though I *knew* which products were going to catch the imagination of the American people."

When neither Leslie nor Ellie replied to this, Madison went on. "I began investing what I could spare from the catalog modeling work that I did while I went to school." Madison paused to take a sip of her coffee. "And when the Internet started, I invested heavily. I was *sure* that thing was going to do well!"

Again, she paused; then, looking up, she gave them a brilliant smile. "To make a long story short, I made millions."

Still, she saw no shock on the faces of Ellie and Leslie.

"I felt that I owed my hometown a lot because, if it hadn't been for their sending me to New York, who knows what would have happened to me? I might have ended up never leaving the place and marrying some guy I hated and . . ." She trailed off, as though the idea were too ridiculous to pursue.

"Anyway, I talked to Thomas about what I wanted to do, and he agreed wholeheartedly, so we invested most of the money in equipment to start a clinic in Erskine. We practiced general medicine for a year or so, but we always knew that we wanted to go into rehabilitation medicine, which is my love. So now, Thomas and I have a small hospital with six physical therapists working for us."

Smiling, she leaned back in her chair. "And you know something? The clinic is not only paying its way, but we make a profit, so we can give our employees fat Christmas bonuses. We get a lot of the ski injuries from the resorts near us, and it's their injuries that pay for the clinic. And our profits also allow us to give free medical care to any resident of Erskine."

She looked at Ellie and Leslie as though waiting for questions from them, but both of them were silent, which encouraged Madison to continue.

"Life is funny, isn't it?" Madison said. "When I was first told that I was being sent to New York to become a model, I resented what I thought of as interference from some meddling old-timers. Truthfully, I thought they wanted me to put Erskine on the map so *they* could profit. It's funny to think of now, but I was even angry at my father—who, by the way, is a nice man and often sees his grandkids—but I was angry that he sent the money for me to go to New York. I don't know what changed my mind, but suddenly, the resentment was gone."

For a moment, Madison looked at them. "You know something? I changed the day we met. After I left the DMV, it was as though the resentment had vanished and I knew what I was to do and where I was going."

"Almost as though someone had waved a magic wand," Ellie said softly.

"Yes! Exactly! I changed after we met. And because I changed my attitude, everything good happened to me. I met Thomas, and we have a beautiful family, and—"

"And your hometown has prospered," Ellie said.

"Yes, they have, but then I owe them everything, don't I?" Madison said. "I wanted to do something to repay them for sending me to New York and for caring about me after my mother died and after my boyfriend dumped me."

"What happened to Roger?!" Ellie and Leslie said loudly in unison, making Madison laugh.

"Poor guy," Madison said, shaking her head. "I feel so sorry for him." For a moment she looked down at the table, then back up at them. "I'm not sure you'll believe this after what I told you about what he'd done to me—you *do* remember that part, don't you?"

"Yes!" Leslie and Ellie again said in unison.

"He called me in New York not long after I got there and told me that he'd been seriously injured by a car running over him. He was a mess, both mentally and physically. He told me he needed me and he begged me to return home to help him. He said that since I'd nursed my mother, I knew all that I needed to know, and that I was the only one on earth who *could* help him."

"And what did *you* say?" Leslie asked.

When Madison looked up, there was a bit of a grimace on her face. "You know, to this day, I still feel a bit guilty about what I did to him. Now that I'm older I realize how much pain he must have been in, but at the time, all I could think of was the way he'd dumped me after all I'd done for him. I'm afraid that I wasn't very sympathetic to his plight. I told him . . ."

Madison had a guilty look on her face. "I told him that his family could afford to hire the best and that I wasn't going to be his free nurse. Pretty callous of me, wasn't it?"

When Madison saw the way that Leslie and Ellie looked at each other, and saw the joy that lit up their faces, she glared at them. "If you two start dancing again, I swear I'll walk out of here. One time was interesting, but two would be embarrassing."

"We'll restrain ourselves," Leslie said.

Smiling, Ellie said, "So what happened to good ol' Roger?"

"*Mmmm*," Madison said. "That's where I *do* feel guilty. He didn't get the care that he needed after the accident. But, worse, he had been misdiagnosed. Right after the accident, he was told that he would never walk again, and it seems that no one questioned that diagnosis."

"You mean that today he's still in a wheelchair?" Ellie asked.

"Yes. It was awful, really. His parents always were the coldest people in the world, and I think that they were embarrassed by their imperfect son, so they put him on the second floor of their house and left him there. He had a male nurse to tend to his basic needs, but no one ever questioned the original diagnosis. And no one ever gave him a MRI after his injuries had healed enough to see that the lesion had not been complete, as they'd originally thought."

Madison paused for a moment. "As I told you, for a while after his call, Roger and I exchanged a few letters, but I think his parents discouraged the correspondence, as they always did think I was of a lower class than their son. Anyway, Roger never recovered from his injuries. His parents died in a boating accident years ago, and Roger inherited their house and lots of money. But it hasn't made him happy. He's been married three or four times—I don't remember which—

and each divorce has made him a great deal poorer.

"I know so much about him because three times a week he travels the distance to our clinic. I was the one who saw that his spinal cord had *not* been severed, as he'd been told. We've worked hard on his rehabilitation, but . . ."

Madison raised her hands in a gesture of helplessness. "The truth is that Roger's heart isn't into the work that it would take to make him walk again. He needs someone to push him and beg him and . . . I guess he needs someone to make him believe that he's once again the captain of the football team and the most popular boy in school. But no one can give that to him. It's too late."

For a moment, Madison looked angry. "Truthfully, it's all such a shame! And such a waste. If his parents hadn't been so cheap years ago and had shelled out for proper therapy, Roger might have recovered. And who knows what he could have been?"

At that Leslie and Ellie looked at each other.

"Yeah, who knows?" Ellie said. "Roger was such a nice guy, wasn't he?"

"I don't think you should judge him just by what he did to me," Madison said. "Sometimes I've wondered what would have happened to me if I'd returned to him that time when he called and—"

"No!" Ellie half shouted, then looked at the table next to them and lowered her voice. "You did the right thing by *not* going back to him."

"Of course I did," Madison said, frowning. "But I still feel that I owe him. If he hadn't dumped me, the town wouldn't have sent me to New York. And if it hadn't been for Roger's letters, I wouldn't have applied at Columbia. And even after I was introduced to Thomas by Dorothy, if it hadn't been for his brother knowing Roger, Thomas and I might not have come to know each other because . . ." Madison smiled. "Well, Thomas *is* from a rich family, and let's just say that he's a bit leery of pretty girls who are friendly to him. Thomas can be a bit intimidating."

"But not to you," Leslie said softly.

"No, not to me. I seemed to understand Thomas from the moment I met him. He and I—" Madison broke off because she could tell her story but she didn't want anyone to see how deeply she felt about her husband, her children, her work, and about her life in general.

"You know something," Madison said softly. "I'm happy. I know it's an old-fashioned way of thinking, but I'm happy. I have family and friends, and I have my work. My life isn't exciting; in fact, it's very ordinary. We have hot dogs on the Fourth of July and I go out trick-or-treating with my children, but I enjoy it. Sometimes people see photos of me, especially the one with the snake, and they can't believe that I gave up a chance to be a 'supermodel' and lead a life of flying to Rome for the weekend for running a clinic in tiny, boring Erskine. But . . ."

Emotion seemed to overcome her, and for a moment she looked away to calm herself. "What about you two?" she asked when she turned back.

"Very happy," Ellie said, as her mind was beginning to clear.

Both women looked at Leslie in question.

"I don't know," she said honestly. "I have some things to do with my life, and since I haven't yet done them, I don't know how they're going to work. Ask me in six months."

"What about—" Ellie began, wanting to hear everything that Leslie had to say.

But Leslie cut her off as she stood up. "I don't know about you two but I am suddenly very tired. I think I'd like to go back to the house and take a nap."

"Sounds great to me," Madison said.

"Me too," Ellie added, but as she said it, she thought, We're all lying. We have things we want to do in private. As for her, she wanted to get to the nearest stationer's store and buy a pen and paper because Madison's story had given her an idea for a book. She wanted to write something about how we all touch each other's lives, about—

"Ready?" Leslie said, and Ellie realized that she'd been standing at the table, lost in a daydream.

Madison walked out first, and Leslie caught up to Ellie. "I want to hear what happened between you and your ex-husband," Leslie said quietly. "What happened in the courtroom?"

"Would it make sense if I said that I need to sit down and *remember* it?"

"Perfectly," Leslie said. "I have to think about what happened to me too."

Ellie looked at Leslie in question. "You

went back, but you decided to change nothing. Did your almost-president turn out to be a jerk? Tell me so when he comes up for election, I won't vote for him."

She'd meant her words as a joke, but Leslie didn't smile. "Actually, he was lovely. I think he is probably nicer than my husband is, maybe smarter, definitely more considerate, and certainly kinder."

"*Yeow!*" Ellie said. "And you left him behind?"

Leslie took her time in answering. "Would you understand if I said that I love my family very much, but at the same time I am fed up with them?"

"Yes, I *do* understand. So what do you plan to do about it?"

Leslie smiled. "I have no idea at all. None."

Ellie laughed. "Okay, so now we're all going to pretend to take naps, but instead we're all going to do things in private. Madison is going to call her family and gush to them about how much she loves and misses them, and you're going to—?"

"I'm going to take a long walk and see if I can figure out what to do with my life as it is. No more withdrawing into a fantasy about a boy from college and what-could-have-been. From now on I live in the present." Leslie smiled. "And you are . . . let me guess . . ." In an exaggerated gesture, Leslie put her fingertips to her temple as though she were thinking. "You're going to write down all the things you thought about while Madison was talking, and you're going to try to put her story into a book—without getting yourself sued, that is."

Ellie laughed. "I'm that transparent, am I?"

"Yes and no," Leslie said seriously. "I think I've finally learned how important *self* is to a person, and with you, those stories inside your head are what makes you you. Take them away and you have—"

"One fat, depressed woman," Ellie said.

"Right," Leslie answered. "Speaking of which, isn't that a nice little clothing store on the corner? Before you leave, I think you should pay them a visit. You don't want to go home to Jessie and Nate wearing clothes twice as big as you need, do you?"

At the thought of having her own body back, Ellie had to turn away for a moment. But it wasn't just having her body back.

Thanks to Jessie, she now had her self-esteem back.

When they reached the house, Madison ran inside, obviously eager to get to a telephone. But neither Leslie nor Ellie went inside. Turning back toward town, Ellie went in search of a stationer's store, and Leslie kept walking down the road, her mind already faraway.

Thirty

Ellie leaned back against the headrest of the plane's seat and smiled to herself. She was back where she'd started, but this time her life was, oh, so very different. It was nearly two days since she'd returned from . . . What? She still didn't know what to call it. Time travel? A sort of mega-sized makeover?

Whatever it was, it had certainly changed her life. She still remembered what she'd been put through the first time with her divorce from Martin, but now that time seemed like a story that she'd read—an impossible story that no one would believe, but certainly not reality.

Now, closing her eyes, she again replayed the story as it had happened the second time around. Last night she and

Leslie had stayed up late, and Ellie had told Leslie all of it.

"It was Jessie who figured everything out," Ellie said, smiling in memory. "Before I could love Jessie, I had to let go of my anger and my desperate need for what I thought of as 'justice.' Once I did that, I could answer the questions that Jessie asked me. And he . . ."

"What?" Leslie asked.

"I didn't realize it until later, but no one had ever looked at my story of the divorce with any logic. I think maybe my self-pity came through so strongly that no one could see anything but what I saw. And what I saw wasn't the truth."

"So what happened this time?" Leslie asked softly as she glanced toward Madison's closed door. They had been careful not to say anything that would make Madison ask what they were talking about. They didn't want Madison to be told anything about her previous life.

"Jessie," Ellie said simply. "I helped him and he helped me."

"Don't tell me you solved a murder mystery?" Leslie asked in horror. "You didn't endanger your life, did you?"

"Well, as a matter of fact, I think I . . . we . . . did. Jessie said that we could do things that the police couldn't, such as put a tap on Sharon's telephone. Actually, it turned out that only *I* could do that because Jessie is a lawyer."

"I thought . . ." Leslie said, then trailed off.

"That he lived off his billionaire brother?" Ellie asked, smiling. "Me too. But I found out that Jessie had left a lucrative practice in L.A. to work for his brother, and, well . . ." Ellie looked down at her shoe for a moment, then back at Leslie. "Let's just say that Jessie may not be a billionaire, but he's not poor, either. And I certainly don't have to worry that he's after the paltry bit of money that I earn."

At that, Leslie squeezed Ellie's hand and smiled at her. "I'm glad for you. So you illegally bugged a woman's telephone, then what?"

"We found out that she had a lover and that all Lew's money was inherited from his father, which meant that if they'd divorced, it would have been his sole property, not community property."

"And she wouldn't have received any of it," Leslie said.

"Right. But she was his heir, so if Lew died, Sharon got everything. That was her motive, but we had to look for proof that she'd done it." For a moment Ellie's mouth twisted in disgust. "I didn't like what Jessie did, but it worked, so everything turned out all right."

Watching her, Leslie thought for a moment. "He made a play for her. She probably knew that Jessie was rich, so if she'd kill for money, she'd certainly marry for it."

"Exactly," Ellie said. "Jessie wanted to stage something like out of an Agatha Christie novel, where he gets her to confess while the police are hiding in the next room. I told him that that wasn't very original, but he said that he wasn't writing a book and trying to get good reviews, that he was just trying to catch a killer."

"Seems he already knows you," Leslie said, smiling.

"Not as well as he thinks," Ellie answered. "Anyway, it worked. Two policemen and I hid behind a door while Jessie enticed Sharon into his house with a bottle of champagne for her and scotch for him; then he came on to her hard. However, the scotch he was drinking was actually tea. When she was getting tipsy, he shocked me by telling her how much he *hated* his rich brother. Within minutes, Sharon started planning ways for Jessie to murder Woody. She said it was easy and that the local police were too stupid to be able to tell a murder from a suicide. A few more glasses of champagne and she was bragging to Jessie how she'd sneaked up behind Lew and started kissing him. She said that he was so glad that she was no longer angry at him that he paid no attention when she wrapped his fingers around the handle of a forty-five."

"I can believe that," Leslie said. "When it comes to sex, men seem to have a one-track mind."

"Poor Lew did. She shot him, then placed the blame on Bowie, who she knew was always skulking around outside their house. But Sharon confided to Jessie that she'd encouraged Bowie by undressing in front of an open window every night at the same time so Bowie would know when to appear to see the show."

"Wow! So you and Jessie solved the murder. But what about your divorce?"

Ellie took a deep breath. "Through all of this I knew that the court date was fast approaching, but there was no way that I was going to leave Jessie alone."

"Certainly not! After all, didn't you say that Sharon was beautiful?"

"With five pounds of makeup on, she looked all right, but she was no Madison, that's for sure." Ellie's words were laced with venom.

Looking down, Leslie smiled. "So did you miss the court date?"

"I hadn't realized it, but all through the days we spent trying to sort out Lew's death, Jessie had been asking me questions about the divorce. I had to fudge a bit about times and such because the things I knew about hadn't really happened yet. I did *not* want to get into telling him about Madame Zoya."

"I don't blame you," Leslie said. "But, in the end, you told him everything?"

"Pretty much. He was a good listener, and I was hungry to talk to someone, especially a lawyer. I know that what was done to me was morally wrong, but I've always felt that, legally, it was also wrong."

Pausing, Ellie smiled. "Sharon was carted off to jail the night before I was to appear in court, and the next morning Jessie flew me down to L.A.—in his own plane, I might add—but we didn't go into the courtroom. You see, I'd been looking at everything wrong. I thought that everyone had believed Martin and that's why he was to be given everything. What has plagued me for these years is that my character was so maligned. But Jessie figured out the truth."

"Tell me," Leslie said breathlessly.

"You remember that I told you Martin had taken a lot of money from me over the years?"

"Yes," Leslie said. "Did you find the money?"

"Yes." Ellie paused to run her hand across her face. "When I look back on it all, I still can't believe that I was so naive about everything. Me! Who writes murder mysteries!

"So, anyway, what Jessie surmised and later proved was that Martin, *on his attorney's advice,* gave that money to a friend of his to hold for him. I told you that it wasn't illegal for him to take that money from me, as, by law, it was considered as much his as mine. But, during the divorce, Martin had to sign a document swearing that he had no hidden money, so his attorney told him to

hand the money over to someone else before he signed the paper.

"But even though Martin didn't have this
money in his possession, he still had control
of it and he used a hundred and fifty thousand dollars of it to bribe the judge.

"What?" Leslie said, eyes wide. "Martin
bribed the *judge*?"

"Yes and no," Ellie said. "It was Jessie
who figured it out. He was puzzled by what
I told him. He said that no one believed anyone in a courtroom and no one cared
whether or not my ex had been the so-
called manager of my career. Jessie asked
me hundreds of questions, and I can tell you
that it was difficult for him to get answers
out of me because I could never get past
the idea that the judge *believed* Martin."

"But it was only money," Leslie said.

"Yes. It was only money. After I went back
to court, this time with Jessie, he told me
what had happened. Martin had gone into
private chambers with the judge and a court
stenographer, and told the judge that he
was going to give a hundred and fifty thousand dollars to his reelection fund. After
Martin made this offer, the judge told Martin
that he was sure that Martin had been the

man behind my career and the judge didn't see why a man of Martin's obvious talents shouldn't be allowed to continue to control my books forever. After all, the judge said that he wasn't at all sure that I was a sane woman."

"Did you say that there was a court stenographer there?"

"Yes. In a way, everything was being done legally."

"I take it the money didn't go to the campaign fund?"

"No. And Jessie knew that it wouldn't. Since everything was so well documented, it was an easy matter to compare dates of when the hundred and fifty was given to the judge and see that he never deposited it."

"And Jessie got this information?" Leslie asked, eyes wide.

"Yes, and Jessie used it to change everything. On the day that I was to appear in court, Jessie wrote a note—and he still won't tell me what he wrote—and had it delivered to the judge in his chambers. Ten minutes later, the judge asked to see Jessie. An hour later, Jessie walked out and we went into the courtroom."

"Then what happened?"

Leaning back on her arms, Ellie smiled, closing her eyes for a moment in delicious memory. "You should have seen Martin's face! When we walked into the courtroom, he was smug, smirking at me, knowing that he was going to be given one hundred per-cent control of all my books—or else I was going to agree to anything to retain control. But three hours later, he walked out with a face black with rage. Everything had been split fifty-fifty, as it should have been."

"And here's an irony. Since Martin had spent most of what I'd earned on what he told the judge was his own 'personal prop-erty,' in the end, he owed me money."

"And what about your house and your books?"

"The house was sold and I was given half the proceeds. And there was never any question that he'd be given control of my books, or that he'd receive any money that I would earn in the future."

"This time, he didn't get the house and you the payments."

"No!"

When Leslie didn't say anything more, Ellie stood up and yawned. "So that's it. I finally found out why Martin was believed and I wasn't."

"And it's freed you, hasn't it?" Leslie said, standing also.

"Yes. It never was the money; it was the injustice that broke me."

On impulse, Leslie hugged Ellie, then pulled away. "So what happened to Martin?"

"Bankruptcy. And he had to go to *work*," Ellie said with a smile.

"Work? Support *himself*?" Leslie said, then they both laughed. "What happened to the money he turned over to his friend?"

Ellie smiled. "Jessie figured out that Martin's lawyer probably knew where that was so during the lunch break, he had a talk with the lawyer. After lunch Martin's lawyer submitted a copy of a bank statement to the court showing that Martin had quite a bit hidden away so I was awarded half of it."

For a moment Ellie closed her eyes, then opened them and looked at Leslie. "The first time around I had all that money taken away from me, but I learned that I could do without it. And the second time the money seemed somehow dirty to me. I didn't want to touch it. I gave every penny of it to help abused children."

For a moment the two women were silent, then they smiled at each other, then they laughed. Then, as though they'd been cued, they once again did the little dance that they had performed in the restaurant. And when they finally went to bed, they were still laughing.

And now Ellie was flying home to Woody's ranch, where they now lived, home to her husband, Jessie, and to her toddler son, a child she had memories of but whom she'd never seen in person, the idea of which made her laugh. She'd purchased three nylon duffle bags to carry all the toys and clothes that she was taking back with her as gifts to Jessie and Nate, Valerie and Woody, and their son, Mark.

Keeping her eyes closed, she smiled in happiness.

Then, in the next moment, her eyes flew open. What if she wrote a story about—

Ten minutes later, she was writing the plot to a new novel fast and furiously.

Thirty-one

When Leslie entered her house, she stood in the entrance and looked into the living room with new eyes—and she saw many things that she didn't like. How pretentious Alan's untouchable antiques looked! He had made what should have been a comfortable *family* room into a room that one could only admire, certainly not use.

"Put them there," she said to the man who was setting her luggage and shopping bags on the floor of the entrance hall. He was the same man who had driven her to the airport, the man who'd flirted with her a bit. She'd been flattered then, but now she felt that he'd just been trying for a larger tip. But, oddly enough, on this second trip, he'd been looking at Leslie as though he really *was* interested in her. And she understood why.

There was a woman at her church who wasn't especially pretty and her figure wasn't nearly as good as Leslie's, but all the men watched her wherever she went. Of course she inspired a great deal of gossip and jealousy among the women, but Leslie had always wondered what it was about the woman that made men look at her. She'd asked Alan.

"I don't know," he'd said in that way that lets a woman know that he doesn't want to analyze something. "It's as though she expects to be looked at, so she is."

At the time, Leslie hadn't understood that, but now she did. Just days ago she'd been a girl again, with a girl's body, and she'd remembered what it felt like to be desirable.

Had she punished herself all these years for what she believed she'd done to the man she loved? Or had she backed down in every argument because she had decided that she was a failure?

Whatever the problem had been, right now, as she entered the house, she knew that, inside, she was a different woman.

"Thanks," she said to the driver, then handed him a ten.

"Thank *you*," he said, then gave her a look that let her know that he was available for further contact.

"Hi, Mom," Rebecca said as she came down the stairs, walking past the luggage and many bags at Leslie's feet. "You forgot to hand-wash my yellow sweater before you left, so I had to send it to the cleaner's. Dad's going to be mad about the expense." With that she sailed past her mother and went toward the kitchen.

For a moment Leslie stared after her daughter. Before her trip to Maine, she would have whined to her daughter that she could have washed her own sweater, but now Leslie felt no such compulsion to say such a thing to her daughter.

Alan came in from the garden. He was wearing perfectly pressed trousers and a crisply ironed shirt. He barely glanced at his wife. "I thought you weren't going to return until tomorrow," he said as he looked through a stack of mail on the kitchen table. "You girls have a fight?" he asked, chuckling at his own joke.

He picked up a couple of envelopes, and

as he walked past Leslie, he gave her an absentminded kiss on the cheek, then started up the stairs. He still hadn't actually looked at her. "I'm going out in about an hour," he said. "Bambi and I have to see a client." At the top of the stairs, he turned into their bedroom.

In the next minute, Joe came down the stairs. "Hi, Mom," he said. "Glad you're back."

At that Leslie smiled, but then Joe told her he was hungry. "When's dinner?" he asked as he went out the front door.

Leslie stood still for a moment. How long had her family been like this? she wondered. When had they become a bunch of strangers living in the same house, with each person caring only about his or her own needs and no one else's?

She went into the kitchen, thinking that Rebecca would be there, but the room was empty.

"I don't *like* this room," she said aloud. It had cost the earth, but she still didn't like it.

Going to the sink she filled the kettle with water and put it on to boil.

Isn't this where I came in? she thought.

Isn't this what I was doing the last time I was in this house?

The water came to a boil and she made herself a cup of tea, then she stood at the window and looked out at the old summer-house in the back. And as she looked at it, she remembered Millie Formund's summer-house. And Leslie remembered what she'd learned in the last few days.

She put her half-finished cup down in the sink, went into the entrance hall, and gathered up six heavily loaded shopping bags, then carried them outside to the summer-house. On the way back from the airport she'd had the driver stop at a local art and craft store, and she'd gone inside and nearly cleared the shelves of merchandise.

Outside the summerhouse, she put the bags on the grass; then she pushed open the door to the once-lovely house and went inside. With the eye of a woman who knew about construction, she looked about the place. Most of the damage inside was from neglect, and it could be easily repaired. There was a leak in the roof and water damage on one wall. But she could fix that.

No, she corrected herself, she could have that fixed.

She looked at what was inside the house. There was little that was hers in there. Alan had removed the upper shelves from the bookcase Leslie had refinished and put in a TV. Of course he'd had to cut a hole in the back for the cables; then the TV had been too deep for the shelf, so Alan had cut a bigger hole, until there wasn't much left of her bookcase.

Joe stored all his old sports equipment in the summerhouse. There were at least three broken skateboards and an old wooden crate held discarded skates. Upon closer inspection, the crate turned out to be a pine washstand that Leslie had found at a flea market. Joe had put the table on its back, opened the doors, and filled the belly with his old skates.

Rebecca had put boxes full of clothes and books in front of the French doors that led into what had once been Leslie's tiny, private rose garden.

For a moment, Leslie wanted to close the door on the whole mess. Maybe it was more than she wanted to tackle. How was she going to persuade her family to clean this place up so she could use it?

But then she remembered the face of that

girl who'd looked back in the mirror at her. That girl hadn't been afraid of anyone or anything.

As Leslie stood with her hand on the door handle of the summerhouse, she knew that right now, this very second, was the turning point of her life. What she did this moment would determine how the rest of her life would go. She had been given a second chance at her life, and she'd chosen this life and these people because she loved them. But she'd also learned that she needed to love herself.

The truth was that Leslie didn't know what was waiting for her in the next months. For a long time now she'd expected her husband to ask her for a divorce so he could marry a woman who probably had the fearless eyes that Leslie had once had. And if he did ask for a divorce, where would Leslie be then? Even more afraid than she had been these last years?

And how would her taking over the summerhouse or not taking it over affect her future life?

"Not one damn bit!" she said aloud, then again looked around the summerhouse. And this time when she looked at it, it was almost as though she saw herself in the old building. She had once been something perfect and beautiful, as this building had once been. But she had been taken over by her family, just as they had taken over this house. It was as though they had pushed her onto her back and filled her belly with refuse.

With a smile, Leslie opened both doors to the summerhouse wide, then she walked to the TV set, picked it up, and jerked the cords out of the wall. Her lovely bookcase had had almost the entire back sawn out of it. Still smiling, she carried the TV through the doorway; then she gave it the strongest heave she could manage. The TV went sailing for a few feet, then hit the edge of the little stone retaining wall that Alan had had put in two years ago, then went tumbling down the slope toward the barbecue pit.

When it hit Alan's oversized brick barbecue and the glass front of the TV smashed, Leslie didn't think she'd ever heard a more satisfying sound in her life. And the sound gave her strength.

She went back into the summerhouse and began hauling out the rest of the rubbish. Joe's skates tumbled down the little hill right behind Alan's TV; then Leslie righted her little washstand and closed its doors. One door's hinge was wrenched nearly off, but she could fix it.

Rebecca's old clothes and her years of pack-ratting went next.

And with each item that Leslie threw out, it was as though she got stronger and . . . well, more of herself back.

"I told you!" she heard Rebecca shout. "She's gone crazy!"

Leslie had her hands full of a broken rabbit cage that the children had dumped into the summerhouse. She gave it a toss down toward the other items that were piling up in front of Alan's beloved barbecue.

Glancing up, she saw the three of them running down the path toward her. Rebecca looked angry, Alan was concerned, and Joe looked amused.

She didn't acknowledge them but went back into the summer-house and picked up a couple of bags of ten-year-old rabbit food. "We might need that," Rebecca had wailed when Leslie had begged her years ago to give it away. But Rebecca held on to every possession she'd ever had and never released anything.

"Leslie, honey. Is everything all right?" Alan said from the doorway. He was using the voice he saved for difficult clients. "The man was crazy," he'd say, "so I talked to him like this." Then he'd show her the voice that he was now using on her.

"Fine," she said, giving him a bit of a smile as she picked up a box of broken Christmas ornaments that Alan swore he was going to repair someday. "Excuse me," she said, then stepped past him and threw the box down the hill.

"Could you stop that for a moment?" he said when she turned back toward the summerhouse.

"No, I can't. I want to get this place cleaned out, so I can set up a studio in here."

"Studio?" he said, and there was mirth in his voice. "Honey, I know that turning forty has hit you hard, but I do think that maybe you're a bit old to start dancing again."

Leslie didn't answer him as she picked up a box full of broken electronic gadgets, the product of many Christmases. When she got to the door, Alan put his hands on the box, but the look she gave him made him remove his hands and step back. But as she prepared to heave the box, Alan nodded toward Joe and he took the box from his mother.

"Thank you," Leslie said, then turned back for more.

Alan stepped inside the summerhouse. "Look, Leslie, honey, if you wanted to clean out this old place, why didn't you tell us? We could have all done it. As a family. And we could have done it in an orderly manner, not throwing things against the barbecue. Did you see that you've damaged it?"

"Damaged it?" she asked softly as she picked up a box of receipts that were dated 1984. "I damaged your barbecue?"

"Yes, you did," Alan said sternly, mistaking her words for caring. "It will have to be repaired."

Leslie went to the door, and while looking at Alan, she gave the box of receipts a hard sling. Pieces of paper went flying all over the lawn and into the trees and shrubs, but Leslie didn't look at them as she stepped back into the house, but she could feel anger rising in her. She looked back at Alan. "*I* damaged *your* barbecue? What about the damage *you* have done to *my* summerhouse?"

"Yours?" he asked in bewilderment. "I thought it was *ours*."

"No, Alan," she said slowly. "The summerhouse was mine, and it always was. You seem to own everything else in our lives, but the summerhouse was *mine*."

Alan nodded to Rebecca and Joe to pick up the papers that were flying about, then he stepped inside and closed the door behind him. "Leslie, honey, I know that turning forty is hard on a woman, but—"

"Turning forty has nothing to do with this!" she half yelled at him. "What is it with you men? For the first half of our lives when we get angry, you say we have PMS. Now what are you going to say, Alan? That I'm heading for 'The Change'?"

"I didn't say anything like that. Could you stop that for a moment?!"

In all their years of marriage, it was guaranteed that if Alan shouted at her, Leslie would cringe. But not now. Now she turned and confronted him. "What's the matter, Alan? Is my little tantrum holding up your rendezvous with Bambi?"

"Bambi? What the hell does she have to do with this?"

"Everything and nothing," Leslie answered, then tried to calm her anger. She'd no idea that she had this much rage inside her. But it was as though it had been building and festering in her for a very long time.

"That makes no sense at all," Alan said, and she could see that he, too, was angry.

In the last days she'd made a decision to not allow her happiness to be tied to *any* man. Ellie and Madison both had careers that they were very successful at, but Leslie didn't. Those two women had themselves, so they could afford to add a man to their lives. But a man was all that Leslie had. In the week she'd spent with Hal and his family she'd realized that if she chose a life with him, that in twenty years' time, she'd be just as she was now. She'd be so involved with *his* life that there would be no room for *her*. And, once again, that girl who had been so fearless would be lost.

"Right," Leslie said, and this time she was calm. "Alan, I can't live as I have been even one day longer. I've given all my life to you and the children, and now that they're nearly grown, I want something for myself."

"And you want this old place?" he asked, still looking at her as though she were crazy. "You could have just said that and not—"

"No!" she shouted. "I couldn't have because you don't *see* me."

"That's ridiculous. Of course I see you. You're right there."

She advanced on him. "No you don't. You don't see *me.* You see a woman who feeds you and buys your clothes and finds your socks and arranges your parties. But you don't see that I'm a person separate from you."

He narrowed his eyes at her. "You went up to Maine and you spent the weekend talking women's lib garbage with those women, didn't you?"

"I want a divorce," she said, then looked at him in shock. Where had those words come from? Where had the thought come from?

Alan said nothing, just stared at her in disbelief.

When Leslie spoke again, she was calm. "I can't take any more of this. I'm sorry that I jilted you, but I should have been forgiven years ago. I've certainly tried to make it up to you over the years. But I can't take this humiliation any longer. If you want her, you can have her."

"Have who?" Alan asked quietly, and she

could see that for the first time in many years, she had his full and undivided attention.

"Bambi!" Leslie spat out the name with all the venom she felt.

"Bambi?" Alan asked. "You think I'm interested in Bambi?"

"The entire town knows about you two, so you—"

She broke off because Alan had smiled—then he began to laugh.

"Me and Bambi? Is that what you think? Is that why you've been so cold to me these last months? Is she the reason you move away from me every time I get near you?"

She wanted to defend herself, but she knew that she had been cold to him. Every time he'd put out his hand to touch her, she'd thought, How long ago was he touching *her*?

Alan sat down on the sofa and a cloud of dust encircled him. Ignoring it, he looked up at Leslie. "I thought maybe you had another man," he said softly.

"Me?" she asked in disbelief. "I'm a middle-aged—"

"You're as beautiful as the day I married

you," Alan said. "And I hired Bambi to make you jealous. Has it worked?"

It took Leslie several minutes to realize what he'd just said. "To make me jealous?"

"There's always been part of you that I could never reach. You've always been so independent. Other wives call their husbands if a mouse runs across the floor, but not *my* wife. No, my Leslie can handle *anything*. Look at this place. It was you who rebuilt it. Do you know how I felt seeing you using a power hand saw when I don't know a blade from a bit? All these years I've wanted to make you *need* me, but I've never succeeded. There isn't anything you can't do and do perfectly."

If she'd thought for a thousand years, she would never had thought that these were problems that Alan had. She sat down on the couch beside him, then waited for the dust to settle. "You weren't angry that I ran off and left you just days before our wedding?"

"Hell, no. I mean, yes, I was, but . . ." He turned to look at her. "It made you worth having. If you hadn't come back to me, I would have been angry, maybe forever, but you did return. And all these years I've secretly enjoyed the ribbing about having a wife who was a New York dancer."

"I failed at being a dancer. That's why I returned."

Alan took her hand in his. "You've never failed at anything in your life. If you think you weren't as good as the other dancers, it's because you missed me so much that you wanted to fail so you could come home to me."

Leslie knew that there was a ring of truth in his words. Madison had been so homesick that she'd run back to a man who she knew was bad. Had Leslie done the same thing? Had she, too, found an excuse to run back home?

After she'd left Hal's family's estate, she'd gone back to college and she'd danced. And there was part of her mind that had wondered how good the girls in New York were if she was considered not as good.

And Leslie had spent two weeks with Alan, a much younger Alan than this one, but the same man. And she had felt the same overwhelming love for him that had been in her heart since she'd met him on the playground in the first grade.

"Alan," she said, looking into his eyes. "I can paint."

"You can do anything."

"No. I mean, on paper. Scenes. Actually, I'm good at people. Watercolors, although I'm going to explore some other media."

He couldn't seem to comprehend what she was telling him. "Do you still want a . . . you know?"

"Do you?"

"Me?" he asked, shocked. "I never wanted a divorce. I just wanted *you* back."

That's the way Leslie felt also, that *she* had been missing for a long time.

When Alan pulled her into his arms, she began to cry.

"I've missed you so much," he said. "And I love you so much. I always have. Remember? I told you that I would always love you."

Yes, she remembered. He'd told her on that first day when they were in the first grade, that he would love her "forever." She'd just stood there by the swings and stared at that boy she'd never seen before, unable to say anything.

The memory made her cry harder, and he held her closer; then he was kissing her neck, and his hands were unbuttoning her clothes. And when Joe opened the door, Alan shouted at him to get out.

It was later, after they'd made love on the floor of the summerhouse, that Leslie said, "Alan, fire Bambi."

"Done," he said; then he began to kiss her neck again.

Epilogue

Thirty-two

❧

Ellie had left Jessie and her son in Bangor as she drove up the coast alone. Jessie hadn't asked too many questions, but she could tell that he wanted to know why she felt compelled to go back to the place where she'd spent just a weekend years before. "It's something I need to do," was all she'd tell him. Something she felt *driven* to do, she thought, but she didn't want to go into that.

She had kissed them both good-bye, then had driven to that town where her life had changed so drastically. But now she'd been in town for three hours and she still hadn't found the Victorian house of Madame Zoya. She'd asked a waitress who said she'd grown up in the little town, but the girl had only laughed at the idea of a psychic setting up business in town.

"You mean a palm reader?" the girl had said.

"She was a bit more than that," Ellie had answered defensively, but she couldn't tell this girl what had happened to her any more than she could tell anyone else what had happened. A couple of times in the last years she'd tried to tell Jessie, but she could see that he wasn't going to believe her, so she'd stopped.

But in the last six months Ellie had felt an overwhelming urge to return to Maine and see the psychic again. It had taken a while to persuade Jessie and to arrange the trip, but she'd managed it.

Ellie left the restaurant and tried to re-member how she and Leslie and Madison had found the street and the house the first time. Before she'd left home, she'd searched everywhere for Madame Zoya's card, but she couldn't find it. She'd e-mailed both Leslie and Madison, but they couldn't find theirs either. Somehow, Ellie wasn't surprised.

She wandered down the main street yet again, looking at all the street signs that branched off, not that there were many, but there was no Everlasting Street. Then, she turned, and there it was.

Smiling, she turned down the street and the house was at the end, just as it had been before, and the house was still as perfect as it had been the first time she'd seen it. She told herself that she was being ridiculous, but her heart was pounding as she knocked on the door.

A small, gray-haired lady answered her knock. She was pleasant-looking, but she wasn't Madame Zoya.

"You must be wanting to see the house," the woman said. "We get so many tourists here, and many of them are kind enough to want to tell me how much they admire my house."

"No, actually," Ellie said, "I was hoping to see Madame Zoya."

"Oh, my," the woman said. "That's a new one on me. Madame what?"

"Zoya," Ellie said.

"I'm afraid I haven't heard of her."

"Have you lived in this house long?"

The woman smiled. "My father built this house as a wedding present for my mother. I've lived in it all my life."

"Oh," Ellie said, feeling deflated. But what had she expected? If a woman who could do what Madame Zoya did were easy to find, she'd be on the evening news.

"Thank you," Ellie said as she turned to go down the steps.

"Wait," the woman said. "You look like you could use a cup of tea, and I could certainly use the company. Won't you come in?"

Ellie thought that she should drive back to Bangor, but instead, she turned and went into the house behind the woman.

"By the way, my name is Primrose," she said; then when Ellie smiled, she waved her hand. "I know. It's such an old-fashioned name, but my parents were old fashioned people. And you are?"

"Ellie Woodward," she said as she looked about the house. It was exactly the same inside as it had been when she and Leslie and Madison had visited. "You don't have a sister or know someone who dyes her hair orange, do you?"

Primrose's blue eyes twinkled. "No, and I do think I'd remember her. In fact, I think that everyone in town might remember her. Now, do sit down. I had just put the kettle on when you knocked, so it should be ready."

Ellie sat down on a sofa, and when she was alone in the room, she had to resist the temptation to snoop, but Primrose was back within seconds, so there was no time anyway.

After she had seated herself and served them both tea and had made Ellie fill her plate with tiny cakes, Primrose said, "I'm sure I'm just being a nosy old lady, but we're quite isolated here, so maybe you could tell *me* what you wanted to tell this Madame . . . What was her name again?"

Ellie looked over her teacup at the woman. She's lying, she thought, and whatever I tell her will get back to Madame Zoya. "I really just wanted to tell her, 'Thank you.'"

"That's all?" Primrose asked, sounding disappointed.

"And I wanted to tell her about my friends, and about me, but if she's not here—" Ellie put down her teacup.

"How lovely," Primrose said. "And how are your friends?"

Part of Ellie wanted to force the woman to tell what she did know, but then Ellie owed Madame Zoya so much that she wanted to get information to her anyway she could.

"They're very happy," Ellie said. "Leslie Headrick is painting full-time, and her husband is very proud of her. Leslie says that she's never been happier. Both her children are in college now, and Leslie says it's like a second honeymoon between her and her husband."

"How nice to hear good in this world. And your other friend?"

Ellie wasn't going to bother to pretend that this woman didn't know who was who and what her story was. "Madison still runs her clinic in Montana, and she's had another baby. She says she'd like to have a dozen if she could.

"The three of us have kept in close contact since . . . well, since we were last here, and I think that all of us are happy now."

Primrose daintily ate a tiny pink cake with an icing rosebud on top of it. "Does that include you? Are you happy too?"

"Yes," Ellie said softly. "Very. I have a wonderful husband and son, and my editor says that the last book I wrote is my best yet."

"Oh, that's good," Primrose said. "Very good indeed." Abruptly, she stood. "Now, dear, you must excuse me, as I have work to do."

"Yes, of course," Ellie said, putting down her teacup, then standing. "It was very nice to meet you, and I hope—"

But Primrose was hurrying toward the front door as though she couldn't wait to get rid of Ellie, and seconds later, Ellie was standing outside on the porch, the door closed behind her.

"That was abrupt," she said, then walked to the street. Digging into her bag, she pulled out her cell phone and called the hotel in Bangor. "I'm on my way home," she said when Jessie answered.

"Good. Nate and I've missed you," he said.

"I've missed you too," Ellie answered as she turned the phone off and headed for where she'd parked her rental car. She was smiling all the way.

As soon as Ellie was out of sight, Primrose dropped the curtain back into place, then walked down the long corridor toward the back of the house. There was a small room with rose-patterned wallpaper on it. The furnishings were sparse, just three fat chairs and a rug on the oak floor. Walking across the room, Primrose pushed on a rose that looked like every other rose on the wall, and a door opened.

Behind the door was a tiny room, hardly bigger than a closet, but inside there was a little table against the far wall, and on it was a large glass globe, what some people would call a crystal ball. On hooks on the left wall were velvet clothes and a bright orange wig.

On the right wall, from floor to ceiling, were photographs of people.

Primrose went to the little table and picked up three brochures and a pair of scissors. Slowly, she began to cut out photos from the brochures.

One picture was of Ellie, clipped from a sales announcement about one of her forthcoming books. Another photo was of Leslie, cut from a program about a showing of her paintings, and one was of Madison, cut out of a brochure of "distinguished graduates" from her Montana high school.

On the wall were the Polaroid pictures

that were taken of the three women years ago, and, now, beside each one, Primrose pinned the new photos; then she stepped back and looked at the differences in the pictures. In the original pictures there was a sadness about each woman that showed clearly in her eyes. But in the new photos the sadness was gone.

Smiling in satisfaction, Primrose stepped further back from the wall and looked at all the photographs. There were over a hundred men's and women's photos on the wall, and beside each one was a new picture. In some, the first photos were better than the second one. But in most, the second photo showed amazing differences in the way they looked out at the world. For a moment, Primrose gazed at the picture of a man wearing dark glasses. He had been blinded in an accident when he was fourteen. Beside the photo of him in dark glasses was a picture of a man who was looking into the camera and smiling.

With a self-satisfied little sigh, Primrose opened the drawer, withdrew three business cards and slipped them into her pocket. She left the little room, closing the door behind her, then made her way through the house to the front door. Once she was outside, she paused a moment to stand on the porch and smile; then she went down the stairs toward the street.